LIVERPOOL LOVE SONG

When Helen Redwood is tragically widowed, she and her daughter, Chloe, move to Liverpool to be closer to her family. But it is tending her beautiful garden with her handsome gardener, Rex Kenwright, that ultimately saves Helen from grief. No stranger to bereavement himself, Rex finds comfort in Helen's company but it is seventeen-year-old Chloe who steals his heart. It is the swinging sixties, however, and Chloe has dreams of her own. When she announces that she is pregnant and moving in with her boyfriend, Adam Livingstone, she has no idea of the effect this will have on those she loves.

LIVERPOOL LOVE SONG

Liverpool Love Song

by

Anne Baker

Magna Large Print Books
Long Preston, North Yorkshire,
BD23 4ND, England.

British Library Cataloguing in Publication Data.

Baker, Anne
    Liverpool love song.

    A catalogue record of this book is
    available from the British Library

    ISBN   978-0-7505-3558-8

First published in Great Britain in 2011 by
Headline Publishing Group

Copyright © 2011 Anne Baker

Cover illustration © Gordon Crabb by arrangement with
Alison Eldred

The right of Anne Baker to be identified as the author of this work has
been asserted by her in accordance with the Copyright, Designs and
Patents Act, 1988

Published in Large Print 2012 by arrangement with
Headline Publishing Group Ltd.

Magna Large Print is an imprint of Library Magna Books Ltd.

Printed and bound in Great Britain by
T.J. (International) Ltd., Cornwall, PL28 8RW

CHAPTER ONE

Spring 1964

It was a sunny April afternoon, the warmest of the year so far, and it was Helen Redwood's forty-third birthday. She sniffed contentedly at the scent of newly cut grass coming in through the open French window of her sitting room. She loved her garden, it had given her back her life.

She could hear her daughter Chloe clattering dishes in the kitchen. Chloe had said at break-fast, 'I'm going to make you a birthday cake, and we'll have a special tea in the garden.' She'd spent half the day baking and decorating it.

Helen knew she had a lot to be thankful for. She'd clung too tightly to Chloe over the years, seeking comfort. She loved her daughter much more than her garden, yet while that had grown and thrived with her care, she'd not always been good for Chloe. But it seemed they'd both turned the corner now.

She went to the kitchen door and was pleased to hear Chloe humming softly to herself, sounding happy as she stacked the tea things on to two big trays.

'Chloe! That isn't the new blue dress you were telling me about?'

'Yes.' Her daughter turned to smile at her. 'It's the very latest style. D'you like it?'

9

'Not a lot, it's indecently short.' It showed rather too much of Chloe's long shapely legs and slim figure. 'I wouldn't call that a dress at all. It's no more than a tunic.'

Helen knew she sounded as shocked as she felt. Chloe was still a few weeks off her seventeenth birthday and the dress made her look even younger. Chloe laughed. 'I told you this style was all the rage. You should shorten your own skirts, Mum, and stay in fashion.'

'At my age I couldn't wear anything like that.'

'Maybe not quite like this, but you'd look a lot younger if you wore more fashionable stuff. Why don't you let me take you shopping?'

Helen tried to smile. 'You know I stopped thinking about things like fashion when your father died.'

'Yes, but that's six years ago now and you agreed we'd both got over it.'

'So we have,' she said quickly. Any talk like this and she was afraid they'd both feel guilty.

'Then why not a new outfit or two? It would do wonders for you. You aren't old yet, Mum. This is the swinging sixties, everything's changing now. If you wanted to, you could still be good-looking.'

Helen smiled. 'That's a bit of a back-handed compliment, isn't it?' She felt she didn't deserve a daughter who tried so hard to help her.

She studied her daughter's face. They shared a strong family likeness. Chloe had inherited Helen's high cheekbones and straight nose, but her eyes were the colour of lavender and had come from John's family. She was more beautiful than Helen had ever been.

Chloe had lustrous tawny-coloured hair that could hang in loose curls halfway down her back, though today she had it tied back with a blue ribbon. Tawny was as near as Helen could get to describing the colour, because there were so many different shades in it, from bright gold through copper to honey blonde and nut brown.

Her own hair had never been anything like that. It used to be plain brown but now it was showing a touch of grey. Helen had grown gauntly thin, while Chloe's limbs were firm and rounded with the bloom of youth.

Helen stopped short. She mustn't feel sorry for herself. Having another birthday had made her remember birthdays past with John. She'd been devastated when he'd been killed; shocked to the core at the suddenness of his end. She couldn't bear to go on living in the house they'd shared; everything there reminded her of him and that terrible accident.

Chloe had been eleven and had just started secondary school. Until then, they'd lived in London. John had left them well provided for, but Helen had sold up and returned to her home town of Liverpool, where she'd bought number 8 Carberry Road, a small detached modern house in the suburb of Woolton. On the next-door gate was a plaque with the name The Farm, as well as the number 9. It was an old sandstone house, set sideways on to the road, and almost all its original land had been sold for building houses.

Because Helen had always had periods of depression, she'd had to learn how to lift her spirits. She'd found gardening soothing and enjoyable and realising there was a three-acre piece of land for sale at the bottom of her plot, she'd bought it to make a new and beautiful garden. It was to be the interest that would help her build a new life.

She'd gravitated towards the nearby large garden centre and seen displayed in their shop an advertisement offering garden landscaping and design. She had noted the telephone number and rung it as soon as she reached home.

She'd talked about what she wanted to a man who said his name was Rex Kenwright. He made an appointment to come round to see her and the pony paddock where for the last few years the ground had been grazed bare and stamped solid.

When he turned up, he'd looked surprisingly young; she'd expected an older man. He told her the garden centre had been started by his parents, and now his father and two younger brothers ran it. Most of the plants and equipment he used came from there, and he found most of his customers by advertising in the shop.

Helen thought him shy but very knowledgeable about gardening, and when he showed her the designs he'd drawn up for her three acres, she could see he had a creative streak. Together they'd discussed his plans round her kitchen table. Rex said the ground needed to be ploughed, rotavated and raked first, then gradually over those early years, the garden Helen had envisaged came into being.

In their first lonely months in Liverpool, she'd wanted to be out working with Rex. Together, they'd dug a pond, planted shrubs and flowers and made a rose arbour. Helen now had a truly magnificent garden and was very proud of it.

On the back of his family's firm, Rex had built up a sizeable gardening business of his own, employing six men. Occasionally he sent one of them to cut the grass and clip the hedges in Helen's garden, but mostly he came himself and spent time talking enthusiastically to her about new ideas and new plants.

'Landscaping is what I most enjoy, and to date, you've given me my largest and most rewarding contract.'

Helen had grown fond of Rex over the years and admired his work. The garden had been her salvation, though she'd been unable to put that traumatic accident behind her and move on. Occasionally she still woke up feeling lonely, helpless and that everything was hopeless. Thankfully these episodes were becoming less frequent.

Chloe was taking a cake out of the larder. 'I hope this is going to be all right.'

'Darling, it will be.'

'It hasn't turned out too well. I hoped it would look better than this.' She'd covered the top with thickly whipped cream. The silver disc in the centre, printed with the words *Happy Birthday*, was rapidly sinking into it.

'It looks fine and I know it'll taste good. You make a very good Victoria sponge.'

'Let's find out. I've set out the table and chairs. Can you carry one of the trays out while I make a pot of tea?'

Once outside, Helen couldn't resist pausing to

admire again the pair of standard rose trees in ornamental pots, her birthday gifts this year. Both were hybrid tea roses, one that would have deep scarlet blooms called 'Red Devil' from Chloe, and one called 'Evening Star' with white blooms from Rex.

It seemed that when Chloe had consulted him about the best rose tree to buy, he'd very generously decided to join with her and get a pair. Helen couldn't wait to see them in flower.

As she crossed the lawn to put the tray down on the table, she could hear the drone of the lawnmower in a distant part of the garden. She went in search of Rex and soon caught sight of him working against the far boundary of trees that were just coming into leaf. She called his name but he didn't hear her and she had to go closer.

Rex Kenwright was tall, over six feet, and wore comfortable jeans and a blue T-shirt. She knew now that he was thirty-one years old and that his youth gave him an advantage. He had plenty of energy and huge enthusiasm for her garden because it was the first time he'd started from scratch on rough land. Physical work had given him a well-honed body without an ounce of surplus flesh. Being outdoors in all weathers had made his skin a healthy bronze colour, which he kept throughout the year. At last he saw her, waved and switched off the mower.

'It's teatime, Rex.' He always had a cup of tea with her if he came in the afternoon. 'Chloe's made me a cake, I'm afraid she'll want you to sing "Happy Birthday".'

He laughed. 'I do wish you a happy birthday

and I'll sing for hours for a piece of your cake.'

He had light brown hair that by the end of the summer would be bleached almost to blond. She thought him a serious young man, gentle, modest and unassuming. Together they walked back to the table and chairs Chloe had set out in the sun.

'That pink aubretia is lovely and so are the forget-me-nots,' Helen told him. 'I love this time of the year. There's so much more colour coming in the garden and you work so hard to make it beautiful.'

'You do a lot here yourself, Helen. Can I go inside to wash my hands?' They were green with grass stains.

'Of course, you know the way.'

Chloe had covered the table with a white cloth to make it more festive and had finished setting out her feast of crab and cucumber sandwiches and gooseberry tartlets. They waited for Rex to come back.

Helen leaned back in her chair and felt the warmth of the sun on her face. 'It's heavenly here today, isn't it?'

Rex returned and sat down between mother and daughter. Today Chloe was acting as hostess, pouring their tea and making sure they had all they needed. She was offering the plate of crab sandwiches round when her arm brushed his. It sent an electric shock coursing through his body that he had to hide. It took an effort to keep his voice steady and say, 'You've even got birthday weather, Helen. Perfect for a tea party in the garden.'

'It's gorgeous when everything starts sprouting in the spring sun,' Chloe said. 'Mum, do we count the garden as finished now?'

'Almost.' Helen smiled. 'I've been thinking about getting a summerhouse. It would look nice here on this very spot and we could use the garden for many more months of the year.'

'Wow! A summerhouse?'

'I'd like one of those you can push round so you can always be out of the wind and in the sun.'

They spent the next half-hour discussing summerhouses. 'There's a good selection in the garden centre at the moment,' Rex told them. 'You must come and see them. They've got the sort on a turntable base that can be swung round. You can have one side completely open or with glass panels that slide across.'

'That sounds expensive.'

'It is. Top of the market, but it makes a real garden room and you'd be able to use it for most of the year.' Suddenly he smiled, 'I hope I don't sound like a salesman working hard for a sale?'

'No,' Helen said. 'Go on, I want to hear about them. I'd really like one.'

'There are more affordable designs. If you like, I'll take you both to see them as soon as I'm finished here.'

'I'd like to,' Helen said, 'but we haven't time. As it's my birthday, my cousin Joan has invited all the family to dinner tonight and we'll need to get changed. I'll pop in myself tomorrow.'

Rex was watching Chloe as she lit the four candles on the cake she'd made for her mother.

'Now, Rex, I need you to sing for Mum,' she

16

said. He could see Helen trying not to laugh. 'Full voice, please, as there's just the two of us. Happy birthday...'

It gave him great pleasure to hear how well his deep voice mingled with her fluting soprano. But it brought an emotional onslaught, waking every nerve in his body. He'd told himself a hundred times that she was far too young for him. She was just a slip of a girl, as slender as a sapling; he didn't understand how she'd come to mean so much to him.

'Now, Mum,' Chloe was all smiles as she set the cake in front of her, 'one puff and blow them all out.'

Helen tried, but one flame continued to flutter. 'In the bright sunlight I can hardly see whether they're alight or not,' she said. That she'd failed made them all laugh.

'Sorry, Mum, it's not a handsome cake.' Chloe pulled a face. 'The cream wasn't stiff enough, I should have whipped it more.' But she couldn't hold back a giggle. The cream had completely swallowed the plastic disc with birthday wishes and was threatening to do the same with the candle holders.

Helen pulled them out. 'At my age,' she said, 'I should be able to blow out forty-three candles, and I couldn't even manage four.' That made them laugh again.

As he took a bite from the generous slice in front of him, Rex said, 'It tastes good. I knew it would, your cakes always do. Gorgeous sponge, absolutely luscious. Food for the gods.'

Chloe's eyes sparkled up at him. 'I wanted it to

be a handsome birthday cake for Mum. It's a bit of a disaster.'

'No, Chloe,' he told her. 'It was a lovely way to mark a special day for your mother.'

He'd have liked to add that he wished she would do the same for him, but knew he mustn't, not yet.

'Absolutely lovely,' Helen agreed. 'And I'm thrilled with my presents. Thank you both.'

Rex went back to pull at the lawnmower until it burst into life. Over the years he'd known this family, he'd become very involved with them; now he wanted to think of them as his own.

Other family members seemed to live reasonably close and came to the house quite often. Helen had introduced him to her mother, Mrs Darty, an elderly lady, frail and ill-looking, and her sister Marigold, who seemed very much older than she was. When Helen made a cup of tea for them, she would invite Rex to join them. He hadn't taken to Marigold; she was thin-lipped and wore her iron-grey hair in a severely mannish style.

From the moment he'd met them he'd thought they were not the sort of people to cheer Helen up. The old lady, poor soul, often dozed off, and there was something hostile, even steely about Marigold's manner. She wouldn't look him in the eye and made him feel he was intruding on their privacy.

Joan Bristow, he liked better. She was jolly, of matronly build, with a pale gold rinse on her immaculately waved grey hair. She shared Helen's love of gardening and would come and spend the whole afternoon outside with her, always bringing a pair of gardening shoes to change into. She knew the Latin names of almost every plant, and quizzed Rex repeatedly on gardening matters.

Helen had said vaguely that Joan was a friend as well as a relation and it took Rex some time to work out that she was a first cousin to her and Marigold. She was about Marigold's age, the daughter of Mrs Darty's deceased sister, but a very different personality.

Joan had been married for only nine years or so to Walter Bristow, who had his own business in Bootle. Sometimes, when his office closed in the late afternoon, he'd come to pick his wife up. But first they would show him round the garden, pointing out all the improvements and the new plants, and Helen would serve them drinks. Joan was the sort of person who cheered everybody up.

Helen had told Rex almost as soon as they met that she had been recently widowed, but it had taken him a long time to see her dark moods. He'd recognised early on that she was looking for support in things unrelated to gardening – her daughter Chloe, for instance.

At that time, Chloe had been an awkward and lost-looking twelve-year-old; he could see she wasn't happy. They'd both seemed vulnerable and in need of help.

It was only after he'd seen Chloe come hurtling out into the garden a few times, red-eyed and rebellious, that he realised she was more troubled than her mother. Rex was afraid they were having the sort of rows he'd had with his family when he'd been growing up, but he couldn't imagine a problem that might cause them.

Rex felt sorry for Chloe, and knew that having a mother who suffered spells of depression must make it harder for her.

'Is she still grieving for her father?' he'd asked Helen. 'Is that what is troubling her?'

'It's what's troubling both of us, I suppose.' Helen was staring past him into space. 'We haven't told you just how bad the accident was.'

He waited for her to go on, but she didn't. 'A climbing accident, you said?' he prompted.

'Yes.' She looked at him then. 'John's hobby was rock-climbing. He was in North Wales with a group of climbers, practising before attempting one of the peaks in Switzerland. He took me and Chloe with him for a few days' holiday. The idea was that we would go walking, but climbing fascinated Chloe. John took her along and gave her a first lesson or two. The other climbers made a big fuss of her and said she was a natural and had real ability. I was always scared for him, but he had no fear and neither had Chloe.

'Then one morning, the climbers were planning to do a much harder climb. John wanted to take Chloe but I stopped him. Climbing scares me and I was afraid for her. I settled down outside with a book and Chloe was watching them through binoculars. I knew she'd gone but it never occurred to me that she'd get a lift over to the rock face and try to climb behind them.

'It came on to rain, and that distracted her and made the rock slippy, and when she reached a more difficult spot she became scared and started calling for help. She'd climbed surprisingly high without help or supervision. Her father and one of his friends came reeling down to help her. She was panicking by this time, so John unfastened his own safety harness to put it on her. She was thrashing about and... Well, he slipped and fell...'

'Oh God, Helen, to his death?'

She flinched. 'Even worse, I think. He broke his back. His injuries were so bad he could never recover. He lingered...'

Rex shuddered. After that he understood Helen's black moods and the clouded horror he saw in the girl's wide eyes.

CHAPTER TWO

Rex finished cutting the grass and was getting ready to go home; he was lifting the lawnmower back into his van when he saw Chloe running towards him. She'd changed into a smart red dress with matching red shoes. He'd never seen her wear high heels before.

His heart began to race. 'Another new dress?' he asked.

'No, you've seen it before.'

'I haven't.'

'I've cut six inches off the hem to bring it up to date. I had to, it's no good having only one dress at a fashionable length. Mum said I was to give you a piece of her birthday cake to take home.

She says it won't keep because of all the fresh cream I put on.'

'Thank you, that's very kind.'

She giggled. 'A bit like a children's party, isn't it, when you get a piece of birthday cake to take home?'

He smiled, 'I'm not too grown up for that. I'll enjoy it for my supper.'

She looked radiant. He noticed with pleasure that she was taking more interest in her appearance; she'd had her hair cut differently and tonight she was wearing a touch of lipstick. It made her look grown up.

'I put it in a Pyrex dish, it's too soft and squidgy to put in a bag.'

He could see it through the glass lid. 'That's a very generous piece. Can you spare all that?'

'Yes, Mum says cake like this will make me fat.'

He laughed, 'You don't need to worry about that yet. I'll bring the dish back next time I come.'

Helen came out and waved to him as he drove away. He felt excited. In six more weeks, Chloe would be seventeen, and now she was wearing make-up; clearly she was beginning to think of the opposite sex.

He could feel himself tingling as he decided he'd waited long enough. She was old enough to be told what was on his mind. He was nervous about doing it because he was afraid she might not feel that way about him. In all honesty, he'd seen no sign that she did. He'd like to start by inviting her to come out for a restaurant meal with him. On her own.

The difficulty was, he didn't want to upset Helen by excluding her. He'd need to talk to her about it first, and just thinking about that made his toes curl with embarrassment. He'd have to tell her outright that he was in love with her daughter. And in view of Chloe's youth and the difference in their ages, would she approve of that?

These days he saw much more of Helen than he did of Chloe. He'd have to wait for the right opportunity to say something like that, but if he looked out for one, sooner or later it would come.

'Rex is nice, isn't he?' Chloe said to her mother as they drove off. 'Very nice,' she agreed. 'A good friend to us both.'

They went first to pick up Gran and Marigold, as Joan and Walter had invited them all to have dinner at their house to celebrate Helen's birthday. Chloe had been looking forward to it.

She was pleased to see her mother smiling and happy. She'd be on top of the world if Mum's spells of black depression were really behind her. It had taken them a very long time to get this far.

Chloe, too, had had her nightmares and her black moods. Her father's absence was a terrible ache and moving up to Liverpool and starting another new school two terms after everybody else had been hard. Mum had brought with her all the furniture and belongings that reminded them of Dad, and had placed photographs of him on show about their new home. She had a way of speaking about him frequently, as though he were still with them.

Auntie Joan and Uncle Walter had been very kind to both of them when they'd first come north. When Chloe's twelfth birthday came round, Mum and Joan had taken her into town. She'd wanted a record player for her own room and they'd let her choose the one she wanted.

Then Uncle Walter had taken them all to the Adelphi Hotel for a special lunch and she'd had ice-cream cake. Before going back to his factory, he'd taken her to a record shop and bought her some of the latest records by Cliff Richard and Adam Faith. By the following year they'd had Beatlemania at school, as had half of England, and Chloe had played their records all the time. She still did, they were her favourites, and every birthday after that Uncle Walter gave her their latest album. 'Love Me Do' was her all-time favourite song.

Every month or so, Auntie Joan and Mum met for lunch in town, and they got together for family celebrations. Aunt Goldie had told Chloe that Joan had made her fortune by marrying Walter Bristow, and she should look out for a rich man too.

Walter Bristow was coming up to retirement age but he was still running the company he'd set up many years earlier. He'd trained as a vet and had very modern ideas about feeding animals. He thought many of the diseases suffered by pets were caused by giving them the wrong diet. He produced foods for dogs, cats, hamsters, rabbits and guinea pigs, each designed to provide a balanced diet to keep the animal in good health. He believed that a dried crunch of ingredients was the easiest way for pet owners to buy and store it.

Her mother drew up in front of Uncle Walter's big house in Freshfield and Auntie Joan came to the door to let them in. She was one of those people who was always bubbling with good humour.

'Hello, Chloe.' She threw her arms round her and pulled her in. 'Happy birthday, Helen.'

Chloe considered Auntie Joan to be one of those women who was still genuinely pretty at fifty. Marigold said disparagingly that it was all done with make-up and that she dyed her hair palest blonde when really it should be grey.

Uncle Walter met them in the hall. He was a big man with a head of thick white hair, pink cheeks and a cherubic face. He gathered Chloe up as usual in one of his big bear hugs, but tonight he wasn't his smiling self.

'Sorry, Helen,' he said, kissing her cheek. 'We've no birthday present for you. I took Joan to the theatre last night and while we were out, thieves broke in and took it.'

'Mum's present?' Chloe wanted to laugh.

'It was a book, Helen. Joan had it wrapped up ready for you.'

'It was that new novel by Rosamund Rogerson,' Joan said. 'I'll buy another copy next time I go into town.'

'You shouldn't be telling Mum what it was,' Chloe giggled.

'Oh dear! I'm not myself today,' Auntie Joan said. 'They took the family silver too.'

'All of it?'

25

'Yes, we think they broke in to get that.'

'You had such a lot, and it was valuable, wasn't it?'

'Walter's father left it to him. He was interested in antique silver and collected it all his life.'

'And now it's gone,' Walter sighed sadly.

'Did they take anything else?' Helen asked.

'Some money, but the police think they were targeting the silver.'

'Don't the rich suffer?' Marigold said sourly. 'It's a comfort to know thieves are unlikely to target us.'

'The best we can say,' Joan added, 'is that it was insured, so we'll get something back.'

'Doesn't the sideboard look bare without it?' Walter sighed. 'I'd like to buy more, but good-quality silver isn't easy to find. And I'm afraid I don't have my father's knowledge. He was never happier than when he was visiting antique shops or grand houses when they were selling off good silver.'

'It's been a hard day,' Joan said. 'The police were here for ages. But it's not the end of the world, and we aren't going to let it spoil your birthday dinner. Come on, Walter, what about the drinks? Gran, you'll have sherry, will you?'

Rex went home to his comfortless bachelor flat and grilled a pork chop for his supper. Afterwards he made himself a pot of tea, ate Chloe's cake and gave himself up to daydreaming about her.

Helen had confided how difficult Chloe had been when they'd first come to Liverpool, and that she was missing her father and also her friends in London. Rex was no stranger to bereavement and knew it could change everything for family members. He'd been bereaved twice, and both times it had been traumatic. His mother had died while he was still a child. Then only a few months before the Redwoods arrived, he'd lost Sylvia, his wife of two years. They'd been visiting her parents, who kept a hotel on Lake Windermere. Almost every time they went there, they'd gone rowing on the lake, but this time they'd been run down by a speedboat. Neither of them could swim and he'd been unable to help her. She'd drowned together with their unborn child.

After Sylvia's sudden death, he was floundering so badly he thought he'd never recover. Nothing had been further from his mind than that he should fall in love with Chloe. He didn't know how it had come about. Over the last year or so, he'd come to accept that Sylvia was lost to him for ever and that if he wanted a wife he must find somebody new. He had in mind a well-balanced woman like Sylvia, grown up and with a mind of her own.

But it was the contract he'd signed with Helen, the garden, and the support and companionship he'd found in her and Chloe that had eventually turned his life round. He'd wanted to do the same for them.

He'd watched Chloe grow up, and it had been like tending a rare plant that had eventually produced one magnificent flower. She was still more girl than woman, but already Rex knew he wanted no other. He loved her and always would.

In those early days when he'd been working in their garden, he'd occasionally seen her come rushing out, angry and rebellious. He pretended not to notice her agitation and tear-stained face and asked her to help with whatever he was doing. A gardening job pulling up weeds seemed to help calm her.

At other times he'd see her come out to cut a lettuce or a cabbage for the table, or even late on a winter's afternoon with a saucepan to cut sprouts for their supper. It seemed she was interested in growing vegetables, perhaps because her mother preferred flowers.

'I'd like to have a vegetable patch of my own,' Chloe had said one day. He'd started her on radishes and sugar peas, which Helen called mangetout, so she'd have something to eat quickly. The sugar peas produced a bumper crop and Chloe had been able to brag that she'd planted them and weeded them and put in the sticks to help them grow up off the ground. They'd proved to be a huge success and she'd planted them every year since.

He saw Chloe as another teenager as unhappy as he'd been. Helen was focused on her own loss and didn't seem to see Chloe's needs. He'd grown to love Chloe without even realising it was happening.

He thought she'd desperately needed a confidant. While they'd bedded out seedlings of lettuce and cabbage, she'd told him of her agony on joining a school where friendships and loyalties had been formed in the months before she'd got there. She'd explained her difficulties with classwork when the curriculum had changed.

'I'm left out of everything. I never quite know what I'm meant to be doing. It confuses me, makes me look a fool.'

'That's the last thing you are, Chloe.'

'I want to do the right thing, I want to join in and be one of them, but somehow I can't.'

'Just keep on trying. The teenage years can be troubled.'

'Were yours? Were you unhappy when you were my age?'

'Yes, I was, but for a different reason.'

'You didn't lose your dad or get moved from one end of the country to the other?' The intense gaze of her lavender-coloured eyes had challenged him.

'No, I lost my mother.'

'Gosh, that's worse. How old were you then?'

'Ten.'

'That's awful.'

It was not Rex's way to talk about his own difficulties. He'd let it be known generally that Horace Kenwright, the owner of Kenwright's Garden Centre, was his father, but that wasn't strictly true. Rex was the eldest son of Laura Kenwright, née Harrington, born before she met and married Horace.

Rex remembered the time when he and his mother had been everything to each other. She'd taken him in her arms to say, 'I'm going to get married. Horace Kenwright will be my husband and your father and we both need him.'

But Rex had resented their new home and the way Horace became the centre of their life. He'd

29

been five when his mother married and he'd started school a week later. He'd had to share his mother's attention and felt pushed out. Over the years that followed, he was aware that Horace found fault with everything he did and carped at his mother. He knew she was unhappy and never allowed to forget her misdemeanour. Horace had adopted him legally and given him his name, but he'd given him precious little else and certainly no love.

Before long, Rex had a half-brother called Simon and felt his mother had even less time for him, though he knew she loved him and did her best to stand between him and his stepfather. When Laura died giving birth to her third child, Gerald, Rex took it very hard.

In later years, he came to understand that in exchange for marrying his mother and adopting him, Harrington money had been forthcoming to set up the garden business and thus support them.

Rex had had an unhappy childhood. He felt Horace very much favoured his half-brothers; they could do no wrong. While his mother was alive, she'd protected him and been very support- ive, but once she'd gone, Rex became the butt of his father's ill humour.

Horace praised Simon and Gerald and sent them to private schools, whilst telling Rex he was an incompetent fool who could not compete with them.

For a time, his Harrington relatives kept in touch with birthday and Christmas gifts, but he rarely saw them. Eventually, there was only his grandfather left, and he was an invalid living in a nursing home.

As a child, Rex had spent his free time making himself useful in the family business, befriending his father's employees and learning from them. He felt he'd grown up without a place in the family, and when the time came for him to leave school, his father had refused to take him into the business.

He'd found himself a job working for the council in their parks and gardens department, and as soon as he could, he'd left home. He was twenty-one when he received a letter from the Harringtons' solicitor telling him that his grandfather had died and that he was the main beneficiary in his will. That changed Rex's life; he knew now what he wanted to do. He enrolled at a horticultural college.

There he met Sylvia, and for a time his star was rising. He decided it would do him no good to resent the Kenwrights, and tried not to feel alienated. His stepfather was still running the business; he'd taken both Simon and Gerald into it, and it was thriving as never before.

He couldn't say all that to thirteen-year-old Chloe. It was too painful to him and he doubted she'd understand, but he told her enough of it to develop a rapport with her.

Helen noticed that Chloe was to be found increasingly often in the garden, chatting to Rex. The vegetable patch grew larger. Chloe wanted fruit bushes, and together they chose and planted blackcurrants and gooseberries and strawberries. Helen too was keen on fruit. Rex took them both to the garden centre at the right time and they bought apple trees and a Victoria plum, a greengage and a damson tree.

In recent years they'd all enjoyed the fresh fruit and Helen had said, 'You're very good for Chloe. She's lost her father, but you're a great father figure for her.'

That made him catch his breath. It wasn't how he saw himself. He hoped Chloe didn't see him in that light, but he doubted she saw him as a prospective husband. The age difference was too great.

One afternoon, Rex was emptying the pond in the lower part of the garden. This had been a rather boggy area, but with a little drainage in the surrounding land he'd achieved a natural pond. Helen had wanted water lilies in it, and though he had a few flowers floating on the water now, the water had grown muddy again.

Today he'd brought some frogspawn, as the tadpoles would eat the algae that was discolouring the water. Emptying and cleaning out the pond was the sort of job Chloe loved. He'd told her he was going to do it. She'd come rushing home from school to shed her shoes and socks on the bank, and still wearing the rest of her school uniform, waded in to join him. He saw immediately that she was upset.

'I hate school,' she told him angrily. 'I loathe all the girls there and they don't like me.'

'Has something happened?' he asked cautiously.

'They hid my gym bag from me and I got into trouble for that, and then I came bottom of the form in a biology test.'

'I'm sorry to hear you have problems at school.'

Chloe sniffed and started pulling out pond weeds. 'I'd rather leave school and help you all day,' she told him. She was sliding about in the mud.

'That's nice to know, Chloe, but you'll have a problem with your mum too if you wallow in all this mud. Shouldn't you go and change?'

She burst into tears at that, so he led her up the bank and sat down on the grass beside her. 'It's not just that, is it?'

'It's everything,' she wept. 'I'm a wicked person, that's why everybody hates me.'

'I don't hate you, and I don't think you're at all wicked. What makes you say that?'

She lifted her hand from her face and he saw her eyes were great pools of misery. 'You don't know how bad I am.'

'Go on then, tell me.'

'I killed my father.'

'What? That's not what your mother says.'

'She's told you about it?'

'Yes. Chloe, she blames herself for your father's death.'

'She blames me, it was my fault. I was big-headed and thought I could climb too.' She started to tell him how she'd slipped away from her mother when she wasn't watching, had gone after her father and caused the accident.

'An accident is an accident. It doesn't mean anyone has to take the blame.'

'If I'd stayed with Mum, it wouldn't have happened.'

'Yes, you made a mistake, but your father wanted to take you with him, and your mum stopped him doing that. She was afraid for you because they were going to do a harder climb. Had she let you go with the climbers, your father would have made sure you were safe, and it would never have happened.'

Chloe sat beside him sniffing but saying nothing.

'And what about your dad? He fastened you into his safety harness and that saved your life. Your mum says that if only he'd stayed in his harness and just hung on to you, nobody would have fallen. You all made mistakes. But your dad wouldn't want you and your mum to be unhappy, would he?'

'We can't help it. We want him back. It's no good saying we must forget what happened; we can't.'

'You'll never forget it, Chloe, it's changed your life. What you must try to do is to put it behind you and move on.'

'I don't know whether we can.'

'I want you to try. Promise me you will?'

He'd treated her as the lost girl she was and he thought she'd responded.

For Chloe, the feeling of personal guilt would not go away, though she'd tried to do what Rex had suggested. She couldn't get away, from the fact that if only she'd stayed with Mum that day, Dad would still be with them. She'd never climbed since, never been near Capel Curig and never wanted to.

She'd grown up feeling lost and mixed up and as though she'd never recovered from her father's death. She knew she disappointed her mother because she'd never shone in the classroom after that.

Mum had wanted her to go to college, but at fifteen she was still all at odds with herself and had no idea which direction she wanted her life to take. All she could think of was leaving school at the first possible moment.

Mum had insisted she go to secretarial college, where she'd learned shorthand typing and book-keeping; after that, she'd drifted into a job in the local office of the Inland Revenue Department. There, she'd finally settled down and made friends, and thanks to Rex and the garden she was now content with her lot. All she wanted was for things to stay this way.

No, that wasn't quite true. She was happy enough, but she knew she wanted more. The girls in the office told her of the exciting times they had with their boyfriends. Chloe had been taken to a dance by one of the young men in the office and to the pictures by another, but she'd found little excitement in their company.

CHAPTER THREE

A few days later, Chloe came home from work to find her mother quite excited. 'I've been to see the summerhouses at the garden centre,' she said. 'They're absolutely gorgeous.'

'Have you made up your mind? About which one you want?'

'I'd like to go back for another look. Why don't you come with me on Saturday? I'd like your opinion.'

Chloe did, but as soon as she saw them, she knew her mother would want the most expensive one. 'Can you afford it?' she asked.

Dad had left them reasonably well provided for, but Mum wasn't as careful with money as she should be. Chloe felt that earning her own salary in the income tax office had made her more aware of the value of money than her mother was. She knew Mum could be very self-indulgent.

'It is a lot to draw out of the bank,' Helen said, 'but I've thought of another way to pay for it. In yesterday's newspaper there was a dealer offering cash for old clocks. I thought we could see how much he'd give me for that grandfather clock in the hall.'

When they got back home, Chloe took a hard look at the familiar clock. 'This name on the dial, Henry Sanderson, London, is that the maker?'

'I'm not sure. Could it be the shop where it was

bought? It kept good time in London but it stopped when we brought it up here and I haven't been able to get it going again.'

'Perhaps it didn't want to come,' Chloe said.

'We've got too many clocks, haven't we?' Her mother led the way into the sitting room. 'I wouldn't mind selling this mantel clock as well.'

'That one keeps good time,' Chloe pointed out. 'How much are they worth?'

'I've no idea. They're old, they belonged to John's father. Enough, d'you think, to pay for that summerhouse?'

'I don't know. You ought to find out what they're worth before you try to sell them.'

Chloe was afraid she would not. Mum was impatient and wanted to get on with things. So during her lunch hour the next day, she went to the reference library, where she found several price guides for antiques. There were even photographs of clocks bearing the same names as those her mother had, and it seemed they were worth a considerable amount.

When she reached home that evening, there was a strange car parked outside, and when she opened the front door, she saw a man shining a torch into the workings of the grandfather clock.

Her mother came dancing down the hall with the energy of a woman half her age. 'He's come to buy the clocks,' she said excitedly.

'You should have waited, Mum.'

The man turned and nodded to Chloe. 'My daughter,' Helen said to him.

He was a tall, well-set-up young man in his early twenties, with dark curly hair worn long and

37

dishevelled in today's popular style, which her mother often deplored on celebrities. He straightened up and came forward to Chloe with his hand outstretched.

'Adam Livingstone,' he said, his face lighting up into a broad, friendly smile.

Chloe met the gaze of his dark eyes as he grasped her hand. She felt she could see right into his soul and felt a tug of attraction such as she'd never known before. It left her breathless.

She pulled herself together. 'So what are you prepared to offer Mum for her clock?' she asked.

'I was just looking at it.' His smile remained as he turned back to the clock. 'It's George III, a fine mahogany case and an eight-day movement. Let me see...'

When she heard the figure he put on it, Chloe pulled up short. It was a lot lower than the price guide had led her to believe it was worth. She saw her mother's face fall.

'Not enough,' Chloe said shortly.

Adam's eyes played with hers as he added another twenty pounds to the price.

'No,' she said. Mum couldn't afford to give him a bargain. Not if she wanted that summerhouse. 'Still not enough.'

'But it isn't in working condition,' her mother put in anxiously. 'It won't be worth all that much, will it?'

'That puts it in a nutshell.' Adam beamed from Helen to Chloe. He was radiating confidence, but Chloe was afraid he was trying to do her mother down.

'I think we'd be better putting it in an auction,'

Chloe said. 'Henry Sanderson, London is a well-known name, isn't it?'

'Yes,' he agreed. 'To those in the trade. Not wildly valuable, though.'

'All the same...'

It didn't seem to faze him that her mum had got him here and now she was suggesting it might be better to sell elsewhere. He was going round their sitting room looking at their ornaments. 'I'm in the market for other things,' he said hopefully. 'Furniture and china.'

Chloe said nothing. Helen pointed out the mantel clock to him.

'I agree, you might get more if you put your clocks in an auction,' he said, and went on to give her the name of their nearest auction room and explain how to go about it. All the time his eyes followed every movement Chloe made. She was beginning to think he was flirting with her.

'It's closed now, of course,' he said. 'But it'll be open tomorrow morning until twelve.' Tomorrow was Saturday. 'I could take you there.' He flashed another wide smile at Chloe. 'Both of you,' he added hurriedly, 'and you could arrange for them to be entered in a sale. How about that?'

Chloe was watching her mother's face. She was keen to sell her clocks and get that summer-house. 'Thank you, that's very kind,' she told him.

'I'll be here at ten o'clock, then.'

Her mother was voicing her misgivings as soon as the front door closed behind him. 'What did you have to do that for? It'll take longer to put it in an auction, and we might get even less that way. There'll be commission to pay and we'll have to get a carrier to take the grandfather clock in.'

'He was trying to cheat you.'

'No, I don't think so. He's a polite and charming young man.'

'Perhaps that's the impression he was trying to give.'

'Chloe! He's going out of his way to take us to this auction room. There's nothing in it for him, is there? He's being very kind.'

She told her mother about the guide prices she'd seen in the library.

'But what good is a clock that won't work? I can't get this one to go.'

Chloe was not convinced until the next day, when Adam turned up on time and did much more than take them to the auction rooms.

'I want to put this mantel clock in the sale too,' Helen said, tucking it under her arm. He helped her fill in the paperwork to enter the clocks in a sale, then offered to ferry the grandfather clock in for her.

He drove them home and expertly removed and dismantled the hood and the working parts of the long-case clock. He produced grey blankets and wrapped the pieces up. 'I'm used to doing this sort of thing,' he said, smiling at Helen now. She was clearly impressed by him.

Chloe helped him carry the pieces out and he laid them flat in the back of his large estate car. On their return to the auction room, he helped her mother book the clock in and then re-assembled it where the staff said they wanted it to stand.

The auction room was open and the goods destined for the next sale were on show to the public. Adam took them round, pointing out the interesting pieces and chatting about them. Chloe was fascinated, and she could see her mother was too. He certainly knew a lot about antiques. But it wasn't just that. His eyes kept trying to meet hers and were full of admiration. Her mother was right, he was charming. Chloe was enchanted.

It was well after midday when they left. Adam paused as they were about to pass the doorway of the pub next door. 'Are you hungry?' he asked, including them both. 'How about a bite to eat in here?'

'It's very kind of you, but no thanks,' her mother told him briskly. 'Chloe and I have things we must do this afternoon.'

By then, Chloe knew he was attracted to her, he was making that fairly obvious. It wasn't that he was giving her all his attention, because he was being careful not to let her mother feel neglected, but she noticed that he turned to listen with extra care to everything she had to say.

She made up her mind. 'I have nothing to do that can't wait,' she said, 'I'd love to have a bite to eat with Adam.'

Her mother straightened up, stiffly rigid.

Adam perked up and asked with suitable diffidence, 'Would you mind if Chloe and I...?'

Chloe could see she'd shocked her mother. Helen was looking from her to Adam with indecision stamped on her face. She wanted to refuse to let them have lunch together, but it would seem churlish when he'd been so kind to them. Chloe thought she was afraid to refuse in case it started an argument.

'I'd like to, Mum. It'll be all right, won't it?'

Helen smiled warily. 'I suppose so. Then I'll see you later, darling.' She kissed Chloe's cheek. 'And thank you so much, Adam, for your help with the clocks.'

Polite words, but her mother's tense back as she strode down the street told Chloe she was unhappy. A thrill ran up her arm when she felt Adam take it to lead her inside. He was a jolly sort of person who laughed a lot, the very opposite to her mother. She could feel herself opening up to him. Her cheeks felt on fire as she told him about herself. In the next couple of hours, they didn't stop talking.

Afterwards, Chloe had no idea what she'd eaten. She was conscious only of him; everything else faded into the background. She thought she'd found the soulmate she'd pined for since she was fourteen. He was her first real boyfriend and she was bowled over.

She saw a lot more of Adam before her mother's clocks came up for auction. He lived in Manchester, and two or three times a week he'd drive over to Liverpool to take her out, usually for dinner in a smart restaurant or to the theatre. He seemed to enjoy the finer things in life and wanted her to enjoy them too.

'It's a long way to come so often,' her mother told him.

He laughed. 'I drive miles all over the country to antique shops and auction houses and to see

42

private clients. I like driving and it's part of my job.'

They were having fun. Her mother had always been strict about the time she came home at night. Ten o'clock was the limit when she went to the pictures with her girlfriends. But Adam called at the house to collect her and asked if he might make it a little later so they didn't have to leave the theatre before the end of the show or rush their coffee in a restaurant.

'She'll be safe with me,' he told Helen. 'I'll take good care of her.'

So that gave them time alone in his car. It was what Chloe enjoyed most. Adam would pull her close and tell her again that he'd fallen in love with her within seconds of first seeing her.

'All my life,' he said, 'I've been hoping to meet a girl like you.' She found his kisses could be tender as well as passionate.

It was Friday, and Rex had spent the afternoon gardening with Helen. During the early part of the week he'd dealt with other clients, but Chloe had been very much in his thoughts. He wanted to tell her he loved her, but he'd have to build up to it gradually, make her see that he was serious about her.

At this time of the year, it grew chilly as evening approached. It had become routine for Helen to ask him indoors for a cup of tea.

They'd chatted about bringing more scent into the garden. He'd told her what plants were available now and advised where they should be planted. Helen had made up her mind about what she wanted. They'd reached what previously would have been a companionable silence, but Rex was unable to relax. The words he wanted to say to Helen had been on the edge of his tongue all afternoon, but he hadn't yet voiced them. He was afraid it would come as a shock to her.

As always, she seemed to welcome Rex's company, and he usually stayed until Chloe came home from work. These days it was the only time he could be sure of seeing her. Tonight she was later than usual. His anticipation was growing; he felt very much on edge. They'd drained the teapot, and Helen had offered him a bottle of beer and poured herself a glass of wine before he heard the front door slam and Chloe came bounding into the kitchen. She brought with her a gust of cold air and seemed to light up the room.

'Hi, Rex,' she said, and pulled a face at his beer glass. 'No tea?'

Helen said, 'You're late, we drank it all. Shall I make some more?'

'No thanks, Mum. Adam's coming to pick me up and I need to get changed.' She rushed noisily upstairs. Helen had seemed relaxed, but now suddenly Rex could see her face clenching with stress.

He couldn't get his breath. 'Who is this Adam?'

'He's arranged to have my old clocks sold at auction. I told you I was thinking of selling them to raise money for the summerhouse, didn't I?' Helen's frown was getting deeper, and for once, he thought she looked her age. 'Excuse me a moment, Rex.' He heard her footsteps running upstairs after Chloe.

So Chloe had already found herself a boy-friend! Rex was shaking as he poured the rest of the beer into his glass. He'd waited too long! How could he have been so stupid as to do that? He could hear their voices now, Helen's was raised in anger. It made him shrink back in his chair. He hated rows like this; they could tear a family apart. It seemed Helen was not happy about this boyfriend either.

Rex was still trying to take in the implications when the doorbell rang. As the voices didn't break off, he got up and went to open the front door.

The handsome young man standing on the doorstep made his anxiety stab up another notch. 'You must be Adam,' he said. 'I think you're ex-pected. You'd better come in, Chloe's getting ready for you.'

It was with a heavy heart that he led him into the kitchen. Adam sat down at the other side of the table on the chair Helen had vacated. Rex was able to study him. He was just the right age for Chloe, a personable young man with plenty of self-confidence and social chatter. Rex found it hard to respond suitably. Adam was his rival. And what a rival! It seemed to Rex very unlikely Chloe would toss Adam aside and turn to him. What a fool he was. Why had it never occurred to him that he might have competition?

Chloe lost no time in getting away and taking Adam with her. Helen was clearly upset. Rex had the impression she was very much against the new boyfriend. He couldn't trust himself to sit discussing Adam with her. He needed to be alone to think about this. He made his escape as soon as he could.

He went home feeling cross with himself for letting this happen. He'd been telling himself it was his duty to wait until Chloe was old enough. He hadn't recognised that he was waiting too long, that he was allowing another man to step in and take her. She was like quicksilver, full of energy and enthusiasm; he was too old and too slow for a girl like her, and this proved it.

On the day her mother's clocks were to be auctioned, Chloe took a half-day off work to go with her. Helen had been edgy with anticipation since breakfast time. Adam met them at the auction hall and escorted them to the seats he'd reserved. The place was buzzing with excitement.

While the long-case clock was being sold, Chloe hung on to Adam's hand and held her breath. The bidding went up and stopped; at what seemed the last moment, it went up further. It made considerably more than Adam had offered for it, though not as much as the figure quoted in the price guide. On her other side, her mother was all smiles to have some of the money for her summerhouse, but it left Chloe wondering.

'It made more than you wanted to give us,' she said to Adam, hoping she didn't sound suspicious.

He laughed. 'I knew it would,' he said easily. 'That's how the trade works. The person who wants the clock to furnish his house is the one who is prepared to pay the most for it. But he expects it to be in good repair, polished up and

46

delivered to his door. I sometimes work on a piece, or arrange for the work to be done.

'If you buy from a fancy antique shop, you'll pay more than if you bid for it at auction, for much the same reason. The shop owner will have put it in working condition and the customer doesn't have to hang about at the auction house waiting for the piece to come up for sale. Dealers like me make our living from these price differences; from our knowledge of the trade and selling, if we can, to the customer who loves it and wants to keep it.'

'Oh!' So it seemed he hadn't been trying to fleece her mother.

The auctioneer announced, 'Lot number five hundred and two.'

'This is yours too,' Adam whispered to Helen.

'Early Georgian ebonised mantel clock with brass dial, by William Webster, Exchange Alley, London.'

'It should do well,' Adam said softly, and gave them his personal estimate of what it would make. It was knocked down for a price exactly midway between the two figures he'd suggested.

Chloe felt that had settled all her doubts about him; it was just that she hadn't understood his trade. She was looking forward to learning more about it, as well as about him.

CHAPTER FOUR

The summerhouse had been ordered. Rex agreed it would look splendid in her garden. It gave him pleasure that he was able to bring good business to his family's firm. Simon, his half-brother, had thanked him for that. Rex was pleased he could show his stepfather that he was capable of earning a living in his own way.

Horace had treated him as though he lacked drive and intelligence because he didn't immediately try to talk customers into buying things in the way he and Simon did. He'd told Rex he was introverted and needed to be brought out of his shell.

Rex was proud that Helen had searched him out for his expertise, and they'd both derived great pleasure from designing and maintaining her garden. It had relaxed her and brought her peace. Rex had always known that gardening soothed him. Nothing suited him better than being outside in all weathers.

The day came for the summerhouse to be delivered. Helen had chosen the biggest and best on offer and it would have to come on a low loader. Her gates were wide enough to get the vehicle through, but once inside, the paths were not. What concerned Rex now was the need to minimise the damage to her garden. He'd had to dig up plants from two borders to save them being crushed. It had been dry recently and the ground was hard, so hopefully the tyres wouldn't churn up the lawn too much.

Rex was proud of the lush green oasis they'd achieved in this residential area. Helen encouraged him to keep coming up with new ideas to hone a corner here or a vista there. It meant more to him than any other job that had come his way. Of course, it meant even more to Helen.

Rex looked at his watch and wished the low loader would come. He'd prepared the base, and the mechanism that would make it turn had been put in place yesterday. What was coming today was the wooden prefabricated building that they'd erect on top. Helen came racing out of the house dressed in her gardening gear of jeans and old check shirt with rolled-up sleeves.

'It's coming. It's coming, Rex!' She was jumping with excitement as she ran to open the gate. She was a good-looking woman, and never more so than now, with her hair bouncing, her cheeks flushed and her eyes shining. She looked a decade younger than her real age. She came running over to him, and behind her the low loader was being backed carefully in.

'I can't wait to see my summerhouse in place,' she laughed.

'It's going to take us a while,' he warned.

But Gerald, his younger half-brother, who'd come with the low loader and brought a gang of three men from the garden centre to erect the summerhouse, said, 'We'll have it up before dark,' and received a little smile of pleasure from Helen in return.

When Chloe came home from work, the floor was in place and the frame was going up. It took Rex's breath away to see her come dancing across to take a closer look.

'Oh Rex, it's going to be lovely. Mum's over the moon.'

But he was so afraid he'd never mean any more to her than he did today.

Rex knew that Mrs Darty and Marigold were invited to Sunday lunch almost every week. On warm days they would sit out in the garden afterwards with the old lady wrapped in shawls.

'Now we'll be able to sit in the summerhouse,' Helen said. 'Gran will be comfortable there for many more months of the year.'

For the next Sunday, Helen invited Rex too. He looked forward to going because he'd be with Chloe for several hours. She'd talk to him and he'd be able to find out if she was as serious about Adam as he thought. When he arrived, Helen was already in the sitting room, sipping sherry with her relatives. Chloe let him in, all smiles and wearing her red dress and high heels again.

'You look very smart,' Rex told her.

'Thank you.' She looked grown up and very beautiful. 'If you'd rather have beer than sherry, come to the kitchen first,' she whispered. He was glad to follow her anywhere; she seemed to dance in front of him. The kitchen was full of delicious roasting scents.

'Lager is what you like, isn't it?' She tipped one bottle into a tankard for him. 'D'you want to take another bottle with you? There's only sherry on offer in there.'

'Better not,' he said.

Marigold gave him a frosty glare when Chloe took him in. Her conversation was mostly about her own aches and pains.

'My back,' she said, 'is riddled with arthritis, and so are my hands.' She held them up to show him how misshapen they were. 'They ache terribly in cold weather.'

'You must keep your hands warm, Aunt Goldie.' Chloe smiled at her.

'It's not that easy when I have the housework to do, and your granny makes a lot of washing for me. She likes pure wool next to her, you know, and I have to hand-wash all that.'

Old Mrs Darty had very little to say. Marigold told Rex that her mother had been fighting bowel cancer for years and that her heart was giving her trouble too. Helen seemed to sense the atmosphere and was more than usually chatty, as if trying to make up for it. She was very enthusiastic about her new summerhouse.

'Chloe and I love it,' she said. 'We'll have our coffee there today, after lunch.'

Rex carved the joint of beef, but his lack of practice showed. Living alone, he didn't buy joints any more. It was a breezy day of fitful sunshine, and when the meal was over, Helen offered to help Gran out to the summerhouse.

The old lady looked round, almost as though she didn't know where she was. 'I don't feel too well, Marigold,' she said. 'I want to go home.'

'We won't wait for coffee today, Helen, thank

you,' Marigold said. 'It upsets Mother's stomach anyway and I think she'd feel better in her own bed. She always goes up for an hour after lunch, as you know.'

'Shall I take you to see my summerhouse first?' Helen asked.

'I can see it from here,' Marigold said, looking through the window. It was at least thirty yards away and partly obscured by bushes. 'I'll take a closer look next time I come.'

So Helen helped Gran into her coat and scarves and took them out to her car to run them home. Chloe started to clear the dishes from the dining room. Rex stayed to help.

'Aunt Goldie does moan,' she said. 'Not a load of fun for you listening to all that.'

'The roast dinner was good, I enjoyed that. So did everybody else, I think.'

'We all tucked into it.' Chloe gave him a quick smile. 'Though Aunt Goldie reckons neither she nor Gran has any appetite.'

Rex managed to say, 'I understand you have a boyfriend now.'

'Yes,' she giggled. 'He's lovely, but I don't think Mum's keen on him.' That cast Rex down; it was bad news for him.

Just as they were finishing the washing-up, Helen brought Adam inside. 'We arrived at the same moment,' she said. 'Adam has come to pick Chloe up.'

It pained Rex to see the way their eyes met, the look of adoration they exchanged. Chloe shot upstairs and came down wearing her coat.

'Bye.' She flashed Rex a radiant smile. 'Bye,

52

Mum.' She dropped a fleeting kiss on her cheek.

Helen sank down at the kitchen table with a sigh as the front door banged behind them. 'Not much fun for you, Rex, I'm afraid,' she said, echoing Chloe's words.

He thought it had been rather a stiff and uncomfortable occasion. Helen hadn't relaxed. Chloe had been her usual self and done more than her share of seeing that everybody was served. But it had been hurtful to see Adam here again and to know they'd arranged to spend the rest of the afternoon together. It seemed he was becoming an established boyfriend and that would end any hope Rex had.

'Let's have that coffee Marigold stopped me making,' Helen said. 'You could do with a cup, couldn't you, Rex?'

He'd been thinking of going home to nurse his wounds and read the Sunday papers, and didn't answer quickly enough.

'Well I'll have one anyway,' she said, switching on the coffee pot. 'I need something to keep me sane.'

'Yes please,' he said belatedly. 'The ladies were having an off day. You mustn't let that get you down.'

'It's mostly how they are. All their days are off.' He could see her hand shaking and knew she was upset. He thought perhaps they'd had a family tiff.

She sniffed into her handkerchief and said in a confidential tone, 'I don't have an ordinary family.'

He'd been about to say 'I don't either,' but bit

the words back.

I suppose you've guessed,' she said. Her eyes, full of misery, looked up into his.

'Guessed what?'

'Marigold is my mother.' There was a catch in her voice. 'She had me when she was sixteen. She was never married.'

That took his breath away. 'But Mrs Darty – don't you call her mother?'

He wished he hadn't said that, it made him sound unfeeling.

'I was brought up to believe she was. It's habit, I suppose. Chloe calls her Gran. I do try to do the same, but sometimes I forget.'

Rex felt tongue-tied. What did one say to such a revelation?

'I was fourteen when I found out. They were having a row. Gran was angry and said enough to set me thinking.' Helen's voice shook; he knew she was only just able to control her tears. 'Eventually I screwed up my courage and asked Marigold. She had to tell me then.'

Rex did his best. 'That was a terrible way to find out. It must have been a shock.'

'Yes.' She nodded. 'I wasn't who I'd thought I was, and my family wasn't either.'

Rex had known from the beginning that Helen was emotionally fragile. 'I did think they seemed very old compared to you.' He jerked to his feet to pour out two cups of coffee, then pushed one in front of her. 'Drink this, it'll make you feel better.'

She was mopping at her eyes.

'All that has come out from behind the net

curtains, Helen,' he went on. 'This is the sixties, there's been a rebellion against Victorian values. These are the days of flower power. There's no shame attached to your situation these days.'

'But there was in 1921 when I was born. Illegitimacy was a very shameful thing and it's been eating into all three of us ever since.'

He understood how corrosive that sort of thing could be. 'No blame could be attached to you. You were the innocent baby.'

'Marigold blamed me. Still does.'

'Yet her mother did it to shield her. To give her a better chance in life.'

'But it didn't. Having me left her paralysed. Held her in limbo. She's done nothing with her life.'

'That's up to her, not you.'

'I don't think Gran realises how much it's affected her. Marigold can't stand men in general. She thinks they're all bad. Did you notice she was a bit offhand with you?'

Rex had, but he shook his head.

'As a family, we couldn't come to terms with it. Gran blames herself for not taking greater care of Marigold.'

'What about Marigold's father? Didn't he help?'

'No, I never knew him. Gran married a sea-going man, an officer in the merchant navy. All went well for the first few years, but when Marigold was four, he jumped ship in Australia and they never heard from him again.'

'Oh my goodness! So they haven't had a happy life.'

'Anything but. Gran managed to find a job, but

55

I know money was short and she found it a struggle to bring Marigold up. Then, just when she thought that job was done, she was landed with me.'

Rex felt full of compassion. Who wouldn't be?

Helen gave him a wan smile. 'They had me in chains from the age of fifteen and were deeply suspicious of any boy I looked at twice. They insisted I brought all boyfriends home for their inspection.'

Rex smiled, 'I bet they grilled them all.'

'Yes, and that embarrassed me and put them off. I had to stop taking them home.'

'But you did marry.'

'Yes, I was only eighteen when I met John, but I knew he was the one and I could trust him.'

'But your family didn't?'

'No, they were over-suspicious, doubted everything he said.'

'They were afraid the same thing would happen to you?'

'Yes, I understood why. I explained to John that they were afraid he'd make me pregnant and then abandon me. Marigold gave me Marie Stopes' books to read so I'd know what I had to avoid.'

'What did John say to that?'

Helen pretended to assume his voice. "They're bound to view me with a jaundiced eye." She laughed; it sounded hollow and mirthless. 'Nobody could have had more honourable intentions than John. He didn't lay a finger on me until our wedding night. He was ten years older than me and wanted us to be married. But we had to have their consent for that. I had to take him home.'

'Surely that's what they wanted for you?'

'Yes, but they didn't share my trust in John. He said, "The only way to deal with this is for us to be married as soon as we can." He'd been offered a transfer to the London office. To start with, he'd been reluctant to go, but we decided that to get away might be the best thing for us.'

'But time showed them his intentions were honourable?'

'We were very happy together, but he was killed, so the result has been much the same. Except ...'

'He left you well provided for?'

Helen nodded. 'That's about it.' He heard the catch in her voice; she was getting emotional again. Did she have more to tell him? He had to put a stop to this before she said too much of what was in her heart. He was afraid she'd bare too much of her soul and later regret it and feel she'd made a fool of herself.

As she pulled the front door shut behind her, Chloe felt Adam's arm go round her waist and pull her closer. She put her lips up to meet his. They were both laughing with the joy of newly found love as he ushered her into his car.

He drove out on the Southport road. 'Have you brought some shoes you can walk in?' he asked. 'I thought we'd spend the afternoon at Formby. It's lovely amongst the sandhills on the beach and there's the nature reserve and so much open space.'

When he parked the car, he tucked a couple of

rugs under his arm and gave Chloe a windbreak to carry. It was a bright and blustery afternoon, too cool and windy for the crowds, so there was nobody much about. The sea was choppy and the wind was whipping up the sand and blowing it about. 'It's stinging my face,' Chloe exclaimed.

'Mine too,' he laughed. 'And it's hard walking in such soft sand.'

'It feels as though I have weights on my feet.'

'Don't worry, we'll find a spot out of the wind and in the sun amongst these sandhills. Then we can sit down.'

Adam knew where to go, and spread his rugs on the sand. They lay down. 'Don't even need the windbreak here,' he said, pulling Chloe closer. She gave herself up to the kisses he was raining on her face. His body felt firm and strong against hers and he made her senses race. They stayed until evening was drawing in and it had grown cold.

'Back to Liverpool now,' he told her. 'I've booked a table at the Adelphi.'

'I'm full of sand,' she protested. 'I need to go home to change.'

'No, I'm starving.' With the car boot sheltering them from the wind, he shook her coat and dusted her down. She combed the sand out of her tangled hair and replaced her Alice band.

'You look great.' He smiled at her. 'I love that red dress. Now, where are your high heels? All you need is a few minutes in the ladies' at the Adelphi and you'll be the prettiest girl there.'

He was stripping off his pullover and replacing

it with a jacket and tie. He'd taken her to the Adelphi Hotel last week, and Chloe had loved the formality of the dining room: waiters in dress suits, starched white damask tablecloths and napkins, sparkling cutlery and china and fresh flowers. She knew it was reputed to be the best hotel in the city. She'd told the girls at work about it and asked if they liked it.

'It's heavy on style,' they agreed, 'and the food isn't bad, but it's very traditional.' They told her where she could get more exciting foreign dishes, but she knew formal and traditional were what Adam enjoyed.

After a wash, and a quick flick of her powder puff and lipstick, Chloe felt fine. Adam ordered wine and they lingered over the many courses while he talked of his career as an antique dealer.

'You're very young to have a house of your own,' she told him. 'Lucky to have achieved it so quickly.' She wanted to know all about it.

'It's in Didsbury, a suburb of Manchester,' he told her. 'It was built in Victorian times but it's in the Georgian style, which I like. You must come and see it.'

'I'd love to, nothing I'd like more.'

'Come home with me now. I could bring you back in time to go to work in the morning.'

Chloe laughed. 'No, Mum would have a fit.'

'You know you'd love to.'

'Yes, but I daren't.'

'Then come on the train on Saturday morning and spend the day with me. I'll meet you at the station.'

The prospect excited Chloe. Since he'd told her

he had a house, she couldn't stop thinking about it.

'One day,' he'd said, 'I hope you'll come and live there with me.'

Any thought of a future with Adam thrilled Chloe. She could feel his love; every day he telephoned her at work, and often he telephoned her again when she was back at home. He was always booking theatre and concert tickets for them as well as taking her to restaurants. When he came to pick her up, she frequently found he'd bought a little gift, sometimes chocolates and sometimes a book he thought she would enjoy.

Chloe was head over heels in love with Adam and knew it had been love at first sight for them both. He hadn't yet mentioned marriage or an engagement, but she felt a more permanent relationship must be on his mind and that they were progressing rapidly towards it.

In order to distract Helen, Rex got up and took both their mugs to the sink and started to wash them. She gazed out of the window. 'Marigold wouldn't even come to look at my new summer-house,' she said sadly.

'Now you've had time to try it, are you pleased with it?' He thought perhaps she wasn't.

'It needs fixing up inside. I put the old garden chairs in, but it needs more furniture and something to brighten it up. Come and see.'

Rex followed her over. He could see what she meant. The inside smelled of new wood, but it looked bare. Helen's wooden garden chairs were shabby, and the cushion covers looked faded.

'At least I don't have to bring them in every night to keep them dry,' she said. 'The summerhouse looks beautiful from the outside, and it's quite easy to swing it round. But I need to buy new furniture for it, make it smarter. What sort of furniture would look good in here?'

Rex looked round helplessly. 'I'm not much good at interior design,' he said. 'Doesn't Chloe have any ideas?'

'All Chloe can think about is her new boyfriend,' Helen said, and looked quite depressed.

Rex would have liked to go home, but felt he couldn't leave her if she was feeling low. 'Do you feel like a bit of gardening this afternoon?' he asked.

She sighed. 'I'm in one of those moods when I don't know what I want.'

'What about a walk, then?'

She gave him another wan smile. 'That would be nice.'

Helen had a lovely house and a magnificent garden, but there was no pleasant place to walk nearby. They could only pace the pavements.

He drove her in his van to Formby and they visited the nature reserve and walked for miles. Helen was fascinated with the red squirrels leaping through the trees and the number and variety of birds. When they got back to his van, her cheeks were glowing scarlet and Rex felt wind-tossed and full of fresh air.

It was early evening as he drove back. They'd mulled over next year's plans for the garden. Helen wanted to get more spring bulbs, so he took her to his stepfather's garden centre and she bought a sackful of daffodil bulbs.

The cafeteria stayed open until seven, so Rex suggested, 'D'you fancy a Welsh rarebit and a pot of tea?'

'Yes please, that sounds lovely.' She seemed more in control now and had quite a long and cheerful conversation with Rex's half-brother Simon.

When Rex ran his van on to her drive and carried the sack of daffodils to the back of her garage, she seemed happier than she had all day.

'It's been a lovely afternoon,' she said. 'I've enjoyed it. Thanks, Rex.'

He got back in his van and waited until he saw her door shut and the lights go on in the hall.

CHAPTER FIVE

When Chloe got home from work on Friday evening, she said to her mother, 'I'm going to Manchester on the train in the morning. Adam wants to show me his house.'

She saw the sudden tension on Helen's face and knew she disapproved. 'I thought you liked Adam,' she said.

'I do, but I don't think it's a good idea to go to his house.'

'Why not?'

'Just the two of you there, you could get carried away and do things you'll later wished you hadn't. I've explained all this to you.'

'Mum, we won't. Don't worry.'

'You're rushing things,' her mother cautioned. 'You're still very young, not seventeen yet. Take your time.'

'I'm taking all the time I need. That's not rushing.'

'Enjoy this part of your life, Chloe. It's your carefree youth. You need time to get to know Adam; let him take you out and about.'

'He does, all the time.'

She felt her mother's twitch of exasperation. 'Will he drive you home, or do you want me to meet you off the train?'

'I'm not sure. If it's to be the train, I'll ring and let you know.'

'Just let him give you a good time...'

'He's giving me a marvellous time,' Chloe said, but marriage was what she really wanted. Perhaps a white wedding in their local church? Mum would enjoy arranging all that for her.

'Just be careful, Chloe.'

'I will, Mum,' she said, knowing Mum couldn't forget what had happened to Aunt Goldie. That had ruled their lives ever since. It wasn't as though it was relevant in today's world.

On the train journey, she could think only of Adam. He was waiting for her in the crowd behind the ticket barrier, his hand raised to attract her attention. Her heart quickened to see him, and moments later he was crushing her in a hug of delight. His house was bigger than the one in which she lived with her mother, and it was furnished with antiques. Chloe was impressed.

'It's a gorgeous house and you have all this

lovely old furniture.'

He laughed, 'It's partly my stock in trade. I haven't got my house furnished exactly as I want it yet.'

She went from room to room, feasting her eyes. He had a better sense of how to make a room look its best than either she or Mum. She told him so.

'You won't think much of the garden, though,' he said. 'It isn't a patch on yours.'

'You don't work at it as Mum works on ours. You have other things to do.'

He'd set the dining room table in readiness for their lunch, with more formality than Mum used when she was expecting company. He used old Doulton china, Bohemian cut glass and sterling silver cutlery, and the table looked fit for a queen. When they were ready to eat, he brought the cold chicken salad and white wine from the kitchen.

'This is lovely,' she told him. He'd even warmed the bread rolls and folded the damask napkins. 'Is this how you live when you're by yourself?'

'I'd like to,' he laughed. 'But I haven't the energy to set things up like this every day. Often, it's a tray on my knee. Is that what you do at home?'

'No, Mum likes to sit up to the table. The kitchen sometimes, for breakfast, the dining room for other meals.'

'I want things to be nice because you're here and sharing it with me. I always will, Chloe. I do love you.'

Afterwards he took her to his sitting room. He'd brewed coffee and served it in a Georgian silver pot on a matching tray. They drank from beautiful cups of eggshell-thin china. Just about the only pieces of furniture that weren't antique were a pair of large supersoft sofas.

Chloe sat down in the corner of one and Adam occupied the other end of the same sofa. He never stopped talking, but somehow he moved imperceptibly closer until he could put his arms round her.

To feel him this close, his breath warm against her cheek, his lips on hers, was what she dreamed of at night in her own bed. The strength of his passion surprised her, even stronger than her own.

Half an hour later Adam whispered, 'Will you come upstairs with me?'

'No,' she said; that was what her mother had been afraid might happen. But she couldn't stop now. His hand moving against her bare skin was making thrills like fireworks explode in her body.

They were lying on a soft rug when he suddenly pulled away from her. She rubbed her cheek against his and tried to pull him back.

'Chloe, are you sure?' His voice was thick with desire.

That rang an alarm bell, she rolled away from him and tried to sit up. 'Yes, but I'm scared we could make a baby. I'd be in terrible trouble, my mother would kill me.'

Adam smiled. 'It's the last thing I want, but it won't happen.'

'It happened to my Aunt Goldie.'

'But years ago. This is the 1960s, all that can be avoided now. You must have read about it.'

'Yes, but I don't know exactly how...'

'I do, and I've got what's needed.' He pulled himself up to the sofa to reach into the pocket of the trousers he'd removed, and showed her a condom.

'That'll stop it?'

'Yes, guaranteed.'

Chloe hesitated, 'I've read that it isn't always reliable, that there's a pill now which is better.'

'We can get that later. This is what I have here and now. It's perfectly safe.'

'But what if it doesn't stop...?'

'It will. I'll take good care that it won't happen. You must relax and not worry about that side of it.'

'You are sure?'

'Absolutely. But talking about it like this – hell, Chloe, it's a real turn-off. Come on, we might as well get dressed and go out. Some other time, eh?'

The following week, Chloe was very much looking forward to Saturday, when she could take the train to Manchester again. She knew now what to expect, and felt she would have the time of her life if Adam made love to her. Being with him was far more fun than staying at home with her own family. They were really quite stick-in-the-mud. She felt she was living at last.

They were still in bed when he ran his finger down her cheek to move her hair away. 'Stay the night with me?' he murmured.

'I couldn't possibly.' Chloe sat up with a jerk. 'Mum would be aghast if I even suggested it.'

'She's an earlier generation, Chloe. In her day,

the only way was to remain celibate, but modern science means we can enjoy the pleasures of life. We don't have to worry about an unwanted pregnancy.'

'When you took me home last week, Mum was really on edge. Well, you could see it, couldn't you?' Chloe had invited him in to have a cup of coffee. 'She's afraid for me, Adam. Afraid I'll get into what she calls trouble. Once it's happened in the family, the horror stays with us.'

'We'll have to give her time to get used to me,' he said. 'She'll trust me eventually.'

Chloe got Adam to drive her home. It was just after half ten when he drew into her drive. 'Mum thinks this is late,' she said.

'The generation gap again.' Adam smiled. 'People of our age think that's impossibly early for a Saturday night.' True,

'She's waiting up for me.' The lights were on in the sitting room. 'Come in with me,' Chloe said.

He was hesitating. 'Last week, she wasn't pleased to see me.'

'She needs to get to know you better.'

She led him into the sitting room, and Adam was as charming as ever to her mother. 'How are you, Mrs Redwood? Well, I hope?'

Chloe went to the kitchen to make some coffee. Her mother, who was not at ease with Adam these days, came to take over from her.

'It's a very late hour to bring visitors in,' she said.

'You need to get to know each other,' Chloe told her. But that seemed to make Helen more uneasy, because it implied Adam was going to be a permanent fixture in her life.

'Can you ask him for lunch tomorrow?' Chloe whispered, so Adam wouldn't overhear and know she'd prompted the invitation. Helen's face told her she didn't want him here again.

'It's the only way, Mum. You'll like him once you get to know him.'

'I've already invited Rex, and there'll be Gran and Marigold too.'

'A good thing if everybody gets to know him,' Chloe told her. Her mother rushed to the fridge. 'I'm not sure the joint will be big enough.'

Chloe almost smiled. 'Mum, that's an enormous leg of lamb. It would feed ten people.'

She got what she wanted, Adam was invited for twelve thirty. That meant they could go out in his car afterwards and have the rest of the day to themselves.

On Sunday, Gran was already dozing in her chair, while Rex was sipping sherry and trying to talk to Marigold about the new Labour government and Harold Wilson's financial policy. He hoped to steer her away from giving another interminable account of the infirmities she and her mother were suffering. Helen was in the kitchen making gravy, and Chloe was pacing restlessly between the window and her chair.

When Rex heard the front doorbell ring, it came as quite a shock to see Chloe rush to answer it and then bring Adam in to introduce him. Helen hadn't told him Adam was invited too. He'd brought a magnificent bouquet of flowers for her and an expensive box of chocolates for Chloe. Rex felt socially lacking; he hadn't thought to bring gifts. He made a mental note to bring a bottle of wine next time he was invited. It seemed Marigold and her mother had not met Adam before, and he got a frosty reception from them.

'A boyfriend?' Gran came to life and adjusted her spectacles to peer at him. 'How long has this been going on?'

Marigold looked shocked. 'You're very young to have a boyfriend.'

Especially one like Adam, Rex thought. He looked sophisticated, almost a man about town in his navy blazer with gilt buttons, silver and navy silk tie and silver-grey slacks.

When he told them he'd driven from Manchester, they were shocked again that he had a car of his own and that he was prepared to come so far to see Chloe. They were bouncing questions at him. How old was he? Twenty-four? What sort of work did he do? How did he meet Chloe?

Rex tried to break the questioning up and help everybody feel more at ease, but before long he realised Chloe was doing a better job at that. It made him disheartened to see how preoccupied they were with each other. Their relationship had developed apace and it had put Chloe out of his reach. He felt she was lost to him. But would it last?

Helen moved them all to the dining room and asked Rex to carve the leg of lamb. It was presented on an enormous platter surrounded with roast potatoes and thyme and parsley stuffing. It had a great bone sticking up, which made it look

69

a more complicated job than last week's beef had been.

Rex hesitated as he approached the table. Chloe noticed and said brightly, 'Adam's good at carving. Would you rather he did it?'

Rex capitulated and said yes. Adam took his place and with great confidence gave a theatrical display of clashing the carving knife against the steel to sharpen it. He then proceeded to carve the joint with professional ease and arrange the servings neatly on the plates. It made Rex feel thoroughly inadequate.

It was a sunny afternoon, and when they'd eaten the apple pie and cream that followed, Helen took them all over to the summerhouse for a cup of coffee.

'I thought it would look better than this inside,' Marigold said. 'Aren't these your old garden chairs?'

'Yes, I'd like to smarten it up, but how best to do it?'

'It needs bright colours.' It was Adam who held forth about a colour scheme of orange, yellow and brown for rugs and curtains.

'Curtains?' Marigold asked suspiciously. 'Why on earth would you want curtains in a summer-house?'

'On a hot day, you might be glad to draw them against the sun,' Adam said. 'And bright colours would bring it to life.' He went on to recommend shops in Manchester where they stocked suitable furniture. 'I'll take you and Chloe and help you choose if you like,' he offered.

'Mum, that would be lovely,' Chloe said. 'The

three of us could go one Saturday and have a day out.'

More than anything else that drove home to Rex that Adam was indeed squeezing him out of the place he'd had in Chloe's affections.

A few weeks later, Rex found the summerhouse had been transformed. It now looked smart enough to provide photographs to grace the centre pages of a luxury magazine. Helen and Chloe said they were delighted with it.

After that, when Rex was invited to take tea in the summerhouse, he'd say to Helen, 'Gardening is dirty work. I don't want my clothes to spoil your lovely cushions.'

'You won't hurt them,' she'd say, but he'd insist on having a clean towel to spread over the seat of the large, well-padded cane chair before he sat down. The primary colours and the cube patterns reminded him of Adam. He didn't care for them.

Adam was coming to Liverpool even more often to take Chloe out, and Rex saw less and less of her. She told him Adam was great fun and that through the summer he'd taken her on trips to the beach at Southport and Morecambe, and he was planning to take her to the Peak District next month. Rex knew she was having a more exciting time than he could give her.

Helen continued to confide her worries to him; they were working together in the garden one Saturday when she told him Chloe was going to Adam's house almost every weekend and that she'd taken the train to Manchester again this morning.

71

'Marigold is almost out of her mind. She's convinced Chloe will make the same mistake she did.'

'You must trust her,' Rex said.

Helen had gone indoors to make them some tea when she came tearing back across the lawn, clearly very upset.

'Chloe's just rung me. She says she's staying the night with Adam and she won't be home until tomorrow. I couldn't make her see reason.'

Rex knew this amounted to a crisis in the Redwood family. He threw his arms round her in a comforting hug.

'The world has changed since we were young, Helen. The 'pill' is changing everything. Young people can live like this now. It's going to become normal behaviour.'

'But it's wrong. I feel she's heading for disaster and she won't listen to me. I've given her the Marie Stopes books Marigold gave me, so she must know the risks she's taking.'

Rex sighed. He'd had to accept that Adam was part of Chloe's life, and Helen must too. 'You can take it that she does,' he said. 'She's been going to his house for weeks. What they're doing is probably no longer new to them.'

The months were passing quickly and Chloe was having the time of her life. She enjoyed her job and she adored Adam. Occasionally one of her colleagues at work got married, and the frequent discussions about bridal matters made Chloe long for marriage too. Aunt Goldie had dropped hints almost from the time she'd introduced her to Adam; now Mum was telling her outright that she should marry him. But Chloe had to wait for him to propose. It was convention that the bride should wait for the groom to ask her. Yes.

He made love to her regularly, and because she was spending one or two nights each week with him, it must be obvious to her family that she was allowing this. One afternoon she was lying in his arms, both of them replete with love, when she said simply, 'Adam, why don't we get married?'

She felt him stir. 'There's no need, is there? Aren't you happy?'

'Yes, but I'd like to be married. It's getting on for a year now, and Mum keeps asking me when it'll be. She says I'm your wife in everything but name.'

He moved away from her and propped his head up with his arm. 'I suppose, yes...'

'I am. So why not make it official?'

He sighed, 'It means nothing, it's only a ceremony and a piece of paper.'

'It's more than that. I'm embarrassed when Mum asks. How can I tell her you don't want to? That sounds as though you don't rate me highly enough. I'm OK as a mistress but would be lacking as a wife.'

'Hey, Chloe,' he was gathering her into his arms again, 'it's not like that and you know it. I do love you, I really do.'

She pulled away. 'But not enough to marry me?'

'Why don't you move in here with me? That would be just like being married, wouldn't it? I've asked you before...'

73

'Many times.' She was out of bed and pulling on her clothes.

His big brown eyes were beseeching. 'Then why not?'

'I'd have to leave my job. I...'

'You'd have to do that if we got married. You could get another job here. What's the difference?'

'My family would be shocked. Terminally shocked. Aunt Goldie would never get over it.' This was the first serious tiff they'd had, and all the warmth and love Chloe felt for him suddenly cooled. 'I want to go home.'

'Now? I've booked a table at the Lansdown for half seven. You said you wanted to go.'

'I've changed my mind.' She was tossing her belongings into her overnight bag. 'I'll take a bus to the station and catch the train home.'

'Don't be like this, Chloe. I'll run you into town if you really want to go. I'll run you home.'

'The station will do.'

On the way, he never stopped pleading with her to forgive him and stay. He told her a dozen times he was head over heels in love with her.

Chloe arrived home to find the house empty, because her mother wasn't expecting her back until tomorrow. She looked in the garage and saw Mum's car was there, so guessed she'd probably gone out with Rex. She found some leftover soup in the fridge and reheated that for her supper.

When she heard the key scrape in the front door, she was slumped in front of the television, though unable to follow the plot of the thriller because her mind was racing with mixed emotions about Adam. She heard Mum and Rex laughing as they came up the hall. It made her feel very much alone.

'Chloe, you're home! That's nice. I thought I must have left the light on. I've brought Rex in for a drink, we've been to the bistro for supper. What would you like, Rex? Beer or a cup of coffee?'

'Coffee, please.'

Chloe could see Rex looking at her in rather a strange fashion.

'I'll make it.' She leapt to her feet, wanting to distance herself before they asked why she'd come home unexpectedly.

They were not laughing any more, and Rex now seemed uncomfortable. He drank the coffee quickly and took his leave. Helen saw him out, then came back to pause in the doorway to gaze at her.

'You've quarrelled with Adam?' she asked.

Chloe was glad her mother had picked up on it and she didn't have to explain.

'You look miserable. I can't think of anything else that would do that to you.'

'Yes,' she admitted, but she couldn't tell her why. Mum would say she'd done the right thing to throw him over and would be pleased.

That night, Chloe cried herself to sleep. The next day Adam rang her twice. The second time Chloe wouldn't pick it up. She told her mother to say she didn't want to speak to him.

As usual on Sundays, Gran and Aunt Goldie came to lunch. They were clearly relieved to hear from Mum that her relationship with Adam was

75

broken off. For Chloe, the following week looked bleak. On Monday, he phoned her three times at the office. She said as little as possible before slamming the phone down. When she'd first told the girls in her office about Adam, they'd been envious; he was the boyfriend who had everything. Now when she told them he didn't want to get married, they sympathised. One said, 'He's a rotter.' Others said, 'Why bother with him? I wouldn't.'

But without him, her life felt empty. She wasn't at all sure that she'd done the right thing. She couldn't stop thinking about him.

On Tuesday, Interflora delivered a magnificent bouquet of red roses. Chloe tore the accompanying note to shreds without reading it. On Wednesday evening, he was waiting outside her gate when she came home from work. She saw him get out of his car as she walked up from the bus stop.

'Chloe, at least talk to me. I love you, I'm lost without you.' His arms went round her and with relief she put her face down on the soft flannel of his jacket and was comforted. Before she realised what was happening, she found herself in the passenger seat of his car. His hugs were balm to her soul, his kisses a joy. She couldn't do without Adam, but she didn't have to. They'd made things up, their quarrel was forgotten.

Chloe shot into the house to tell her mother not to cook for her because Adam was taking her out for dinner. She found her with Rex in the summerhouse. Neither seemed to welcome the news.

CHAPTER SIX

Life went on as before and Chloe gave herself up to enjoying everything it brought. In October of 1965, Adam suggested a two-week holiday on the island of Kos, and Chloe, against her mother's express wishes, agreed to go. They had long, lazy days in the golden autumn sun; it was the best holiday of her life and she was heartened to find other unmarried couples in the small hotel.

They enjoyed it so much, they talked about it all winter and planned to return to the Greek islands the following year. This time they wanted real heat in the sun and booked for the last week in August and the first in September. Again they had a wonderful time and returned home feeling relaxed and refreshed.

Her office colleagues said her holiday tan suited her and she looked the picture of health, but almost immediately, Chloe began to suspect she could be pregnant. The thought of it terrified her. Surely this couldn't be happening to her!

She waited another week, hoping and half expecting to find it was a false alarm. She knew Adam was confident he had all that under control. However, the passing of time did nothing to ease her worry. When she did tell him, she found him equally shocked.

'You can't be,' was his first comment. 'You know I've taken precautions every time. You're mistaken, you must be.'

But it became increasingly obvious that she was not. She told nobody else. She was filled with a growing dread that she would end up like Aunt Goldie. The family would be able to say, 'I told you so.'

'What am I going to do?' she implored Adam.

'Move in with me,' he said. 'You know that's what I want. I'll look after you.'

Mum would be hurt and distressed that she'd let it happen to her, and as for Gran and Aunt Goldie ... it would be the disaster they'd always expected. Chloe knew only too well that the only outcome her family would find acceptable was for her and Adam to be married.

When she went to Manchester to spend the weekends with him, she no longer wanted to go to restaurants and eat fancy meals. Morning sickness bothered her long beyond the first few months. Hiding that from her mother was difficult, and keeping a clear head when at work equally so. She lost her energy and enthusiasm for shopping trips and outings to theatres and cinemas. She was even off lovemaking, but she chose the moment when Adam was relaxed and happily satiated with it to close her eyes and say, 'Adam, I want you to marry me. Please do this for me.'

She felt him freeze and he said nothing. Panic was rushing up her throat when he said, 'You've always known I'm not the marrying sort.'

'But this changes everything. There'll be a child to consider.'

He turned his face away from her. 'Couldn't

you get rid of it? Have an abortion? It's legal now, you know.'

Chloe felt tears sting her eyes. 'That's what you want?'

'It's what you want too, isn't it?'

'I want not to be pregnant, but since I am...' He was staring silently up at the ceiling. 'I've no idea how to go about getting an abortion.'

He sat up. 'You haven't even been to your doctor yet. First you must do that and make sure you really are pregnant. You could be worrying for nothing. Then tell him you want an abortion.'

'I can't!' The thought of explaining her predicament to Dr Harris made her toes curl with embarrassment. She'd known him for years, and he lived quite close. 'Mum's always seeing him about something, he'll tell her.'

'Well, you could change to my doctor. I could make an appointment for you. He's open several evenings each week.'

Chloe knew she couldn't just bury her head in the sand over this. 'Yes,' she said, three days later. 'Make an appointment for me.'

She'd already read everything she could find about abortion, but now she went to the library in her lunch hour to see if there was anything more there that would shed light on how she should go about getting one. There had been a lot on the subject in the newspapers a few years ago when it was made legal, but she thought it wasn't available on demand for all who might want it.

Adam had to collect her from the office and

drive her straight to the doctor in order to get her there in time for his evening surgery. She had the facts straight in her head by then. Abortion had been made legally available in Britain, but only within strict medical guidelines and not for social reasons. Chloe could see that would rule her out. The journey gave her time to talk it over with Adam.

'Anyway, I've left it too late for an abortion; that has to happen in the first few months. For me, it isn't possible. I'll have to have this baby.'

'Well,' Adam said, 'now I've got used to the idea, I think I might like to have a baby. It's quite exciting, isn't it?'

Chloe relaxed a little. 'Yes, it'll be a whole new way of life for us.'

'Move in with me. You know I've always wanted that.'

'Adam, I'd like us to be married, that would make everything perfect.'

He sighed heavily. 'I wish you wouldn't nag me about that.'

Chloe wouldn't let herself think about Adam's stand against marriage. How could he say he loved her and then refuse to marry her when she was pregnant? The only logic in that was that he didn't love her enough. But she had to do something. She decided moving in to live with him was her best option, really her only option. The alternative was to throw herself on Mum's goodwill.

She didn't mention abortion to the doctor, and he confirmed she was over four months pregnant. She joined his list and gave Adam's address as her own. Further appointments were arranged to take place in local clinics, and delivery was booked at a nearby hospital.

Chloe felt in limbo. She continued to put off telling her mother; she needed to think how best to do that. She couldn't tell the girls at work and she couldn't leave her job. With less than five months to go before the birth, she couldn't look for another job in Manchester. She had no savings and the baby would need clothes and a cot and a hundred other things.

'We'll get them,' Adam assured her. 'Don't worry about money. I'll take good care of you.'

Chloe felt no less anxious. He'd been taking care of contraception, and look how well he'd managed that. She felt torpid and inert, it took all her energy to get through each day as it came. She wished, how she wished, that when he'd told her he wasn't the marrying sort last year, she'd stayed well away from him. He had warned her, Mum had warned her; why oh why hadn't she listened to them?

Spring 1967 was well advanced. Helen's hedges were bright with forsythia and the daffodils were out in their droves. Rex was raking her grass to remove what remained of the snowdrops and crocuses he'd planted in the lawn around her summerhouse. They'd heralded in the spring at the beginning of the year. Now he wanted a perfect lawn for her in the coming summer.

He'd expected Helen to be gardening with him this afternoon, but he'd forgotten until he got here that she did charity work two afternoons a month. She'd invited him to supper tonight. At least once each week he took her out for a meal, and she cooked for him on another evening. Now that Chloe was spending so much time with Adam, he and Helen had been thrown together more. He was glad to have her company and knew they were growing closer.

Helen was very unhappy about what her daughter was doing and spoke of her often. Rex had to hide his own hurt and wished things had remained as they were. It was as much to reassure himself as her that he mentioned again, 'These days there's no shame in how Chloe lives her life. Young women count it their right.' It didn't make Helen's pursed lips relax.

He was some distance from the house and had paused to admire the carpet of self-sown blue-bells under the trees when he saw Chloe and Adam coming over to him. He hadn't seen her for a while and was immediately struck by the change in her. She didn't look well; she'd lost her bounce.

'Chloe,' he said. 'How nice to see you.' He nodded to Adam; he too looked subdued.

'Is Mum about? Is she gardening too?' The garden was of such a size that there were many places where she'd have been out of sight.

'No,' Rex said. 'I expected she would be, but I'd forgotten it was her day to run that charity shop.'

'Oh no! I'd forgotten that too.'

'We can come back another time,' Adam said and took Chloe's arm.

Now Chloe was close, Rex could see she was pale and looked washed out. 'How are you?' he asked, and saw her lip quiver. 'Is something the matter? Shouldn't you be at work?'

'Yes.' He saw her swallow and for the first time she looked him in the eye. 'I've finished work, I gave in my notice last month.'

'Goodness!' He could see tears welling in her eyes; her distress was obvious. 'I thought you liked working there.'

'She did,' Adam put in quickly. 'We're having a baby, Chloe's had to give up working.'

Rex felt his stomach turn over, acid was rising in his throat, making him gag. 'Chloe!'

His gaze went down. Her long legs in nylon tights were as shapely as ever, and her fashionable short tunic dress gave little hint. He understood only too well how upset Helen and her family would be about this. His mouth was suddenly dry.

'I'm so ... so sorry it had to happen like this.' Rex stopped. Shouldn't he have said congratulations? Something to cover up that he knew this baby was not what she wanted? He could feel her embarrassment, but his own was greater. And greater than that was the hurt he felt that this had happened to her.

He wanted to take her in his arms to comfort her, but Adam slid an arm round her shoulders and pulled her closer. That cut him like a knife, adding to his pain.

'I came home to tell Mum and pack up some of my things,' she said.

Adam was defiant. 'It's some time off yet. You'll all have time to get used to the idea.'

'It's due at the beginning of May,' Chloe told him.

'Goodness, that's only...'

'Five weeks off. Will you tell Mum for me? I kept trying to tell her,' she shook her head miserably, 'but I couldn't. She'll hate me for doing this.'

Rex took a deep breath. 'Why don't you wait and tell her yourself? She'd want you to.' He had to stuff his hands in his pockets to stop himself reaching out for her. 'Chloe, what you do is up to you. All your mum wants is for you to be happy.'

He stopped. This wasn't making her happy; the exact opposite. What could one say in these circumstances?

'It'll all be forgotten once you're married. The baby will be welcomed. You'll be a little family.'

Chloe was biting her lip and Adam looked positively dour. 'Helen won't approve, but Chloe's going to move in with me,' he said.

Rex gave a very audible gasp. Did that mean there would be no wedding? He hurried on, 'That's as maybe, but this changes everything. Look, Helen will be home soon, probably in the next fifteen minutes. Please wait and see her; she'll be upset if you don't.'

Adam glared back at him, showing his reluctance.

'Let's go inside and make a cup of tea.' Rex took them to the kitchen. They both sat down and let him put the kettle on and get out the tea things. He felt terrible. He couldn't possibly tell Helen news like that. Chloe would have to do it herself.

They were all silent as he poured out three cups of tea. He served them and sat down at the table in front of the third cup. He closed his eyes and thought of Helen. Please hurry up, we need you here, he prayed.

She came at last, smiling happily until she sensed the atmosphere. Rex poured her a cup of rather stewed tea and left them to it. He was glad to get back to his gardening, and within moments the rake was tearing furiously into the grass. He knew his anger was for Adam, that he'd done this to Chloe.

Adam's car was heading towards Manchester. Chloe sat in the passenger seat, rigid with tension. She couldn't get her mother's face out of her mind. She'd never seen her look so hurt and shocked before, and to make matters worse, Helen had grown quite agitated.

'You shouldn't have swept me outside so quickly. You should have given us time to talk it through.'

'Chloe, we'd been over everything three times and were going round in circles.'

'I told you how raw my family is about illegitimate babies. I knew Mum would take it hard.'

'She's got a chip on her shoulder.'

'She was angry with me. I should have stayed until I'd made my peace with her.'

'I couldn't stand any more of that,' Adam said. 'Better to give her a couple of days to calm down, then ring her and make your peace.'

'She might not want to by then. She might not forgive me.' Chloe was trying to blink back her tears. 'It was awful telling her, embarrassing. She was all of a flutter when I told her I was nearly eight months gone and she hadn't known.'

'She'll get over it.'

'Even worse, she assumed we'd be getting married and so did Rex; they were absolutely racked to hear it wasn't even being planned.'

'You did the right thing by pretending you didn't want to.'

Chloe couldn't keep the note of urgency out of her voice. 'But I do, Adam. I do. I wish I could change your mind. I don't understand why you're so against it.'

He was staring out at the road ahead. 'I keep trying to explain that marriage just isn't my sort of thing.'

'It's not as though there's a reason why we can't.'

His sigh was impatient. 'Everybody will soon be used to the idea and we'll be very happy, you'll see.'

'I'd be happier now if we could be married. So would Mum. It would solve everything. She'd accept you then.'

Adam was irritable. 'I wish you'd give over about getting married, Chloe,' he barked. 'It won't make any difference in the long run; it's just a ceremony and a certificate.'

Chloe leaned back in her seat and squeezed her eyes tightly shut. She knew he hated to see her cry. When they'd first met, she'd thought Adam wonderful, their relationship had seemed perfect. He'd been passionate about her and done his best to give her a good time. Having his own very nice house and earning his living the way he did, she'd thought him a man of the world. But really, he wasn't as sophisticated as she'd thought.

He'd been genuinely shocked when she'd told

86

him she was pregnant. He'd never considered that he might father a child unintentionally.

'I'll do the right thing by you,' he'd told her. 'You mustn't worry, you can move in with me just as soon as you like.'

Chloe had put that off as she'd put everything else off. As time went on, Adam no longer seemed as keen to drive into Liverpool to take her out on the town. She was doing her best to hide her pregnancy, but she thought he was no longer proud to have her on his arm. It was only when her pregnancy was becoming obvious and she felt she could no longer work that she was forced to make the move.

The need to tell her mother had been like a wall she couldn't see beyond. But the other side seemed brighter. She was looking forward to moving in with Adam and devoting herself to him and his lovely house. She comforted herself by thinking of her coming child. Once it was born, it would bring them closer. She would have her own little family.

When they were nearing his house, he said, 'Come on, love, cheer up. At least that's over. You've got it off your chest; we can both relax now that everybody knows.'

Chloe could feel tears stinging her eyes and couldn't prevent one rolling down her cheek.

'I know,' he said. 'We'll go to the Cavendish and have a slap-up dinner and a bottle of wine. That'll cheer both of us up.'

Chloe swallowed hard. Indigestion was troubling her now, but Adam still wanted rich and heavy dinners. She'd have to accept that this was how things were going to be.

As soon as Rex heard Adam's car start up and drive off, he went back to the kitchen. He knew Helen would need to be comforted. He found her at the kitchen table with her head down on her arms. When she lifted her face, it was ravaged with tears. She looked even worse than he'd expected.

He sat down next to her. 'You're going to tell me,' she sobbed, 'that the world has changed and there's nothing wrong with Chloe living with that man as though she's his wife, but I know it's making her very unhappy.'

'I know, but...'

'It's what happened to Marigold. She and Gran will be shocked, devastated. I'm horrified at what they've done. Chloe went into this with her eyes wide open. She knew the risks she was taking, sleeping with him before they were married.'

Tears were coursing down her cheeks. Rex pulled out his handkerchief and gave it to her. A couple of blades of grass fell on the table from his hand. She swept them on to the floor.

'I kept telling her to insist he marries her. That she'll have no legal rights unless he does. She says she doesn't need legal rights, that she's happy with things as they are.'

'I don't believe that,' Rex said slowly. 'She was in tears. Now there's a baby on the way, they'll get married and all will be well. Soon this will seem just a storm in a teacup.'

'No it won't; they aren't going to get married. Heavens, Rex, if they meant to get married they'd have done it months ago. I wouldn't have minded if they just sneaked off to the registry office without telling anybody.'

Rex's stomach was churning. 'Is Adam already married?'

'No, he just doesn't want it. Doesn't see the need for it. He says we're old-fashioned and that nobody bothers about marriage these days.'

'And Chloe's going along with that and pretending she doesn't care?'

'Yes, she's going to live with him in Manchester from now on. "My partner", she calls him. She'll have the baby there. She's got all that arranged.'

Rex could sit still no longer. He was boiling with fury at the way Adam had treated Chloe. He could accept that Adam had got her pregnant by accident, but if he loved her, why didn't he want to marry her? Chloe had been upset and embarrassed enough to keep her pregnancy a secret. There was something very wrong with the way Adam was behaving.

Rex ached to help her, but Adam had put her beyond his reach. Why hadn't he spoken up before Adam had come on the scene? Let her know what was in his mind? He would have loved and nurtured her. Her happiness would have been his first aim. Adam was a man who thought only of his own pleasure and not of Chloe's welfare. That was not love. True.

Helen's eyes were red and her face was blotchy. She looked anything but her elegant self.

'Come on.' He took her hand, pulled her to her feet and led her to the door of the downstairs cloakroom. 'Dry your eyes and wash your face, it'll make you feel better. You've had a shock, you need a drink.'

He went to the drinks cabinet in the sitting room and poured her a tot of brandy. It showed how badly this had thrown Helen, who was usually very thoughtful for her guests. He poured another tot for himself and waited for her to come in, then put one glass in her hand and showed her the other.

'I hope you don't mind. I'm in need too.'

'Rex, I'm sorry, I'm not thinking straight.'

He raised his glass, 'For medicinal purposes.'

She sipped cautiously. 'Chloe is nearly eight months pregnant and I didn't even know. She couldn't tell me.' Her voice was bitter. 'I find that hurtful.' He could see the agony in her swollen eyes. 'Why didn't I guess? The signs must have been there. I've failed as a mother, haven't I?'

'No, Helen, you haven't, you've been a good mother over the years I've known you. Chloe loves you.'

'But she doesn't want to live with me any more. She's moving in to live with him. How d'you think that makes me feel?'

'I can see how you feel, but you're wrong. You mustn't blame yourself. Chloe doesn't. She blames herself and she's full of guilt. She knows she's hurt you.'

'But I should have been able to protect her. I tried to warn her.' Her voice was a wail of protest.

Helen's tears were coming again and Rex didn't know how to console her. They'd sat down at opposite ends of the sofa; now he slid closer and felt for her hand.

'I blame Adam,' she said. 'He's talked her into this.'

Rex sighed. 'I blame society as a whole. First the Victorians drew heavy curtains across everything to do with sex. Girls must be kept innocent and pure. But now with the pill, the need for that has gone. Youth can no longer see the point. This is the swinging sixties; they think they can push marriage aside, take all that life can give them when they want it.'

'They don't realise how hurtful their parents find it.'

'They don't realise they can hurt themselves and each other,' Rex said gently.

He didn't remember putting his arm round her and pulling her close, but now Helen's head was on his shoulder. He felt her shudder occasionally in the aftermath of her stormy tears and dropped a kiss on her forehead.

'Chloe's no longer a child,' he said. 'She wants to go her own way. I'm afraid you'll have to accept that.'

Rex had had to, and he was finding it painful. He stayed as still as he could, feeling Helen relax against him. He knew she was calming down.

He'd become tightly involved with Helen and Chloe; they'd become his closest friends. And yes, he'd needed their support over the years. Helen snuggled closer. It was almost an hour later when she raised her head.

'What am I thinking of? I asked you to supper, and here I am making no effort to get it on the table.'

Rex rubbed his shoulder, which had begun to

ache. 'Would you like to go out instead? The bistro, perhaps?'

'No thanks, I feel awful and I probably look a sight.'

'Course you don't,' but that made him take another look. Helen was nearly forty-six now, and painfully thin. Her face was tearstained and he could see more grey creeping into her hair.

'Maybe you aren't looking your best tonight.' He smiled. 'Can I help you cook?'

He followed her to the kitchen. He was hungry. She showed him two steaks in the fridge and gave him the bottle of wine he'd brought to open. With a full glass in her hand she sank back on a chair to sip it, too spent to busy herself with the cooking. It was Rex who scrubbed the new potatoes and washed the mangetout she'd gathered from her own vegetable patch.

He set about grilling the rump steaks, which turned out to be the best he'd ever tasted. Helen had prepared a confection of cream and chocolate sponge to follow. The wine cheered them both, though Helen's self-control was as brittle as eggshells.

'A magnificent meal,' he told her. Helen didn't drink much and they'd never before opened two bottles of wine on the same evening. But tonight was different; he thought for once it wouldn't come amiss. They took their coffee back to the sofa in the sitting room.

Helen put on some soft music and sat down beside him to put her head on his shoulder.

'Thank you,' she said and kissed him. 'You've got me through one of the worst afternoons of my life. What would I have done without you?'

Helen was twelve years older than Rex, while Chloe was almost fourteen years younger. Rex lay back against the cushions wondering if age was all that important, and whether, in lieu of Chloe, living here with Helen would be better than his monastic existence in his poky flat.

He didn't go back to it that night. She was clinging to him; she said she needed him. In the early hours of the morning he went upstairs with her to her bedroom and made love to her three times. They were both hungry for it.

He was awake well before Helen. He watched her for a while, sleeping peacefully under her satin covers. Then he slipped out of her bed and quietly got dressed. He drank two glasses of water as he passed through the kitchen, then let himself out into the garden. In the cold light of morning, he felt hung-over and shocked at what he'd done. It had changed for ever the relationship he'd had with Helen. True

Yes, he was fond of her, but did he love her?

CHAPTER SEVEN

For the best part of an hour, Rex circled the vegetable patch, crossed the lawns and tramped round the boundary. The vistas of colourful flowers and trees bursting with new leaf no longer delighted him; he couldn't even be bothered to pull out the odd weed he saw. This was the first time Helen's garden had failed to bring him pleasure.

Helen had never stopped telling him it had been her salvation, and really, it had been his too. It had given him a friend. Helen was outgoing and chatted as they worked, but that was not his way. He'd opened up to Chloe but not to her mother. He'd listened to Helen's confidences but given out little of his own troubled circumstances in return.

She knew he'd lost his wife, but nothing of the months of empty loneliness, his feelings of searing loss, or how bleak the future had seemed. He felt he was supporting Helen through similar troubles, and to tell her now his version of grief and loss would be piling on the agony.

It was only when the summerhouse came in view that he remembered. He'd made an appointment at ten o'clock to see another client at the garden centre who wanted to buy a summerhouse. Since his stepfather had built the new extension there, Simon had persuaded him to set aside a small office where Rex could meet his clients before taking them round to see the goods and plants he proposed using. It was good business for both of them.

Rex hurried indoors to boil the kettle and take a tea tray up to Helen's bedroom. She was just waking up and smiled sleepily. 'Stay with me today,' she murmured.

'I'm afraid I can't.'

'You're already dressed!' She sat up.

'Yes, sort of. I need to go home to bath and shave,' he said, and told her about his appointment.

Her face clouded. 'I'm worried stiff about Chloe. Marigold will go spare.'

He poured them each a cup of tea and sat down on the end of her bed. 'You have to accept it, Helen. You have to let go and let Chloe live in her own way.'

'But she's ruining everything.'

'We don't know that. Many would say there's nothing wrong with what she and Adam have done; that they stand the same chance of happiness as any newly married couple.'

'No...'

'It's human nature, after all. Didn't we do exactly the same last night? And we don't have the excuse of...' he almost said 'love', but managed to change it to 'youth'. The last thing he wanted was to hurt her feelings.

'Come back,' she implored. 'I'll cook dinner for us again tonight.'

When Rex left, Helen tossed and turned in bed for a long time. Yes, she was agonising about Chloe and the mess she'd got herself into, but thinking about Rex soothed her. He'd been a pillar of strength to her for years. There had been times when she'd begun to hope he'd see her as more than a friend, but she'd never so much as hinted of that to him. She'd feared he might not feel the same way.

But last night, whether it was the thunderbolt Chloe had dropped or too much wine, she'd let herself go. She'd encouraged him, kissed him, clung to him. She'd needed him.

It had turned back the clock for her. His body

95

was young and strong and vigorous. It had been a revelation to her; she knew he could make her happy. She didn't care that Marigold would be derisory if she knew, and call him her toy boy. Rex was wise beyond his years, and gentle and kind, and the garden gave them so much in common.

For a long time she'd been wondering how he saw her. She felt close to him and he seemed pleased to accept her little invitations and always tried to repay her so she could ask him again. But did he love her? Last night, for the first time she'd begun to think he did. He'd been passionate. It warmed her to think about it and helped to blot out the awful trouble that had befallen Chloe.

Helen had felt bad enough when Chloe had stayed overnight in Adam's house and brazened it out. Marigold had had plenty to say about that since the day she discovered it was happening. Helen had told Marigold what Chloe had said to her, that science had made such strides that nobody needed to get pregnant today unless they wanted to.

The truth was that nothing had really changed. This was the last thing Chloe wanted. Helen and John had longed to start a family. They'd been trying for years before it had happened, and then there had been only Chloe when they'd wanted more. She'd believed her daughter would have a similar experience and that had reduced her anxiety. How silly that was, now she thought of Marigold and her own birth.

Chloe had been wrong to believe modern methods could save her from the consequences of what she was doing. How could she and Adam be so careless as to let this happen to them? And then keeping it hidden for so long had cut Helen completely out of it. Worst of all was seeing Chloe made so utterly miserable and unable to talk about it.

Helen knew she'd stayed in bed too long; she felt terrible. She made herself get up eventually, though her head ached, her eyes were red again and she felt exhausted. It surprised her to find it was bright and sunny. She went out into the garden and spent most of the morning there. It was so large that there was always work needing to be done on some part of it. As always, it soothed her.

That evening, Helen was busy in the kitchen making a chicken pie for their supper. Rex came back after work, wearing the pullover she'd given him last Christmas.

'How are you?' he asked, presenting her with a box of chocolates.

'I'm all right. Fine.'

'Have you spoken to Chloe today? Made your peace?'

Helen had to shake her head. 'I've been trying to put all that out of my mind.' It was only by thinking of Rex instead of Chloe that she'd been able to keep her tears at bay.

He came and took hold of her hand. 'Ring her, Helen, I want you to.'

'She's deserted me, she's the one who...'

'She knows she's upset you; she knows she should have told you sooner and she's full of guilt.'

His earnest urging was more than she could take. She was biting her lip till it hurt.

'Keep the lines open or this will fester and be between you for years. I think you should stay in touch.'

That made her swallow hard. 'I will, I will, but not now...'

'The sooner the better. What's her number, do you know?'

She walked out to the phone in the hall. 'She wrote it down for me.'

'There you are, then, it's what she wants. What she needs.'

'But what can I say that I didn't say yesterday? I don't want to start it all up again.'

He lifted the handset, dialled the number she'd shown him, then pushed it into her hand. 'Ask her how she is,' he said and went back to the kitchen.

She heard it ring and Chloe's voice answer. 'It's Mum,' she said softly. 'Chloe, are you all right?'

She heard Chloe's tears. 'Mum, I'm sorry. I knew you'd be horrified. Please forgive me.'

For Helen, the following days passed in much the way they always had. Rex gardened with her and they did all the things they used to do. She felt they were closer, but he made no move to make love to her again.

She asked him to lunch on Sunday. 'I haven't told Gran and Marigold about Chloe yet, but she won't be here. They're bound to ask where she is, so I'll have to tell them. I'd like you to be on hand to help me.'

For once, he did not seem delighted with the invitation. 'Please, Rex,' she urged. 'I need you.'

'Of course I'll come,' he said then. 'You know I'm always glad of a good dinner.'

His presence probably prevented Gran making too much of a scene, but she did say that she was feeling ill again. Marigold burst into tears, saying it was history repeating itself, and Helen found, as she'd expected, that it was very hard to keep her own tears under control.

Rex did his best to comfort Marigold and said his bit about it being the swinging sixties now and that nobody took that sort of thing to heart any more.

The impact of the news about Chloe was softened by Gran saying in her quavery voice, 'Helen, I want you to promise to look after Marigold when I'm gone.'

Marigold was indignant. 'You'll be here for many years yet, you know you will.'

'I don't think so.' Gran shook her head. Her white hair was very sparse now, her face wizened with wrinkles. 'Marigold will need help,' she went on to Helen. 'She won't be able to manage on her own. She won't be left well provided for as you were.'

Helen could see that that had taken Rex by surprise, but she was used to little digs from her family. She did her best to smile from Gran to Marigold. 'Don't worry,' she said. 'You know I'll do all I can.'

Helen felt that Sunday lunch had been wretchedly embarrassing for them all. They could talk of nothing but Chloe's plight and how she and Helen had ignored their warnings. Marigold said she'd hoped Helen would be a better mother to Chloe than this, and that shocks like this were bad for Gran's health. Gran seemed switched off and left most of her dinner on her plate. Only Rex looked interested in food.

Helen was bringing in the bread and butter pudding when Marigold suddenly leapt up and said they must go home straight away. Helen felt shocked and gave in to the tears that had been threatening.

It was a relief when Rex got to his feet. 'I'll run you home, Marigold,' he said. It was he who brought in their coats, and buttoned Gran into hers.

Helen kissed them goodbye and whispered to Rex as he passed, 'Please come back.'

'Of course,' he said. 'I won't be long.'

She was a miserable wreck when he got back. 'Come on,' he said. 'A brisk walk along the beach at Formby, that'll make you feel better.' They were out all afternoon and though he tried to cheer her up, she was still very much on edge when they got back.

'I'd like you to stay for supper,' she said, 'but I haven't much to offer. Would it be OK if I fried up the Yorkshire pudding and potatoes left over from lunch to have with the cold beef?'

'That'll keep until tomorrow,' he smiled. 'I know a pub that's open on Sunday nights where they do good food. You need a little treat.'

She felt more herself when he drove her home; she could see he meant to drop her at the gate and drive on. 'Stay with me tonight, Rex,' she pleaded. 'I don't want to be by myself.'

Once they were indoors she put on some soothing music and sat with him on the sofa. 'You've been very kind to me today,' she said, and kissed his cheek. 'I don't know what I'd have done without you.' They were late going upstairs to bed and she fell asleep in his arms.

Helen was woken by the telephone ringing and ringing in the hall below. It felt like the middle of the night. Beside her she heard Rex stir.

'This happened once before,' she told him. 'It was a wrong number.'

'Shall I answer it?'

She put on her bedside light and looked at her alarm clock. It was five fifteen. The ringing stopped. She sighed and sank back against her pillows. 'No need.'

She was about to switch her light off when the phone burst into life again and rang relentlessly on.

'I'd better go,' she said. 'You aren't supposed to be here at this time of night.'

She was afraid Chloe might have had an accident or the baby was coming early. She jerked herself out of bed and ran down to the hall. 'Hello,' she barked into the phone.

She recognised Marigold's voice immediately, though it croaked with fear. 'Thank goodness I've got you, I've been trying for ages, I thought you weren't there.'

'Where else would I be? I was asleep. What's the matter?'

'It's Mother, I can't wake her up...'

'Leave her, it's much too early.'

'Helen, I think she's dead!'

'What!' Helen felt the hall begin to eddy round her. 'Oh my God! Are you sure?'

'No, no, I'm not. I need you to come and help.'

'Oh my goodness! Ring the doctor, Marigold. I'll be there as soon as I can.' She flew back upstairs.

'It's Gran, Marigold thinks she might be dead but she isn't sure. She's in a flat spin. She wants me there.' Helen started pulling on the clothes she'd worn last night.

Rex leapt out of bed and threw his arms round her. 'I'm so sorry, this is terrible for you. Another shock on top of Chloe's bombshell.'

Helen pushed herself out of his arms and shook her head. 'I'm stronger than Marigold. Gran knew she'd need me.'

'How can I help?' Rex started to dress too.

'You can't. You aren't supposed to be here. Stay in bed a bit longer and then go to work. I don't know when I'll be able to come back.'

'You must feel awful, as though the bottom has dropped out of your world. Are you all right to drive?'

Helen was a bit shaky and she could see he was concerned. 'My knees feel like rubber.'

'I could take you.'

'No, Rex.' She had to stand on her own feet. 'I'll need my car to get back, won't I?' She was strapping her watch on.

'It was only yesterday lunchtime,' Rex said. 'Mrs Darty said it wouldn't be long. She must

102

have had a premonition.'

'I took no notice,' Helen lamented, as she pulled on a coat and ran out into the cold early dawn.

The only dead person she'd ever seen was her husband, John, but one look at Gran and she had no doubt that she was dead too. Marigold was in floods of tears and walking round in her nightie with bare feet.

'What about the doctor?'

'He said he'd come.' Marigold was shivering, her hands and feet were a mauvish colour and the house itself was freezing cold. Helen led her to her own bedroom, pushed her arms into her dressing gown and knotted her into it. She found her a pair of Gran's bed socks and made her put them on before her slippers. She pulled the eiderdown from her bed and wrapped it round her.

'Come on downstairs and I'll make a hot drink.' Helen had grown up in this house; it always had been a cold place. She took their tea to the shabby living room. The grate was filled with cold ash and there was no other source of heat. Helen groaned. She'd lost the art of laying fires, if she'd ever had it.

She was relieved to see a car pulling up outside behind her own. 'Look, here's Dr Harris.'

'Thank goodness.' Marigold shot to open the door before he knocked, but was then too upset to be able to tell him clearly what had happened.

Helen knew Dr Harris well; he'd been their family doctor for years. He was painfully thin, and his tired grey face made him look more ill than many of his patients. On being consulted regarding some indisposition, his soulful grey eyes would stare with benign intensity into those of his patient. Helen followed him upstairs, recounting how they'd both been to her house for Sunday lunch where Gran had eaten nothing; how a friend had brought them home and helped Marigold get Gran to bed for her afternoon rest.

'What happened after that?' the doctor asked.

'She went to sleep,' Marigold said. 'I helped her take off her skirt first, so she wouldn't crease it. It was her best one.'

Helen turned down the bedclothes and was shocked to see that Gran was still fully dressed apart from her skirt.

'When did she wake up?' the doctor asked.

'Well she didn't. I made her tea – she likes scrambled egg with some soft bread and butter on Sundays – but I couldn't wake her up to eat it.'

'Marigold!' Helen was horrified to think that Gran might have died yesterday.

'I tried to ring you, but you weren't there,' Marigold wailed. 'Rex took me out for a walk.' Helen was defensive.

'I tried again and it was getting dark; you couldn't have been out walking then.'

'And out to supper afterwards.'

'Was your mother breathing, Marigold? Can you remember?'

'Yes, but it sounded different. Slower and deeper somehow.' Tears were streaming down her cheeks. 'I sat here with her for a long time. I held her hand

and kept talking to her, but she didn't answer.' Marigold clucked with distress. 'I couldn't wake her.'

Helen shivered, tears stinging her eyes. She could understand why Marigold was upset now.

Dr Harris smiled gently at her. 'You did right, Marigold. If your mother could hear you, that would have comforted her.'

He looked at Helen then. 'It sounds as though she lost consciousness and slipped away peacefully in her sleep.'

They followed the doctor down to the icy living room. Helen watched numbly as he wrote out a certificate and left it on the table.

'She's been failing for some time, as you know, and she's had a very long life. Perhaps she's glad to be at rest now.'

As he saw himself out, Helen collapsed on a chair and made no effort to stem her tears.

Rex had made himself tea and toast and gone to work as Helen had suggested, but he couldn't settle. He knew this had come at a bad time for Helen; she was still smarting because of Chloe's pregnancy, and at the best of times she had little emotional strength. He was worried about her.

The morning was passing. He rang her home, but as he'd half expected, she wasn't there. He knew where her family lived. They had a small garden and he regularly sent a man round to maintain it. He got in his van and drove round.

It was Marigold who came to the door, with red eyes and a blotchy face. He found Helen still weeping at the living room table.

'Life has to go on for you two,' he told them. 'Have you had anything to eat?'

It was he who lit the fire and made them a brunch of eggs and bacon. He rang the vicar of their church, who promised to call round. Then, as it seemed neither had any idea what to do next, he found them a local undertaker, who also said he'd call.

Rex was preparing to leave when Helen lifted a stricken face. 'Chloe,' she said, 'I haven't let her know.'

'Do it now.'

'I can't, I don't know Adam's number. She wrote it down for me but I'll have to go home to get it.'

Rex drove her home and promised Marigold he'd deliver her back again. She spent a very tearful ten minutes talking to Chloe on the phone, and there was no possibility of drying her eyes after that. She was full of guilt that she'd been out enjoying herself with Rex, instead of being available to help Marigold.

'A hot bath will make you feel better,' he told her. 'You left without even cleaning your teeth this morning.' He ran the bath for her and she got out some clean clothes. While she was in the bath, he collected her make-up for her to take with her. By the time she was ready to leave, she was much calmer.

He drove her back to Marigold's house and promised to return at six that evening to take them both out to the bistro for supper. When he did, it was Chloe who opened the front door to him. She looked pale and exhausted, and for the first time, he thought she looked heavily pregnant.

'Thank you, Rex,' she said. 'Mum tells me you've been a cast-iron support to her and Aunt Goldie. You did what I should have been here to do.'

He rested his hand on her arm for a moment. 'I only did what anyone would do. How are you?'

'I'm fine,' she told him with a wry smile.

'Would you like to come with us for a bite to eat?'

'Yes, if you don't mind.'

'Of course I don't mind. We're all glad to have you here,' he said.

Chloe's presence made the simple meal the highlight of the day for Rex, though the women were quiet and had little to say. He was glad he'd encouraged Helen to keep in touch with her daughter. He'd feared a rift between them, because that would mean he'd never see Chloe.

Afterwards, he took them back to Helen's house. As it seemed they all intended to spend the night there, Rex knew he could not. He went back to his lonely flat to dream of Chloe.

Chloe grieved for Gran. In her early teens, when she'd first come to Liverpool, she'd found her sympathetic and a comfort. But Aunt Goldie seemed to view her death as the end of everything and went to pieces. Her mother too seemed incapable of functioning normally. Chloe would have liked to go back to Adam's house to escape from their grief, but felt she couldn't leave her mother until the funeral was over. They wanted that to take place as soon as possible, but Chloe knew they were dreading it as much as she was. Her mother was clearly looking for support.

Rex came round as usual and Chloe was surprised to find him discussing everything from the service to the flowers with Mum and Aunt Goldie. The earliest date they could get for the funeral was seven days hence. It was to be at half past eleven in the morning, and Mum decided to follow it with a light buffet lunch at her house for the mourners.

'What about Auntie Joan? Have you told her?' Chloe asked. 'She'll be upset, Gran was her aunt.'

'Oh heavens, no! How could I forget Joan?' Helen rushed to the phone.

'Tell her about me too,' Chloe called after her. She wanted them to know of her problem before they saw her.

Mum was on the phone for ages. Chloe heard her say her name several times and she knew they were discussing her. But when they came round later that day she was swept up into comforting hugs.

'You mustn't worry about it love,' Auntie Joan told her. Chloe thought they were particularly kind to her. It was Auntie Joan who took over organising the funeral lunch.

Chloe rang Adam later that day. 'I'm missing you,' he told her. 'When are you coming back?'

She told him about the funeral arrangements and suggested he came. 'You could take me back with you after the lunch. I'll have everything packed ready.'

'I don't like funerals,' he said. 'They give me the creeps. Tell your mother I'm sorry but I have to go to an auction on that day. An important one I can't afford to miss.'

'Oh!'

'She won't care whether I'm there or not.'

'I care.' Chloe thought he should come. 'You must if you're ever to be considered one of the family.'

He said, 'You could catch the train back and I'll meet you at the station.'

To Chloe, the days of waiting seemed interminable. Aunt Goldie came to stay with them in the third bedroom, but she complained that it was poky and the bed uncomfortable. Rex encouraged Chloe to take her mother out for walks and on trips to the shops to buy their daily provisions. They cooked together, and Rex usually joined them for their evening meal.

Adam rang her every day. 'I do love you and wish you were here,' he told her. 'It's lonely without you.'

But on the day before the funeral he said, 'If you come back tomorrow afternoon, I won't be able to meet your train, because the sale I told you about is in Edinburgh.'

'I thought that was just an excuse for you to avoid the funeral.'

'Of course not.' He sounded disconcerted. 'The sale is at Hampton's in Edinburgh, I told you that.'

'I don't remember.'

'Why don't you stay over till the next morning? There's a train you could catch that gets in about twelve. I could meet you and take you to lunch in Manchester before we go home. That would be nice, wouldn't it?'

'Yes,' she agreed. 'All right, that's what I'll do.'

When the day of the funeral came, it was pleasantly warm and sunny. Rex drove them to the church in Mum's car and was very attentive to them all. Gran had been in her eighty-sixth year and had outlived or lost touch with most of the friends she'd had, but she and Aunt Goldie had been regular churchgoers all their lives, so the church was not empty, as many of the congregation attended the ceremony.

As Helen's house was some distance from the church, only the vicar and two or three of the congregation came for refreshments, and they didn't stay long. That left the family party, which included Auntie Joan and Uncle Walter. Soon Mum and Rex were showing them round the lovely garden. Chloe made afternoon tea in the summerhouse for those who stayed on, and spent quite a long time talking to Auntie Joan.

Helen was relieved when she could take Marigold home and have the funeral over. She missed Chloe when she went back to Manchester, but was pleased she was maintaining contact with her. The following week, Chloe rang several times to ask how she was, and then invited her to come for afternoon tea and see where she was living.

'I'd love to,' Helen said. 'How do I find you?'

'I could draw a street map and post it to you. Or you could come by train and Adam will pick you up from the station.'

'Easier to drive, provided I can find you.'

'What about Rex? He's almost one of the

family, isn't he? Would he like to come too? Then you'd have him to map-read.'

'Yes, I'll ask him.'

Helen found Rex was quite keen. 'I'd like to see where Chloe's living now, and it would be a day out for us.'

After much deliberation, they decided on a Wednesday afternoon. 'Come here around half twelve,' Helen told him. 'I'll make us a light lunch, salad or something, and we'll get on our way as soon as we can.'

They had no difficulty finding the house, and Helen was impressed when they drew up outside. It was a stately Georgian-style building of smoke-blackened stone, with the sun glinting on the tall windows.

'Is it a flat they have here?' Rex asked.

'Chloe said it was a house.' It was a substantial one.

She'd been watching for them and came out to greet them. She seemed more relaxed and happier now she'd made her move.

The hall took Helen's breath away. It was vast, with white walls and a chandelier; the furniture was of the period. Chloe showed them round. It was all beautifully and expensively furnished. The kitchen and bathrooms were ultra-modern and there was central heating, though now it was summer it had been switched off. The sitting room was sumptuous.

'Adam says he had to have modern sofas and easy chairs,' Chloe told them. 'Antique soft furnishings are hard to find and they aren't very comfortable.'

'It's luxurious,' Helen said. 'Is it his family home?'

'No, he was brought up in Bournemouth and his mother still lives there. She's a widow now.'

'So Adam lived here alone before you came?' Rex asked.

'Yes.'

'This really impresses me, when I think of my own comfortless two-bedroom flat. He could be an interior designer, he has very good taste.'

'Antiques are an obsession with him.' Chloe smiled. 'They're his hobby as well as his means of earning a living.'

'He's a perfectionist,' Rex said.

'It's all lovely.' Helen had not thought Chloe would improve her living standard by moving in with Adam, but she had to accept that she had.

Chloe chatted away about her coming baby and showed them the Georgian mahogany cot Adam had found and the layette she was putting together. Helen immediately offered to knit a matinee jacket for the baby.

It pleased her very much that Chloe was showing nothing of Marigold's attitude of shame. Rather she seemed to be looking forward to the birth and to be content with her lot.

She'd made them a chocolate cake and little savoury sandwiches of prawns and cucumber. She served the tea in a Georgian silver tea service on a silver tray and they used exquisite china.

Adam returned and greeted Chloe in a way that showed how much in love with her he was. He too seemed more relaxed now that their position was accepted by Chloe's family. He chatted pleasantly about his day and offered them sherry.

On the way home, Helen said, 'I didn't realise Adam had money.'

Rex sighed. 'We needn't worry about Chloe after all. She'll be all right with him.'

'All they need to do is get married,' Helen said.

CHAPTER EIGHT

Helen felt she couldn't neglect Marigold now she was alone, and called round to see her. It was almost lunchtime but Marigold was just lighting her living room fire. She looked as though she'd neither washed nor combed her hair this morning.

'I had a wakeful night,' she said, 'and then I fell into a deep sleep when it was time to get up.'

'Have you had any breakfast?'

'All I want is a cup of tea.'

Helen went to the kitchen to put the kettle on. She knew Marigold must be feeling her loss because her life had always been so tied up with Gran's. She moved the remains of her last three meals from the table and started washing the dishes. It shocked her to see Marigold neglecting herself.

'Gran was old, Marigold,' she said. 'It's not as though her life was cut short by illness. She was old and often in pain. She probably didn't want to live longer.'

'You don't understand.' Marigold's face showed

113

signs of long-dried tears.

'We all have to go in the end,' Helen added.

'I know that.' She sounded impatient. 'What I don't know is how I'm going to manage without her.'

Helen had given little thought to that. She felt her relationship with Marigold had been permanently distorted because she'd been brought up to believe that she was her older sister. Even now, that was how she saw her.

Certainly she thought Marigold had had a sad life. Having an illegitimate daughter when she was sixteen had never been spoken about, but had provided all sorts of undercurrents in the family. Helen had been unable to understand this until she was fully adult. While Gran had had her health, she'd been a real matriarch and made all their decisions for them. Marigold had been her subservient daughter, and had never had another man in her life.

Last year, when she'd turned sixty, she'd retired from her job as a sewing machine operator and her time had been filled looking after her ailing mother. Now suddenly her days were empty. She could go to church on Sundays and chat to the vicar and others in the congregation, but she had no real friends.

Helen made her some tea and toast, poured a cup for herself and led the way back to the fire, which was now drawing up. She felt tea and sympathy would fill the bill.

'I've nothing but my old age pension to live on,' Marigold told her. 'Mother worked in the council offices for most of her life and she earned a pension from them, so with that and both our old age pensions, we survived.'

'You lived in modest comfort,' Helen corrected. 'Gran said you had all you needed.'

'Yes, but her pensions have died with her.' Marigold made it sound as though she'd been singled out to suffer like this.

Helen looked round the shabby room. She'd been brought up in this house and nothing had changed in all the years. She'd thought it draughty and comfortless then. It was a Victorian bay-windowed terrace house, one of the many thousands in the outer districts of Liverpool.

'They keep putting the rent up,' Marigold complained. 'It's too much, I can't afford it.'

'Won't social security help?'

'I don't want to live on social security.' She was indignant. 'It's not what our family do.'

'There's no harm in claiming help with your rent if you need it,' Helen said sharply. 'That's false pride in this day and age.' She could sense what was coming.

'You've had a much better life than I have, Helen.' Marigold sounded envious.

'That was due to John's greater earning power.' Helen didn't find it easy to forgive their hostility towards him.

Marigold pulled herself up on the sofa cushions. 'Wouldn't it be a good idea if I came to live with you?'

Helen froze. It was the last thing she wanted. If Marigold was always in the house, Rex wouldn't come. Her presence would be off-putting even if he did. She very much missed having Chloe

115

about the house, but it did mean that if she invited Rex to stay the night, nobody else need know. She wanted to go on having her house to herself.

'We'd be company for each other, wouldn't we?' Marigold said. 'You'll be lonely too, now Chloe has left you.'

Helen went home feeling depressed. She felt she'd been pummelled by the events of recent weeks, and now it seemed she had a new problem. She'd given little thought to how Marigold would manage on her own.

Today had promised to be a pleasant one. Rex had said he'd come in the late afternoon and spend an hour or so working in her garden.

'I'll get some steak and make dinner for us,' she'd told him, and then, feeling greatly daring, she'd added, 'And not just dinner, bring your overnight bag.'

Rex had given her his shy smile, kissed her cheek and said, 'Thank you.'

Helen felt her love for him was growing. She'd relied on him and he'd provided the support she'd needed for years. But everything had changed the night Chloe had told them she was pregnant and left with Adam. Helen felt she'd be less than honest if she didn't admit to herself that she'd encouraged Rex into her bed. He was a diffident man and would never push himself on anybody, but since then, he'd been showing her real love.

This deepened relationship was still so new to them that they were both a bit shy of talking about it. He'd told her that it had brought a new dimension to his life. Helen wanted it to develop naturally. She wanted him to say the words 'I love you'. Even more, she wanted him to suggest marriage. She felt sure that in time he would.

She set about preparing their evening meal, but when she looked up, she saw him through the kitchen window trundling a wheelbarrow across the grass. She went running out after him. 'Rex!'

He turned, smiling, and opened his arms to her. She felt them tighten round her in a hug and his lips came down on hers. She stifled a sob.

'I'm glad you're here.' Marigold's difficulties were clouding everything for her.

He held her away from him. 'What's the matter? Has something happened?'

'It's Marigold,' she told him. 'She wants to come and live here with me.'

Rex was smiling at her, not taking her seriously. 'She can't. It would be too embarrassing.'

'I know.' Helen couldn't help a wail of distress. 'I feel awful about it. And if I let her move into Chloe's bedroom, where will Chloe sleep when she comes to stay?'

'But you have three bedrooms, haven't you?'

'The third one is very small. I do have a single bed there, but Marigold complained it was cramped when she slept there recently, and I tend to use it as a box room and dump things there.'

'Why does she want to come here when she has a place of her own?'

'She says she can't afford it. She reckons that without her mother, she's living on the edge of poverty.'

'Is she?'

'She has only her old age pension and she's too proud to ask social services for help with her rent. I'm afraid she'll not be satisfied until she's in Chloe's room. But how can I have you in my bed if she's in the next room? She'd be angry and never stop telling me it was wrong.'

'She'd probably blame me,' Rex said. 'She'd think I'd talked you into it.'

'I don't want us to stop.' Helen smiled at him.

'Neither do I.'

'I think we're entitled to our pleasures, don't you? We aren't hurting anybody, and if we enjoy it, why shouldn't we?'

'No reason at all.' Rex gave her another hug.

'Oh dear, what am I going to tell Marigold?'

'Helen love, only you can decide that.'

'I know,' she sighed. 'But what if she won't take no for an answer?'

'We must find a way to keep her in her own home. I could make her an allowance.'

'No way, I can't let you do that. I'm pretty sure social security will pay her rent. She was quite uppity when I told her that, but I'm going to get the forms she'll need to apply, and offer to help her fill them in.'

Rex gave her another hug. 'That does make us look a little selfish, doesn't it?'

'All her life Gran coddled her, did everything for her. It would have been better if she'd made her stand on her own feet.'

He smiled. 'You can't say that. These last few years, Marigold has had to look after her mother, had to do almost everything for her. Anyway, it makes you sound very hard-hearted.'

'That's what I am.'

'No, Helen, you're not.'

Later that May evening, Helen was dishing up the sherry trifle she'd made for dessert when the phone rang. 'Who can that be?' she said as she went to answer it. She recognised Adam's voice immediately.

'I took Chloe to hospital at two o'clock and she had a baby girl at six this evening.' He sounded ecstatic.

'A girl!'

'She weighed seven pounds and we're going to call her Lucy.'

'That's wonderful! How's Chloe?'

'She's fine. They both are. An easy birth, so they say, no problems.'

'Excellent, I can't wait to see the baby.'

'They'll be home in a few days. I'll let you know.'

Helen rushed back to tell Rex. A wide smile lit up his face. 'I'm glad Chloe's well. A baby girl, eh? What time is visiting? We could run up to the hospital to see them both.'

Helen dished out two large helpings of trifle. 'Adam more or less put me off doing that. He said they'd be home in a few days.'

Chloe had thought that once Helen had accepted her pregnancy and she was living with Adam, her troubles would be over. But Adam liked to be out and about, while Chloe needed a quieter life.

She'd been dreading the birth, and though it

119

wasn't as bad as she'd expected, she was very glad to have that and the whole business of pregnancy behind her. Hospital had not been much to her taste either, though Lucy had been the most beautiful baby on the ward. To hold her in her arms almost made it seem worth while.

She was pleased when the time came for her to return to the comfort and elegance of Adam's home. They'd both enjoyed introducing Lucy to the new nursery they'd fitted out for her in the bedroom next to their own.

Chloe had thought that having a child would bring her and Adam closer, but nothing could have been further from the truth. A baby did not fit into Adam's lifestyle. They could not go out together on the spur of the moment; it needed planning, and they were too far away from Helen to have a babysitter on call. Chloe had neither the time nor the energy to serve and prepare fancy meals for when Adam came home, and the smart house lost some of its sparkle.

While Chloe doted on Lucy from the moment she was born, she soon realised Adam did not. Lucy cried a lot and kept him awake at night; he said he wished they'd made her nursery further away from their own room, preferably on the other side of the house. And during the day he complained she was always there between them, a demanding and bawling presence.

Chloe had looked forward to showing off her new baby to Mum and Rex. On the day she'd invited them to come, she'd dressed Lucy in the smart gown Adam had bought for her and she didn't cry once. They brought gifts for the baby:

Mum had managed to finish knitting her a white matinee coat and Rex presented her with a silver-backed hairbrush.

Mum was clearly thrilled to hold her, and billed and cooed over her. Lucy had a soft covering of golden down on her head, neat regular features and round eyes of the darkest blue. It surprised Chloe to find Rex carrying the baby round the room marvelling at how beautiful she was.

Adam was at home and made tea for them in the silver teapot. 'Sorry,' he said, 'I've had to buy a cake, Lucy takes up so much of our time.'

'More than we expected.' Chloe smiled.

'She'll get easier to manage as she gets older,' Helen comforted.

'The house doesn't look as spick and span as it did,' Adam said ruefully. 'I'm going to ask Ruby, my cleaning lady, to work two extra mornings if she will.'

'You have a cleaning lady?' Rex sounded amazed.

'For two mornings a week up to now. It helps me keep the place tidy.'

'You keep it looking like a show house.'

'No point in having a nice place and not looking after it,' Adam said tartly.

On the way home, Helen said, 'They seem happy, don't they? She may be all right. Anyway, I'll have to get used to her being an unmarried mother.'

'She's certainly living in luxury there.' Rex shook his head. 'To think of Adam employing a cleaner for two mornings a week when he was living there alone.'

'And not much more than a lad, only twenty-five,' Helen said. 'He's done very well for himself.'

'He'd no doubt be shocked to see how I live,' Rex said. 'He'd probably think my flat was a slovenly mess.'

'It isn't,' Helen said.

'But it's cramped and not at all smart.' Rex flashed her a smile. 'The baby's lovely.'

'Adorable,' Helen agreed.

In the weeks that followed, Chloe settled into motherhood and thoroughly enjoyed caring for Lucy. She hadn't expected to miss going to work, but she certainly missed the company of the office girls. Adam couldn't do without his visits to top Manchester night spots and took to going out without her once or twice a week. When he returned home, she'd usually been in bed for an hour or so, and it meant he woke her up. Sometimes he woke Lucy up too.

Chloe tried not to show her irritation about this. She felt he should involve himself more with Lucy, but he wasn't drawn to her, he didn't want to feed or nurse her. Neither did he want to get up to her when she woke up in the night, which was most nights.

He said, 'You don't have to get up to go to work, Chloe, so it's only fair you should see to the baby.'

Chloe was always tired and felt she and Lucy spent a great deal of time on their own. She wished her mother and Rex were nearer; the garden would be a pleasant place to take Lucy on a hot afternoon.

'You need to get out more in the day by yourself,' Adam told her. He'd provided a large Silver Cross pram for Lucy's outings. Super.

'I know, I know. Couldn't you take the odd afternoon off so we could all go out together?' she asked Adam.

'That could be difficult.'

Chloe thought the next best thing would be to go to an auction with him, so one day he drove her and Lucy to an auction room in the Peak District. Chloe was fascinated, but Lucy was restless and wouldn't settle in her carrycot. It was too long for a baby to be in a noisy and unfamiliar place, and Adam said he couldn't concentrate on the buying and selling.

'I'd get you a car, if only you could drive,' he told her. 'What about driving lessons?'

'Who would look after Lucy while I was learning?'

'You could ask Ruby.'

Ruby was now working for them four mornings a week, and Adam, who was very fussy about cleanliness and order about the house, thought she needed every minute of that. But she was working for someone else in the afternoons and occasionally they asked her to babysit of an evening as well.

'Couldn't you have Lucy on the back seat in her carrycot?'

'I don't know whether I could cope with that,' Chloe said. 'How could I concentrate on what the instructor was telling me if she was crying in the back?'

When she saw the look of impatience on

123

Adam's face, she gave up.

Rex had stayed overnight with Helen for the last three nights and was cooking egg and bacon for their breakfast while she took a bath. She had hinted that she'd like him to move in permanently, but he knew she was worried about Marigold, and they'd have to decide what was to be done about her first.

He felt guilty. He was increasingly fond of Helen and he recognised that she was giving him her heart. He didn't want to lose her – his life was vastly improved now she had a larger part in it – but it was Chloe who haunted him still. If it weren't for Chloe, he'd ask Helen to marry him. Make an honest woman of her, as the saying went. Then Marigold could come and live with them, if that was what Helen wanted.

But Rex couldn't commit himself to Helen while he still held feelings for Chloe.

Helen came downstairs in a cloud of fragrant bath scents and put the bread in the toaster. She'd had a storm of tears yesterday when Marigold had told her she was having nothing to do with social security; she was not going to be a burden on the tax-payer. He could see Helen frowning over this.

'I've given her money but that doesn't satisfy her. She says she's getting old now and needs physical help.'

'No, Helen,' he told her. 'She's perfectly capable of looking after herself. For heaven's sake, she was taking care of her mother as well, only a few weeks ago. She hasn't got over the shock of that yet. Give her time.'

'She doesn't want time, she's impatient with me. She thinks I should have her here. She is my mother, after all.'

Rex sighed. 'I suppose that house is too big for her.'

'The house is awful, I can't just leave her where she is. She thinks this is luxury.'

'I do too.' Rex dished up their breakfast and pulled up a chair in front of his plate.

'If Marigold were here,' Helen said, 'having you round for a meal wouldn't be the same. We wouldn't be able to talk, would we?'

Rex felt as though he had his back to the wall. He hadn't expected Gran's death to catapult him and Helen into an impasse. He couldn't make up his mind what to do for the best. The last thing he wanted was to hurt Helen's feelings.

'Our problems are the result of Victorian thinking,' he said. 'What's happened in your family and what's happened in mine wouldn't happen today. It won't happen to Chloe; she's much more up front and in tune with the times.'

'But it's still affecting you and me, and how do we stop that?' Her eyes were pleading with him across the table. He knew it was on her conscience that she'd done nothing about settling Marigold.

It came to Rex in that moment, and he almost laughed outright. 'I must get myself a house that's halfway decent. Heavens, Helen, when I saw how Adam had set himself up in the grand style, it made me feel I was being silly to live the way I do. My business has prospered over the years and yet I spend little of the profit. I could afford to buy myself a house with some comfort now. I'm going to do that, and when we want to be together, you can come and stay overnight with me.'

Helen's jaw had dropped. 'But I love this place and the garden...'

'You must keep it. This is your home. I'm not going to try and duplicate the garden. Another good thing is, it'll stop me feeling I'm sponging on you by always coming here.'

'You don't, you often take me out.'

'Will you help me find a house and set it up?'

'I'd love to.' Helen's eyes were sparkling with anticipation.

'I'm not good at that sort of thing, but you are. It'll be a place we can share.'

'I'm being greedy.' She was biting her lip. 'I want to share your new house and to keep my own too. But it's all very exciting. Let's start looking for it today.'

'I have to go to work, Helen. Things I must do.' He laughed. 'But you can.'

'Shall I see if the local estate agent has anything to suit?' she asked.

'Yes please. We need it near here. I must put my flat on the market too.'

It turned out to be an exciting time for both of them, almost as though they were setting up home together. They pored over street maps and visited one estate agent after another. Looking at houses around the neighbourhood meant they were out and about more. And once out, they

126

tended to stay out to have meals and drinks in the local pubs and cafés. Rex found it invigorating and had new energy; he thought Helen had too.

They looked at umpteen houses before they found Newburn Cottage. It was in a quiet backwater, tucked away behind a church. Rex had thought he wanted a modern house until he saw a photo of this one in an estate agent's window. It was late Victorian, almost turn of the century, but it had been well worked over recently and had a large kitchen, three bedrooms and two bathrooms in the very latest designs. There was central heating too, as well as an open fire, so they need never be cold.

'It doesn't need much doing to it,' Helen said. 'It's all in tip-top condition.'

'I like it very much.' Rex went from room to room, overawed by what was going to be a huge change in his life.

'It's just a question of moving your own furniture in,' Helen said.

Rex laughed. 'You've seen my furniture, so you know there isn't much I'll want to bring.'

That started them going round the big Liverpool stores looking at carpets and furniture. Afterwards, they usually had a cup of coffee in some nearby café to discuss what they'd liked and what would be suitable. Helen made notes, and later they made their choices and returned to buy.

'I'm going to have an absolutely beautiful new home,' Rex told her. 'I'm thrilled with it.'

It upset him when Helen's enthusiasm left her

like a burst bubble. 'But the more I think of inviting Marigold to live with me, the less I like the idea. She's never really pleased with anything.'

'You're right to think carefully about that.' Rex patted her hand. He had in mind the fits of depression she used to suffer and thought her wise not to rush into it.

'I wish I wasn't such a selfish person.'

'You aren't that,' he said. 'I've been thinking about it, and there is another alternative. What about my flat? It hasn't sold yet; would Marigold like to live there? It's small and easy to manage.'

Helen's face brightened. 'I could ask her, couldn't I?'

'Why not? She might like it. We must take her to see it. Persuade her.'

Rex felt much better about things now he had somewhere to entertain Helen. But Marigold was still pressing her to let her move into Chloe's room and he wanted to help her.

He and Helen went round his flat deciding which of his shabbiest furnishings should be thrown out, and Helen brought a few pieces from her house to smarten the place up. Then one Sunday, after Helen had provided the three of them with a good lunch of roast lamb and apple tart, they took Marigold to view it.

'It's small,' Rex told her. 'Just right for one person and very convenient for the shops.'

'There'd be much less housework for you, as there'd be no fires to light,' Helen added.

Rex drove them there in Helen's car as his van had seats for only two people. When he drew up outside, he saw Marigold looking up at the newish pink-brick block without enthusiasm.

'I don't like the area,' she said.

Helen pushed that aside. 'In a block like this, you'd be closer to other people. You wouldn't be lonely here.'

'There's a lot of stairs to get up to it.'

'It's only on the first floor.' Rex knew Marigold was going to turn it down. Her lips were straightening into a hard line as they led her from room to room.

'You can have warmth at the touch of a button,' Helen said. 'You'll love that.'

'But how much is it all going to cost?'

'It's very economical to run.' Rex flung open the bathroom door. 'Hot towel rails here, and I had the largest possible bath fitted.'

'You like it, don't you?' Helen asked.

'Well it won't do for me. I couldn't come to live in Princes Park, could I?'

'Why not?' Helen asked.

Rex said quickly, 'It's a very quiet neighbourhood and you have the park just round the corner. And Sefton Park isn't far either. It would give you some nice walks, it's a good place to live.'

'But I've always lived in Anfield. How would I get to church on Sundays? Hardly any buses run on Sundays, you know.'

'There's a big church within easy walking distance of this flat,' Rex assured her. 'We could go and see it now.'

'No thank you. I'd rather go to the church I'm familiar with, and be amongst people I know. No,

Rex, your flat is nice enough but I don't think it's for me.'

Helen drove her home to Anfield after that. 'Think about it, Marigold,' she said as she got out.

'Do you care what I think?' she retorted.

'Of course.' Helen was subdued in the face of such confrontation.

'Then much the most sensible thing would be for me to move in with you. You must be lonely now that Chloe's left.'

'I live a fair step away from your church,' Helen pointed out gently.

'Yes, but you have a car. It would be nice for us both to go on Sunday mornings, wouldn't it?'

CHAPTER NINE

From time to time Chloe spoke to her mother on the phone and knew she was sympathetic about the difficulties of getting out and about with a baby.

She said to Adam one evening over supper, 'I'm afraid Mum might feel I'm neglecting her because I've made no effort to take the baby to see her. I'd like to do that, perhaps stay a night or two if she's willing.'

'I don't like you staying away overnight,' he said. 'I miss you.'

'Just one or two,' she persuaded. 'You could eat out, see a show or something. You know you'd

130

enjoy that.'

'Well, you do need a break. Just this once, then.'

Chloe was keen and went to ring her mother. She was surprised to hear her voice spilling over with good spirits.

'I'd love to see you both, darling,' she said. 'Babies grow so quickly at this stage. Why not come for a week? That would give you a break and a change.'

'Two nights, Mum. Adam doesn't like me staying away too long.'

'Right, then I'll come to Lime Street station to pick you up. If you can't spend long with us, I don't want you to waste time coming up on the bus.'

Chloe saw her mother the moment she got off the train and thought she'd never seen her look so alive. She'd smartened herself up and was wearing her clothes fashionably shorter. She looked younger and happier than she had.

'You look very well, Mum.' Chloe couldn't believe it; she'd been half afraid her mother would miss her and grow depressed again.

'I've been in town all morning,' Helen said, taking Lucy from her arms and trying to hug Chloe at the same time. 'I've bought a new dress and had my hair done.'

She made a great fuss of Lucy as they walked to where she'd parked her car. 'Isn't she beautiful? And so like you when you were a baby. She's really coming on, lovely blonde hair.'

'She's sleeping through the night now, so I'm able to as well.'

Helen hoisted Lucy higher on her shoulder to

131

unlock her car, and then paused. 'Are you happy, Chloe?' she asked.

'Yes, yes.' Chloe tried to sound more enthusiastic about her changed circumstances than she really felt. 'I've missed you and your lovely garden. I can't wait to see it again, it's always gorgeous in the hot weather at this time of the year.'

'It is, I absolutely love it.'

'And Rex, is he OK?'

'He's fine. When I told him you were coming today, he said he'd arrange to work in my garden so he could see you and Lucy. I've asked him to have dinner with us.'

'Jolly good.'

'And guess what? He's sold the little flat he had and bought himself a lovely old cottage. It's behind the church in Rossmere Road, do you know where I mean?'

'Yes, I think so.'

'I've been helping him with the furnishings. We think it looks gorgeous. Perhaps we'll have time to take you to see it.'

'I'd like that,' Chloe said. It was a relief to find her mother was all right living on her own. In fact she seemed to be finding life more exciting than Chloe was herself. She pointed out with enthusiasm the two hybrid tea rose trees in their ornamental pots on her patio.

'They've improved every year,' she said. They were in full bloom again. 'You and Rex gave them to me for a long-ago birthday.' Red Devil had deep scarlet blooms and Evening Star was white. 'I love them.'

Chloe felt the garden was an oasis of peace. She

took a deckchair down near the pond and spent a lot of time sitting there in the shade. They ate breakfast and lunch in the summerhouse each day.

'Lucy is absolutely adorable,' Mum kept telling her, and she could hardly tear herself away from the baby. Rex was fascinated by her too and they virtually cared for her between them. Chloe felt she had a complete rest.

She spoke on the phone to Adam each day and it seemed he wanted her to return. When the day came, she was down in the hall all ready to leave for the station when the phone rang.

Her mother lifted it as she was passing. 'It's Adam,' she said, handing it to her.

'I'm glad I've caught you, Chloe.' He sounded tense and hurried. 'Something's come up. I won't be able to meet your train. Why don't you stay another night with your mother?'

She would have loved another night here, but now it made her laugh. 'It's a bit late for that. I've stripped my bed, packed my case, and as we speak, Mum's backing the car out of the garage to take us to the station.'

'No, Chloe, I won't be able to meet you.'

'I'll get a taxi.'

'Wouldn't you rather I drive over tonight and pick you up?'

She thought he sounded anxious. 'What's happened?'

'Nothing really, nothing to worry about. I'm rushed now, I'll explain when I see you.'

'Better if I come now and use my return train ticket,' she said. 'Mum's got something else on tonight. She's tooting for me to come, can you hear her?'

Her mother drove her into Liverpool to catch the Manchester train. Travelling with Lucy meant she had to cope with a lot of baggage. She wondered why Adam had changed his mind about wanting her to come home today.

It was a peaceful journey. The gentle rocking of the train, and later the taxi, kept Lucy contentedly asleep past the time when her feed was due. Chloe knew she'd need feeding as soon as she got home.

When the taxi drew up at her gate, she saw a car she didn't recognise parked in their drive and assumed a client had come to call on Adam. Lucy woke up and started to cry as Chloe manoeuvred her and her baggage indoors. With the babe on her shoulder she went to the kitchen to make her a feed. She filled the kettle and set it to boil. Then she went to find Adam. The door to his study was firmly shut. She gave it a tap and put her head round.

'Hello,' she said. 'I'm back.' She sensed immediately that there was something wrong. There were two men with Adam, one much older than the other. They seemed vaguely threatening.

'My partner,' Adam told them. Lucy opened her mouth and let out a lusty cry. Chloe knew she was capable of keeping it up.

'Do you want me to make a tray of tea?' That was usually what Adam asked her to do.

'Better see to the baby first.' Adam was stiff with tension. She noticed there were no antiques spread across the desk between them.

'You are Miss Chloe Redwood?' the older man asked.

'Yes.' She was conscious of Adam shrinking back in his chair.

'And you live at this address with Adam Livingstone?'

'Yes.' Chloe felt her heart beginning to beat faster. 'What's all this about?'

They flashed their warrant cards at her and introduced themselves as police officers. 'Mr Livingstone is helping us with our inquiries,' the older one said smoothly.

Chloe froze. Lucy was howling at the top of her lungs by now and flailing her fists and feet. She could no longer think straight.

'Were you here on the night of May the fifteenth through to the morning of May the sixteenth?'

'Yes, I've lived here since the end of March.' She looked from one to the other. 'Why?' She was afraid Adam was in some sort of trouble.

'Mr Livingstone tells us he spent that night here alone with you. And he definitely did not go out between ten and midnight. Can you confirm that?'

'Yes,' she said. 'Yes, why d'you want to know?'

'It would help us with our inquiries.'

Lucy's cries rose to a climax. 'Look,' Chloe said, 'I've got to see to the baby. She's hungry.'

Full of alarming suspicions, she rushed to the kitchen to make up a bottle. Lucy was distressed and scarlet in the face. Chloe was heading upstairs to the nursery with her when she heard Adam showing the policemen to the front door. She sank down on the nursing chair. There was sudden peace as Lucy took great slurps from her bottle.

She could hear voices from the hall for a while, then the front door was shut and Adam came up looking much more relaxed.

'Thank you,' he said, rubbing his hands together with satisfaction. 'I'm very grateful for that.'

Chloe felt she'd given the policemen short shrift. Her attention had been elsewhere. Now she straightened up. 'Grateful for what? Why were those policemen here?'

'Routine stuff.' Adam was smiling at her. 'Every month they make up a list of stolen property and circulate it through the trade in the hope that if some of the articles come up for sale, we'll recognise them. I couldn't help them.'

Chloe was full of suspicion now. 'It sounded more than that. They were asking about you.'

'No,' he said, 'not really. I'll start to cook. I've got some steak for dinner.'

Feeding Lucy always gave Chloe a quiet time to think, and it seemed obvious to her that Adam was trying to pass off the police visit as one of little importance. But he'd not wanted her to come home and find them here. He'd been very anxious; she'd felt his tension when she'd gone to his study and he'd been extraordinarily grateful for what she'd told the officers. What exactly had she said?

It came to her then like a bolt from the blue. May the fifteenth? When had Gran died? Lucy finished her bottle, and Chloe tucked her under her arm and ran down to the kitchen to consult the calendar. She'd not been here on May the fifteenth. She'd stayed in Liverpool with Mum, waiting for Gran's funeral.

She could feel the strength ebbing from her knees; they felt like rubber. The police had been asking her about Adam's movements. Without thinking, she'd provided him with a false alibi. That was why he'd been so grateful.

Adam was at the stove. She whirled round on him. 'What were you doing on the night of the fifteenth of May? It was you they were checking on, wasn't it?'

'There's no need to worry, Chloe...'

'I wasn't here that night. Why did you let me say I was? I wasn't thinking. The police will think I've lied. I've got to tell them it was all a mistake.'

She was heading for the phone in the hall to look up their number in the directory. Adam's arms came round her and the baby in a hug, pulling her to a halt. 'No, there's no need, love.'

'Yes, they could charge me with wasting police time.'

'It wasn't all that important.'

'But it is...'

'No, that wasn't about me. You've got it all wrong. They'll just drop whatever it was they were inquiring about. It's all over now.'

'Are you sure?'

'Yes, no need to give it another thought.'

Chloe was afraid that Adam was not as honest as he should be. That he could deny he'd done anything wrong with such an appearance of innocence made her want to believe him. It was what he'd said on the phone beforehand that gave her grounds to worry, and the fact that clearly he

137

didn't want her to contact the police. It left her anxious, but she did nothing, and as he'd predicted, they heard no more from them.

Chloe couldn't bring herself to do anything that might cause a rift between her and Adam, but it took her a while to put the incident out of her mind.

As the weeks went on, Chloe began to feel better. She had more energy and with a little experience she found taking care of the baby was easier. She pushed Lucy to the shops regularly, and once a month or so she took the train to Liverpool to see her mother. She'd struck up a friendship with another girl called Dulcie, who'd been in the same ward having a baby at the same time. They took their babies to the child welfare clinic to be weighed and to the local park on fine afternoons.

Chloe didn't want another baby for a while and knew that Adam's precautions were unreliable. It seemed that Dulcie was of like mind, so they went together to the family planning clinic to get the pill. Adam thoroughly approved of her taking over that responsibility.

He spent the odd day working from his study, phoning and catching up with his paperwork, but the telephone often rang while he was out. He was relying on Chloe to take work-related messages for him from clients, shops and auction houses. She was interested in what he was doing and offered to type letters for him on the portable type-writer he had. Adam seemed glad to take her up on that and gave her books on antiques to read so that she'd understand more of what it was all

138

about. Occasionally, clients and colleagues came to see Adam at home and Chloe would help to entertain them. She tried to involve herself more with his business because it was an interest she and Adam could share.

She felt she'd settled down to motherhood and was enjoying her very comfortable station in life. She was proud of Adam's ability to provide so well for them and eager to learn as much about it as she could.

One morning, Adam had arranged to visit a saleroom in Derbyshire. Before he set out, he ran upstairs to the nursery, where Chloe was dressing Lucy.

'Chloe,' he said, 'a man by the name of Newcombe is going to bring in a clock and some silver this morning. Get his phone number and tell him I'll ring him back this afternoon when I've had time to look at them.'

'Are you going to buy these things?'

'It depends on what they are. Mr Newcombe says his son is ill and has mortgage difficulties. He's trying to raise money urgently for him.' He dropped a kiss on her head and then one on Lucy's. 'I'll see you later. Bye bye.'

About an hour later, Chloe saw an old car draw up on the drive and a very elderly couple come towards the front door, each carrying a bag. She ran to open it and asked, 'Mr and Mrs Newcombe?'

She thought they looked a rather sad pair and took them to Adam's study, where she helped them unpack their bags and lay out what they'd brought on his desk.

'We've had these all our married life,' the old lady said. 'To us they're a slice of our history, but are they any good?'

Mr Newcombe smiled at her. 'Mr Livingstone said he'd give us instant cash for top-quality goods, but if they aren't what he wants, we'd have to wait for them to be sold at auction.'

The clock was very similar to the mantel clock her mother had sold to help buy the summer-house. 'I think he might be interested in this,' she told them.

Chloe felt she could value it, but knew better than to say so to its owners. Adam was very fussy that she should not talk prices to customers. 'It raises their hopes,' he'd told her, 'and you could get it hopelessly wrong.'

She wrote down their phone number and said, 'My partner will ring you later this afternoon when he gets home.'

When they'd gone, Chloe went back to take another look at the things they'd brought. Their clock seemed to be of good quality. It had a different name on the dial to that her mother had had, and she knew that could make a big difference to what it was worth. There was a silver tea and coffee set; each piece was hallmarked, but the marks conveyed nothing to her except that they were solid silver and not plate. She got out Adam's list of hallmarks and tried to fathom them out, but it wasn't easy and Lucy wouldn't let her concentrate.

Adam was home before four, in good time to have afternoon tea with her. When he went to his study to view the goods, Chloe followed him and stood in the doorway, interested to hear his opinion. He took the silver coffee pot to the window, where the sun was beaming in.

'Nice stuff.' He was enthusiastic. 'George IV five-piece service, yes, 1827, by Charles Fox.'

'How much is that worth?'

'Quite a lot, a good maker. It depends to some extent on how much silver is in it.'

'It's an attractive design.'

'It's a good weight but I haven't got big enough scales to find out exactly. It has its matching tray, though, and trays are often lost. I have a client who might like this. Yes, I'm sure he will.'

'And the clock? That's like the clock Mum had, isn't it?'

He picked it up. 'Same period, early Georgian. This one's by William Webster. Very nice brass dial. It's worth more than your mother's.'

'I'm glad,' Chloe said. She'd felt sorry for the old couple.

Lucy had crawled after her, but finding her mother's attention was elsewhere, she let out a howl of protest. Chloe picked her up and kissed her to comfort her. She'd taken only a couple of steps along the passage when she heard Adam speaking on the phone. There was no enthusiasm in his voice now.

'Of course they are worth something,' he said, 'and I'll be happy to buy them from you. But I have to tell you that silver is losing its popular appeal; housewives don't want the bother of cleaning it these days. That means it's losing its value in today's market. The clock? It's handsome, but dozens of similar ones were made and that also affects the value.'

Lucy was chuckling softly and rubbing her face against her mother's. Chloe waited silently, listening for the amount Adam was about to offer for them. In order to learn, this was what she needed to know.

When Adam named the figure, it rooted her to the spot. She'd expected him to offer at least twice that. She was filled with sympathy for the owners, who no doubt had hoped for more in order to help their son. Adam was still talking. It seemed the couple were about to accept his offer.

'I'll make out a cheque for you,' he said. 'You can either come round and collect it, or I'll put it in the post for you.'

She heard the phone click down on its rest and went back to the doorway.

'I thought that stuff would be worth more than that,' she said, balancing Lucy on one arm so she could pick up the teapot. 'It's pretty, I like it.'

She turned to face Adam, and the look on his face spoke volumes. She sucked in a deep breath. This surely must be proof that Adam was not honest. 'That's not a fair price, is it?'

He looked guilty and blustered, 'I have to do the best I can for myself.'

'But that's cheating.'

'I've told you, haven't I? We dealers have to make our living on the price difference between buying and selling.'

'But other antique dealers price their stock fairly for their customers.'

'None of us could stay in business if we didn't,' he maintained.

'You cheated the Newcombes. They must be in their eighties,' she went on slowly. 'Selling their belongings is not something they've done before. They don't know what their things are worth and even less about the antiques market. They're in a hurry, and you could be reasonably sure they wouldn't try another dealer.'

So this was how Adam was able to afford the fine house and the good life. He was buying top-class merchandise and giving its owners a fraction of what it was worth. Hadn't he tried to do that to her mother? Why hadn't she seen this straight away?

'They didn't try to push me up.'

'No, you'd have given them a pound or two more if they had, but it would still be a bargain for you. It's a form of fraud.'

'Don't be ridiculous,' he said angrily, and tried to justify what he was doing. 'Sometimes I win and sometimes I lose.'

'Mostly you win.' Chloe's voice was sharp. 'You make sure the odds are in your favour.'

'I have to. We all have to. It's not like the civil service. We're living on our wits.'

She was frowning. 'I was proud of you, doing so well. You have this fabulous house.'

'I've bought it on a mortgage,' he said. 'Not everything goes the way I want it to. Sometimes I make a mistake and sometimes I back a loser. It's not always easy.'

'Think of the people you are defrauding out of what is rightfully theirs.'

'Most have more than they need.'

'It's not a question of what they need. Most

don't understand the value of what they're letting you have.'

'More fool them.'

'Adam, you have to keep abreast of values to stay in business. That's your job, but values are changing all the time and the people you deal with are often old, like the Newcombes. They could have owned what they're selling you all their lives; some things have been passed down the family.'

He was impatient. 'I know all that.'

'You're cheating them.'

'Almost everybody cheats one way or another.'

'No they don't. Most people are honest.'

'Chloe, everybody is out to feather their own nest. I've been in this business a long time and I've seen it time and time again.

'Last year a man rang me up and asked me to value the contents of a big house. He wanted it done urgently because he meant to sell everything as soon as he could. He took me from room to room, but when I went to push open one of the bedroom doors, he said, "Not in there, my father's in bed."

'As it was mid-afternoon, I said, "Sorry, is he ill?"

'"He died last night," he told me. "I need to move everything to an auction room before I tell the rest of the family, or they'll strip the place out before I get a look in."'

Chloe stared at him in disbelief.

'At another place, I was followed round by eight members of the family when I went to value the contents. All of them were scared stiff they

144

weren't going to get their fair share of the pick-ings.'

Chloe choked. 'Adam, I'd like to think I could trust you.'

'Well of course you can. I went to another house where they had hidden money behind the wall-paper and the house was so damp, brown mildew and fungus was growing through pound notes. Not everybody comes from a polite, honest, well-to-do family like yours.'

'My Aunt Goldie is not well-to-do, but I believe her to be honest.'

'Everybody has to look out for himself in this trade.'

Chloe tried to see things squarely. She no longer admired what Adam had achieved, she didn't like his methods, and on top of this, the police had been making inquiries about something he'd done. He'd lied to her about that and she'd pro-vided him with a false alibi.

She knew she should have done something to correct that, but having Lucy bonded her to Adam. She couldn't earn her own living and take care of her daughter; her only logical course was to stay.

It cooled things between them for a while, but on a day-to-day level they rubbed along together fairly well and things picked up again. Chloe told herself that mostly Adam was making his living by legitimate means. He was generous and he wanted them all to have a good time. It was just that he always seemed to be on the lookout to make the extra pound anywhere he could.

CHAPTER TEN

Helen was feeling happier about Chloe. She seemed contented with Adam, and Lucy was thriving. For herself, she'd really enjoyed helping Rex set up his new home. It wasn't quite finished; perhaps it never would be. It was very pleasant to prowl round the shops together seeking exactly the right table lamp or some pretty china. He needed another armchair to complete the sitting room and a blanket chest to stand on the landing.

Rex said he was very comfortable there and should have made the move years ago. He cooked meals for her and she found he was keen on curries, though she hadn't realised that until recently. She spent the night with him quite often, and at other times he'd come to stay the night with her. At last he had a buyer for his flat and the sale was going through without a hitch. He told her he was happy and couldn't ask for anything more.

As far as Helen was concerned, the one fly in the ointment was Marigold, who was now in the habit of calling round to see her without giving any warning. She'd come by bus and stay for meals. From time to time Helen had to tell her she had other plans made and offer to run her home. Today she arrived about eleven, in time to have coffee in the summerhouse.

'You have a lovely house, and the garden is fantastic,' she said, lying back on a lounger. 'I need to find somewhere better to live. I wish you'd help me.' That made Helen feel guilty. She wanted her house and garden to herself and so had put off doing anything for Marigold. 'You've had a much better life than I've had.'

This was something she said from time to time, with envy clear in her voice. 'You promised Gran you'd help me, but you haven't.'

Helen felt the heat run up her cheeks. Marigold wasn't usually so blunt. 'I got social services to help with your rent,' she told her, equally blunt. 'You have enough to live on now.'

'You know I'd like to move from that house. It's too big for me on my own.'

'There's a block of small flats being built not far from you. Would you like us to take a look at those? See if–'

'You know what I want, Helen. I'm getting old and I can't do all the things I used to.'

'Old? You keep telling me you're only sixteen years older than I am. That's sixty-two, not all that old.'

'I need help.' It was a cry from the heart.

The implication was clear. Marigold considered it Helen's duty to look after her now.

'The most sensible thing would be for me to come here and live with you.'

Helen bit at her lip. How could she keep saying no?

'It's the most economical thing to do.'

Helen stayed silent.

'I am your mother.'

'I know you are, Marigold, but somehow...'

'You don't love me.' She made it a bitter accusation, her cheeks flushing with anger.

Helen found that too near the truth and could hardly get her words out. 'It's not that. I know it'll only upset us if we go over and over it, but I find it hard to think of you as my mother. I was brought up to call you Marigold and regard you as my big sister. That's permanently engraved on my mind.'

'But you know differently now.'

Helen went on the offensive. 'Yes, but what I don't know is the first thing about my father. You've always refused to tell me anything about him.'

'Mother thought that was the best thing for me. That I forget all about him.'

'But what about me? You must have realised I'd be curious. You asked Gran about your father, and all the time I thought he was mine too that was all right. But suddenly I found he was my grandfather.'

'You were too young to understand, only fourteen.'

'I'm not too young now. I'm forty-six and you've never told me. I mean, what sort of a man was he? How did he earn his living? What happened that he didn't marry you?'

Marigold's face was flushed. 'He was already married to someone else, so it wasn't possible. He was a real rotter. Mother said I'd be better off without him.'

'But I'm his daughter as well as yours. That could make me a bit of a rotter too, couldn't it?'

'Don't be silly, Helen.'

'You don't understand. It's something I need to know. He's provided half my make-up and you're the only person who can tell me about him.'

Marigold's face was working with anger. Helen wasn't going to let that stop her. 'For you it was all over years ago, but for me it isn't. Why won't you talk about him?'

'If that's what I have to do to make you see where your duty lies, then damn it, I will.' Marigold didn't stop to take a breath; it all came out in a rush. 'I worked for a small garment-making business, blouses mostly. His name was Harold Waters, he was my boss and twenty-five years older. He already had two children but I didn't know about them at the time. He took advantage of me and I admit I was a fool to let him. He ruined my life and I've never forgiven him for what he did.'

Helen was shocked to find how wound up and intense she was.

'Marigold, it happened forty-six years ago. You've had plenty of time to come to terms with it. You should have forgiven as well as forgotten.'

'How could I? You were always there to remind me.'

That took Helen's breath away. Marigold got up and rushed towards the house. 'I can't stay, I'm going home.'

Helen followed her. 'But it's lunchtime and you said the egg salad I made for us looked nice.'

'No, I'm too upset now.'

At the back door, she turned, and Helen saw that her face was ravaged with tears. She said, 'I'll get the car out and run you home.'

'No, don't bother. I don't want to trouble you for anything.'

'Marigold!'

'Just leave me alone. I'll use your cloakroom and then go home on the bus. I'd rather.'

Helen went back to her summerhouse and had a little weep. What sort of a relationship was that to have with one's mother? When she'd been in her teens she'd pleaded with both Marigold and Gran to tell her about her father, and though she'd learned his name at long last, it gave her no satisfaction. She said it aloud: 'Harold Waters.'

Gran was right after all, he needed to be forgotten. Not that Marigold had forgotten him; she had all his details in the forefront of her mind. They'd been fermenting there for years, souring everything for her and for her family. Poor Marigold.

Rex had said he'd come to work in her garden this afternoon and she waited for him to arrive. As soon as she saw him unloading plants from his van, she rushed to tell him what Marigold had said to her.

'You mustn't let her upset you.' Rex gave her a hug. 'She's very unhappy, we should feel sorry for her.'

'We don't get on,' Helen agonised. 'But this all came to a head because she wants to come and live here with me.' She let out an impatient sigh. 'Oh dear, what am I going to do about her?'

'Helen love, only you can decide that.'

'I know,' she sighed.

'I prescribe an hour or so of gardening for us,'

he said. 'After that, I'd like you to come to my place and cook our dinner. I bought some fillet steak this morning.'

Helen was nodding. Rex knew what would make her forget her troubles.

'And not just dinner. If you will, I'd like you to stay overnight with me.' Rex had given her his shy smile and kissed her cheek.

'Thank you,' she said. He was a wall of comfort to her.

A day or two later, Rex was drinking tea in Helen's kitchen when the phone rang in the hall.

She went to answer it. 'Chloe, how are things with you?' Hearing Chloe's name spoken made him move to the kitchen door.

Helen looked up and smiled. 'Lucy's learned to walk,' she told him. 'She can do three steps without holding on.

'I knew she wasn't far off,' she said into the phone. 'It's her first birthday next Friday, isn't it? I've got her a teddy bear. Are you planning anything special?' Rex watched Helen's face while she listened.

'Do bring her to see us that day, and the cake, of course. We'll have a little party in the summer-house. Well, just Rex and us. Yes, I'll meet your train. You'll come on the one that gets in at half ten as usual? Yes, look forward to seeing you. Take care, love.'

Helen's face was all smiles as she came back to the kitchen. A visit from Chloe always cheered her up.

That night, Rex didn't sleep well. Chloe was

very much on his mind. He hadn't yet proposed to Helen and he hoped that seeing Chloe again might help him to decide how much she really did mean to him. If she was an obsession he was getting over, he'd be able to devote himself to Helen.

The grass in her garden needed to be cut and Rex went to do it early in the morning before Chloe arrived. These days he brought his own sit-on lawnmower. He had several large gardens to look after and it saved him time and energy. But he didn't start straight away; he had a little walk round to savour what he'd created and see what work was needed.

Now in May, Helen's garden was looking its best. His favourite flower was the peony. There were few other plants that could provide a heady fragrance and such a marvellous display of colour. In his first years in this garden he'd planted a long bank of them shading from Pink Delight through to the deep rose of Gaye Lady to the black-red of Wilbur Wright. They were all in full flower and looked magnificent. Every year, Helen remarked on them.

He walked on to the pond. The water lilies that Helen had wanted were a magnificent sight, with flowers and leaves floating on the water. He'd put in several sorts of iris but they had all flowered and died back now.

Some animal life had arrived of its own accord, whirligig beetles, newts and pond-skaters. Helen had also wanted goldfish, so they'd chosen several varieties and they seemed to be thriving.

To start with, the pond had needed cleaning

out several times. Recently Rex had been trying out various aerating plants to supply oxygen, and now he'd got the pond balanced so the water stayed clear.

He loved this part of the garden. The trees had grown and in some places provided a canopy of leaves overhead. It was cool and restful on a hot day like this. But he was idling instead of cutting the lawns. He walked back and started his mower. It was lovely to work outdoors in weather like this.

He was thinking about Chloe again, anticipating their meeting. The put-put of the mower engine was shutting out all other sounds. Suddenly he looked up and saw Marigold rushing towards him, waving and calling and clearly in great distress. He swung the mower round and drove towards her before shutting it off and jumping down.

'Where's Helen?' she was calling. 'Where is she?'

'She's gone into town to meet Chloe. She's bringing Lucy over to see her today.'

Marigold burst into tears. She seemed to be losing weight, her face was stern and grey and her eyes were dark pools of unhappiness. She looked frightened, and it sent a shiver through him. 'Has something upset you?'

'Yes, I've had my purse stolen. I've lost all my money and my house keys. I can't get back inside, but the thief can.'

'That's terrible. What happened?'

'I was...' She could hardly get the words out. 'I was in the high street. Outside that big butcher's shop, the one that sells cooked meats as well. I was looking in his window, wondering whether to buy mince again or get myself a pork chop. I was afraid it might be tough...'

'Yes, but how was your purse–'

'As I turned to go, a youth jolted into me. He didn't say sorry or anything. When I came to pay for my half-pound of mince, I found my purse had gone.'

Rex took her by the arm and led her back towards the house. 'Where was it?'

'I had it in my shopping bag. It has a flap over it, it couldn't be seen. I thought it would be safe there.' Her voice rose in distress.

'Have you informed the police?'

'No, I didn't know what to do...'

'You must do that. Have you lost anything else, your chequebook?'

'I don't have one. But my pension book, yes, that's gone too. And I hadn't drawn my pension for this week. I was saving it to buy myself some new shoes.'

He led her to the back door. 'It's locked,' she wept. 'I tried it.'

'Helen locks up when she goes out, but she leaves a key for me here.' He lifted one of the plant pots on the patio and unlocked the door.

'She's trusting, isn't she?' Marigold's tone had become frigid.

'She thinks I might want to make myself a cup of tea. And right now, you need to use her phone to contact the police.'

He sat her down beside it, found the number in the book and dialled it. When he heard it ringing, he handed the phone to her. 'Report what happened,' he told her.

She still had trouble getting her words out. He went to the kitchen to make her a cup of tea. She sounded shocked and very much in need of it.

'Jostled, yes. That did surprise me because... A young man, twenties I'd say.' A note of anger crept in. 'I didn't notice, I didn't think it was important. I didn't realise at the time. I've lost over three pounds, all the money I had. The police station? I don't know where that is. Yes. Yes, all right.'

She came unsteadily to the kitchen. When the tea was ready, Rex pushed the cup in front of her. 'What did they say?'

'They'll send an officer round to take the details.'

'Round here?'

'No, to my house. Should I have told them I was here?'

'When is he going to come?'

'How should I know?'

Rex rang the number again and was told the officer would visit when he had time, possibly later today or tomorrow.

He was glad to hear Helen's key in the front door, and then Chloe was standing in front of him, her lavender eyes smiling at him, more beautiful than ever. 'Hello, Rex, long time no see. How are you?'

She was pleased to see him. Chloe put little Lucy to sit on the hall rug and he watched her pull herself to her feet on the umbrella stand.

'She can walk round the furniture now, but she can move more quickly on all fours,' Chloe told them.

Lucy took three wobbly steps and sat down with a bump. Rex picked her up. Her eyes, almost completely round and deep blue, stared straight up into his. He thought she was lovely as he led the way to the kitchen.

Marigold hadn't moved; she was still in tears. Rex told them what had happened to her and they all sat round the kitchen table listening to her story.

'He's taken my purse, but that's not the worst of it. He's got my front-door key.'

'I've still got mine,' Helen said. 'We can have another cut for you from that.'

'But don't you see?' Marigold wept. 'He can come in any time he wants to and take the rest of my things.'

Helen took Lucy from Rex's arms and led the way out to the summerhouse. 'Happy birthday, darling.' She kissed her. 'I've left the present I've bought for you out there.' They all enjoyed seeing her tear off the fancy paper from the teddy bear.

'She loves that.' Chloe laughed. 'I bought her some plastic ducks for her bath and Daddy gave her a drum.'

It rather surprised Helen to see Rex bring out a soft white rabbit for the baby. She hadn't expected him to show such interest in her. It looked as though he'd have made a good father and family man. He took Chloe off to see the garden and collect a few vegetables to take back with her.

For Helen, Marigold's plight quite spoiled Chloe's visit. Marigold couldn't stop worrying about her loss. She went on and on about it.

Chloe was being kind to her. She pushed a few pound notes into her hand and whispered, 'To make up for your loss.' But even that didn't quieten her. The theft had shocked poor Marigold and her nerves were raw.

Helen had decided it was just the day to have lunch in the summerhouse, and when Chloe came to help her carry the dishes out, she said, 'I've had to invite Marigold to eat with us. She's been very low since Gran died. This is going to knock her for six.'

Marigold's tears and woebegone face cast a blight on what should have been a very happy occasion. Rex and Chloe made the afternoon tea at four o'clock and brought it out to the garden. They sang 'Happy Birthday' for Lucy and tried to teach her to blow out her single candle, but she didn't understand and Chloe had to do it for her.

After that, Marigold began to fuss about getting home to make sure nothing more had been taken from her. It shocked Helen to hear her say, 'I can't walk into the house on my own. You'll have to come with me in case the thief is inside.'

'You'll be all right,' Helen told her. 'I have to take Chloe for the five fifteen train.'

'I'll run you home, Marigold,' Rex offered. 'And we'll make sure there's nobody inside.'

Helen was impatient with Marigold. It seemed she didn't appreciate how much others had to do for her.

'I don't think I'll be able to stay in that house on my own,' she told them all. 'Not now I know the thief has my key.'

'If you put the bolts on, Aunt Goldie,' Chloe said as she kissed her goodbye, 'he won't be able to get in.'

CHAPTER ELEVEN

Chloe had not enjoyed her day out as much as she'd expected. Aunt Goldie had worked herself up into a terrible state and moaned about everything. Having her purse stolen had upset her, of course, but that was no reason to go on at Mum as she had. Chloe hadn't realised how jealous Marigold was of Helen's luxury life and fantastic garden. When Rex had wanted to take her round it to see the improvements, she'd refused to budge from her chair.

She'd made it horribly obvious she wanted to move in and share what Mum had. Chloe knew that had been on the cards since Gran had died, and she couldn't blame her. Aunt Goldie had had a hard life and her house was miserably cold in winter. But Mum had spent years getting her place just as she wanted it, and she'd have to be a saint to want Aunt Goldie permanently with her.

When Adam had driven her into Manchester this morning, they'd discussed the situation.

'Marigold and Mum have never got on,' she'd said. 'I don't think it would be a good thing for them to live together.'

'That's only half the reason.' Adam had turned

to smile sardonically at her. 'Rex is probably stay-ing there at night, doing with your mother exactly what you and I are doing. The sixties have loos-ened everybody up, you know. And why not?'

'I don't know about that.' Chloe was doubtful. 'I can't see Mum...'

'You're as strait-laced as the rest of your family,' he'd laughed.

Adam had called him, 'Your mother's toy boy,' but when Rex had put them on the train, he'd kissed Chloe and Lucy goodbye almost like a father.

'I like Rex,' she'd told him.

Rex had gone out of his way to cheer things along, but he hadn't succeeded. He'd kept Lucy amused for most of their visit, and now the rocking of the train was lulling her to sleep.

When Chloe got Lucy and her pushchair off the train in Manchester, Adam was waiting for them. She was tired and her skin felt tight after being out in the fresh air for most of the day. She was glad she'd prepared a cottage pie for tonight's dinner. All she had to do was put it in the oven to heat through and brown the top, and she'd brought a spring cabbage from Mum's garden to have with it.

'I'm tired too,' Adam said. 'I've been out all day as well.' While he opened up the house, she lifted Lucy to carry her in. That woke her up and made her cry. Chloe knew she'd be hungry too by now.

Adam was irritable. 'Shut her up for a minute. There's a strange noise, can you hear it? A sort of drip-drip?'

He went to investigate. Chloe had Lucy on her shoulder as she hurried to light the oven. The most urgent thing was to find Lucy some supper, but for that she had to put the child down. She'd brought a rug to the kitchen so that Lucy could stretch and roll on the floor to get a bit of exercise. It wasn't what she wanted now; she drummed her heels on the floor and opened her mouth to scream with all her might.

Chloe had thought Lucy could share some of their cottage pie, but she was in no mood to wait for that to heat up. She was in the habit of making up batches of baby food and freezing them until they were needed. She brought out a packet of fish pie with peas and was about to fill the kettle when Adam came rushing down in a panic.

'We've got a leak. Total disaster. For God's sake, shut the baby up. I can't think while she's making this racket.'

He pushed Chloe out of the way to get under the kitchen sink and turn off the water supply.

'Come and help me. I can't believe the mess. There's a leak in the loft, the water's pouring through the ceiling in one of the spare bedrooms.'

Chloe followed him upstairs. 'Thank goodness it's not over our bedroom or Lucy's.'

'It's a bloody disaster wherever it is. The bed is saturated and so is the carpet on the landing. It's been dripping most of the day. Look at the ceiling!' It was bulging.

'Oh my goodness.' Chloe was as shocked as he was.

'I'm going up in the loft. Find me some buckets or bowls, something to catch this water in.'

Chloe rushed back to the kitchen to get them. It went through her to hear her baby crying like that, and it was almost more than she could bear to ignore her, but she ran back to Adam with a bucket and a washing-up bowl. He'd pulled a table underneath the trap door and balanced a chair on top; now he was ready to swing himself into the loft. She handed up the utensils.

'At least it seems to be stopping,' he said between clenched teeth. 'Push that bed out of the way, will you?'

She did what he asked before shouting, 'I'm going, I've got to see to Lucy.'

Lucy was still screaming at the top of her lungs, her face was scarlet and she'd rolled off her mat. Chloe picked her up and tried to comfort her. She felt hot and sticky and looked totally woebegone. 'Sorry, love. Sorry – a domestic emergency.'

She found enough water in the tap to fill the kettle and put it on to boil in order to heat Lucy's fish pie. Then she took her to the bathroom to change her. There was just enough water left to sponge her down before putting on her night clothes. Lucy was still having an occasional shudder against her shoulder. The fish pie was thawed but barely warm when she took her back. Lucy didn't care, she gobbled it down.

Chloe warmed some fresh milk and put it in a bottle, then took Lucy up to the nursery and sat down to feed her. The baby was soon sucking hard; Chloe knew this would settle her. She closed her eyes, feeling bone weary.

Adam came to rest his head against the door frame.

'What a day,' she said.

He'd calmed down. 'I've found a plumber, he says he'll be round in about an hour. It's the one who refitted the kitchen for me last year.'

When she'd put Lucy down for the night, Chloe went downstairs to see about dinner. The cottage pie was golden brown and filling the kitchen with mouth-watering scents, but there was no water to boil the cabbage or even wash it.

Adam was slumped at the table drinking beer. He got up to refill his tankard and poured a glass of wine for Chloe. 'Never mind the veg,' he said. 'Let's eat what's ready, we're both famished.'

'We'll have it here in the kitchen,' Chloe said. They ate their meals in the dining room in considerable style, but it took time and energy to organise.

'OK, we'll feel better when we've eaten.'

The plumber arrived while they were finishing off last night's gooseberry pie. As Chloe tidied up the kitchen, she could hear them going up into the loft and running down again to fetch equipment from the van outside. She checked on Lucy and found her fast asleep, looking her angelic self.

Chloe's feet squelched on the landing carpet and Adam came to the trap door in the ceiling to speak to her. 'It could be worse. I thought the main water tank had burst, but it's not that.'

'It's pretty bad,' she said. 'Everything's dripping on this side of the house. What caused it?'

'The plumber thinks it's too much modern technology on old pipework. He thinks the thermostat failed and the water's been boiling in the hot water tank. He's replacing some of the pipes.'

Chloe climbed up on the table to look into the loft. The plumber was crouched over the pipes using a blowtorch on them. Adam was busy moving boxes and packages out of his way. She was surprised to find so much stuff had been stacked up there.

'What are all those parcels?'

'Nothing,' he said, dropping his voice.

'They have to be something.'

'Just stock.'

'Why bother bringing stock up here?'

He turned uneasily to look at the plumber, but he was making too much noise himself to hear what they were saying. 'To get it out of the way.'

'But it's difficult to reach when you want it.'

She'd never seen Adam go up into the loft until now. He often kept pieces of porcelain and silver in his study, and occasionally a piece of furniture was put in the conservatory.

'Yes, but I wanted to store it for a while. The market for this sort of thing was depressed. I thought it might improve.'

'Has it?'

'Yes, a little. Can you pass me up some towels?' he asked. 'There's a couple of pictures here that need wiping down. The last thing we want is water damage on them.'

He brought them down to the landing to unwrap the wet packaging and dried them very carefully. Then he slid them under their own bed, where it

163

was dry. Chloe was puzzled. She'd had time to study the paintings. They were in matching ornate gold-painted frames, and looked like nineteenth-century oil paintings of a family. One showed them in a garden with a grand house in the background. The other depicted them with horses and dogs. She was curious.

'I like them,' she said. 'Who is the artist?'

'Nobody you'd have heard of,' he said easily. 'Fortunately I'm insured, so I'm not too upset.'

Nevertheless, the leak gave them a good deal of extra work. The damaged bedroom ceiling had to be taken down and replastered. The wet carpets had to be replaced both in the bedroom and on the landing. Adam counted himself lucky that he'd only recently recarpeted the stairs and was able to match the pattern exactly.

Fortunately, too, it was summer and they could have all the windows wide open to hasten the drying of things that couldn't be taken out. Adam believed in doing the job properly and had considerable redecoration done at the same time. Soon his house was immaculate again.

It was autumn before Chloe saw Adam bringing down some of the boxes and packages she'd seen stored in the loft.

'I'm going to put these in the next auction at Deepdene's in Chester,' he told her.

She saw he'd brought out the two paintings he'd stored under their bed. 'Is that a good sale to put paintings in?' she asked.

'One of the best.' He smiled.

He was out all day and told her he'd entered

quite a lot of stuff in the sale. He was out all the following day too. When he came home, he came to the kitchen where Chloe was preparing their evening meal.

'Things were going for good prices in Chester today,' he told her. 'Most of my stuff made more than I expected.' He was rubbing his hands together in high good humour.

Chloe was surprised. 'The Deepdene's sale was today?'

'Yes, that pair of pictures did especially well. They were a real sleeper.'

'They'd have suited this house. I'm surprised you didn't want to keep them.'

Adam was getting a bottle of beer from the fridge; he sat at the kitchen table to drink it. 'I wasn't that keen on them.'

He was busy emptying his pockets and sorting out the bills and receipts he'd need to put in his accounts to keep them up to date. That done, he threw his empty beer bottle and some papers he didn't need into the kitchen rubbish bin and headed towards his study. The bin was full and the sale catalogue slipped off the top and on to the floor.

Chloe picked it up, and on the spur of the moment flicked through it, looking for the stock Adam had put in. He usually pencilled in the margin the prices his pieces made, and she wanted to know if the artist and the family she'd seen pictured had been named.

She couldn't find any of them. She went back to the front of the catalogue and looked through it more methodically, keeping an eye out too for the silver candlesticks she'd seen Adam packing up to take. None of his things were listed in the catalogue. She felt mystified and took it along to his study to slide it on his desk.

'The things you entered in the sale aren't listed,' she said. 'Why not?'

He looked up at her, no longer in high spirits. 'The auction house had already sent the list to the printers when I took them in. I was too late.'

'You only took them yesterday,' she said, more mystified than ever. Adam was very organised; he was usually on top of his job. 'Why didn't you put them in earlier?'

'I forgot all about the stuff in the attic.'

Chloe wasn't sure she believed him.

As the months went on, Chloe was learning more about the antique trade and finding it fascinating. Adam found books for her to study and talked her through any interesting pieces that came his way. She'd also learned how to get out and about with a toddler in tow, and Adam often took them with him when he was working.

Lucy was beginning to say a few words. She was now a pretty little moppet with thick blonde curls, and both she and Chloe were becoming known in the auction houses and antique shops of the north-west. Chloe found that the staff made a great fuss of Lucy, and were only too willing to answer her own questions and teach her the finer points of the trade. She felt that living with Adam was giving her a fuller, more interesting life and she was enjoying it.

They went with him to a small auction house

near Congleton where he went regularly. Even Chloe was beginning to feel on friendly terms with the staff. The sale was over for the day and she was waiting for Adam to pay for what he'd bought and load the pieces into his car. She had Lucy on her hip and was passing the time of day with one of the auctioneers when a policeman came in with some printed lists and gave him a copy.

Lucy said, 'Me, me,' and put out her hand. The policeman made a great show of presenting her with another copy. 'Tank you,' she lisped.

'Just the May list of stolen property,' the police officer said to Chloe as he chucked Lucy under her chin.

'To make sure we don't auction off stolen property.' The auctioneer smiled.

Lucy began to suck on the list. Chloe took it from her and examined it. 'Do you see much stolen property?'

'No, not here. But we need to keep our eyes open and be aware that it could happen. We act as agents, you see, and though we might be perfectly innocent, if stolen goods appear in our catalogue we might be charged with fencing.'

'But it can't be that easy to auction off stolen property,' Chloe pointed out. 'After all, the goods are on display to the public for days before the sale. That gives everybody time to pick out anything suspicious.'

'It should, but the canny ones bring their goods in as a late sale. Probably the day before the auction takes place. That way they miss having stolen goods described in our catalogue and there are fewer records by which stolen property can be traced.'

Chloe held her breath. Was this what Adam had done?

'Once the sale takes place,' the auctioneer went on, 'the stolen goods go to a new home and the new owner believes them to be rightfully his. Possibly he'll keep them for decades. It's very unlikely then that the thief will ever be caught or the goods recovered.'

Chloe could feel perspiration breaking out on her forehead. This explained why Adam had kept stock hidden in their loft for months if not years, and then brought it in as a late sale. It had to be, there was no other reason. The staff at the auction houses saw a lot of him and probably thought he could be trusted to put things in late. Her heart was pounding and she was struggling to appear her normal self.

Fortunately the auctioneer started to play with Lucy. He told her his wife was expecting their first baby and he was hoping for a daughter as pretty as hers.

She was glad when Adam came looking for her, but she couldn't look him in the face. Once Lucy had been strapped into her car seat and he'd started to drive home, Chloe settled herself in the passenger seat and closed her eyes. She was shaking inside. She'd had to quell her suspicions about Adam more than once in the past, but this brought them all rushing back. She had a dragging feeling in her gut. Adam was handling stolen property, he was a petty crook. She needed to think hard about this.

When they reached home, Chloe gave Lucy her supper, bathed her and put her in her cot. She got their dinner of beef casserole on the dining room table and had a glass of red wine in her hand. Then she was able to push the police list of stolen property across the table to him.

'Tell me, Adam, what you kept hidden in the loft, was that stolen property?'

He was gulping down his food, ignoring her, but a guilty flush was spreading up his cheeks.

'I'm pretty sure it must be. Otherwise why enter it for auction the day before the sale?'

He was angry. 'It was convenient that way.'

'It was stolen!'

His cutlery crashed down on his plate. 'What if it was?' he barked.

Chloe swallowed hard. 'Did you steal it?'

'No, I did not.'

'Then you must be fencing it, and that's no better. Now I know how you can afford all this,' she said, waving her hand round the exquisitely furnished dining room. 'This is worse than conning pensioners to part with their property for a fraction of its value, though you no doubt continue to do that. It's a criminal offence, Adam. It could get you into trouble.'

'You do exaggerate.'

'Don't try to play it down. You could be caught and sent to prison.'

'I take care not to get caught, and I'm not sure it would rate a prison sentence if I was.'

'I don't know about that, but it's completely dishonest. What about your reputation? If this

169

becomes common knowledge, people won't want to deal with you.'

'And your reputation is whiter than the driven snow, of course.'

'I don't know about that either. If you were charged with fencing, the police would look at me again. Don't forget I mistakenly gave you a false alibi.'

'More fool you.'

Chloe shuddered. 'Would I be able to convince them I was innocent? I live with you and must see what you're up to. They'd think I was helping you handle stolen property, and that scares me.'

'Oh for God's sake, don't start worrying about that, it isn't going to happen.' He started to eat again. 'And stop nagging, I can't stand it.'

Chloe took a deep breath. His aggression was hurtful. 'Mum sings your praises because she thinks you've done well for yourself. If she knew, she'd be horrified.'

'She won't know unless you tell her.'

'Give it up now, Adam, before you're caught.'

He refilled his wine glass, took a good swig and rolled it round his tongue. She knew from the look on his face that he had no intention of giving it up.

To think of what might happen in the future was terrifying, and to stay with him now would condone what he was doing. She shuddered. She ought to leave and take Lucy with her, but that was a huge step in the dark too. She was frightened to stay and frightened to leave.

CHAPTER TWELVE

Once in a while, Helen enjoyed getting dressed up and going into town to meet her cousin Joan for lunch. Today she'd arranged to meet her in the restaurant in George Henry Lees. She was a little early but found good reason to pause as she walked through the shop. It was her favourite, and she bought many of her clothes here. She was studying a black and white linen two-piece when Joan caught her up.

'That would suit you,' she told her.

Helen shook her head. 'Too formal for me. I prefer something simpler. How are things?'

They'd been shown to a table when Joan said, 'Not a lot is going on. Walter is still taking me around the antique shops looking for silver. We've had our insurance money for ages.'

'You're now looking for more to replace what you lost?'

'We've been looking since it was stolen. We've bought a biscuit barrel and a bonbon dish, but we'd like a tea and coffee service and other things too. We haven't seen anything to compare in quality to what we lost.'

Helen and Joan had discussed Chloe's boyfriend at great length on previous occasions. Now Helen said, 'Adam might be able to help you.'

'Yes, he's an antique dealer, isn't he? Walter suggested I ask you about him.'

'I don't know whether he specialises in silver,' Helen said slowly, 'but he certainly knows a lot about clocks and furniture.'

'Do you have his phone number? I could give him a ring.'

'At home, yes. I'll talk to Chloe and ask her to get Adam to ring you tonight.'

'Thanks. No harm in finding out if he has anything that would please Walter.'

Adam was delighted when, in due course, he spoke to Walter and Joan. He said to Chloe, 'Your uncle sounds like the perfect customer. He has money in hand to replace what he's lost, and he's looking for high-quality antique silver of every sort.'

'He used to have a lot of silver teapots and bowls and things.'

'He said he wants a full tea and coffee service but he's looking for almost anything as long as it's top of the market. I told him I had a nice stirrup cup in the shape of a fox's head, but he wasn't too sure about that.' Adam laughed. 'I told him I'd see what else I could find and that I'd be in touch with him in a week or so.'

Once Adam knew he had a client ready to buy, he let other dealers know what he was looking for. In an auction sale he picked up a nice claret jug of silver and cut glass made in 1860, and after visiting an antique fair and spending two weeks searching through various shops he came across a footed bowl by George Jensen. It had open-work leaves and ivory round the stem, setting off a plain bowl. Adam thought it an outstanding design, but it was hallmarked 1924 and not yet an antique. He bought it but had to pay more than he wanted to, because he could find little else that he thought might excite Chloe's uncle.

He knew there was no shortage of tea and coffee pots and neither were matching sets rare, but though many were nice enough, he wouldn't say they were top of the market. He widened his search and came across a George IV cake basket by John Edward Terry that he liked; he thought Walter would like it too.

Then he got chatting to an elderly man who'd been a dealer for decades and was known in many auction houses. Adam had dealt with him once or twice, and asked him if he knew where he could find good-quality silver.

'I might,' he said, and told him about a contact he had in Liverpool. 'I've sold him a few things over the years; he's a collector. He rang me the other day and said he wanted to sell some of his pieces.'

'Good stuff?'

'Very, he bought only the best, but I'm not sure I want them back. Getting a bit past it now and the market for silver's going down, isn't it?'

Adam was interested. 'Nobody wants to clean it these days. Who is he?'

'A man called Leo Hardman, a strange fellow. I reckon he's in need of money.'

'Strange in what way?'

'Not the sort you'd expect to invest in antique silver, but he's got a good eye for it.'

'Do you think he might have what I'm looking for?'

'Yes, and he might want more for it than it's worth.'

'Doesn't everybody?'

'He's a canny fellow and he knows all there is to know about silver.'

'He's not in the trade?'

'No, he said he works in a big hotel.'

Adam paused. 'This stuff, it is all right? He's not fencing or anything?'

The dealer pulled a face. 'I'd say it was clean. He made sure he wasn't buying anything dicey from me.'

'Right, can you give me his phone number?'

He smiled. 'For a small consideration, I'll even ring him up and tell him I'm sending a buyer round to help him.'

'OK – if he's got what I want and I buy.'

It took Adam a day or two to set up an appointment to call on Leo Hardman. He seemed to be ringing a shared number in a public part of a building. When he finally managed to speak to him, Hardman said, 'I work nights. I'd like you to come as early in the morning as you can, so I can get to bed.'

Adam got up very early on a wet Saturday morning to drive to Liverpool. He was surprised to find Leo Hardman's flat in a crumbling Victorian house in a poor and shabby part of the city. He saw several bells, each with a curling scrap of paper beneath from which the writing had faded. He rang two of them and then found that the front door opened to his touch. As he went inside the building, he could hear a child crying and an enraged woman screaming at it. He cringed at the thought of having close neighbours like that.

Leo Hardman came rushing downstairs to meet him; Adam didn't know what to make of him. He was small and thin and wore scruffy jeans with a faded red T-shirt; he was not at all the sort of man he'd expect to own fine silver. Adam was afraid he was wasting his time until he followed him into his bedsitter.

One glance at the silver laid out on the table blew his breath away. There was the tea and coffee service Walter Bristow had specially asked for.

'It's George III, by Samuel Wood. Every piece hallmarked London, 1763.'

Hardman's voice had thickened with pride; Adam thought him a real enthusiast. He picked up the sugar bowl for a closer look. 'It's a good shape.'

'It's very attractive, and it's complete with its matching tray, not one somebody's tried to marry up.'

Adam knew Walter Bristow would love it. He picked over the other pieces.

'A pair of gadrooned shell butter dishes on periwinkle feet. London, 1810,' Hardman told him, 'by Rebecca Eames and Edward Barnard.' He held up a bonbon dish and told him where and when it was made and even the weight of silver it contained. He did the same with some vegetable dishes and followed that with a cigarette box. His hands lovingly cradled each piece.

A boat-shaped cake basket caught Adam's eye; he leaned over to pick it up.

'That's a real gem,' Hardman said. 'By Paul

Storr. London, 1802. And I have a honey pot by him too, yes, here it is, silver gilt, beehive shape, cover and stand. That's 1798. You can't get better than Paul Storr.'

Adam had to agree. He could hardly believe his eyes; he'd never seen so much fine silver in one place: a rose bowl, a chocolate pot, a decorative table centre. He was looking at an Aladdin's cave of treasures. His hand came to rest on a set of four wine coasters.

'Those are by William Plummer,' Hardman told him. 'George III, 1777.'

It went on and on. A caudle cup hallmarked London, 1666. Silver salvers, sauce boats, and every piece sparkled and glittered under the one low-powered ceiling light.

Adam could see the man was passionate about quality silver. It seemed he could read the dates and other information in hallmarks. He had a bookcase stuffed with books on the subject and none about anything else. The room had originally been designed as the drawing room of the house and was light because it had a big window. If it were clean and tidy, it could have an air of faded gentility.

'It must take you a long time to clean all this.' He was trying to make up his mind on how to handle him.

'I enjoy doing it, no point in having things like this unless they're looking their best.'

Adam was asking himself if there would be too much here for Walter Bristow. He picked out a selection he thought would most appeal to him. Then came the question of what price he'd have to pay. Leo Hardman knew exactly what everything was worth and haggled over each item. But Adam was well used to this and felt equal to it. He carried a notebook for transactions and listed each article he was buying and what he paid for it. At last they came to an agreement and he brought up boxes and blankets from the boot of his car to carry his purchases. Hardman produced a plentiful supply of old newspaper for wrapping.

Adam had gone to his bank yesterday to withdraw cash, because he knew that was what all sellers to the trade preferred, but he hadn't withdrawn enough. Hardman was willing to take a cheque for the small shortfall. He also helped him carry the silver down and lock it in the boot of his car.

He was feeling rather light-headed at the overabundance of his purchase, but thought he could unload it on other clients should Walter Bristow not want it all. He drove until he saw a telephone kiosk, then he pulled in to the kerb and gave ten minutes' thought to the figures on his list. He needed to work out the selling price he'd ask; once he'd done that, he wrote it in against the figures he'd paid.

He couldn't help thinking about Leo Hardman. The man had sparkled with interest and enthusiasm for his silver, but he'd hardly said a word about himself, except to confirm that he worked in one of the main city hotels. But through the night? Adam felt he knew virtually nothing about him.

He got out of his car then and rang Walter

Bristow's number, asking if he could come round immediately to show him what he had. He felt buoyed up, excited even by the dazzling quality of what he'd managed to get, and counted himself lucky to find both Joan and Walter at home. As he opened up his boxes in a room they called their snug, he could feel their excitement building up until it eclipsed his own.

They exclaimed over every piece as it was revealed. Joan was absolutely thrilled with the George Jensen bowl he'd bought earlier. Soon the room was littered with screwed-up paper. They bought most of the silver and Adam couldn't believe his luck. In one morning he'd managed to earn himself a generous profit.

Not only that, but the Bristows seemed grateful to him. He knew he'd delayed their lunch, because he could hear Walter's stomach rumbling and it was after two o'clock.

'I'm sure you must be hungry too,' Joan said. 'Would you like to join us? It's only salad and cold beef. I think there'll be enough for you too.'

Adam was starving and thought it an excellent meal. They were up on cloud nine with the silver he'd found for them.

'It's all lovely,' Joan told him, 'and I know Walter's thrilled with it, but we used to have a pair of candlesticks sitting one each end of the sideboard here, and I would have liked to replace them.'

'Surely this is enough, Joan?' Walter smiled.

'It's more than enough and I'm delighted, but candlesticks...'

To amuse them, Adam told them a little about

178

the man he'd bought most of the silver from, and of course they talked about Chloe. After the meal he asked if he might use their phone to ring her and tell her what time he'd be home. After all, he had something to celebrate. He asked her to book a babysitter so they could have a night out on the town.

On the way back to Manchester, Adam stopped off and sold what remained of the silver he'd bought from Leo Hardman. He felt he'd had an excellent day and was in an expansive mood when he got home. It was only when he was facing Chloe across the tray of afternoon tea that he started to tell her what they were about to celebrate.

He saw her face change. 'You sold a lot of silver to Uncle Walter? I thought you were having difficulty finding pieces to please him?'

'I was.' He told her then about finding Leo Hardman, his hoard of silver, and what a strange character he was. 'They were thrilled with every piece, over the moon in fact. They even invited me to have a bite to eat with them at lunchtime. It was a jolly meal, they were really pleased.'

'You didn't overcharge them?'

'No, of course not. It was top-of-the-market stuff, they're very lucky to get it.'

Chloe groaned. 'If you want to celebrate, you must have made a killing. I'm not sure I like you doing deals with Uncle Walter.'

'They're celebrating too,' Adam said coldly.

Leo Hardman felt depressed watching Adam drive away. He hated having to part with so many pieces

179

of his beloved silver; it was like parting with old friends. He'd been feeling very low anyway.

It was another of those bad times when he was urgently in need of money and could see no other way of raising it. He had to take care of Bernie Dennison's wife and baby while he was in prison. Bernie had asked it of him and he owed him that. Whatever anybody said, there was honour amongst thieves.

The police had caught Bernie and charged him with robbing a jewellery shop in Dale Street. Leo had been with him, and it had given him nightmares to imagine the arms of the law tightening round him. Bernie had slipped up and left evidence behind, and though they knew he must have had an accomplice, he'd denied it and kept on denying it. He'd said he was working on his own and Leo's name had never passed his lips. Bernie prided himself on being strong enough to withstand police questioning, and he'd kept mum. But Leo had sweated and worried for weeks that they'd break him down, and the fact that they had not left him eternally grateful.

Bernie had known Leo had been clean for two years and to be charged with another robbery now would be a disaster for him. So Leo had to pay his dues and look after Bernie's wife; it was the only way he could thank him.

Leo reckoned that bad luck and lack of money had dogged him all his life. He'd still been at school when he first felt the need to earn money. A mile or so away from his home was a pub called the Cheshire Cat and he'd heard they were seeking bar workers for Friday and Saturday nights. He'd had to lie about his age when he presented himself to the publican, as he was only fifteen at the time. He'd expected to be asked to provide proof, so he'd borrowed his brother's birth certificate without his knowing and took it with him.

His brother Jeffrey was nearly four years older than him and he'd got away with it. He'd answered to the name of Jeff for nearly nine months. The job suited him perfectly; he enjoyed it and found the pub a jolly place. His fear of being found out had long since gone when a friend of his brother, already well tanked up, came in for a drink. The publican overheard him calling Leo by his real name. He'd had plenty of time to work out a logical explanation and told his boss that it was his mother's pet name for him, because he was a lion-hearted lad. But Jeff's friend filled him in with the true facts and his boss didn't believe him.

Leo had left school without qualifications and had taken jobs that kept him at the bottom of the feeding chain. He'd never earned much. He'd been a van driver, where he'd augmented his wages by fiddling free petrol for his father's car until he'd been found out. They'd put him on probation for that.

He'd had a job in a shoe shop then but had been caught stealing shoes from his employer and selling them more cheaply on a market stall. That earned him three months in a youth detention centre, which he hated.

But he came out and managed to get taken on as a clerk by an insurance company, where he

181

mostly did book-keeping. He felt he'd taken a step up in the world because he worked in an office. He kept that job for a couple of years, and he was even managing to divert a little of their cash for himself, but it ended in dismissal and three months in jug.

A social worker working with discharged prisoners helped him get training as a bus driver. He kept that job for several years, even after he'd managed to work out how to keep for himself some of the cash the public paid for their tickets. Eventually, though, that earned him another six months in prison, and it was bad enough to make him determined not to end up there again. Prison had provided some benefits: there were classes designed to equip him to hold down a job when he was released. He took English language, with particular emphasis on writing it, and also book-keeping. He learned even more from his fellow inmates.

By using his brother's clean identity again, he managed to get a job as night desk attendant in the Exchange Hotel, a Victorian railway hotel of luxury standard in the centre of Liverpool. He had very little to do except talk to the night security guard. Occasionally late guests arrived and he acted as receptionist, then showed them to their booked room and acted as porter. He was also responsible for room service and took up sandwiches and other cold food. Quite a few guests came in late and he handed out their room keys, but his duties didn't keep him busy.

He had many night hours to roam through the main office, but the desks and file cabinets were

182

locked. He examined the hotel register at length and discovered that some guests gave details of their credit or debit cards so eventually the hotel could draw the cost of their stay directly through those. He studied them minutely, hoping to discover some way he could draw a little too.

Gary, the security guard, had the keys to the main areas and many of the storerooms. They both went regularly to the kitchen and helped themselves to the same luxury food as the guests.

'This isn't a bad life,' Gary said with his mouth full of smoked salmon. Leo wasn't so sure. Working here, he could measure what he had against the life of luxury enjoyed by the guests. What he could afford was not enough to keep a woman happy. His wife had called it poverty and left him for a better provider, and so had the woman he'd found to take her place.

'You've got to look on the bright side, mate,' Gary said. 'You've got a place of your own?'

'Well, a rented bedsit.'

'A nice one?'

'Not bad.'

'It's hard to rent anything these days, and in a bedsit you'll have plenty of company round you. Friends, like.'

'Too much company sometimes,' Leo said. 'Students banging about day and night.'

'They're not all young, though, are they?'

'No, there's a fellow who works on the trains, but he's a bit dour, I don't like him much.'

'You can't like everybody, Leo. There must be some you like.'

'Well, the landlord's all right.' Most of the time

Gary was all right too. They helped themselves to delicacies from the hotel's freezers and store-rooms to take home.

'Helps us save on food bills,' Gary said as he locked the door behind them. 'I reckon we have a pretty good life here. It's a question of making the best of it.'

Leo went home. As he let himself into the house, divided into flatlets, he met his landlord, Conor Kennedy, in the hall. Conor was in his sixties and had a bald and shiny head and a hale and hearty manner. He clapped Leo on the shoulder and said in his Irish accent, 'My friend, is everybody here behaving themselves?'

'You can see we are.'

Conor used to live in the bedsit Leo now rented on the first floor, number four out of eight, but he'd moved out round the corner into a two-up, two-down of his own. He came back to check on his tenants almost every day and Leo met him often in the nearby Irish pub. He played the occasional game of darts with him.

'Aye, it's all quiet contentment here this morn-ing.'

'It's rarely quiet,' Leo told him. 'That student in the next room to me had a woman in with him all last weekend.'

'Did he now? Well, that's not illegal.' Conor wanted to know what was going on in his pro-perty, but was fairly relaxed about what his tenants did. They had to get on with each other and there was to be strictly no fighting. No drugs either, and they had to pay the rent on time.

'That kid on the ground floor was bawling its head off yesterday,' Leo said. 'It's right below me, and when I asked its mother to keep it quiet so I could sleep, she gave me a right mouthful.'

'The kid's ill,' Conor told him. 'She's taking it to the doctor this morning. Poor Maisie's got a lot to put up with.'

Leo knew Conor Kennedy was sympathetic towards all his tenants, perhaps because he was living on the rents they paid him. But he was extra kind to Maisie. She had the bedsit next to the front door and it was her duty to make sure it was locked at night. They were a feckless lot here on the whole. Maisie also cleaned the shared bathrooms and the stairs. Leo thought she got something knocked off her rent for services like that.

But Conor was friendly enough. He'd occasionally buy Leo a glass of Guinness at the Irish pub, and that was a friendly place too. The landlord there, Tommy McWilliam, welcomed them all. He and Conor had this thing about how wonderful the Irish were: the songs, the food and, of course, the Guinness. Leo told them his mother came from Dublin; he wanted them to like him.

CHAPTER THIRTEEN

One evening, Leo went to work to find four members of the day staff in a state of shocked agitation and in no hurry to go through the handing-over routine. They were chattering together behind the reception desk.

'Our chief accountant's been killed,' one told him. 'Isn't it terrible?'

'Francis Clitheroe, do you know him?' asked another.

'No,' Leo said. He'd never heard of him. Gary, the security guard who usually worked with him, came in.

'He's really nice, very friendly. He was on holiday, we had this postcard from him yesterday.' It was pushed into Leo's hand. The picture was of a Majorcan beach resort.

'What's happened to him?' Gary asked. The day staff all spoke at once.

'He went on a jeep safari.'

'It went off the track, rolled down the mountain and turned over.'

'It killed both him and his wife.'

'It's awful, isn't it? You never know the moment.'

'They're being flown home tomorrow.'

'But in Majorca?' Leo asked. 'That's all beaches, how could...?'

'The safari was to the mountains in the north. There are huge mountains there.'

It took the day staff much longer to get on their way home. The security guard was still talking to one of them. Leo turned off most of the lights and, still musing about Francis Clitheroe, went to the main office to sign in. To be chief accountant for a hotel like this, the fellow had done pretty well for himself, but he should never have gone on that jeep safari. His luck had been out that day.

The office supervisor left the signing-in sheets on top of her desk. Leo was used to seeing the other desktops cleared by their owners before they went home, and everything locked up. But tonight, as he picked up the pen to sign, he could see that the supervisor had forgotten to lock her desk. The centre drawer was slightly open. He pulled at it and it slid back, revealing a file clearly marked with the name Francis Lovell Clitheroe.

'Wow!' he murmured to himself. Nosiness welled up inside him. He wanted to know more about this man, and here was something that would help him while away the long night hours. He took the file out and slammed the drawer tightly shut.

The bell on the reception desk pinged, letting him know that a guest was seeking his attention. Leo held the file under his arm, making it as inconspicuous as possible, as he hurried back. He passed Gary on his way to sign in. Spending so much time with him, Leo felt they were on chummy terms, but Gary was responsible for security, it wouldn't do to tell him everything.

There were plenty of hiding places behind the long mahogany reception desk. Leo was able to keep the file out of sight until the place grew quiet and the guard had gone round the hotel on one of his security checks. He chuckled to himself as he opened it. Francis Clitheroe's sudden death must have thrown everybody off kilter.

He flipped through the contents and the first thing he saw were copies of the man's birth certificate and educational certificates. Clitheroe had a degree in economics and was a chartered accountant. Leo felt a surge of excitement. Even his bank account details were here, together with the amount of salary that was paid in monthly. It was enough to make his mouth water. Nobody had ever offered him a salary like that.

He hadn't realised that Francis Clitheroe had only been working at the Exchange Hotel for two months. He'd come with a history of long-time employment in an insurance company in London. Here was a letter from them recommending his services. He was said to be efficient, hard-working and honest. Yes, honest. Leo took a deep breath and stepped back, his heart pounding. Information like this could prove invaluable, and he wondered how he could put it to best use.

Two guests came in and asked for their room key. They kept him chatting for a few moments, but all the time his mind was racing. The question of how he could benefit from Francis Clitheroe's personal details closed it to everything else.

Leo wondered if he could take Clitheroe's identity and get himself a better salary. He remembered how he'd borrowed his brother's birth certificate to help get a job in that pub. It had worked and nobody would ever have found out, not even his brother, if his friend hadn't come into the bar and opened his mouth too wide.

Could he pretend he was Francis Clitheroe? Apply for a job in his name and get away with it? He'd be a trusted member of management, wouldn't he? No longer the gofer, tea-maker and sweeper-up. Could he do whatever an accountant did? If he wasn't looking for a career, could he do it for long enough to get his fingers in the till? Well, they'd tried to teach him basic bookkeeping in prison and he'd concentrated, thinking he might find it a useful skill. He'd done some when he'd worked for that insurance company, too. Clitheroe had worked for an insurance company. Would anybody doubt him when he had authentic details like this? Leo was simmering with excitement. He could be on to a good thing.

At midnight, Gary locked the front doors. From now on, guests would need to ring the night bell. This was when they went to the kitchen to rustle up some supper. Gary took out his keys and unlocked the main fridge. They made smoked salmon sandwiches and took out a handful of quail's eggs that had been hard-boiled.

'They taste like ordinary eggs.' Leo was disappointed. 'But they're fiddly, and it's twice the trouble to get the shells off. Not worth bothering with.'

There were several trays of individual servings of chocolate mousse, meant for tomorrow's lunch menu and left in the fridge to set firm overnight. They had one each and voted it excellent. The chef left out a tray every night for them to make tea. Leo made a pot for them to share. They were supposed to bring their own food.

Every night, they took it in turns to have a couple of hours' kip. Gary did his rounds and brought a blanket and pillow from the store cupboard. He took off his shoes and left them under the reception desk, peeled off his jacket and hung it neatly on the back of an upright chair. Then he padded across the lounge and lay down on a large sofa in the shadows at the far end, pulling the blanket over him.

Leo made himself comfortable behind the reception desk and gave more thought to Francis Clitheroe and the information he had about him. It wasn't going to be that easy to get money out of his bank account; he'd need to know his mother's maiden name. Asking a customer to give that was becoming an essential part of bank security.

It occurred to him then that in his position, Francis Clitheroe would probably have a private office. He might be able to find out more about him if he could get into that. Leo knew where the hotel manager's office was and he thought he'd seen others along the same corridor. He heaved himself out of his chair and listened; he could hear soft sounds of contented sleep coming from Gary's sofa. He edged over to where the security guard's jacket was swinging on the back of a chair and felt in the pocket for his keys. He'd done this once before, when he'd taken a duck from the freezer for his Christmas dinner. He knew he had to get a tight grasp on the keys before he moved them so they wouldn't rattle.

He picked up the powerful torch Gary used in the semi-gloom, unlaced his shoes and crept silently away to look for the accountant's office. It wasn't hard to find, Clitheroe's name was on the door. Leo was about to slip the key into the lock when he pulled up short. Fingerprints. It might not make the slightest difference if he left them plastered everywhere inside the office, but he'd learned enough when he was in jail to know that if ever the police were called in, it could be his downfall. He went swiftly back to the kitchen to get a pair of rubber gloves and felt immediately safer.

He closed the office door behind him and switched on the light. Mr Clitheroe had left his mackintosh swinging on a peg on the door; he'd have that for a start. It took him a few moments to get the desk open – he had to force it – but what he saw made him glad he'd thought of coming. Here was Clitheroe's security badge with his photograph and fingerprints. Leo studied it. Clitheroe looked a smart professional gent. He also found a new hardback novel, a romance by Rosamund Rogerson. It seemed an unlikely choice for a chief accountant. On the title page the handwritten message read: *To my son Francis. You were wrong to bet I'd never get it published. Read it again, hope you enjoy it this time.*

Leo looked at the book with new eyes. It appeared to have been written by Clitheroe's mother. It would be very useful to know his mother's maiden name, so the book was an amazing find. But how could he find out if Rogerson was her real maiden name or just a nom de plume?

On the flap of the back cover was a picture of

the author, who looked no spring chicken; well, she wouldn't be if Francis was her son. It said she was married to John Lovell Clitheroe, a university professor, and went on to extol his claims to fame. Leo didn't care about him; he could feel a surge of warm triumph stealing through him. That made her Mrs Clitheroe, so there was a good chance that Rogerson was her maiden name.

He saw Clitheroe's diary and fell on it with eagerness, hoping to learn more, but it was a desk diary and recorded only appointments and professional meetings. At least he knew something of Francis's family history.

He stuffed the novel in a pocket in the mackintosh, threw it over his arm and helped himself to an expensive-looking pen before locking up carefully. He returned to the main office and found a large manila envelope; he meant to take the whole file away, including Francis's postcard. It would be as well to know what his handwriting was like.

Having packed together what he wanted to take home, he went back to the kitchen to make another pot of tea, and poured out two cups. He could hear Gary now, snoring heavily. It was time to wake him up so he could have his turn on the sofa; two hours of comfort. Before doing that, he returned the keys to Gary's coat pocket and ensured his torch was exactly where he'd left it. Then he padded across the lounge to shake him awake and present him with his cup of tea.

Shortly afterwards, Leo pulled the warm blanket over himself and settled down to give Francis Lovell Clitheroe more thought, but almost immediately, he could feel sleep creeping over him.

As the summer months slipped slowly away, Chloe tried to make up her mind what to do. She felt tense and unhappy, but she tried to pretend to her mother that all was well.

She and Adam were going over and over the same ground and having arguments that escalated into shouting matches and major rows. The level of conflict seemed to rise daily. She'd thought herself to be head over heels in love with Adam, but her doubts about him had worn her love down. His dishonesty was altering everything. She couldn't rely on the life they had continuing in the same way. There were risks she hadn't known about.

Chloe knew that if she left Adam, she'd have to go home to Mum. She had no other practical option. Mum would have her, she didn't doubt that, but it would be embarrassing all round. Helen hadn't wanted her to live with Adam; she'd wanted them to marry. She'd warned her against doing what she had. But the way things had turned out, Chloe could see that marriage would have solved nothing. It would have made leaving him harder, because it would have meant getting a divorce.

Compounding her problem was that caring for Lucy took up all her time and energy. If she left Adam, she'd need to get a job to support herself and her child. She didn't feel she could expect her mother to do that, and thought it unlikely that Adam would hand money over to her if she left him. Not with his dishonest ways of increasing his income.

Autumn brought a long spell of cold, damp weather. Adam caught the flu and took to his bed, and Chloe pushed their problems behind her to look after him. Lucy went down with it a week later and she had two fractious patients to care for. Lucy was ill enough for Chloe to get the doctor out to her, and he prescribed antibiotics.

By the time Chloe began to feel ill, Adam was recovering, and because they had a generous amount of domestic help, hot meals could be provided and they were able to cope.

But Chloe took longer to get better and had pain when she breathed in. Adam drove her down to see the doctor and he gave her antibiotics too. It was November before she felt well again.

She felt one good thing had come from it: she and Adam had had to forget their differences to look after each other and were getting along with less friction. Life at last got back to normal. She wasn't sure whether he'd given up fencing or whether he was being careful to hide it from her.

She was helping him run his business again and going to sales with him. They were back on friendly terms and he became the ardent lover he used to be.

By December, Chloe was suffering bouts of nausea. She felt as though she was pregnant but dismissed the idea as impossible. She was sure she'd never missed taking her daily pill; she was very careful about that. The feeling didn't go away, and in January, Adam drove her to her doctor's surgery.

'I have to tell you you're about fourteen weeks pregnant,' the doctor said.

She'd suspected it, but confirmation shocked her to the core. 'I can't be,' she wailed. 'I've never failed to take the pill.'

'I'm afraid there's no mistake.'

'Fourteen weeks! But how can I be?'

'It does sometimes happen; if you're taking one drug, it can be affected by something else you take.' He studied her notes. 'Yes, I prescribed penicillin in the middle of October.'

'Penicillin? I wouldn't have taken it if I'd known.'

'I'm sorry, but we in the medical profession are only just finding out the effect one drug can have on another. I wouldn't have prescribed it for you without explaining this if I'd known. It takes time for these side effects to become apparent.'

Chloe felt ill. Another baby! This rocked her confidence. She'd been so sure the pill would prevent this. Another pregnancy! She was not ready to go through all that again. She walked slowly back to the car, knowing Adam would not welcome her news. Lucy was asleep in her car seat; he was reading a newspaper spread out on the steering wheel.

'I'm fourteen weeks pregnant,' she announced.

'Oh my God! Not another? It's the last thing we need.' He spun round at her. 'I trusted you to be careful. You said you were taking your pill.'

'I was, I never failed, but it seems I'm not the first person this has happened to. It's not always one hundred per cent–'

'Oh hell and damnation!'

Chloe was very churned up. Her second pregnancy had come as a shock, but even worse was hearing Adam's reaction to the news. It drove home that he felt no responsibility for fathering another child. She needed his help, craved his support, but he'd dropped her and Lucy back home and driven off again.

That could only mean he no longer loved her. The days went on and he was going out more and leaving her alone with Lucy. She gave up going to auction sales or trying to help with the business. Adam said there was no point; business was falling off. It was getting harder to make a living, and the prices achieved at auction sales were lower than they had been. They were both irritable and starting to argue about things of little importance.

At the clinic, they kept telling her she'd find the second birth easier than the first, but she felt low and despondent. The weeks of waiting dragged, and she felt unable to do anything until it was over. She looked on it as something to be endured and did not welcome another baby.

Chloe felt fat and frumpish, took less interest in her clothes and let herself go. She no longer looked smart. Adam seemed to be making a life apart from her, and she was afraid he'd want her and the children to leave. She'd thought it difficult to leave Adam with one baby, but with two it looked virtually impossible. She felt trapped. What was she to do? Lucy didn't allow her much rest and she felt chronically tired.

With the approaching birth of her second baby, Chloe felt her relationship with Adam had fallen away. He was spending many evenings out in smart bars and restaurants, but he no longer asked her to arrange a babysitter and go with him. Instead she was left alone to take care of Lucy.

She did manage the occasional day trip to Liverpool to see her mother. The garden was gorgeous, Mum seemed happy and full of life and Rex was usually there. He told her she didn't look too well and seemed concerned. She thought he was trying to draw her out, but how could she confess that her relationship with Adam had gone pear-shaped when she'd insisted on living with him against their advice?

On one occasion Auntie Joan was there too. She recounted a few problems, though Chloe thought they were minor compared with hers.

'Walter's worried about his business. I wanted him to sell it and retire. He put it in the hands of an agent, but nobody seems interested.'

'But Joan, he said he was happy to carry on,' Helen said.

'He is really – he's not sixty-five yet and he's strong and healthy - but his accountant, Tom Cleary, is a couple of years older and he'd like to go. They've been advertising for an accountant to take his place, but so far no luck. They haven't found anybody they think would be suitable.'

Chloe tried to show Joan she cared, but it just wasn't there.

'You'll feel better when your baby's born.' Joan patted her arm. 'How much longer is it?'

Chloe's time came at the beginning of June. Adam ran her to the hospital and afterwards took Lucy to Liverpool, where her mother had offered to care for her. She found the second birth took longer and was more painful than the first.

'A baby boy,' the midwife told her. 'He weighs six and a half pounds.'

Chloe hadn't wanted him, but when he was put into her arms to hold and she looked at him for the first time, she felt quite different. Her face felt hot with mother love.

'A perfect baby son for you,' the midwife enthused. 'Strong and healthy.'

He had a sweet face and just fluff for hair. Chloe was marvelling at his tiny hand when it closed round her finger and squeezed it. He was a lovely baby and she gave him her heart. Adam chose his name. He was to be Zacharia Adam James Livingstone, Zac for short.

On the day they were due to leave hospital, Mum and Rex brought Lucy home. They both walked round the sitting room nursing Zac, telling Chloe with more enthusiasm than Adam could muster that he was a gorgeous baby.

Adam had provided a fancy afternoon tea with cake and tiny sandwiches served in his usual style. Chloe was cheered by the company and the pleasure of being back home and reunited with Lucy. As soon as Helen and Rex had gone, she felt tired and would have liked to rest.

Adam surveyed the sitting room of which he was so proud and said, 'What a mess, and you've only been back a couple of hours.'

Certainly it was no longer an elegant room. Zac's carrycot stood on the coffee table and Lucy's toys were strewn round the carpet. She'd spilled milk and crumbs on the sofa and there were bibs and shawls everywhere. Chloe set about tidying up.

For her, the first weeks with Zac on one routine and Lucy on another were very hard work. She didn't know how she'd have managed without Ruby to help with the housework. Lucy kept her on the go most of the day and Zac broke her sleep at night.

She was alone with the children for much of the time. She was seeing less and less of Adam. Apart from Ruby, she'd hardly spoken to an adult since coming out of hospital and certainly she'd not had time to think of smartening herself up.

She felt her mother was her lifeline; she often rang up for a chat and she was sympathetic. 'Your problem is you haven't yet had time to recover from the birth. With a new baby to care for and a toddler of two who never stops, it's hard going. Why don't you come to me and have a week's rest? I can look after Lucy and you can sleep when the baby does and stay in bed late. You'll feel better afterwards; it'll put you back on your feet.'

Chloe thought a short break would help not only her but Adam too. He was suffering from the broken nights as well, and was often tetchy with them.

Later that day, she suggested it to him. 'Mum keeps ringing up and asking how we are. She'd love to see how Zac's getting on.'

'Yes, well, at the moment money's a bit tight for holidays.'

Chloe knew Adam was finding things more difficult, but didn't believe money was as short as he made out.

'It would only be the train fare and a bit of

pocket money. It's more a change and a rest than a holiday.'

'Even so...'

Adam's income had always ebbed and flowed, but now he said he could do nothing right. He was passionate about antiques and good at dealing. He loved being his own boss, and when he had money he was generous, but his present problem did crop up from time to time.

He'd gone to a recent private house sale and been so impressed with the quality of the furniture and the prices it was being knocked down for that he'd not only sunk all his working capital into it, but borrowed more.

He'd had a private client who'd asked him to look out for a George III dining table with a set of matching chairs, and he'd expected to have no problem selling it to her, along with some of the other items. But the table was a rectangular drop leaf and now she said she particularly fancied an oval one. Though he managed to sell two occasional tables, he'd failed to sell the more important pieces to any of his contacts, so he'd entered them in an auction sale.

'If they sell and I make a reasonable profit, you and the kids can go,' he agreed. 'Hopefully, it'll do you good.'

W39 9foot

CHAPTER FOURTEEN

Within a few hours, Leo had a clearer idea of what might be possible. All his life he'd been trapped in lowly jobs and small-time theft; this was his chance to go big-time.

If he took someone else's identity before he stole anything, it would shield him, keep the police away from him. If it came to the worst and the theft was traced to Francis Clitheroe, he could disappear, revert to his own identity and the police would find it very difficult to pin anything on him. It was the smart way to avoid arrest.

In the meantime, Francis had been killed only yesterday; there was a good chance his bank had not been notified yet. Leo decided he had enough information to open a charge account in Clitheroe's name at one of the large department stores. But if he was going to do that, he'd need to move quickly; the sooner he did it, the safer it would be.

It was four in the morning and the time at which he and Gary ate another meal. Leo could smell savoury scents coming from the kitchen as he locked the blanket and pillow back in the housekeeper's cupboard.

Gary was frying. 'Tomato soup with hot bread rolls,' he said. 'Then these fillet steaks with fried eggs on top to follow.'

'With chips?' Leo asked.

'No, too much damn trouble to make, though I'd like them. We can finish off with black forest gateau and lashings of cream.'

All the time he ate, Leo was pondering on opening a charge account – or several accounts. He decided he'd try Watson Prickard to start with; they sold the high-class clothes Francis would have chosen. And if he was to take his identity, he would need them. The problem was, he didn't know whether the real Francis already had an account there.

He was glad when knocking-off time came round. He left his anorak hanging on its peg in the staff cloakroom, walked out of the building with Francis's mac folded over his arm covering his file, and went home to his bedsit in the cheaply converted Victorian house. He sank down to rest on what was supposed to be a sofa during the day, converting to a bed at night. It spent most of the time as a bed; it was too much trouble to return it to its guise as a shabby sofa. With his hands behind his head, he stared up at the stained ceiling and allowed himself fifteen minutes to get what he planned to do straight in his head.

Then he polished up his only pair of Oxford lace-ups, washed and changed into a clean shirt and added a tie. He found the pullover he'd nicked from Lewis's last year and hoped that with Francis's mac he'd appear to be a respectable member of the professional class. He was feeling jittery by now, and hungry again, so he made himself a cup of tea and ate the contents of a tin of baked beans, cold and straight from the can.

The one advantage of his bedsit was that it was

very central and he could walk to all the main shops, hotels, theatres and cinemas in town. He found himself outside Watson Prickard's before he had his nerves totally under control. But he wasn't going to get cold feet at this stage; this was an opportunity too good to miss. He studied the clothes in the windows and then went in and did the same round the shop. What did he fancy, and what would Francis Clitheroe choose?

'Can I help you, sir?' A sales assistant approached him.

This was the part that scared Leo. He smiled. 'Yes. You have some very nice suits here. I was wondering if it would be possible for me to open a charge account?'

'Yes, sir, come this way, will you?' Leo could feel his heart pounding, though he'd worked out exactly what he'd say if it turned out Francis Clitheroe already had a charge account here. It would be almost impossible to sound convincing; he'd need to make a quick getaway.

He was led to a seat at a small table and handed over to an older man, who brought out a ledger and some forms and began asking questions. What was his name and address, his profession, his salary and his employer's name? Leo had memorised all that but he couldn't stop his pulse racing.

Entries were being made in the ledger and forms being filled in on his behalf. Leo saw his hand trembling and pushed it deep into his mackintosh pocket. The questions went on. Did he have a bank account? If so, where? What credit cards did he hold and what was his mother's maiden name?

The man asked Leo to wait a few moments. In his absence, Leo took out his handkerchief and wiped the perspiration from his face. There were butterflies in his stomach too. The man returned with a smile on his face, and Leo began to feel a little easier. Another form was pushed in front of him; a pen was offered.

'For your signature, sir. You will see from this that you are allowed credit of up to three hundred pounds.'

Leo was able to breathe normally after that. Clearly Francis had not previously had a charge account here and they would not hear he'd been killed until they contacted his bank. Feeling elated, he returned to the racks of high-class suits. He bought himself one in pale grey wool of the sort Francis would have worn. Then he chose several shirts and three silk ties, and finally two pairs of shiny formal shoes.

He'd never bought so many clothes at one time and felt he needed to come up for air. Once they were wrapped up and the bill signed, he left the shop and made for the nearest café. His mouth felt dry and he was cold and quaking inside. He told himself it was because it was the first time he'd ever done such a thing and that it would be easier next time. He knew if he was going to do it again, he must do so straight away. He ordered a cup of coffee and allowed himself fifteen minutes to get his nerve back.

He rushed home to drop his parcels and decided he'd go to Lewis's next. If all went well there, perhaps he'd have another go in Owen Owens.

It wasn't difficult to get credit; everywhere he went, they bent over backwards to serve him. He was gaining confidence. Francis's job, his address and the salary he earned seemed to do the trick. He was handed bills that took his breath away. The agreement was that he'd be given thirty days to pay off the full amount, or make a minimum payment and be charged interest on the balance. He wasn't planning to do either.

His plan was to spend close to the limit they were prepared to allow. He bought more clothes of every sort, pullovers and T-shirts, shorts, swimming trunks and good-quality underwear, new loafers, a trilby and a mac that fitted him, of the same make Francis had had, as well as a wallet, a watch, a leather briefcase and a portable type-writer. He would have liked a television and a small fridge, but they would have to be delivered, and his address would be different to the one shown on the application form. Sooner or later they'd realise this was fraud, and he didn't want his bedsit pinpointed for the investigating officers. Reluctantly he decided a new television was impossible.

As it was, it was better than half a dozen Christmases; he'd never had so many new belongings. He spread them round his bedsit, trying first one thing on and then another. When he tried to pack everything away out of sight, he found he hadn't nearly enough storage space. He had to put his packages in a corner and cover them with a blanket.

He must not wear his new clothes yet; he couldn't risk his neighbours noticing and thinking he'd suddenly come into money. Many of them were students, bright lads who might envy his new gear; he must keep his plans fail-safe.

He took out Francis's identity tag and studied his photograph. He knew he must try to make the same impression. It wouldn't matter that their features were quite different; this was just about whether the public would think he looked like a chief accountant. Right now, Leo had to admit he did not.

He could see from the birth certificate that Francis had been born on the second of February 1931. That would make him thirty-six against Leo's twenty-nine, so he needed to make himself appear older than he was.

He couldn't remember when he'd last had his hair cut. The Beatles had made longish hair fashionable for men, and for the last year or so he'd asked the barber to do him something similar to Paul McCartney's cut. It had grown rampantly and needed to be reshaped, but that wouldn't do for Francis. When the time was right, he'd have his wild brown mop cut into the style shown in Francis's photograph. Not exactly a traditional short back and sides, but still quite restrained. And he'd find himself some heavy spectacles with clear glass in the frames; that should give him a more academic appearance and hopefully make him look older.

That evening, Leo did not feel like turning up for work as night desk attendant at the hotel. He'd had a busy and exciting day with very little sleep. But he'd have to go because his plan was to change nothing until the time was right for him to adopt the persona of Francis Clitheroe.

For that, he needed to find a job for Francis and get himself hired to do it. That wouldn't be easy, but if he could find just the right niche, he would not only be paid a good salary but hopefully be able to tap into company funds and help himself. A chief accountant he thought would find that possible, but he'd need the top job; it would never do to have a boss who was a qualified accountant peering over his shoulder all the time.

Leo thought about it some more, it would not be easy to pull the wool over the eyes of any accountant, even if he were considered his junior. Particularly one who had been passed over for promotion and who might therefore resent him. What he needed was a job where Francis would be the only qualified accountant in the business. Therefore, it would need to be a small- to medium-sized firm.

There were always lots of newspapers left lying around in the hotel; Leo never needed to buy one. Both he and Gary picked up enough to give them all the reading they wanted through the night hours. Sometimes they disagreed over who should have first read of the tabloids and magazines. There were many more broadsheet papers, this being an expensive hotel.

Tonight Leo wanted to look through the situations vacant columns to find a job Francis Clitheroe might apply for, but he didn't want Gary to see him doing it. He waited until the security guard had settled down for his two-hour nap, then fished out a copy of each of the main broadsheets.

He realised almost immediately that most of the jobs advertised were in different parts of the country. Here was one that looked hopeful, but it was in Sheffield, and there were many more in London.

He sat back and thought about it. It would be safer to move to London, but Liverpool was where he'd been born and brought up; he had local knowledge here, and it was where he felt at home. He would be less at ease anywhere else. Francis's new job, he decided, must be in Liverpool.

He took the broadsheets to the rubbish pile and selected instead the *Liverpool Daily Post*. Accountants, he found, were much in demand; there were several firms advertising for their services. Being local meant he'd be able to check the businesses out before he applied. It was at that point that he thought about his address. Nobody earning an accountant's salary would live where he did.

He turned to the property pages. There was little to rent, and dare he attempt to buy a house? He shivered at the thought. He wasn't planning a lifetime career, only one lasting a few months until he could get into the firm's bank account. Finding a new home would need more thought, more money and probably more study.

The next morning Leo went to a theatrical costumier and bought himself a pair of spectacles with heavy black frames and clear glass lenses, and then went straight to the library to look for a book on accounting procedures.

Chloe had been looking forward to going with

Adam to Wentworth's auction rooms, which was in the suburbs on the other side of Manchester. He always seemed to enjoy the auctions he went to and she was keen to know whether the proposed visit to Liverpool would be possible.

The sale day was a wet Thursday morning. Apart from a quick pram push to the local shops, this was Chloe's first outing with her three-week-old baby. They arrived early because Adam wanted to be there when his furniture went under the hammer. He knew a lot of the people in the trade and was walking round talking to them, leaving her and the children sitting on the end of the back row in the packed hall.

Chloe was trying to keep Lucy amused with the toys she'd brought, but she was more interested in the Steiff teddy bear and antique dolls that would shortly go under the hammer. Zac was restless in this strange place, though she'd fed him before coming. She was finding the waiting tedious.

Her eye was caught by the scene reflected in a row of gilt-framed mirrors hanging along the wall. She was able to pick herself out, but she wasn't flattered. Her hair was untidy and badly in need of a trim and she looked hot and harassed and older than her twenty years. She would have liked to take off her new blue anorak, but Zac had regurgitated his feed on the pullover she was wearing underneath. *Ugh —*

Lucy chuckled with delight when she too noticed their reflection. She snuggled closer to Chloe, pulling faces and waving at herself. 'That's me, Mummy.' In her best pink coat and bonnet with golden curls showing round it, she was a very attractive toddler.

At last the auctioneer announced the first of Adam's lots, 'Fine-quality mahogany dining table.' Zac chose that moment to start throwing his arms about and making ticking noises, which Chloe recognised as a sign that he was about to cry. She picked him out of his carrycot on wheels, hoping to forestall him. The place was already noisy enough for those trying to hear what the auctioneer was saying. Zac opened his mouth and let out a wail of protest.

In an effort to comfort him, she lifted him to her shoulder, rocked him and patted his back. He belched audibly and followed that by expelling another mouthful of his feed down the back of her new anorak. Knowing she'd failed to get his wind up after his feed made her feel incompetent as a mother.

Zac began to cry in earnest, and Chloe was afraid he must still feel uncomfortable. She stood up, knowing she'd have to take him out; his cries of distress were disturbing others. She laid him back in his pram and, catching hold of Lucy's hand, tried to take them both out, but Lucy refused to walk past the Steiff bear and wriggled free, lifting her arms towards it.

'No, love, you must come with me.' Chloe took her hand in a firmer grasp and half dragged her towards the door. Lucy let out a scream of protest and started to jump with rage. Now both her children were crying noisily and people were turning to stare at them.

Chloe turned to look imploringly at Adam; she

wanted his help, but his handsome face was flint hard and his lips mouthed the words 'Get them out of here.'

Now Lucy tossed herself down and drummed her heels on the dusty floor in a full-blown temper tantrum. Zac joined in his sister's crescendo of screams. Picking up her squirming and kicking daughter, Chloe tucked her under her arm and pushed the pram to the door. It was a relief to get out into the busy street, with the rain cooling her cheeks. Mortified with embarrassment, she stood Lucy on her feet and brushed what she could of the dust and dirt from her back.

'Don't you dare lie down on this wet pavement,' she told her. 'It'll ruin your pretty coat.' Lucy was still playing up. 'I'll spank you if you do. You've even got dust on the back of your bonnet.'

But she couldn't stay out here in the driving rain; they were getting drenched. She pulled up the hood on her anorak and drew back into the porch. The advice they handed out at the clinic for dealing with a temper tantrum was to ignore the child, walk away from her and deny her what she wanted.

Chloe sighed. That was hardly practical here. An old lady also sheltering in the porch offered Lucy a jelly sweet. But that would be a reward, so Chloe had to say no thank you, and try to comfort her daughter with hugs instead.

Zac was quietening down and looked as though he might doze off. Chloe had a big bag of baby equipment attached to the pram and was able to drag out Lucy's rain cape and reins. Once she had those on her daughter, she felt she'd be able to cope.

She was angry with Adam for refusing to help. What did he expect her to do now? He'd brought them here in his shooting brake, but if he was planning to stay much longer, she thought she might try going home on the bus. She pushed open the door to the hall and was in time to hear his chairs being knocked down for a price she knew would please him.

An elderly couple came out. 'Do you know what the Georgian table made?' Chloe asked, but they shook their heads. It didn't matter; it had reached its reserve before she went out and the bidding had still been going up. Adam would have made enough to buy her a train ticket to Liverpool.

Her eyes searched him out in the crush of people at the back of the hall. Yes, there he was, with his back towards her and his attention firmly fixed on a slim young girl in a red pullover. Chloe wheeled the pram inside and headed towards him.

As she drew near, she heard him say persuasively, 'We must do it again. What about tomorrow night?'

She felt her stomach lurch. The girl had seen her, and said to Adam, 'I'd better get back to the office.' She turned on her heel and left.

He replied, 'I'll come and see you before I go.'

It was only when Lucy swung on the bottom of his jacket and said, 'Daddy, want to go home,' that he noticed them. He seemed shocked to see Chloe so close.

'Who was that?' she asked.

He recovered his suave manner immediately. 'She's the cashier here.'

Her heart was pounding. 'Pretty girl,' she said. Did Adam have a new girlfriend? She was afraid he might have.

'Good prices, you can go to your mother's.'

'Are you going to stay here much longer?'

'For a while.'

'Want to go home.' Lucy tugged at him again.

'Not yet, there's a nice pair of decanters coming up soon.'

'In that case,' Chloe told him, 'I'll try and get back on the bus.'

'Shouldn't be too hard,' he said. 'You need to get back to the centre of the city, then catch the usual bus to Didsbury.'

Chloe's knees felt shaky as she pushed the pram to the nearest bus stop.

Riding on the bus, Zac went to sleep and Lucy was sulky. Chloe was distressed; she felt as though her life was falling apart. Adam had told her that when he went out without her in the evenings he met a group of his old schoolfriends, men he'd known for years who enjoyed each other's company. But now it seemed he'd found another girlfriend, and that made everything a hundred times worse. Chloe didn't know if he was serious about the girl, but it had sounded as though he was spending a lot of time with her.

'We must do it again,' he'd said. 'What about tomorrow night?' What else could that mean?

Chloe fretted that if what she supposed was right, Adam would not want her living here with him. He didn't seem to care at all for his children; they didn't fit into the life he wanted to lead. The future suddenly looked frightening.

By the time she reached home, she felt exhausted and absolutely drained of energy, but she knew she'd feel better if she ate. Ruby had been and the house was neat and tidy. Chloe was heating up some soup she'd made yesterday when the phone rang. It was her mother.

'How are you all?' she asked. Chloe couldn't tell her the truth; she was too uptight and she had to be sure of Adam's intentions before she said anything. She made herself sound more upbeat than she was.

'Everything's fine, I'm just tired. I've talked it over with Adam and I'd love to bring the children and stay with you for a week.'

'Good, when will you come?'

She knew it would take four days for the auction room to pay out, and then it probably meant a cheque in the post. 'How about the middle of next week?'

'That's excellent. There's just one thing. I've had to let Aunt Goldie come and live with me.'

'Mum! Have you got room for all of us?' Chloe had been blithely supposing that she could use the spare room for Lucy and have Zac with her in her old bedroom. She'd even thought about going to live there permanently, if things got any worse.

Mum didn't sound too happy either. 'We'll all squeeze in. Marigold's in the spare room, but I'll make up a little bed on your floor for Lucy. I'm glad you've decided to come.'

'I thought you didn't want Aunt Goldie with you?'

'I was being silly, afraid we'd get on each other's nerves, but she's been a wreck since she had her purse and key stolen. Rex changed the lock on her front door, but that didn't help. You saw how upset she was. Somehow she can't put it out of her mind. Poor Marigold, I couldn't hold out against her any longer.'

'Are you sure it's all right? Me and the children coming too? It'll mean a lot of work for you.'

'Of course it's all right, Chloe. I'll love having you here. I can't wait to see how the children have grown.'

Chloe put the phone down feeling as though Aunt Goldie had cut the ground from under her feet. How could she possibly suggest to Mum now that she move in with her permanently?

All the same, she was glad she'd be having a week away from Adam. Things were getting a bit strained between them. He never stopped carping about the mess and the noise the children made in his house. She packed the necessities for a week away, and tried not to think about the future.

The night before she left, Adam didn't come home until nearly eleven. Chloe had fed Zac and was settling him down for the night. Adam lost no time in getting into bed and seemed to be asleep by the time she got there. He'd agreed to take them to the station the next morning.

Chloe was up early to get the children ready and to make their breakfast. Adam said little until they were all in the car, then as he put it in gear and pulled away, he dropped a bombshell.

215

'Chloe, I'd rather you and the children didn't come back.'

'What?' She'd been rushing round to get them ready in time and felt flummoxed.

'You heard. I don't want you or your kids back here. We aren't getting on any more, are we?'

'But you can't put us out like this, on the spur of the moment.'

'It's not the spur of the moment for me. I've been thinking about it for a long time. Everything's gone sour between us, so what's the point of carrying on? You aren't happy any more, in fact you're as miserable as sin. A pain in the neck really.'

Chloe gripped the edge of her seat. 'I can't stay longer than a week. We won't have enough clothes, and there's all the children's stuff.'

'I'll pack everything up for you and leave it in the conservatory. You can send somebody to pick it up.'

Chloe couldn't get her breath; she felt in shock. 'But I've no money, how am I going to manage?'

He reached in his pocket and brought out a wad of notes, which he flung on her lap. 'This should get you started. Anyway, your mother's got plenty of money. She won't see you starve.'

Chloe felt as though he'd kicked her. Tears were stinging her eyes.

'You've got another girlfriend?'

'What if I have? You don't want to come out with me. You've been no fun recently.'

CHAPTER FIFTEEN

Chloe spent the whole train journey gripped in a void of cold terror. She couldn't stop her teeth chattering, although the carriage was warm. She couldn't believe Adam would do this to her. She'd loved him and thought he loved her. He'd said their arrangement was exactly the same as marriage but without the ceremony and the certificate. She'd assumed that meant it was permanent.

'Mummy crying?' Lucy tugged at her sleeve. 'What's matter?'

Chloe was conscious of nearby passengers turning to look at her. 'Just something in my eye,' she whispered, and was glad she could bury her face in Zac's shawl. She couldn't think straight.

'Want to sit on your knee, Mummy.' Chloe put Zac back in his carrycot and took comfort in hugging her daughter and responding to her baby talk.

She felt no better when the train pulled into Liverpool Lime Street. The elderly man who'd been sitting opposite helped her lift the carrycot containing the sleeping Zac down to the platform. Gripping Lucy's reins firmly, she looked round for her mother, who'd said she'd meet her.

Helen, wearing a smart red coat, was waving to them from behind the ticket collector. Chloe knew she'd have to tell her what had happened and throw herself on her mercy. She'd nowhere else she could go.

'Nana,' Lucy shouted. 'Hello, Nana.'

But though Mum kissed them all and gave them a warm welcome, she was not in her usual happy mood. 'Marigold can be a trial,' she said, taking charge of their case and hurrying them towards her car. 'I'm sorry she has to be with us. I meant you and me to have a lovely relaxing week. You look as though you could do with a rest.'

Lucy was gripping her grandmother's coat and told her, 'Mummy crying,' but her words were not heard.

'Marigold never throws anything away, you know,' Helen went on, 'and she's brought so much stuff with her. I'd no sooner got her installed in the spare bedroom... D'you know what she said?'

Chloe was beyond saying anything.

'"It's silly, isn't it, to squeeze me into the box room, when Chloe's bedroom is empty?" I had to remind her quite sharply that you come to stay for a few nights once in a while. She said, "I can move out when we know she's coming." So I'm glad you're here to prove my point.

'Lucy, my pet, I've got you a car seat. I thought I'd better get one to keep you safe. Let me lift you in. There now, we'll soon be home.'

Chloe climbed into the passenger seat. Her eyes were prickling and she was struggling to control her tears.

'You're very quiet.' Her mother glanced up from the road. Chloe could hold them back no longer. Tears streamed down her cheeks. 'Chloe, darling!'

'Mummy sad,' Lucy said.

218

'I'm in terrible trouble, Mum,' she wept. 'Adam doesn't want us to go back, and I don't know what to do.'

She felt the car's momentary jerk. 'You've had a quarrel?' Anxiety scraped in her mother's voice.

'It's more than that.'

'Darling, a week apart and it'll all calm down. You'll both feel differently.'

'Mum, it's over between Adam and me. I can't go back and I've nowhere else to live.'

Chloe knew that had registered as a shock. There was horror in Mum's voice. 'You can live with me, you know that.'

'Careful, Mum!' Chloe felt a moment of panic, but the brakes slammed on and Mum stopped an inch away from the back of a bus.

'I'm so sorry this has happened,' she said. 'Let's talk about it when we get home. You mustn't worry, I'll see you're all right.'

Chloe's bedroom had always been a place of refuge when she was in trouble, though it didn't seem quite the same, with the mattress for Lucy on the floor in the corner. She put the carrycot down on her bed and sank down beside it.

Her mother came running up with their suitcase and bags and threw her arms round her. 'Marigold's looking after Lucy. Tell me what's gone wrong.'

Chloe felt terrible. It took her a long time to get it all out. She wept on her mother's shoulder and felt a large handkerchief being pushed into her hand.

'I've left everything behind, all our clothes and

the pram and cot. How am I going to get them here?'

Adam's business meant that they were always arranging for goods to be picked up or delivered. She knew how to arrange it, but she also knew what it would cost.

'Ask Rex,' Helen said. 'He has a van, he'll be only too glad to help you.'

'Are you sure? It'll take up his time, and then there's the petrol...'

'Diesel. You could offer to pay for that, but he'll want to do it.'

Chloe took out the roll of money Adam had flung at her and counted it.

'You'll be all right.' Mum patted her hand.

'But this is all I've got,' she wailed. 'And I've two children to bring up now. I feel terrible throwing myself on you like this.'

Her mother touched the roll of money.

'You're not penniless.'

'Adam's given me a hundred pounds.'

'There you are, then.'

'I don't know if there'll be any more.'

'Of course there will. It's his duty to support his children.'

Chloe shivered. 'I've a feeling this is all I'll get.'

'Chloe darling, you mustn't be so negative.' Helen walked round the room and came back. 'I can make you more comfortable here. Oh dear, if only you'd married him.'

Chloe sniffed. 'Right at the beginning you warned me, you said we must get married.'

'It would have made you both think harder before you'd decided to part.'

'We weren't getting on, Mum. Staying with him isn't an option any longer. I've been scared about what he's doing. Afraid the police will catch him and we'll both find ourselves in court charged with fencing.'

'Oh God! How long has that been going on?'

Chloe shrugged, 'All along, I think. Anyway, he's got another girlfriend.'

'Marriage would have given you legal rights.'

'And the need for a divorce.'

Zac began to stir and make his ticking sound. Chloe picked him up out of his carrycot. 'It's time for his feed,' she said. 'I should have left Adam ages ago, before I had this one. I wish I had.'

'You mustn't say that, love. Zac is here now, and he's a beautiful baby. You stay here and feed him, have a rest if you can. I'll go and break the news to Marigold and see about some lunch.'

'What a mess I've made of my life.'

'Darling, you know I'll help in every way I can. We'll arrange something for you.'

The bedroom door closed behind her. Chloe lay down on her bed and began to feed Zac. It made her keep still, but nothing could calm her. She couldn't stop thinking about Adam. She'd thought he loved the children. She'd seen him as her husband even though he wasn't. She'd truly thought of him as her partner for life.

Had he ever thought of her like that? Or had he deliberately avoided marriage so he could move on when he tired of her? He'd let her down, kicked her in the teeth, altered the whole course of her life. Ruined it. He'd rejected her and there could be nothing more painful than being rejected by a lover. She'd trusted and given freely of all the love she had. She was a failure as a lover, a failure as a homemaker and probably also as a mother. Chloe felt she was touching bottom.

When Zac went off to sleep again, Chloe made herself go downstairs. She had to; she knew from the clatter of dishes that lunch was nearly ready. She'd have preferred to stay in her room and forgo that; she wasn't hungry. But she had to live here, so there was no way she could hide from Aunt Goldie. She found her reading 'Cinderella' to Lucy.

'Well, Chloe,' Marigold said, straightening up as soon as she saw her. 'I'm sorry to hear about your trouble, but you must know how shocked and shamed I felt when you brazenly went to live with a man who didn't want to marry you.' Her grey eyes flashed with unforgiving severity. 'I did my best to warn you. You should have taken heed of what I said, and now I'm proved right. You've brought shame on us all and saddled us with these two little children to bring up.'

Her mother came rushing in. 'Lunch is ready,' she said. 'Will you bring Lucy in, please, Marigold?' She stood back to usher them all to the dining room.

'She could do with a high chair,' Marigold said. 'I don't suppose you bothered to bring that, Chloe?'

'I've put a cushion on this chair for Lucy,' Helen said, but nothing could stop Marigold's tirade.

'You had a very comfortable life here with your mother. You should not have been in such a hurry to turn your back on it.'

'No,' Chloe agreed. How she wished she hadn't. She was only just in control of her tears, and she wouldn't be able to stand much more of this.

'She gave you everything you could possibly have wanted. Holidays at the seaside, visits to the ballet, trips to art galleries.'

'Would you like some mayonnaise on your salad, Marigold?'

'Yes please. You should not have let yourself be led astray by that Adam fellow. Whatever made you do that?'

Chloe bit back. 'I understand you did exactly the same, Aunt Goldie, so it's in my genes. You can't push all the blame on me.'

Marigold's cheeks flushed puce. 'How dare you say—'

'Give over, both of you,' Helen burst out. 'If you're going to live with me, you'll have to live in peace. I want no more of this.'

There was a subdued silence until Lucy piped, 'What's Mummy done wrong?'

'Nothing, darling,' Helen said. 'I've asked Rex to come for dinner tonight. He usually comes in the afternoon to do a bit of tidying up in the garden. We should all get out and enjoy the sun.'

'Bringing shame on the family,' Aunt Goldie muttered under her breath. 'You'll be paying for this mistake for the rest of your life.'

Chloe cringed and struggled to swallow the cold beef.

'You mustn't let Marigold faze you,' Helen said to

her daughter while they were washing up together afterwards. 'I'm sure Gran accused her of shaming the family, and she doesn't realise how things have changed. Neither does she remember how painful it was at the time.'

'You're wrong, she's never forgotten,' Chloe said. 'She's been bitter and twisted all her life. Never got over it.'

'Take no notice of what she says. In the old days, when it happened to Marigold, it was hard to pick yourself up afterwards. It's easier now; it'll be quite different for you.'

She could see Chloe was struggling to hold herself together. 'Marigold is surprisingly good with Lucy. Give her credit where it's due.'

'That's not easy either.'

'If I'd known you'd be coming back to live with me, I wouldn't have let her come. It would have been the perfect excuse.'

'I should have said something sooner. Let you know that things were getting impossible between me and Adam.'

'I wish you had. By the way, I rang Rex before lunch to put him in the picture. I thought it would be easier if he knew before he came.'

'Thanks, Mum.' Chloe wiped her eyes on the tea towel. 'I've made a mess of my life. Sorry to have landed you in it too.'

Rex was outraged at the way Chloe had been treated. He ached to tell Adam what he thought of him face to face. Just thinking about it made his hands clench into fists. He'd like to make him suffer.

He'd persuaded a young and innocent girl of barely seventeen to have sex with him. Lured her into living with him in his fine house and sired two children with her. Now it seemed he didn't want her or her babies any more. He'd got himself another girlfriend. Rex didn't call that love; he thought Adam had abused Chloe.

Her children were delightful, especially little Lucy, who could charm her way into anyone's heart. Even Marigold had taken to her. How could her real father turn his back on her? He must have a heart of stone.

Rex had meant to spend an hour on his business accounts, but he couldn't settle to the work, so he drove over to Helen's garden earlier than he'd intended. He parked his van beside her garage, and though he'd meant to do some gentle hoeing to keep the weeds under control, he set about knocking back some nettles that were taking hold near his compost heap. He slashed at them furiously, trying to get the anger out of his system. He'd deal with their roots later, when he was calmer. He ached to help Chloe. In a way, he blamed himself for what had happened to her.

Why hadn't he taken up with her before Adam had come on the scene? His reasons sounded stupid now: he was so much older than she was; he'd been afraid she'd think him dull, too old for romance, past all that. He'd been waiting for her to grow to maturity.

Like a fool he'd hung back, but she'd have been his adored wife, he'd have cherished her. He'd have done everything to make her happy. Life

225

would have been good for her and marvellous for him.

And if only he'd waited, been more patient once Chloe had gone to Adam, he'd be free to comfort her now. Once she'd recovered enough, he'd have been able to plead his case, but he hadn't foreseen a disaster like this overtaking her. Chloe might find a staid older husband more acceptable after this. He'd never stopped loving her, and he'd love her children because they were hers. He'd help her bring them up; he'd have a ready-made family.

What he really wanted to do was to turn everything round for her. But no, he could not. He mustn't even think of it. He'd consoled himself by getting into Helen's bed and he'd taught her to rely on him. He'd taken what he'd thought of as second best, but he cared deeply about her too, and he couldn't push her away now and turn to her daughter. Helen would be distraught. She and Chloe were fond of each other, supportive of each other. What would that do to their relationship? If he asked Chloe to marry him now, it could destroy everything for her mother.

'Rex?' He knew it was Chloe calling his name; he turned to see her coming towards him, carrying the baby, with the toddler at her heels. She looked washed out, grey-faced, and he could see she'd been crying. He wanted to gather her in his arms to comfort her.

'Chloe, I'm so sorry. Your mother's told me. Such bad news.' He could see her face screwing in an effort to keep her tears back. 'You deserve better.'

'Mum's being kind. She's done her best to welcome me back.'

'I wish there was something I could do to help.'

She was blinking hard. 'There is, as a matter of fact.'

He'd heard enough from her mother to know she was traumatised by being put out of Adam's house and worried about her future. He wanted to ask her what had happened, what had gone wrong. But she might think he was prying. 'I'll help in any way I can,' he said. 'You know that.'

'I've brought very little with me. Just clothes for a few days. Would you take me back to Manchester in your van to collect the rest? There's Zac's big pram and a pushchair, a cot and a high chair for Lucy. Oh, and her rocking horse and all their clothes and other paraphernalia.'

'Of course,' he said. 'I'll be glad to, but not tomorrow, I've made an appointment – I'm hoping to get more work.'

'The next day?'

'Yes, that's fine.'

'I'll ring Adam and tell him we're coming. Thank you, Rex. Mum said you'd help or I'd have never dared ask such a favour.'

'Chloe, I've told you, I'm glad to do all I can for you.'

Chloe waited until she thought Adam would be home from work before ringing him.

His first words were 'I haven't changed my mind. I don't want you back here, so it's no good asking.'

That felt like another kick from him. 'I wouldn't

227

dream of asking,' she retorted with all the dignity she could find. 'Wild horses wouldn't drag me back now. What I do want are my belongings, my clothes and all the children's things. Cots, prams and toys. I won't be able to manage without them.'

'I've already packed up most of your stuff. I'll leave everything in the conservatory. You can arrange for it to be picked up.'

'Rex is bringing me in his van on Friday.'

'I won't be here, I'm going to a sale in Derbyshire on Friday.'

'Good, there's no point in meeting, is there? I've still got the keys to your house.'

'So you have. Be sure to leave them behind. You'll have no need of them after this.'

'I'll do that,' she said and put the phone down, relieved that it was arranged. She still felt very uptight and wished she didn't have to go back to Adam's house, but she couldn't afford not to collect her things. Rex had been sweet, but all the same, she'd be glad when the Manchester trip was over.

During the first days back at her old home, Chloe wasn't able to relax and she couldn't sleep. It didn't help that Lucy kept asking, 'When is Daddy coming to see us? When are we going home? I want my bike and I want Daddy.'

Aunt Goldie had said some horrible things to her, but now she and Mum were bending over backwards to be kind; they couldn't do enough to help.

Chloe got up early on Friday morning to wash

and dress the children. She'd arranged for Rex to pick her up at half ten, so that Ruby would have time to clean up and go.

Mum and Aunt Goldie had offered to look after both the babies, but she elected to take Zac with her. He was a hungry baby, needing to be fed every three hours, and she was breast-feeding. She had loads of milk and would be uncomfortable and leaking if she didn't feed him.

Rex arrived at the appointed time and strapped the carrycot behind her seat. He was dressed smartly today. 'Nice silk shirt,' she said as they started off.

'A Christmas present from your mother.' He turned to smile at her. 'Too good for gardening.'

'You're very kind to take me to Manchester. It'll take up a lot of your time.'

'I always enjoy a day off doing something different.'

'Adam won't be there, but I'm not looking forward to this.' She felt at ease with Rex; she'd known him for years and saw him as a family friend, part of the old life she'd turned her back on two and a half years ago.

'He's treated you very badly.'

'He's a crook. That's how he can afford an expensive lifestyle. I couldn't stay.' She told him how she'd found out, and about the false alibi she'd given him.

'Then you had to leave him.'

'Yes, I was afraid that sooner or later it would all blow up in my face. That we'd both be charged with fencing and I'd be in big trouble.'

Rex's heart turned over that she'd confided that

229

to him. 'I didn't realise you had that sort of problem. I thought it was the usual, you know, not getting on.'

'That too, when I couldn't persuade him to give up. It all went sour.'

It upset Chloe to see again the lovely home she'd thought of as hers. 'At least it's locked up and there's nobody here,' she said to Rex. 'Come on in.'

Nothing had changed, except for the collection of baby equipment, cardboard boxes and bags waiting in the conservatory for her to take away. She helped Rex carry the things out to the drive, 'There's a lot here,' he said.

'There's probably more,' she told him. 'I bet he'll have forgotten half the nappies and cot sheets. I'm going to check the airing cupboard and my wardrobe. I don't want to leave any of my clothes here.'

She left him to load his van and went upstairs. The airing cupboard was stacked high with things that belonged to her and the children. She tied them into cot sheets and stuffed them into pillowcases. Then she dragged Lucy's toy box containing her bricks and colouring books and other bits and pieces on to the landing.

Warily she went into the bedroom she'd shared with Adam. Trying not to look at the vast bed, she opened the door of what had been her wardrobe. It made her gasp to see the garments hanging inside, only two or three, but they were not hers. She slammed the door shut and turned round to see fluffy white slippers by the bed and a whole collection of cosmetics on the dressing table. So Adam *had* had another girl here. To move her in this quickly, he must have been carrying on with her for months.

She took her alarm clock from the chest of drawers, and recognised the exotic bottle of perfume standing beside it. She picked it up, opened it and sniffed at it. She'd never cared much for it; the scent was too heavy for her.

Rex appeared in the doorway with Zac in his arms. 'He was starting to cry,' he said. 'I think he needs changing.'

'This was my Christmas present from Adam,' she said, and hurled the bottle of perfume at the skirting board as hard as she could. It didn't break the glass, but the stopper rolled away and a heavy cloud of cloying scent rose into the air. She shut the door on it.

'I'll change Zac in the bathroom, I've done all I can here.' She put her clock in the toy box before taking the baby from him.

She didn't want to spend a minute longer in the house than she had to. As soon as she was sure Rex had loaded everything belonging to her and the children into his van, she double-locked the front door and posted the keys back through the letter box.

CHAPTER SIXTEEN

Rex climbed into the van, started the engine and began the drive back. He'd felt Chloe's tension from the moment he'd followed her inside the house. Now the van was full of her raging emotions.

He tried to comfort her. 'You'll be all right now.'

She was unbuttoning her blouse, getting ready to feed her baby in the passenger seat beside him. He glanced at her before he could stop himself. One exquisite rosy breast was being offered to the baby. He heard Zac's satisfied sucking.

He sat up straighter, gripped the steering wheel harder and took a firm grip on himself. Chloe didn't realise what she was doing to him. He anchored his gaze on the road ahead.

'I don't know how I'm going to cope.' Rex thought he could hear tears in her voice. 'Mum's trying hard not to say "I told you so". Well, of course I knew the family would hate me for living with Adam.'

'No,' he said. 'They feared for you, they knew how difficult it would be if things went wrong.'

'They couldn't help but know, could they? It's Aunt Goldie's mistake over again. Look what one unsupported baby did to her life. And I was daft enough to double the handicap.'

'Chloe, you mustn't think of it as a handicap.'

'Actually, it's a disaster. How else would anybody see it? If only I could put the clock back. I'd give anything to be back working in the civil service.'

'Hindsight makes everything clearer.'

'It would be hard enough even if I didn't have two children.'

'You mustn't regret having them. Show them you love them and they'll grow up level-headed and contented. They won't always be babies, they'll be real people who'll love you for the care and affection you give them now. Many would envy you your family.'

He could see that Zac had finished feeding and Chloe was buttoning up her blouse again, but she couldn't put him back in his carrycot unless Rex stopped the van. The baby was dozing off in her arms.

'Are you hungry?' he asked. 'There's a café round here somewhere. We could have a bite to eat.'

'Yes, there's one on the next corner.'

It was only when he tried that he found he couldn't get the carrycot out without first unloading the pram and rocking horse.

'Never mind, Rex. I can manage a sandwich with him on my knee.'

They went inside a fancy little café and he ordered bacon sandwiches and a pot of tea. While they ate, he told her about his own unhappy upbringing.

'Once my mother died, nobody seemed to care about me, certainly not my stepfather. That made me stand on my own feet from an early age, but I didn't find it easy. At least you have your mother.'

She sniffed into her handkerchief. 'But what am I going to do? I can't sponge on Mum for the rest of my life.'

'Don't worry about that for the time being. You've just gone through a bad patch. You need to give yourself time to get over this knock.'

Did it sound as though he was belittling her difficulties? he wondered. She was facing more than just a knock. She looked quite ill.

He went on more gently. 'Then you need to think about what you want to do. You still have choices, there are things you can still achieve.'

'I could have had anything once, but now... I've messed everything up, haven't I?'

'Not necessarily. Having two babies changes things, but it doesn't mean all is lost.'

Two tearful lavender-blue eyes stared into his. 'Come on,' he said, putting a hand under her arm to help her up. 'Let's get on home, you'll be more comfortable in the garden.'

He unlocked the van. It was hot inside, and when he took the baby from her to lay him down in the carrycot, he could see mother and baby had been sweating against each other.

'Get in, we'll open all the windows.'

They set off. 'Chloe, you must give yourself a few months to weigh everything up,' he advised. 'Take it slowly but make your decisions.'

She was twisting her lips in agony. He could see her mopping at her eyes with a screw of damp lace. He'd brought a clean handkerchief with him, half expecting something like this. 'A man-sized one,' he said, pushing it towards her.

It brought a storm of tears he hadn't expected.

234

'You're trying to be kind, buck me up, but whichever way you look at it, I've ruined everything. Made a real mess of my life.'

Her hand was beside him on the bench seat; he patted it. 'What counts is how you pull it together again.'

'How can I possibly?'

'You can, you'll manage. You must think about what you want from life.'

'I don't know what I want, I only know it's not what I've got now. I've made a bad mistake. I thought I wanted Adam.'

'Make the best of what you do have. Your mother will help all she can and so will I. You're not alone, Chloe.'

That opened the floodgates; soon the tears were pouring down her face.

'It takes courage to pull yourself up and get on with life,' Rex said. 'Don't see yourself as a victim. You mustn't think like that. And don't blame Adam. You got carried away too.'

'I got pregnant,' she said through clenched teeth. 'That changed things for ever.'

She'd quietened down by the time he was running his van alongside her mother's garage. He started to unload so that she could unstrap the carrycot. Zac was fast asleep.

'Thanks, Rex,' she said. 'You talk a lot of sense. If anyone can save my reason, it's you. I'm grateful.'

Rex knew she'd never needed him as much as she did at this moment, but she didn't recognise that he ached almost as much as she did. He wanted to gather her and her baby into his arms

235

and kiss them.

Chloe felt she was going to pieces. She didn't feel well and both her body and her mind were acting strangely. Rex seemed to understand and was trying to buoy her up with kindness. He helped her carry Lucy's bed upstairs and make it up with the bedding from the nest Mum had made for her on the floor. It was while he was trying to erect the big cot for Zac that his hand touched hers and she felt the tingle of electricity run up her arm. It had been just the same in that café when he had helped her to her feet. He was really very sweet. Mum was very lucky to have a friend like him, someone she could trust.

Chloe found the first weeks at home hard going. It was taking all her energy to get through each day as it came, though she knew her family was rallying round. Whenever Rex came to work, she'd go out to talk to him if she could, and give him a hand in the garden.

'The only way forward I can see,' she told him, 'is for me to get a job.'

'Not yet,' he advised.

'But I need to support my children. I'd feel better if I was doing that. At home here with Mum and Aunt Goldie – well, they cosset me.'

'They're trying to show you their love and that all is forgiven.'

'They treat me like a child. They offer advice about baby care all the time, although I've had as much experience of that as they have. If Zac cries and I can't quieten him within moments, they try to take him over.'

Rex laughed. 'Most parents believe they know better than their children. Your mother is doing her best to help you. All she wants is for you to be happy.'

'I know, but look at the mess we're making in her house. She always kept it spick and span, everything neatly in its place, but now it's littered with toys. She used to display her Royal Worcester china ornaments in the sitting room; now they've all been put away because Lucy's inclined to hurl her teddy bear about.'

'Helen loves Lucy too. She's more important to her than pretty ornaments. She can spread them all out again when Lucy's older.'

Another day she said to him, 'The easy thing would be for me to stay at home with the kids, but in a way it's too cosy. I feel I'd like to see more people and do other things. A job would be quite a good thing for me.'

'It might be, but first give the children time to grow a little older and yourself time to recover and get really fit.'

'You're very wise, Rex. You always say the right thing. Comforting, too. I'm glad you're here. You keep me afloat.'

Chloe had always known that the relationship between her mother and Aunt Goldie was not entirely sunny. There were times when she could feel Aunt Goldie's jealousy and resentment. She made frequent verbal jabs at her mother and occasionally it boiled over into an argument.

'You've had a more comfortable life than I have. I worked hard to give you better chances and look what you've got now; you have this lovely home and a car to drive round in. Money enough to spend on extravagances like your garden, while I'm entirely dependent on the crusts from your table.'

Chloe watched Mum walk away from many of these exchanges in order to keep the peace. She hadn't expected much help from Aunt Goldie, but to her surprise, she was acting almost like a nanny to Lucy. They seemed to enjoy each other's company, and that gave Chloe more freedom to nurse her baby and sit out in the garden as Rex had suggested. She tried hard to think about her future but couldn't come up with any plan to improve matters.

Money was a problem for her. Adam had made no offer to pay towards the children's maintenance and so far she'd been too proud to ask for it. Mum was buying necessities for the children, but she couldn't let her go on doing that, not when she was already providing food and shelter for them all.

She made herself dial Adam's number, but he didn't want to speak to her. He said, 'Please don't ring me, it's over between us, Chloe,' and put the receiver down. Writing letters had no effect either. The only conclusion she could draw was that he had no intention of giving her more money.

Apart from the essentials that she couldn't avoid buying for the baby, Lucy would need new shoes and warmer clothes now that autumn was on the way. Chloe's little nest egg was being used up. She applied for social security and got it.

'That's living on the state,' Aunt Goldie said in shocked tones. 'I had to accept help with my rent when Gran died and her pension with her, but I hated having to do it. Where is your pride?'

'I can't afford it,' Chloe retorted. 'I understand that a lot of old people feel like you, but I'm not too proud and neither are others in my position. That's why help is made available to us.'

'You shouldn't bring children into this world and expect others to support them.'

'What did you do when you had Mum?' Chloe had answered, expecting to hear that Gran had given her money.

'I went back to work when she was a month old. I had to hand her over to Gran to look after. Can't you find yourself a little job?'

'I'd like to.'

Mum had been listening to this, and said, 'But there's no hurry, Chloe. You'll have plenty of time to work when Zac is older. He needs you now.'

Chloe eased her frustration by fiddling with her hair. It was growing long and she couldn't afford to visit a hairdresser. She was practising putting it up in a more sophisticated style, one she could wear when she finally went to work.

Rex had dinner with them at least once a week. Chloe looked forward to his visits and knew her mother did too. He made opportunities to walk Mum around the garden so they could have a private chat. Sometimes he asked her out for a meal on her own, leaving Chloe at home with the children and Aunt Goldie.

He invited them all round to see his new home. Aunt Goldie praised it loudly and Chloe loved it. She noticed that her mother was very much at

239

ease there and actually made tea for them.

It brought to mind what Adam had said about Rex, that he was probably Mum's lover. At the time she'd thought that highly unlikely. She couldn't imagine Mum in that situation. Mum believed wholeheartedly in marriage, and as Rex was a widower, if they loved each other she could see no reason for them not to marry.

Perhaps they were working up to it? But no, they'd known each other for donkey's years, they had no reason to delay. In fact, Helen had every reason to go full steam ahead, as it would get her away from Aunt Goldie. All the same, the way she smiled at Rex made it look as though she was in love, and he was always drawing her aside for a chat. They were clearly very close.

Rex would make a kind and dependable husband. Chloe smiled to herself. He was already trying to be a father to her. If they did decide to marry, she'd give them her blessing.

Although Helen and Aunt Goldie had made a fuss of the babies to start with, as the weeks went on even their patience frayed occasionally.

Zac was teething; he cried more and wasn't sleeping so well. Lucy didn't seem to settle; perhaps it was all the changes in her routine. She was still having temper tantrums. One afternoon when they were all in the summerhouse, making the most of the fitful sunshine, she had a particularly demanding one. Aunt Goldie had stopped her trying to lift Zac from his carrycot.

'Zac's asleep, you must leave him alone,' she told her. 'You aren't big enough to lift him out.

You might drop him and hurt him.'

Lucy pulled at her mother's skirt. 'Want to play with Zac,' she said.

'No,' Chloe told her. 'Aunt Goldie's right. You mustn't try to lift him out of his carrycot, that isn't safe. He'll play with you when he's older.' She pushed the stuffed rabbit Lucy was fond of into her arms.

She was defiant. 'Want Zac. Get him up.'

'No, babies need to sleep. We'll get him up later.'

'Now,' Lucy screamed and hurled the soft toy at the sleeping Zac with all her force. Then she threw herself at the carrycot and tried to push it off the coffee table. Chloe had to leap to her feet to stop her.

'No, Lucy, that's naughty. You'll hurt Zac if you do that.'

Lucy screamed even louder and tossed herself down on the rug in a fury, throwing her arms about and thumping her heels. The wooden floor resounded like a drum. Helen covered her ears with her hands and they all tried to ignore Lucy and the racket she was making.

'Let her get on with it,' Aunt Goldie said. 'She mustn't be allowed to get her own way by making a fuss like this.'

Chloe hated these scenes; they distressed her almost as much as they did Lucy. The little girl began tearing at her clothes and scratching herself. That made Chloe gather her into her arms and lift her on to her knee. The child's face was scarlet, she felt hot and sweaty, and for the first time Chloe noticed that she had some biggish spots on her thighs. She looked under her clothes and found more on her back and tummy.

'Heavens, Mum, is this a rash? Is she ill?'

'Oh! It's a rash all right, but I don't know what it is.'

'It's not measles.' Aunt Goldie was peering over her shoulder.

'We need to know what it is, don't we?'

'Yes, I'll go and ring the doctor,' Helen said. 'It could be something infectious.'

Lucy was sobbing softly in Chloe's arms. 'We don't take her out much, how can she catch anything infectious?'

A few minutes later her mother was hurrying back. 'Dr Harris says to bring her down and park the car outside the surgery. If one of us lets him know when we're there, he'll come out and have a look at Lucy. He says there's a lot of chickenpox about at the moment and it could be that.'

Chloe carried Lucy to the car and her mother drove them round.

'Yes, that's chickenpox,' the doctor confirmed. 'Stop her scratching if you can. That can cause scarring. She might want to sleep more than usual. Give her a light diet for a few days. Keep her away from other children until all the scabs are off.'

'I don't know where she could have caught it,' Chloe said. 'She's mostly at home with us.'

'The incubation period is fourteen to twenty-one days, and it's very infectious before the rash comes out.'

'She has a baby brother. Will he catch it?'

'How old is he?'

'Five months.'

'If you had chickenpox as a child, most likely not. He'll get immunity from you. I'll give you a prescription; it's an oil that will help the scabs come off more quickly.'

'Well at least we know what it is,' Helen said as she drove home.

'I've been thinking,' Chloe said. 'I took Zac to the clinic to have some test, and Lucy came with us. They have a slide there and some toys, she loved it. And there were other children.'

'When did Marigold take us to church? For the harvest festival? That's about the right time too. There were lots of children there as well. It's bound to happen from time to time, one of the joys of parenthood.'

'And chickenpox isn't serious, is it?'

Lucy had gone to sleep in her arms by the time they reached home again. Chloe took her upstairs and laid her down on her bed, where she slept for an hour.

She came down for her lunch, ate almost nothing but wanted to stay down with them. Aunt Goldie took her out into the garden and played with her in the shade. Lucy was noticeably more crotchety than usual, but she wasn't really ill.

When the last of Lucy's scabs was off, Chloe thanked Aunt Goldie for looking after her so well. She really had been a great help in keeping her happy. But soon Marigold herself began to feel unwell, and Chloe felt she owed it to her to be sympathetic. Goldie was querulous and demanded a lot of attention. The next day she announced she had a rash round her midriff.

Helen took her to see the doctor. He confirmed it was shingles, caused by the chickenpox virus.

By this time Aunt Goldie was in considerable pain and was angry. 'I didn't realise Lucy was a source of infection, I should have stayed well away from her. But I tried to be kind and help you and look where it's got me.'

Helen and Chloe took turns to dab the lotion the doctor had prescribed on her rash. She complained a good deal, was quite short-tempered with everybody and said some hurtful things. When she tripped over Lucy's toy dog on wheels, she turned on Chloe. 'I hope you're going to stay away from men in future. We can't cope with any more babies here.'

Helen chided, 'Marigold, you're very fond of Lucy.'

'You needn't worry,' Chloe said. 'I'm off all men.' But she felt very bad about Aunt Goldie catching shingles, because she'd virtually nursed Lucy back to health. She did her best to be polite and kind to her at all times, though Aunt Goldie took weeks and weeks to recover.

To get away from her one morning, Chloe went out to the vegetable patch to gather salad vegetables for lunch, and found Rex was there planting out seedlings for winter cabbage.

'Aunt Goldie's driving me up the wall,' she told him. 'I need to get away. I've decided it's time to start looking for a job.'

'The children need you here, Chloe.'

'There are other things they need more. As you know, Adam hasn't been near and neither has he paid a penny in maintenance.'

244

'I can't believe he hasn't come to see his children.'

'Neither can Mum, but it's up to me now, isn't it?'

'Shouldn't you be here to look after them?'

'Mum and Aunt Goldie have offered to do that. It's asking a lot, I know, but Goldie's good with Lucy. Once I'm earning, I might be able to find a girl to help them.'

Rex sighed. 'Look, if it's money, your mum and I would be happy to help.' That made her eyes search his face. 'Wait another six months, at least...'

'That's a very kind thought, Rex, but no.'

'I wouldn't miss the money.'

'Mum's supported me and my brood since I came home, hasn't she?'

He nodded. 'She wants to.'

'She feels she has to, and I feel I've lost control of everything. Things are happening in my life. I'm being tossed and turned and rushed along by them and I have to do something about it. You've helped me see it this way, by telling me to think about the future and make plans.'

'Chloe, I didn't mean that you had to get a job before Zac was even a year old.'

'I know, but I've brought two children into the world and it's my responsibility to bring them up. I'll feel more in control if I'm earning and can pay for their keep.'

'Well I think I'd feel the same. You'll go back to office work?'

'It's all I know, but I'm afraid I'll be rusty at it. I stopped work before Lucy was born, and that's two and a half years ago now.'

'Was it shorthand typing you did in that civil service job?'

'I did a few letters, but I worked in the accounts department and mostly it was bookkeeping. I should be able to do anything like that.'

'You could get your textbooks out and refresh your memory,' he suggested.

'Of course I should. Thanks for reminding me. I'll get them out today.'

That afternoon she felt she'd made a start at taking control of her life. Zac was six months old now and she was able to start him on solids and cut down the number of breast-feeds he had. A week later she rang the office where she used to work and spoke to her old boss.

'I'd be glad to have you back, Chloe, but it isn't possible just now. Sorry, we have our full complement of office staff.'

That knocked her back a bit, but she started studying the situations vacant advertised in the local newspapers. There didn't seem to be very many. She thought perhaps a part-time job might suit her better to start with. It would give her a chance to get her hand in again, and Mum and Aunt Goldie would not have to look after her kids all day.

She didn't get the first two jobs she applied for, and as a result she had to fight the feeling that it was all hopeless. She had to force herself to carry on.

CHAPTER SEVENTEEN

Helen had arranged to meet Joan in town for lunch and tried to persuade Chloe to go with her. 'You'll feel better if you get out and about,' she said. 'It's not a good day for the garden. Marigold will look after the babies if you ask her.'

'I know she will, Mum, but I'd rather stay in the summerhouse and take it easy.'

So Helen went alone feeling low, and let all the problems with Chloe and Marigold come gushing out. Joan was sympathetic.

'You've done your best for both of them, Helen. You mustn't let them upset you.'

'It's hard not to. Chloe's in quite a state. She was in love with Adam and gave him everything.'

'To have his children and then be told he doesn't want her living with him must have been hell for her.'

'It still is, and he's not helping to maintain his children. That really bothers her, though I've told her not to worry about money; that I'm very happy to have them all live with me.'

'Chloe sees them as her responsibility, not yours.'

'Yes, and she feels she's ruined her life and can't see any way out of the mess she's got herself into.'

Joan sighed. 'I wouldn't know what to suggest either.'

'Rex is very good with her and Marigold is helping with the babies. Anyway, enough of our troubles. How is Walter? Has he managed to find a new accountant?'

'No, it's an ongoing saga, I'm afraid. As you know, Tom Cleary has been his accountant for the last fifteen years and a good friend to Walter. Tom said he wanted to retire and he's been advertising for a replacement for him ever since.'

'I thought you'd found somebody?'

'So did we. Walter and Tom picked out the best one from those who applied and told the others the position had been filled. At the last moment it turned out the replacement had been offered a better-paid job elsewhere and turned them down.'

'Oh dear, so Walter's back to square one?'

'Yes, he's advertised again and hopes he'll find somebody soon. Poor old Tom is getting impatient. He had his sixty-fifth birthday two months ago but he's working on until Walter can find someone to take his place.'

'Walter's had no luck trying to sell the business?'

'No, not a bite, but he's happy to carry on for the time being, as long as he can get help.'

Everything changed for Chloe when she applied for a part-time job in the office of a Liverpool department store. She was delighted to be called in for an interview and found it was a temporary appointment to cover the maternity leave of a member of staff.

'We filled this vacancy some months ago and thought we'd chosen well, but unfortunately our stand-in was injured in a road accident last week and so can't carry on. We need somebody immediately and it's for four months only, I'm afraid. Would you be interested?'

'Yes,' Chloe said immediately. Four months would be long enough to get her up to speed again. Long enough to find out if it was practical to go to work when the children were so young.

'Can you start tomorrow morning?'

She agreed, and was shown round the office and introduced to some of the staff. Feeling cock-a-hoop, she browsed round the shop and looked through the rails in the children's department for warm clothes for Lucy.

Mum and Aunt Goldie were as excited as she was at the news. Rex was invited round and a special celebratory dinner was prepared. He brought a bottle of wine to drink to her success.

By the next morning she was full of trepidation about whether she could cope with the work. Worse, she felt guilty at walking away from Zac, and to make her feel worse still, Lucy cried when she kissed her goodbye. Chloe told herself she should have expected that and she must get used to it. She should be able to manage anything if it was only for four months.

To start with, she felt lost without the children tugging at her and demanding attention. But Aunt Goldie told her that once she was out of sight, Lucy and Zac seemed to forget about her and were perfectly happy. She began taking them to the child welfare clinic and seemed to enjoy having responsibilities in the family.

Without the children, Chloe found she could

concentrate on the work she was given. Her job was in the accounts department and her hours were from nine until one. She didn't find it easy, but once she understood their accounting system, she began to relax and enjoy having more to do. Life as a working mother was totally different.

When she discovered she was entitled to staff discount on what she bought, she fitted Lucy out with a winter wardrobe. Zac's needs, she decided, would be largely met by what Lucy had outgrown. She bought herself a new mackintosh and some smart shoes to wear to work.

She found that the girls in the office were friendly. Most of them were smartly dressed and efficient. All were interested in boyfriends and clothes and going to concerts and theatres and having meals out and holidays. For Chloe, that was a world that had ceased to exist. Yes, she was tempted to be drawn back into it, but she knew she must not. She had responsibilities now. Two of them, as Aunt Goldie kept pointing out, and she had no alternative but to take care of them.

What she most wanted was a home of her own in which to bring up the children, but it was hardly practical at the moment. She needed Mum and Aunt Goldie to look after them, but perhaps one day, if she saved, it might be possible.

Chloe was sorry when the four months were up. She felt she'd coped adequately with the work. She was employable again and was promised a reference. She'd taken a big step forward and felt better about everything; she had more energy and was happier.

Being rejected by Adam had been a bitter and

painful experience that had left her feeling adrift, but she'd proved she could manage without him. She'd start looking for another job, a full-time one. She knew where she was going now. She was in control again.

Leo Hardman was lying on his bed studying the contents of Francis Clitheroe's file. He'd already done marvellously well out of it by applying for storecards in Clitheroe's name. He'd provided himself with all the clothes and personal possessions needed, but Clitheroe's bank would have been notified of his death quite quickly, so Leo could milk nothing more that way.

He drew out Clitheroe's security badge bearing the image of a smart professional middle class man. From the first moment Leo had seen it, he'd been sure he could make the fortune he'd always dreamed of by taking Clitheroe's identity. Over the last few months, it had become an obsession and he'd spent hours and hours searching for the right job to suit Clitheroe's qualifications and his own needs. At last he thought he'd seen it advertised, but before he could apply he needed a better address. No qualified accountant would live in a well-known inner-city slum as he did. A prospective employer might be put off before he even saw him, but moving house would cost money he didn't yet have. It came to him while he was having a smoke after Gary had gone off on one of his rounds that lodgings might provide the cheaper option.

He decided he'd go for lodgings that provided supper, bed and breakfast from Monday to Friday.

He'd live there in the week and tell the landlady his home was in the Isle of Man or somewhere miles away, and he'd had to move to Liverpool to get a job. He'd keep this bedsit on and come back at the weekends. The neighbours here would be unlikely to miss him during the week because he'd been working nights for months, and it would do him good to be able to unwind from being Francis.

Leo found what he wanted in Gateacre, a more prosperous part of the city, and was able to book lodgings for Francis to move into three weeks hence, at the beginning of next month. If he found a job, he need never mention he was in lodgings; the address was all he'd need to give.

The big advantage was that if he failed to get a job, he'd just cancel his lodgings and stay where he was. If he started work and something went wrong later on, he'd be able to ditch his new identity in a hurry, and have a safe getaway route already set up.

Another difficulty was that he didn't have Francis's original certificates of qualification. The copies he had looked as though they'd been made by the hotel. Any new employer would more than likely want to see the originals.

He could say he'd lost them. That he'd had a fire in his house... No, that was too obvious. He'd say he'd lived on a boat on the Thames for a while, that he'd had an accident, a collision and it had sunk. The river authority had lifted his boat because it was causing a hazard to other river traffic but everything he owned had been soaked and much of it ruined and somehow his papers had been lost in the mess and must have been thrown out.

He'd apologise and suggest his employer write to the Institute of Chartered Accountants in Moorgate, and ask them to confirm that his name was on their list. He could give the date and all the details because he had a copy. That should do the trick.

Leo had made up his mind. He was keyed up and full of hope as he applied in the name of Francis Clitheroe to five different companies advertising for an accountant. He knew one would suit his purpose better than others, but it depended whether they'd take him on.

Leo waited impatiently for the best part of a week before he went round to the lodging house to see if he'd had any response to his letters of application. As an excuse, he took a suitcase full of his less important belongings and asked the landlady if she would store it for him. She handed him two letters that had come for him.

He couldn't get out quickly enough to read them. One invited him for an interview tomorrow morning at ten thirty. He felt his stomach begin to churn; it was what he'd aimed for and hoped for, but it left him feeling shocked. And he'd only just collected the letter in time!

The company was called Bristow's Pet Foods Limited. A family firm, based in Bootle. He immediately caught a bus to Bootle and went to look at the place.

It seemed quite a big building, old and of smoke-blackened brick. It was busy; there were vans pulling into the yard behind with the firm's name emblazoned on their sides. It made him feel quite heady to think of what he was about to do.

He went home and went to bed to work out exactly what he was going to tell Bristow's tomorrow. He felt exhausted, and as he was used to sleeping for much of the day, he drifted off before he'd decided anything, but woke up at four o'clock with a clear mind.

The next step loomed. He couldn't see any firm taking Francis on without a reference from a previous employer. He thought of writing an open To Whom it May Concern type letter, but that was old-fashioned now, especially for a professional man.

He got out Francis's file and studied it again. He'd heard nothing at work about it being missing, but it was likely the office staff were being blamed. The hotel had required two references from Francis when he'd gone to work for them. One was a character reference from a vicar who'd thought very highly of him, and the other was from the insurance company in London where Francis had been employed for nine years. That was written in glowing terms too, but both were addressed to the manager of the Exchange Hotel.

Francis had been working there for only a few months. Leo wondered if it would be feasible to ask the insurance company to send another letter of reference to Bristow's Pet Foods, saying the hotel job hadn't worked out and he'd changed his employer. But Francis didn't seem the type to flit from job to job, and after nine years with the insurance company he might have made friends there who knew of his death. Leo decided that would be too risky. He must give the matter more thought.

The best he could come up with was to provide copies of the references in Francis's file, addressed to Bristow's Pet Foods and with the right date. But Bristow's had asked him to bring the names and addresses of his referees with him when he came for interview. That was the first hurdle he'd have to face.

For Francis's most recent place of employment, he chose a well-known insurance company with branches in London. Leo had once worked as a lowly clerk in a Liverpool insurance office and felt that gave him a little background knowledge of the industry, which might be an advantage if he was questioned about it.

He drafted out the name and address of a fictitious clergyman living in Chester to provide a character reference. That was the best he could do, though he knew it was his weakest link and if he made a hash of getting references it could kill off the whole plan.

Evening came and he got up and went to work. He spent many of the night hours wondering what would happen to the requests for references if the person they were addressed to had never heard of Francis Clitheroe. They could write back and say so, or they might just ignore it. Ignoring it would be fine, but the other option would result in disaster for him.

In the early hours of the morning, he took a shower and washed his hair. The facilities were better at the hotel than those he had at home. He raided the hotel fridge and helped himself to some sausage and black pudding to take home; he'd need to set himself up with a substantial breakfast today.

When the day staff came on, Leo hurried home feeling exhilarated and on top of his form. He kept his mind focused on what was to come as he prepared himself. He ate his breakfast, then packed his new briefcase with what he thought he might need before getting changed into his pale grey suit for his interview. He must be on his toes, ready to take any opportunity that came up.

Chloe thought she'd enjoy a week or two at home with the children. It would be a rest and a change. This time she gave some thought as to where she'd like to work, because she wanted a permanent job. The department store had been lovely; she'd like something similar, or a job in one of the city-centre hotels. She answered three advertisements, and was invited for one interview, though she didn't get the job.

Her enforced rest was dragging on longer than she'd expected, and Aunt Goldie seemed to resent not having full charge of the children in the mornings. Chloe felt a pang when she saw Zac turn to Goldie for comfort after a fall, but told herself it was only natural. She saw that Goldie's strict, no-nonsense attitude was doing them no harm and was good for discipline.

She continued looking for a job, but felt at a loose end. At this time of the year, it was cold out in the garden, but she helped Rex dig over the vegetable plot and decide what should be planted for spring. When her mother arranged to meet Joan in town again for lunch, Chloe was persuaded to go with her.

Joan was bubbling over. 'At last Walter thinks he might have found an accountant to take over from Tom.'

'That'll be a weight off his mind,' Helen said.

'Yes, though nothing's decided yet. Judging from his application, Walter thinks he could suit. This is a young man, and Walter says he should have more energy than Tom. He's coming for an interview tomorrow.'

Leo set off in plenty of time, not wanting to feel rushed, but he was on tenterhooks as he entered Bristow's premises. Walter Bristow towered over him, a large and gentle-looking man with a handclasp like that of a bear. Leo thought him friendly and old-fashioned. He explained how he'd started the business twenty-five years ago, how he'd trained as a vet and suspected that many of the sick animals he treated had been overfed on the wrong food. That had led him to formulate what he considered to be an ideal diet for each species.

Leo found the questions polite and courteous but none the less deeply searching. He felt wide awake and very much alert. He answered each one as fully as he dared, putting in authentic details when he was asked about his duties in the insurance company; he thought he acquitted himself well. After half an hour or so, Mr Bristow said he'd take him on a tour of the offices. Leo was glad to move; he felt stiff with tension.

He'd noticed as he'd gone through that five

257

women occupied the large room adjoining the boss's office.

'This is Mrs Parks,' Bristow told him, 'our accounts clerk.' A stout middle-aged woman had been deftly working a comptometer; now she smiled up at him. Leo froze. She could prove to be a danger; he'd not appreciated there could be clerks working on the same accounts.

Then he was being introduced to the four secretaries. Leo missed the names of the first two, but registered that Bristow's secretary was called Miss Gibbs.

'Miss Tomlin is designated as your secretary, but I encourage them all to be flexible and share the work out.'

Leo tried to smile and appear amiable. All four were quite attractive girls, but the last thing he needed was to make friends here in the office. He must keep his distance from everybody.

Next he found himself following Mr Bristow down a corridor to meet the retiring accountant, Mr Cleary, who was elderly and courteous too.

'Have a seat,' he said. 'Make yourself comfortable.'

Leo took in that the second-floor office, though small, was comfortable and private; it had a big window looking out on to a busy street. This would be his office if he were hired.

'Tom will explain what the duties of our company accountant are,' Bristow said, and left.

Tom Cleary was pedantic and explained the accounting set-up at length. Leo concentrated hard on everything he was being told. He'd make notes on this when he got home. He might be glad of the information. Mr Cleary took him back to the boss's office after that, where the generous salary and other benefits that could be his were set out for him.

Walter Bristow's eyes were watching him closely from the other side of his desk. Leo saw him push his shock of white hair back from his forehead and smile at him. 'I think you'll fit in here very well. I'd like you to take the job. What d'you say?'

Leo felt his heart jolt; he hadn't expected to be offered the job straight off. His head was whirling. He accepted with great enthusiasm, almost losing the clamp of control on his tongue, but it was probably a good idea to be keen at this stage.

'Subject to medical examination and references being satisfactory, of course.'

The word 'references' brought him down to earth and sent a cold shiver down his spine. But he'd thought this through and was fishing in his briefcase to find the paper on which he'd written the names and addresses. Bristow perused it and then buzzed for Miss Gibbs to come in.

'Write the usual notes asking for a reference,' he told the girl. 'As you did for the cleaner we took on last week.' Leo dictated the addresses to her.

Bristow then turned to him. 'Mr Clitheroe, we'd like you to start work as soon as possible. Do you have time to see our doctor today for a medical examination?'

The appointment was made for him to visit the doctor straight away. 'Come back afterwards and I'll show you round our factory,' Bristow added.

'We close for lunch between one and two.'

Leo was glad to get out into the fresh air. Despite the coffee he'd been given, his mouth was bone dry. He'd been on his guard for hours and felt drained, but now he could relax a little. For the moment there was no need for him to hang on to every word he heard; he had no worries about his health.

He'd been directed to the doctor's surgery, which was only a few hundred yards away, and was seen without having to wait. He felt tired when he came out, and headed straight to a café he'd noticed on the corner. It was busy and noisy, but perhaps that was just as well, because more than anything else, he felt in need of sleep. He ate a hot dinner and drank two more cups of coffee. It was the worry about his references that kept him awake.

He was pleased and surprised that Bristow's wanted him to start work as soon as possible. It seemed that Tom Cleary had a trip to New Zealand planned and was anxious to start handing over to his successor as soon as possible. That had speeded up the process, but it would all come to naught if there was a hiccup over Francis's references.

Leo tried to put his mind to what would happen next. Was there anything he could do about the references now? He made sure he was back in the office a few moments before two o'clock. The front door was closed and he had to ring the bell, but a clerk let him in. He found his way back to the secretaries' office, where all four desks were deserted. He was about to search through Miss Gibbs's out-tray, but he saw that Walter Bristow's door was ajar and he was at his desk. He tapped, pushed it wide and went in.

Leo didn't know how he stayed alert and attentive that afternoon. He was introduced to the production manager, John Walsh, who took him round the dusty factory, clanging and pounding with machinery. Walsh carefully explained every operation they were carrying out. It was a busy place and Leo had a blinding headache when at four o'clock he finally escaped and went back to Mr Bristow's office to finalise things.

The secretaries' office was deserted again and the door to Mr Bristow's room was firmly shut. Leo flicked through the contents of Miss Gibbs's out-tray. There were some dozen sealed and stamped envelopes ready to be posted. With shaking fingers he picked out the two with the addresses he'd given for referees and slid them into his briefcase. The rest he put back exactly as he'd found them.

When he knocked on the boss's door, he found Miss Gibbs was taking dictation. Mr Bristow stopped to shake Leo's hand and tell him he was pleased to welcome him to the staff. It was agreed that he should start work on the first of next month, which was only three days off.

Leo was glad to get out into the street. His head felt as though it was bursting. He was a nervous wreck but at the same time ecstatic with triumph. He'd achieved what he'd wanted, it was all fitting together nicely. He could write his own reference letters now.

He went home and fell into bed. He'd need to go to work tonight to copy out Francis's references. He had no suitable notepaper at home, and although he'd provided himself with a portable typewriter on one of the storecards, he'd never tried to use it. Also, he'd give the hotel his notice, saying that his mother was desperately ill, and that he'd have to go home to the Isle of Man to look after her.

He hoped he'd also have time to make some notes about what had passed between him and Cleary on accounting procedures. He was so weary that night, he could hardly move himself to hand out the occasional room key or take a plate of sandwiches up to a room. Nevertheless, when Gary settled down for his nap, he went to the main office. There were several typewriters, each covered for the night with a plastic cover, and he sat down in front of one of them. He had to force the lock on the stationery cupboard to get some blank notepaper and a couple of envelopes before he could start.

He'd never tried to type before and it was harder to produce a fault-free copy than he'd thought. He spoiled many sheets and had to return to the cupboard for more paper. He usually looked forward to the time when he was due to wake Gary, but tonight it came before he was ready. He had only one letter copied to his satisfaction, which meant he'd have to come to work again tomorrow night. He helped himself to more notepaper and took all the sheets he'd spoiled home to destroy.

His head was clearer the following night because he'd slept all day, but it still took him an age to copy the vicar's letter without making a mistake. Now he had everything ready to move into his new job, he could leave this one. The only good thing about it had been the lovely food he could help himself to. He'd had more than his fill of night work.

CHAPTER EIGHTEEN

For the first few days at work, Leo felt a nervous wreck, because Tom Cleary was there beside him watching everything he did. It took him some time to see that Tom's mind was on taking him step by step through the files, cash books and ledgers he kept. There were a vast number; storage for them took up a lot of space in his office.

Cleary opened books and spread documents in front of him and his explanations came at a bewildering pace. Leo asked questions but not as many as he would have liked; he was afraid of revealing how little he knew. He blessed the time he'd worked as a bookkeeper. At least he knew what double-entry bookkeeping was, and some of the terms sounded vaguely familiar. Cleary was assuming he understood more than he did.

Leo was seeing quite a lot of Mrs Parks, the accounts clerk. It put the wind up him to see her being handed figures to collate. It was something he'd have to do soon. Cleary assured him she was very efficient, but that did nothing to settle his nerves. She would be in a better position than anybody else to monitor what he was doing.

He kept a notebook and wrote down what seemed to be important facts in front of Cleary, it didn't matter that he looked over-careful. Though he mustn't be seen to be recording facts that any accountant would regard as mundane.

There was a little send-off in the office for Tom Cleary. The staff had collected to buy him a clock. Leo felt everybody was friendly and welcoming towards him; nobody seemed to have any suspicions. Mr Bristow was hosting another celebration that evening for the senior staff, who were invited together with their ladies to a farewell dinner. Leo was relieved to find he was left out of that.

In the first few days after Tom Cleary left, Mrs Parks pointed Leo towards the routine work that needed to be done. Leo felt he was floundering; he was more scared of her than he'd been of Cleary, because she'd be staying. It was a comfort to know he could get out of all this and disappear if he had to, and a further comfort to know how he could take payment for all the effort he was putting in.

He was thankful that his office was private and nobody could see what he was doing once he had the door shut. He was spending a lot of time dithering, which might seem odd behaviour to other staff.

The bills were flooding in and the method of paying them was clear enough. It gave him a job to get on with. Mrs Parks kept the wages book and drew up the figures for those who were paid weekly. Leo found that it was his job to check her figures and also pay the more senior staff their monthly salaries. He was amazed at how much everybody earned when he compared it with what he'd scraped by on in his lowly jobs.

He set up a new bank account in the name of Francis Clitheroe, into which he meant to pay his salary in due course, but in order to maintain a safe distance he opened another account in a different bank in the name of Alistair Jackson. It was his job to make out the cheques, and only those over two and a half thousand pounds had to be countersigned by Mr Bristow. The regular bills for supplies fell comfortably below this threshold.

He studied the figures in the company's bank accounts and realised he was working for a very profitable company. He made up his mind that he'd spend the first week or so finding his feet and earning Mr Bristow's trust. He got out the collated figures for the previous year, found the exact week and knew he had to produce figures that were very similar.

He went back to his digs every night, and with the other lodgers ate his high tea of meat and two veg, followed by a pudding. He then retired to his room to write up all sorts of details while they were still fresh in his mind. This notebook was one he wouldn't take to the office. He had to be ultra-careful.

At nine thirty a jug of cocoa and a plate of biscuits was put on the dining room table. After partaking of that, he went to bed early to ponder on what he could do to get the best return for all this effort.

It was easy enough to take money out of the company accounts – part of his job was doing just that. Hiding the fact from old Bristow and Mrs Parks was the difficulty.

He thought about making out a cheque for just under two and a half thousand pounds to Alistair Jackson at the beginning of the month, then moving it out of that account as soon as he could and making a run for it. But what he did next would be traceable through bank records, unless he drew it all out in cash. He'd already noticed in the small print of their literature that banks required prior notice if a client wanted to withdraw a large sum, and that would give them time to check back and find out it was fraud.

Also, he'd been hoping for more money than that. He realised that what he'd set up was a long-term drip-drip way to take the money, not a grab-it-quick job. But he wouldn't be staying any longer than necessary; it was too nerve-racking. His plan now was to hang on here for as long as possible, hopefully at least six months, and drain off as much as he could. He wanted to get enough out of this to buy himself a cottage somewhere quiet, and perhaps a car.

Joan was very interested in Helen's garden and came round to see it every few weeks. Chloe enjoyed her company and was pleased when Mum told her she'd be coming the next day. She spent the morning baking scones and a chocolate cake, and decided she'd put on afternoon tea in style, as she used to in Adam's house. Mum had a silver tea service she displayed in a cabinet in the dining room but never used. Chloe took it out and got it ready.

Auntie Joan had no children of her own, although she said she wished she'd been married soon enough to have them. She and Uncle Walter had married late in life; until then, she'd taught history at Blackburn House, a notable Liverpool grammar school for girls. Mum thought Joan had achieved more in her life than she had herself.

Joan arrived with a picture book of fairy stories for Lucy and a cloth book for Zac. Chloe admired her discreet make-up and thought she looked really elegant.

'I'm sure you must have found it hard to go to work and leave your two babies,' she said to Chloe. 'They're very sweet.'

Chloe pulled a rueful face. 'I did find it hard to start with, but it was a temporary job and it's over now. I managed fine; Aunt Goldie looked after the children.'

'She's looking much better. Seems more cheerful, too.'

'She enjoys taking care of the kids. I think she wants to be needed, but doesn't like to admit it.'

'She's good with them.'

'Yes, I feel they're safe with her. I loved going to work,' Chloe said, 'and to be honest, I need the money. I'm looking for another job, but there's a general slowing down in the economy and I've not had much success so far.'

That brought Auntie Joan's blue eyes to meet hers. 'Walter's finally found an accountant, but now he's looking for a replacement for his secretary. She's getting married and going to live in Portsmouth. That's your sort of work, isn't it?'

Chloe was ready to reach out for any job now. 'It is my sort of work,' she said. 'But I'm afraid Uncle Walter will think I don't have enough experience to be his secretary. I can do shorthand and typing, but my jobs have been mostly working with figures. They always put me in the accounts department.'

'Well, Walter has an accounts department too. Why don't you write him an official application for a job? I'm sure he'll be glad to fit you in if he can. I'll tell him about you tonight. It can't do any harm, can it?'

'Thank you,' Chloe said. 'I'd appreciate it if you would.'

Auntie Joan praised Chloe's cake. 'And the elegant way you serve afternoon tea. Your mother does it very nicely too, but I don't get the best china and the silver with her.'

Helen laughed. 'You know you get the everyday cups and saucers.'

Joan lay back in her garden chair. 'I love your summerhouse, it's perfect on a day like today.'

'We use it even in cool weather,' Marigold told her. 'It stops the children making a mess in the house.'

Rex joined them, and he and Auntie Joan discussed Britain's ongoing financial problems arising from the low amount of exports and the huge bill for goods being imported. 'Walter is very concerned,' she told him. 'The country can't pay its way.'

Afterwards, they all took Joan on a tour of the garden. Rex dug up a root of heather she'd admired for her own garden, and gave her some of the bedding plants he'd grown from seed to put in her patio pots.

Chloe felt very much more hopeful as she waved Auntie Joan off.

'Walter can promote one of his more experienced girls to be his secretary,' Marigold said as they watched Joan's car go down the road, 'and find you something within your capabilities, a slot in the typing pool or something like that.'

Chloe sat down immediately and wrote the letter to Uncle Walter that Joan had suggested. A few days later, she received his reply on official company notepaper, inviting her to come along to see him in his office to talk about her application.

Chloe felt nervous as she went up the steps into the entrance hall at Bristow's. It was silent and deserted. She saw a notice on the desk inviting visitors to ring for attention, but just then a young girl with red hair came scurrying through with a pile of files in her arms, so she asked her the way to Mr Bristow's office.

'I'll take you up in a moment,' the girl said. 'I'm Angela Smith, the office junior. I just want to drop these files into the sales department first.'

Within moments Chloe was being escorted through corridors to a large office containing four desks with secretaries seated behind typewriters. Only the clatter of typewriter keys disturbed the silence.

'This is Mr Bristow's secretary,' her guide waved towards one of the desks, 'Maureen Gibbs,' then she went to sit down in her own place.

Miss Gibbs was a little older and more sophisticated. Chloe was impressed when she said, 'Are you Miss Redwood? Mr Bristow's expecting you,' and buzzed through to tell him she was here. It seemed his office opened off this one. He came to the door.

'Do come in, Chloe.' He stepped forward to meet her. 'Would you like a cup of coffee?'

'That would be very nice.' His secretary was asked to arrange it, and Chloe relaxed. 'It's good of you to see me like this,' she said.

He closed the door and went back to his chair behind a large partner's desk. Chloe had called him Uncle Walter since she was a child and had seen him regularly at family get-togethers, though she saw more of Auntie Joan while he was at work. His silvery hair was still thick and heavy and his gaze kindly.

'So you want a job?' he said. 'I think we'll be able to fit you in somewhere.' His office was large and light, with two large windows. 'Have a seat. How are your two babies?' She found herself telling him that Aunt Goldie was happy to look after them while she came to work.

'Helen tells me that your children have been Marigold's salvation,' he said. 'They've helped her get over her bereavement, settled her down.'

'Yes, she's better. It's as though she needs something to keep her busy, and the kids love her.'

'Well then, I shall find something to keep you busy too. We have four secretaries here as well as Mrs Parks, the accounts clerk. Miss Gibbs looks after me and Miss Tomlin, Lydia that is, works for the accountant. The sales manager and the buyer share Miss McDonald, and Angela Smith works for the production manager. She also floats and fills in where she's needed. Well, all the girls do, they're very good like that.'

He was studying her now across his desk. 'I remember you doing a secretarial course some years ago. Then you went to work for the civil service. Goodness, time passes so quickly. Tell me about the work you did there.'

'My previous jobs have been mostly book-keeping, but I can do office work of every sort.'

'Miss Gibbs will be with us for another fortnight. Why don't I ask her to show you what she does? Two weeks should give you time to pick it up, d'you think?'

'You're going to let me take her place?' Chloe was astounded. 'She has the top secretarial job here.'

'Yes, you could manage that, couldn't you?'

'Yes,' she said with as much confidence as she could muster. 'Yes, I've got my shorthand and typing speeds up by doing the temporary job at Owen Owens.'

'The other girls will help you until you find your feet.'

'It's just that I'm more used to working with figures.'

'Chloe, if you have two children to support,' his manner was paternalistic, 'you need a job that pays a reasonable salary. I understand that child-ren can be very expensive.'

'They can.'

'Let's do that then, and see how you get on. You

agree? If you find it too much, I could promote Miss McDonald and give you her job.'

'No, I'd like to try working for you.'

'Good.'

'You're very kind to me, Uncle Walter.' Chloe could feel tears scalding her eyes. 'I'll do my very best.'

Maureen Gibbs came in then with the coffee. Chloe was relaxed enough to look at her now and found that she was pretty and not much older than she was. It made her feel she'd be able to do her job.

Uncle Walter took her round the offices and introduced her to the staff. She knew she wouldn't remember all their names; there were just too many at once. He said, 'I'm afraid the accountant, Francis Clitheroe, is not in this afternoon, so you won't see him until Monday.'

Then he showed her round his factory, and Chloe was captivated. He pointed out the mounds of barley, wheat and maize waiting to be crushed, the dried meat, the linseed oil, the brewer's grains, the yeast and the fish meal that was used in cat food. She was introduced to John Walsh, the production manager, who explained how the various recipes were made up and vitamins and minerals added. He took her through the drying rooms, where she saw the chopped meat, fish and vegetables being prepared; then on to the packing department, where the colourful labels were being attached to the different packages, showing whether it was intended to feed hamsters and guinea pigs or cats and dogs. It was a busy place.

When she was leaving, she said, 'Thank you, Uncle Walter, for giving me this chance. I'm very grateful.'

'Monday, then,' he said. 'Nine till five. I'll put it all in writing for you, as I do for other employees.'

'Yes. Is it all right for me to go on calling you Uncle Walter?'

He pondered for a moment. 'Perhaps Mr Bristow would be better while we're here.' His smile was both broad and friendly, and she wanted to kiss his cheek as she did when she visited his home.

Monday morning was very wet. Rain was splattering against the windows as Chloe tried to dress both Lucy and herself. She needed to look her best for her first day at work, because Miss Gibbs and the other girls she'd seen working there had looked very smart. She piled her fair hair up into a large bun on top of her head. It was a style Mum thought suited her very well.

'Shall I run you over to Bootle in the car?' Helen offered as they ate breakfast. 'You'll get wet through in this.'

'No thanks, Mum. I give you enough trouble as it is, and I've got to get used to going on the bus.'

'Take my umbrella, then, it's a big one. You'll need it if you have to wait at the bus stop.'

Chloe wore her new mackintosh and carried her new shoes in a bag. She was glad of the large umbrella, though it was heavy and she could hardly see where she was going. The bus was all steamed up inside, and when she got out, the rain was coming down in sheets. She joined the steady stream of workers hurrying along the street to their offices.

She'd only been once to this part of town and almost missed the entrance. At the last moment she veered across the pavement towards it, closing her umbrella. She heard an involuntary gasp of distress, and once she was in the dry she turned to find the cause.

'I'm sorry,' she faltered. She could see that she'd doused the office worker following her with rainwater off her umbrella.

He followed her inside the entrance. 'I took that full in the face,' he told her, mopping at it with his handkerchief.

'I'm so sorry.' She knew exactly what she'd done. She'd half closed her umbrella and then flipped it open and shut it quickly in order to shake the rain off. It was what she always did. 'I didn't realise there was anyone close enough ...'

He'd taken off his spectacles and was drying them too. 'It's all right, no real harm done.' He replaced them, shook the rain off his hat and half smiled at her. 'I haven't seen you before, have I? Do you work here?'

'As of today.'

'Just starting? A secretary?'

Chloe felt that his heavy glasses screened his face and she had to look twice to see anything more of it. He looked polished, as though he spent a lot of time and energy turning himself out smartly.

'Yes,' she said. 'Where will I find the ladies' cloakroom?'

'Oh, we've just passed it, sorry.' He retraced his

274

steps to point it out.

Inside, Chloe met up with Miss Gibbs. 'I'm Maureen,' the older woman said as she showed Chloe where she could leave her wet clothes. Then she led the way to the office she shared with the other secretaries and introduced her. 'Everybody, this is Chloe Redwood, who's to take over my job.'

They all smiled and said hello. 'This is Lydia Tomlin, she works for the accountant, and this is Clarice, Mrs Parks, our accounts clerk.' Both women were already hard at work.

'We have a new accountant.' Mrs Parks smiled. 'He's reviewing everything and wants all our duties listed. He's working us to the bone.'

'This is Rosemary McDonald.' She was dark and slender. 'She's shared between the sales manager and the buyer. And this is...'

'Angela Smith,' Chloe said, nodding at the young redhead. 'I met Angela the day I came for interview.'

'She works for the production manager.' Maureen Gibbs pulled a spare typewriter from a cupboard and set it up on a table. 'You can work here until I go. It's not the best of typewriters, I'm afraid, but it does work.'

'I hope I'll remember all your names and what you do.' Chloe was struggling to smile and look at ease.

They were all trying to explain the set-up to her when Chloe heard a buzzer. 'That's Mr Clitheroe, the accountant,' Maureen Gibbs said. 'It means he wants something. He probably has letters to dictate.'

'Oh lord!' his secretary groaned. 'He never stops.'

'Today there's help at hand.' Maureen Gibbs went hastily to the cupboard again and pushed a new shorthand pad and a couple of pencils into Chloe's hands. 'We all muck in together here, and Mr Clitheroe is a good place for you to start. His letters are all short and to the point. Is that all right?'

'Yes, fine.'

'Oh, and Mr Bristow said I'm to be sure to introduce you, as he wasn't in when you came on Friday.'

Chloe took a deep breath. This would be a nervous moment for anyone starting a new job. She had to prove she could do it.

'This building is a bit of a warren,' Maureen Gibbs said over her shoulder as they climbed stairs and hurried along dark corridors. 'I hope you'll be able to find your way back to us.'

Chloe tried to concentrate on where she was being taken. Miss Gibbs threw open a door and ushered her inside.

'Mr Francis Clitheroe,' she said, and then turned to him, 'this is Miss Redwood, who will be taking my place when I go.'

Chloe raised her eyes to meet those of the man she'd recently doused with water. He was staring at her. She couldn't stifle her groan of dismay, but she managed to move forward to shake the hand he offered. Maureen had things to tell him, and when she took her leave, it seemed he was ready to dictate. In a daze Chloe sat down on the chair he waved her to, opened the pad on the first

276

page and grasped one of the pencils. Her hand was shaking. She felt she'd got off on the wrong foot.

Concentrate, she told herself sternly. You've got to get the shorthand right. You've got to produce clean and accurate letters for him, you mustn't give him any reason to complain about your work. He must already think you're a clumsy fool.

When the office door closed behind Chloe, Leo took a deep breath and leaned back in his executive leather chair. He'd made up his mind before taking up this job and becoming Francis Clitheroe that he'd form no close relationships with the staff; it wouldn't be safe.

Until today he'd taken no interest in the girls, but Chloe Redwood was different. She seemed diffident; she'd looked at him shyly through her long lashes. She was a stunner and might be just his type. But he'd heard she was related to the boss, so he needed to stay well away from her.

He'd turned down the offer of going for a drink after work with the sales manager, Alan Bryant, pleading that he had other things he had to do, which was true. But he'd been unable to avoid walking to a local café at lunchtime with John Walsh, the production manager, to have a bowl of soup and a sandwich.

To his dismay, he'd found the other managers collected at a large table there. They didn't all go every day, but there was always some of the staff there. Leo was running out of excuses to avoid going, but he couldn't let it develop into a regular habit. He found it very hard work, keeping his ears open and a close watch on his tongue at the same time. It suited him better to go for a walk on his own and buy something to eat, or slip into some other café. He needed to switch off in his lunch hour.

He felt as though he'd been walking on eggshells since he'd started the job. He could never relax and let himself go. He'd had to keep his nerves on a tight rein; he was senior staff and had to show calm confidence at all times, even if he was dithering inside. He studied every letter addressed to the accountant, and thought through every reply before he dictated it. He went back to his lodging promptly at five o'clock to study accountancy in all its forms, but most of all the accounts of the previous year put together by Tom Cleary.

One of the first things Cleary had told him was that the company's financial year had ended in December and that the accounts had been audited then. He saw that as a blessing. It gave him time to put his plans into action and be well away before the current year ended.

Leo felt cock-a-hoop. He'd managed the hard part; now he could concentrate on the fun part. He'd been working out how he could shift some of the company's money into his own account, and now was the time to start doing it.

CHAPTER NINETEEN

During the days that followed, Chloe settled in. She found the other girls welcoming and friendly; Lydia Tomlin never stopped talking. 'I'm not keen on our new accountant,' she told everybody. Chloe could see that he wasn't popular with the other girls.

Only Clarice Parks said, 'He's only been working here for a short time, he hasn't found his feet yet.'

'He's cold and stand-offish,' Lydia said. 'I've tried to be friendly but I'm wasting my time.'

'He's like a fish out of water,' little red-haired Angela Smith said. 'I don't think he knows what he's doing.'

'He gives me the collywobbles.' Rosemary McDonald was taller than he was. 'He looks at me as though he's afraid I'll bite him.'

Chloe understood that; he made her feel uncomfortable too. Whenever she was with him, she could feel his dark eyes behind their heavy spectacles following every movement she made.

Uncle Walter said that he was very pleased with him; he worked hard and had taken to studying the accounts from previous years so he could get to know the business thoroughly.

Chloe, however, thought him dour. He conformed to what she thought a senior accountant should look like. He was not much more than her own height, and lightly built. His dark hair was neatly brushed back, his face was narrow and his forehead high. His heavy glasses seemed his most noticeable feature. He wore suits by Daks – her days at Owen Owens enabled her to distinguish between brands – smart shirts and always a silk tie and polished shoes.

One day he asked for somebody to take his letters when Lydia was down in the factory working for the production manager, so once again Chloe went along.

He had ready a heap of files on his desk. Opening them one by one, he dictated short letters in a flat, expressionless voice, then built another pile of files for her to take away with her. She was delighted to find she had no trouble keeping up with him.

When he'd finished, he pushed the files across his desk to Chloe. As she scooped them up in her arms, she heard something drop to the floor. She stooped to pick up a silver propelling pencil and couldn't help but notice the initials LH engraved on it.

'Is this yours?'

'Yes.'

'Very nice,' she said, putting it back on his desk. His reaction surprised her; his thin face had gone white and stiff, and suddenly she could feel his tension. He was positively radiating it.

'A special pencil?'

'Very special.' Mr Clitheroe was recovering. 'It belonged to a friend of mine.' Chloe thought him rather a strange person.

Uncle Walter dictated fewer but longer and more

complicated letters, but she had no difficulty with them, as he stopped to think and spoke more slowly. He was paternalistic to all the staff and they couldn't do enough for him. Chloe was trying to see him not only as her uncle but also as her boss. She thought that once she'd settled in and got to know what was expected of her, she'd be able to relax and be happy here.

Maureen Gibbs left, and Chloe heard a full report of her wedding from other members of staff. They each received a sliver of her wedding cake. Gradually Chloe was getting to know the people she worked with and picking up facts about them. Rosemary had a boyfriend who worked in the sales department. Lydia was engaged to a chemist. There was an undertow of gossip, of affairs between different members of staff, and on the whole they all got along in harmony.

Chloe began to enjoy their company and her busier days. She felt in control again, and that she could put her bad times behind her.

A few weeks later, Rex said to Helen as she brought two mugs of tea to a seat in the garden, 'Chloe's settled down, she seems happier.'

'Yes, and so does Marigold. She was absolutely awful when she first came, and then when Chloe had to come home with her two I thought I'd made a big mistake and there'd be no peace for any of us.'

'But it's all worked out,' Rex said. 'You've settled down very nicely together.'

'It's the tranquillity of this garden.' Helen sighed with pleasure and listened to a thrush singing in the oak tree behind them.

'I think Marigold is happier because she now has some purpose in life.'

'Who would have thought she'd take over responsibility for the kids like this?' Helen asked. 'She's quite strict with them, and they're good for her. Chloe was notified that Zac was due for vaccination, so she's taken them to the clinic this afternoon. Goldie was used to looking after Gran, and now they've taken her place.'

'But it's changed our lives,' Rex said gently. 'I can't have you to myself any more.'

'I know, we're both missing out. I can't have you to spend the night with me.'

'But that's why I bought Newburn Cottage. So you could come to me.'

Helen put both hands to her face. 'I feel a bit embarrassed about doing that. I tell them you've asked me out for dinner.'

'Well usually I have, even if we eat at my house. You come for a few hours, but you never stay overnight with me. I miss that.'

'So do I.' There was a real weight of feeling in her voice. 'But Marigold has a sharp tongue. There'd be no hiding it from her if I stayed out all night.'

She was looking up at him half dazzled by the sun. Rex felt a sudden surge of pure love for her sweep through him; it knocked him off balance. But why should it surprise him? He'd been making love to her regularly, it was impossible not to be drawn closer and closer to her. Helen was a warm and loving person; he knew her through and through and he didn't want to be separated from her in this way.

'We're allowed to live as we please too,' he said with a catch in his voice. 'I love you, Helen. I want us to be together.' He felt for her hand; she moved closer and rested her head against his shoulder. For years he'd been thinking of her as a friend, but what he felt for her went much deeper than friendship. It had grown slowly and steadily; he did truly love her.

'Why don't I book a table somewhere nice and then you can come back with me for the night?' His voice shook. 'Couldn't you say to Marigold, I might be late tonight, or I might not come back at all, and then walk straight out before she or Chloe can say anything? It would be kinder that way, wouldn't it? They won't be worried if they find your bed hasn't been slept in.'

She smiled, 'You think of everybody's feelings, Rex.'

He wanted to spend the rest of his life with her. 'Helen, love...' he was about to propose marriage. It was on the tip of his tongue but he felt her pulling away from him. He looked up to see Lucy heading across the grass to them, followed by Marigold with Zac in her arms.

'I'll do it,' she said quickly. 'I'll stay overnight.'

That evening, Rex watched Helen's car pull into his drive. He could see her triumphant mood as she came striding to his door, swinging her overnight bag.

'I've done it,' she giggled. 'I've burned my boats. Why should I let my family stop me doing what I want?'

'You shouldn't. You bend over backwards to do your best for them.'

'You should have seen Marigold's face! It was a picture.'

Rex had booked a table at a new nightclub in town called the Red Balloon. It was quite dark and had an intimate atmosphere. The music wasn't loud, but it had a beat that throbbed and there was a small dance floor. He ordered a bottle of champagne. Everything was going their way at the moment; they were in high spirits and they had reason to celebrate.

The floor show started as their first course came to the table. The food was excellent and dancing began again as they finished their chocolate mousse. They took their time over everything and were quite late going home.

Rex knew that Helen was as happy and relaxed as he was. He kissed her as he closed the front door behind them, then hung their coats up downstairs and took her by the hand to lead her to his bedroom. She'd been here many times over the last months, but as she always wanted to be home by midnight, they never seemed to have enough time. He always drove her home afterwards, which meant he couldn't relax with her in his arms. Tonight he was looking forward to that.

Helen was unbuttoning his shirt; she knew how to get him in the right mood. 'It doesn't matter what Marigold thinks,' he whispered.

'Or Chloe,' she said, putting up her lips for a kiss. He pulled her into a close hug to push the image of Chloe out of his mind. Tonight he only had thoughts for Helen.

He slipped her blouse off her shoulders. 'You've got a lovely figure, something to be proud of.' He reached both arms round her to unclip her bra. She had a slim waist, a flat tummy, and she'd not put on much weight over the years.

He was running his fingers over her soft body, trying to give her the same joy she gave him. He stroked her nipple and felt her sensuous flesh beneath his fingers, heard her sigh of pleasure. He stopped abruptly. Something felt wrong.

'What is it?' she murmured in his ear.

He put his head down on her breast. Surely it couldn't be? He needed to unwind, to think calmly about this. But Helen wouldn't let him. She was nuzzling against him, showing him she didn't want him to stop. He didn't need a second invitation. In the heat of that moment he forgot everything else. Helen knew how to make love.

In the warm aftermath they lay together silent and still. It was ten minutes later when he felt again gently down the side of her right breast, this time with no trace of passion.

She lifted his head. 'Is something the matter?'

'I don't know.' He took her hand and with it covered the same area round her breast and under her arm. 'Can you feel anything?'

She sat up with a jerk. 'A lump? Is it a lump?'

He felt again carefully. 'It feels lumpy, doesn't it? But it might not be of any importance.'

He couldn't see her in the darkness, but he knew that had changed everything. She put her arms round his neck and pulled him close. 'I'm frightened. It could be cancer. It's quite a big lump. Why haven't I felt it before? I never have.'

'Don't worry about it now. In the morning you must go to the doctor, see what he thinks.'

He knew she was shocked. He'd planned a night of indulgent bliss for them, but that lump had ruined his plans. He spent the rest of the night holding Helen in his arms, trying to stay her fears. Neither of them could sleep.

In the morning, she didn't want to get out of bed. 'I feel exhausted. I want to pull the blankets over my head and curl up here.'

'I'll run a bath for you while I shave,' Rex said.

He went downstairs to make breakfast for them, but she hardly ate anything. Her face looked drained and paper white. All the life had gone out of her, and she seemed to have no energy. He was afraid that if he went to work, she'd just sit here and do nothing about it.

He rang the surgery and spoke to Dr Harris, telling him that Helen had found a lump in her breast and was very anxious.

'Bring her in straight away,' he was told. 'I'll see her before I start morning surgery.'

'I'll have her there in about fifteen minutes,' he replied.

Helen was clinging to his hand with a grip that made him ache with sympathy. Fear was paralysing her; she didn't want him to leave her side. When the receptionist sent her in, he went with her. Dr Harris examined her first sitting and then lying on his examination couch.

'Is it cancer?' she asked. Rex heard the catch in her voice.

'Not necessarily,' the doctor replied, pushing his grey hair back from his greyish face, 'but we must have it investigated.'

'What will that entail?' Helen's eyes were wide pools of horror.

'I'll make an appointment for you to see a specialist. He'll want to examine you and probably to send a sliver from your lump to the laboratory; that will give us a diagnosis. Until we have that, we can't be sure. As I said, it might not be cancer. Many lumps I see turn out to be benign. You can get dressed now, Mrs Redwood, and don't worry.'

Dr Harris withdrew to his desk. Rex drew the curtains round Helen and followed him.

'She can't help but worry,' he said in a low voice. 'Could she see the specialist as soon as possible?'

'Yes, of course,' the doctor agreed, 'but it might take a week or so.'

'Would she get an earlier appointment if she went as a private patient?' Rex knew that waiting to find out would be hell for them all, and worse by far for Helen.

'Does she have insurance?'

'No, but I'll be happy to pay for it.'

'Right.' The doctor dropped his voice even further. 'But I have to say, it may not be necessary for you to do that. The need for urgency in this case will be recognised. She'll be seen as soon as possible.'

Rex's heart lurched and his voice was a whisper. 'What are you saying?'

The doctor was full of concern. 'I'm sorry, but I think you should be prepared for the worst.'

Rex had been holding his breath. Now he let it come out in an agonised gasp. 'I still want her to be seen privately,' he said.

As they walked out to his van, Helen said, 'What were you and Dr Harris talking about?'

Rex told her that he'd asked that she be treated privately. 'It might cut down the time you have to wait. We'll all be worried until we know.'

'You're very kind, Rex.'

He drove her back to Newburn Cottage. She'd left her car outside his front door and she needed to pick up her overnight bag. He knew she was having a little weep in the passenger seat of his van, but when they arrived she gave him a wry smile and seemed to have her tears under control.

'Cup of coffee?' he suggested, but she shook her head.

'You'll want to get off to work.'

'Are you all right to drive?'

'Of course,' she said, but she was covering her face with her hands. 'Thanks for coming with me.' She reached up to kiss his cheek. 'Thanks for everything.'

It seemed to Rex that after that, for Helen everything careered on at breakneck speed.

Helen knew that Chloe would have gone to work by this time. Marigold met her in the hall with Zac on her shoulder. Her attitude was aggressive; she looked as though she was spoiling for a fight. 'Where've you been?' she demanded. 'You stayed out all night.'

Helen couldn't cope with her anger. In a low, defeated voice she said, 'I found a lump in my breast. I'm worried.'

'You've got to go to the doctor.'

288

'Rex took me this morning.'

Marigold's shocked face stared back at her. 'Is it serious?'

'I'm afraid it might be, but I'll know better when I've seen a consultant.'

'Oh, Helen! How awful for you.' Zac was dumped on the carpet and Marigold's arms went round her. 'What terrible troubles we all have.'

Helen wasn't going to whine in the way Marigold always did. 'It might be a benign lump, we don't know yet.' She put on a brave face, but inside she was already bracing herself to face the worst.

Time hung heavily. Marigold could talk of nothing else, but she was full of sympathy. Chloe wept in her mother's arms when she came home and heard the news. Helen felt buoyed up by their affection.

The telephone rang. Chloe answered it, but it was for Helen. She thought it might be Rex to ask how she was. It was the secretary of a consultant offering her an appointment with him.

'Nine thirty the day after tomorrow? Can you make it that early?'

Helen thought she'd have no difficulty with that. She knew Rex would take her and that he'd ask her to spend the night before at Newburn Cottage with him.

When they saw the consultant he asked if Rex was her husband. 'As good as,' she said, smiling at Rex. 'My partner.'

The consultant, a rotund fellow with ruddy cheeks, looked grave as he examined her.

'I want you to come into hospital in two days'

time and I'll operate the following day,' he said. 'I want you to sign a form giving me permission to make a small incision just here.' Cold fingers circled round her lump. 'I'll take some sample slides and send them straight up to the laboratory for immediate diagnosis.

'You'll have a light anaesthetic for this, then if the lump turns out to be benign, you'll wake up in bed half an hour later and that will be that. If on the other hand the lump is invasive, you'll be given a deeper anaesthetic and I'll have to remove it.'

Helen felt she was hardly taking in what it entailed. 'A mastectomy?' she faltered. 'Is that what you call it?'

'Yes, it means taking away part of your breast.'

It was what she'd expected, but her mouth had gone dry. 'How much?'

'I'm afraid that depends on what I find. I won't take more than I have to, but cancer spreads, and if that's what it turns out to be, I'll need to take out every bit I can. I may also have to cut into your axilla, up here under your arm, to remove some of your lymph glands. It can spread up there too.'

Helen was appalled. She could hardly get the words out. 'Then I won't know when I'm being taken down to theatre whether I'll wake up whole or without my breast?' She had both hands on it, pressing it flat.

'Yes, I'm sorry, but this way you'll have less anaesthetic and there'll be less delay. It's the best way for you.'

Helen was stunned. Rex was feeling for her

hand. 'If the news is bad,' he whispered, 'the sooner it's done the better.'

'Yes.' She'd wanted it done quickly, but this had turned into a nightmare rush.

Rex found the hours of waiting unbelievably long and he knew the others did too. They all worried. Chloe said, 'Think how much worse it must be for Mum.'

He tried to take Helen for a walk, but her energy had suddenly gone. He suggested taking her out for a restaurant dinner, but she didn't want to go. Marigold said she was eating very little. Helen just wanted to lie on a lounger in her summer-house, and fortunately the weather was fine enough for that.

On the morning of the operation, Rex insisted that Chloe go to work as usual and he took Helen to the hospital.

'I'm praying he isn't going to take off all my breast,' she said as he was about to leave her. 'I won't feel a whole woman; you'll not want to sleep with me if he does.'

'I will,' Rex assured her. 'Don't you worry about that. It won't make the slightest difference to the way I feel about you. I love you, Helen.'

But he couldn't keep his mind on his work that day. He went home at lunchtime and stayed there. The consultant had said he'd telephone him when he'd finished operating. It was four o'clock when the call came.

'I'm very sorry to have to tell you,' he said, 'it was cancer, and more advanced than I'd expected. I've performed a radical mastectomy.' Rex felt rooted to the spot, unable to say anything. 'I'm afraid she'll need a course of radiation later, to make sure there's no further spread.'

'How is she?'

'Not fully round from the anaesthetic as yet, but the operation went as expected; she stood it well.'

'Can I come in and see her tonight?'

'Of course, if you wish, but she's had a lot of anaesthetic. She'll probably be drifting in and out of consciousness and won't be able to pay much attention to you. I'd advise you to leave visiting until tomorrow.'

'She will get better, won't she?'

There was a telling pause. 'I hope so. There's no reason why she shouldn't enjoy life again, but she'll need to take it easy for a time.'

Rex shuddered. This was horrific, far worse than he'd anticipated when he'd first felt Helen's lump. He rang Chloe at work to tell her, trying to sound more upbeat than he felt. Then he rang Marigold. He knew he'd destroyed their hopes. He threw himself down on his sofa in despair, but he was on his feet again a few minutes later. He felt like a caged lion. He went out to work in somebody else's garden and stayed cutting hedges until the light went and he could no longer see what he was doing.

It didn't get any better. The following day when Rex arrived to see her, Helen's face looked grey against her pillows. She seemed sluggish, inert and in pain. When Rex went in the day after that, he could see she'd been crying. She wept again when he tried to comfort her; she was upset to find just how radical her mastectomy had been. Her recovery was slow.

They were taking it in turns to visit her, so that she'd not have too many hours alone in her private room. To start with they didn't stay long, as she tired easily. Rex went in most mornings before he started work, taking flowers for her, until one day she smiled, thanked him and pointed out that her room was like a florist's shop already.

In the afternoons, Joan went in herself or looked after the children so that Marigold could go. Chloe visited in the evenings after she came home from work. They found the staff kind and efficient.

Rex discovered that he knew Sister Carey, the sister in charge. He'd barely recognised her to start with, having only seen her wearing jeans and sweaters before. She was approaching middle age, unmarried and very down to earth. She lived at home with her elderly parents; theirs was one of the many gardens he looked after regularly.

He was glad to find her ready to pass the time of day with him and report on Helen's progress. She gave him a better understanding of Helen's condition.

'She's going to need long-term care, possibly for years, and she'll need a lot of treatment after this. I wouldn't continue paying privately for her,' Sister Carey advised Rex. 'It could turn out to be very expensive indeed, and she'll get exactly the same treatment on the NHS.'

'She'd lose her private room.'

'Yes, but being with other patients often helps them recover. They don't have so much time to

293

dwell on their own problems. Some find a private room lonely. Anyway, I know you work hard to earn your money.'

'I wanted her to be seen quickly, to have the best possible chance.'

'That was important.'

'And to have the best attention.'

'She'll have that, and you could spend your money taking Mrs Redwood away for a good holiday when she's feeling better. She'd like that, wouldn't she?'

Rex decided that Sister Carey was very sensible, but what she'd said made him feel worse. She'd spoken as though she expected Helen to be ill for years. The doctors had made no mention of a complete and rapid recovery either.

He told Chloe something of what Sister Carey had said about private care. She was very troubled about her mother. 'You've been a tower of strength, Rex. Helping to get Mum seen and her treatment started quickly. Thank you.'

Two weeks later, they went together to fetch Helen home, but she was only to have three weeks to convalesce after the operation, and then she was to start a course of chemotherapy.

'I'm dreading it,' Chloe said. 'It'll make all her hair fall out, won't it?'

'Your mother's facing up to it,' Rex said. 'Being very brave about it. We don't talk about the side effects.'

Once she started on chemotherapy, Helen said, 'It's making me feel really ill. I think the treatment is worse than the disease itself.'

'I know it is,' Rex comforted. 'I can see how it

affects you, but the doctors say it'll give you the best chance of complete recovery.'

He took her in his arms and she clung to him like a limpet. 'Once the course is over, you'll find you begin to feel better.'

He patted her back and stroked her hair. Helen had lovely hair; it was thick, strong and curly. He'd never forget the look of total horror on her face when she combed it and clumps of it started coming away in her hands.

'They told me this would happen,' she sobbed, very distressed. 'That the chemotherapy would make my hair fall out.' Oh,

'It'll grow back,' Rex consoled her. 'The doctors say it will.'

'I know, but they don't say when,' she groaned. 'It's going to take ages. I thought I was prepared for it, but it's going to make me completely bald. I'm going to look awful.'

'You'll still have a pretty face,' he assured her. But they both knew that wasn't entirely true; her complexion was now a greyish yellow. She looked really ill.

'I feel a travesty of myself, losing my hair as well as one breast.'

'I still love what's left.' He kissed her cheek.

'It's a very cruel disease.'

'It's ghastly for you, but you'll get over this part.' He tried to smile. 'Things will get better. I'll be able to take you out for meals again. We'll go away on holiday somewhere nice. You'll enjoy life again, you'll see.'

Helen seemed happiest on a lounger in the garden if the weather was sunny; if not, she liked to be in the summerhouse. Rex spent a lot of time working in her garden, often stopping to chat to her.

Chloe cooked Sunday lunch these days, and Rex was always invited. He worried about Helen, as did all her family. He couldn't understand why it had taken him so long to find that terrible lump. The disease had been well advanced by the time he had.

CHAPTER TWENTY

Leo had planned a relaxing weekend in his own bedsit, but as soon as he got home, he could hear peals of childish laughter coming up from the flat below. That was followed by a heavy thump as something was knocked over. It irritated him; he couldn't stand the racket the damn child living in the bedsit below his was making. He decided he might as well go to the pub straight away.

When he went to use the communal bathroom, he found somebody had been sick there and not cleaned it up. Maisie, the woman downstairs, spent too much time playing with her screaming kid instead of attending to the chores she'd agreed to do.

On the way out, he hammered on her door. When it opened, the sound of scampering feet, together with peals of laughter, resounded round the hall.

'I can't stand the noise your kid's making,' he

said, and saw the smile fade from Maisie's face.

'Sorry, Lulu's four today and she's got her friend here to tea. They've been playing hunt the thimble, but I'll stop them now.'

'You shouldn't have kids running around in here making such a din. Sounds like there's ten of them,' he complained. 'The rest of us want a bit of peace when we come home from work.'

'I'm sorry, I'll read them a story now.'

'Also, our bathroom is in a disgusting state.'

'I cleaned it yesterday.'

'Well it needs cleaning again.' Leo went out, slamming the front door behind him.

It didn't please him to find the Irish pub just opening. With only two customers, the place was dead. He walked on to the burger bar to eat his tea there, then, feeling rather unsociable, continued further along the row and went into the news theatre to see an hour's show of short topical films.

It didn't cheer him to watch Concorde, the needle-nosed aircraft, take off for its first flight, or Cunard's liner *Queen Elizabeth 2* receiving the final touches before her maiden voyage. It would be some time, Leo thought, before he could afford to travel on either of them. To see the newly married John Lennon and Yoko Ono hold a press conference in bed depressed him further. He had no chance of that.

Leo stretched his legs and sighed. The show was not holding his attention, because he was upset. He should never have let Chloe see his silver pencil. He'd been very stupid to take it to work and careless to let that happen. He used it

297

to lightly pencil in any figures until he'd double-checked them. He'd watched the girl twirl it between her fingers, and in case she'd noticed the engraved initials he'd been quick to say it had belonged to a friend. All the same, it had given him a shock. He'd use an ordinary pencil in future and leave that one at home.

When he went back to the Irish pub, the music was belting out. This was more like it; he needed cheering up. Once inside, Conor Kennedy's heavy hand went round his neck.

'My friend, how are you? We haven't seen much of you recently. Maisie says you're spending your week nights away.'

Leo cursed inwardly. That woman again! 'Got myself a girlfriend,' he said. 'She's very hospitable.'

'Thinking of leaving us? Moving in with her altogether?'

'No, I like my own place.'

'Good for you.' He called to the barman, 'Patrick, a pint of Guinness for my friend here.'

'Thanks, Conor. Good health to you.' The tape machine was playing 'Paddy McGinty's Goat', and Conor went behind the bar to turn up the volume.

For Leo, Monday morning came all too soon, and he had to think himself back into the persona of Francis Clitheroe. He settled himself at his office desk and pulled his comptometer forward. Should anybody come in, it made him look busy if he had a few columns of figures on the print-out.

He'd had to teach himself to use it. Fortunately, it was a recently bought piece of equipment and

298

he'd found the instruction booklet in a drawer in the desk. Not that he was much good at it. Mrs Parks put him to shame; she could make the figures bubble out of it. He wouldn't dare use it in front of her. She was not all that quick on the uptake, but even she would notice he needed more practice.

Otherwise things were going well. He felt confident about his plans; they were as foolproof as he could make them. One of his duties was to settle the large number of bills that came in. Many were for the ingredients they used to make their pet foods, and the names of the suppliers appeared in their accounts over and over again.

The buyer, Don Tyler, was ordering regular supplies of cereals such as wheatings, bean and pea meal, oats and millet, from companies with names that were not dissimilar: Cheshire Farmers' Cooperative, Fylde Farmers' Cooperative, Fylde Grinding Mills and such like.

Leo now put into action his plans to set up a fictitious firm called Cheshire Crushing Mills. He'd spent all the previous Saturday finding a small printing firm and ordering bills and some headed notepaper in that name. He'd designed them to look very much like the genuine articles and he meant to keep them in his bedsit. Today, when he came to the office, he set up a file for this company amongst the others.

To test out his system, he'd typed a letter enclosing a bill from the Cheshire Crushing Mills, charging Bristow's Pet Foods four hundred and ten pounds for a delivery of flaked maize. He folded both together, creasing them so they'd look as though they'd come out of an envelope. Then he put them in the file he'd created and pushed it into the middle of a whole armful of genuine files containing genuine bills. Next he called in Lydia Tomlin and dictated a short letter to each company saying that he was enclosing a cheque in payment of their bill, and let her get on with it.

When she brought his letters back to be signed, he took out the company chequebook.

She wrinkled her nose and said, 'Mr Cleary made out the cheques first before he dictated the letters.'

That was a heart-stopping moment for Leo, but he managed to keep his voice level and say firmly, 'I prefer to do it this way.'

When the door closed behind her, he took a deep, steadying breath. He hoped she'd think him pernickety and over-fussy. Better that than find out that the cheque due to the Cheshire Crushing Mills would be made out to Alistair Jackson and slipped in to his own pocket. The bank at which he'd opened an account in that name was round the corner from the office, to make it convenient to pay in. Leo could see no reason why the ruse should not work smoothly. As he was the company accountant, the bank would eventually return the cashed cheques to him; he'd bundle the genuine ones up neatly and destroy the fraudulent ones.

He felt sure that the theft was well hidden and that nobody would notice that he'd removed the money from Bristow's Pet Foods to an account he could access privately. The only weak spot was that Cheshire Crushing Mills might be noticed as a company from which nobody had ordered supplies.

Leo didn't mean to let money build up in any of his personal accounts, where it might attract attention from the bank staff. He drew it out in small amounts and soon found himself swimming in cash. His dreams of what he might buy with it were expanding. The cottage he'd once hoped to own had grown into a sizeable country house with a few acres of land. He'd need a car, too; he meant to set himself up in a new life well away from Liverpool.

One of the first things he'd like to do was to buy himself some more silver to replace what he'd had to sell. Bernie Dennison's wife had been very grateful for his help and told him that Bernie sent his thanks. Leo had missed his fine silver, though he'd never had anywhere to set it out on show. Even if he had, he wouldn't have trusted his neighbours not to nick it. He used to keep it wrapped in newspaper in an old trunk. One of his pleasures had been to take it out from time to time, polish it up until it sparkled and then gloat that such exquisite silver belonged to him.

He felt he had to limit his monthly withdrawals via Cheshire Crushing Mills to the average amount of the genuine bills he paid. Bristow's Pet Foods was providing the richest seam he'd ever been able to access, but at this rate he'd have to stay here a long time. He set up another fictitious company in order to double the amount he could take.

Bristow's bought in yeasts and brewer's grains in large amounts, and had dealings with several

301

large brewers with well-known names. A similar company name would be easy to replicate. Northampton Brown Ales, for instance; that sounded genuine enough. They were also buying in meat meal and dried blood, sometimes from abroad... But no, he mustn't go ahead too quickly; he didn't want the boss to pick up on what he was doing.

But old Bristow was already freewheeling downhill to retirement. He'd been running this profitable business for the last twenty-five years and thought he could do it in his sleep. He was no longer as careful as he should be. And that went for Don Tyler, his buyer, too. A couple of old has-beens. It looked as though this could be a walkover.

The phone on his desk rang, tearing him away from his reverie. He recognised Mr Bristow's voice. 'Could you come along to my office? I'd like a word.'

'Yes, of course,' he said, but it caused his heart to race and a jangle of warning bells to ring in his head. If trouble was to come, this would be the way. But he daren't delay, not even to pull himself together.

He knew the moment he saw Walter Bristow's smiling face that he hadn't been found out. He was able to relax as he was waved to a chair. There were a few pleasantries and then Bristow said, 'Our accounts are usually audited in December for the end of our financial year, but since then our cash flow seems suddenly less and I'm a bit concerned. I'm thinking of asking our auditors to come in and spend a day looking over the figures to see if they can pinpoint any reason.'

Leo felt his head spin. He'd known an annual audit took place in December. It hadn't occurred to him that Bristow might arrange an earlier snap examination of his accounting. Even more scary was the fact that Bristow had noticed there was less money coming in. Leo felt this as a crisis.

'Before I arrange a date for this, do you have a preference?'

An auditor would go through everything with a fine-tooth comb. Leo feared that his newly learned accounting skills would not stand up to such scrutiny.

'No,' he said, then added hastily, 'Not the end of the month, of course; the salaries ...'

'Tom Cleary didn't like them in at the end of the week either, because of having to pay the wages. They take two or three days as a rule. Shall we say Monday and Tuesday the week after next?'

Leo made his escape as quickly as he could, knowing that he must not show how agitated he was. This could finish off his grand plan.

Leo told himself not to panic as he strode back to his own office. He slumped down at his desk and opened up all his account books. For the first few months he'd been here he'd taken nothing, but more recently he'd set up three fictitious files and had written cheques transferring company funds to an account he'd set up in a false name, amounting now to over three thousand pounds.

He thought he'd hidden what he'd done, but would it be noticeable to an auditor that fraud was taking place? He was afraid it might be. It depended on whether they found the fictitious files.

And what about his way of working? Would an auditor know it wasn't the work of a chartered accountant? Just the words profit and loss and bank reconciliation sent him into a cold sweat.

Leo was very careful what he allowed Mrs Parks to see. To think of a team of auditors examining every entry horrified him. He circled the dates they'd come on his calendar; goodness knows why, it was unlikely to slip his mind. If only he could write a cheque for one massive amount and do a runner, he could disappear and hope not to be found. But no, that wouldn't work for several reasons.

He had brought his two textbooks on accounting to the office to help him get his figures right. He got them out now for guidance.

He read that an auditor would check the figures in his ledgers against the monthly bank statements, to make sure they balanced. That terrified him, though it seemed they were seldom in total agreement anyway, because cheques could be sent out but not all would be presented for payment by any given date.

He didn't calm down until he'd returned to his lodgings and eaten his tea of stew, potatoes and cabbage. He didn't want to do a runner now. This was the best chance he'd ever had of getting himself a house of his own and financial security. He thought that with a bit of luck, he might still survive. He'd take his textbooks home and pack up all his personal belongings ready to run at a moment's notice if things went wrong.

Two auditors from a very well-known firm, both confident young men, arrived promptly at nine o'clock on the designated day. To Leo it felt like an invasion; he found it agonising to sit at his desk and watch them check the figures in his ledgers. They asked questions too, and he had to think carefully before he answered. He was worried stiff that he'd show his ignorance.

The two auditors laughed and talked together. Leo ordered frequent cups of tea and coffee for them and took them to the café where the rest of the staff gathered at lunchtime. By the end of each afternoon, he was exhausted and in a lather of sweat. He hoped that what he'd be able to take would make all this worth while.

One of the auditors did point out that some of his records were incomplete, and showed him which figures must be carried through. Leo told them he'd only just started this job and the figures were largely put in by someone else. He was sweating with relief when the accounts were counter-signed as correct. He went back to his lodgings that night full of triumph. He'd got away with it, and found it calming to know that no suspicion had been attached to his figures.

Now was the time to take as much as he could as quickly as he could. He must get it out of the account he'd set up in the name of Alistair Jackson too. He had to assume that the money could be traced through the bank's records as coming from the Bristow's account.

To muddy the waters and make his access to the money safer, he opened another account, in the name of Arthur Worboys, at yet another bank. Then he started drawing out large sums in cash from Alistair Jackson's account and paying it into that of Arthur Worboys. He meant to make it as difficult as possible for anybody to find out how it had been done, or to be able to make any connection with the name Leo Hardman.

He knew that if Walter Bristow discovered the money was missing and reported it to the police, the fraud squad would be called in.

Chloe knew that her mother was putting on a brave face and trying hard to appear her normal self. Before she went to work, she took breakfast up to her in bed, but after that, Helen got dressed and ate her other meals with the family. She said she was feeling better. Chloe had seen her laugh and play with the children, and that seemed a good omen.

Yes, Mum's hair had gone, but she'd been fitted with a wig, chosen to suit the shape of her face, and it didn't look too obviously false. She'd also been measured for a special bra, to hide the fact that she'd had one breast removed. Her bustling energy had not returned, and Chloe suspected that underneath, these things distressed her as much as ever. Mum used to do the cooking and run the house, but now she couldn't even garden. That made Chloe's heart go out to her. All the housework was falling on the rest of the family.

'I feel guilty,' Chloe told Rex. 'I go off to work every morning and leave Aunt Goldie to cope with my children as well as all the extra work Mum's illness makes.'

Rex's sympathetic eyes looked into hers. 'Do you want to stop work and look after your mum?' he asked.

'Of course I do, I feel I should.' Chloe covered her face with her hands. 'But I talked Uncle Walter into giving me this job, and now that I've been there long enough to make myself useful, I don't want to walk out on him. I think he's got enough worries about the business at the moment.'

'Then your other alternative is to get some household help.'

'A cleaner, you mean?'

'Yes, but you need someone to give all-round help.'

'A mother's help? Does any girl want that sort of work these days?'

'You need a capable woman, not a young girl. I might know just the person...'

'Rex! That would be marvellous.'

'I've had a gardener working for me for years, and he told me the other day that his wife is looking for a job. She's worked as a cook-general for an old man for ages, but he's just gone into a home. She's a motherly sort of person, has brought up five children of her own, but they're all grown up now. She's a cheery sort.'

'She sounds ideal. I would feel happier if there was another pair of hands here to help out. Rex, you always know the answer to everything.'

He laughed. 'I wish that was true. I'll try and bring Mrs Wilson round to see you and Goldie at the weekend.'

He brought her on Sunday morning while Chloe was trying to get a leg of lamb into the oven for Sunday lunch.

'I'm Peggy,' she said. She was stout and in her fifties, with a shock of iron-grey hair. 'I've heard a lot about your garden; my hubby comes to work here sometimes. Here, let me give you a hand with those runner beans. Are they from your garden?'

Chloe took to her, and thought that if she came for five mornings a week, they'd be able to manage. Rex suggested five full days, nine to five.

'Those are the hours Peggy's looking for,' he whispered, and manoeuvred her into agreeing. 'I think you'll suit each other.'

He swept Peggy out to the summerhouse to introduce her to Helen, Goldie and the children.

'As it's Sunday, why don't I pour you ladies a glass of sherry to cement the bargain?' he suggested. 'Then I'll run you home, Peggy.'

In the weeks that followed, Chloe felt she'd eased the burden on Aunt Goldie, who was coping better with the children. Peggy was running the house, helping to look after her mother and also preparing the evening meal for them so Chloe had less work too. She had only to serve it up when she came home from work.

Goldie told her that Peggy was kind to Helen and good with the children. They all began to rely on her, and she soon became almost one of the family.

A month or so later, Rex was delighted to find that Helen was looking much brighter. She was smiling and joining in family discussions in a way she hadn't done for a long time. Her appetite had improved too. He took her for walks round the garden, and she never tired of seeing how it changed from one season to the next, but she was not all that steady on her feet when they got away from the paths.

'I think you're well enough to come out for a meal with me,' he said. That brought a broad smile to her face. She suggested lunch, saying that she grew tired towards the end of the day.

They had lunch out twice a week for a while, though she couldn't eat all that much, neither could she walk far.

'It'll take time to get you really well,' he told her. 'But you are getting stronger.'

He took her to the seaside or for little country drives. They ate in village pubs and Helen seemed to enjoy it. They progressed to early-evening meals at the garden centre, and from there to the bistro.

'I'm so pleased,' Rex told her, 'that we're getting back to our old ways.' He thought Helen was enjoying life again. 'How about coming to my place and staying the night with me?' he asked.

She smiled, but she wouldn't be rushed. 'I'm pretty useless by bedtime,' she said. 'Too tired for anything. That's why I like you to bring me home early.'

'We'll give you another week or two to get stronger,' he said. 'You're improving all the time.'

He sensed that she didn't want him to see her body, that she was shy about it, but he continued to invite her. Eventually she said, 'You'll find me off-putting. You won't like my operation scars and bald head. You won't see me as a lover any more.'

Rex was filled with compassion. 'I will, Helen.

Underneath you're the same person.'

'But mauled and cut about by illness.'

'With the lights out, I wouldn't see any of that. You could just go to sleep in my arms.'

She smiled. 'I would like that.'

'Tuesday,' he told her. 'I could bring something to eat from the garden centre and we could have it here. Would that be less tiring for you?'

She nodded. 'I'm still having very early nights.'

'That's no problem. I go to bed early myself.'

He fetched her and served the meal he'd kept warm. She told him that Peggy had been preparing a stew for the rest of the family and that Lucy had taken the carrot tops with their green plumes and planted them back in the garden, thinking the bottom part would grow again.

'Perhaps she'd be interested in having a little garden of her own.' Rex laughed. 'I'll try and encourage it.'

It seemed almost like old times, though Helen wouldn't take a glass of wine with the meal. At bedtime, he saw her take a new satin nightdress from her overnight bag, but she got into bed wearing her wig and the surgical bra.

'I can't bear to let anyone see.' She clung to him, not far from tears. 'I have to hide behind my props.'

'You don't have to hide from me,' he told her. 'You know that.'

In the past, Helen had always been keen on making love. Tonight, he would not have made the first move, but shyly she did. Rex felt very needy and on an emotional knife edge. Helen's illness had swept up on them and advanced so quickly.

He'd never been more passionate, over the top really. Afterwards he had the empty feeling that she'd done it to please him. That really she was no longer interested in sex.

CHAPTER TWENTY-ONE

Leo was pleased when Mrs Parks told him she was about to take two weeks' holiday. 'Are you going away somewhere nice?' he asked.

'No.' She was a decade or more older than the secretaries, a widow with three youngish children. 'I'm going to have a rest. Well, as far as I can while the kids are off school.'

He'd been nervous of Mrs Parks to start with, knowing that she was in the best position to see through what he was doing. With time, he'd realised she was wrapped up in her children, and though the work she did was adequate, she was not the type to be curious or to give it more than minimum attention. All the same, her absence would give him some much-needed freedom. He knew she thought him fussy and rather odd.

Leo was inclined to grow more edgy as each month came to an end. At that time, Walter Bristow received bank statements for his business accounts. In addition, he required Leo to provide copies of some of the accounting documents he drew up. From these it would be possible for the boss to assess how his business was progressing.

To Leo, taking the documents to Mr Bristow's

office on the first day of the new month felt a bit like putting his head into the lion's mouth. It couldn't fail to draw Bristow's attention to his figures. To start with he'd taken comfort that the audit had confirmed that all was correct. But the months were passing, and he was transferring more and more company money to accounts he controlled. He made sure he was ready to shrug off the persona of Francis Lovell Clitheroe at a moment's notice, should it prove necessary.

At the beginning of August, he delivered his figures to Bristow, then went back to his office and waited with some trepidation for the boss's reaction. It was a long wait. Just when he was thinking of locking his desk and going home, Mr Bristow came to his office to toss some papers, including the bank statements, on to his desk without comment. When he'd gone, Leo studied them and realised why. They'd made a bigger than average profit the month before and the healthy credit balance had hidden the sum he'd stolen.

He couldn't believe his luck. He'd found the perfect company to employ Francis Clitheroe. At this level, he could probably work here for years and treble his salary with little danger of being found out. But it was nerve-racking. He'd stick to his original plan, take as much as he could as quickly as he could and get out.

The following weekend in his own bedsit, Leo created three more files in order to double the amount he could take each month. Having six fictitious companies did increase the risk, but he thought it was a risk worth taking.

Don Tyler, the buyer, would know the names of the companies from whom he ordered and might be expected to pick out any false ones amongst them. But his responsibilities ended when he'd checked what was being delivered against his orders. John Walsh, the production manager, used the supplies to manufacture the pet food and would possibly recognise some of the companies' names. He might even prefer one company's goods over another, but he didn't have access to Francis Clitheroe's accounts.

When Walter Bristow asked Leo when he wanted to take his two weeks' holiday, he was taken by surprise and almost said he didn't want any time off. The truth was, he was scared of leaving his fictitious files unguarded for a whole fortnight. But the boss had clearly never had an employee who didn't want a holiday before.

Leo tried to cover it up. 'Am I due for a holiday yet? I mean, I've only been working here since February.'

'Of course.' Bristow was showing more surprise. 'You can take it any time during the year. Tom Cleary used to work out the wages, get everything ready and leave it to me to pay them at the end of each week.'

Leo shut up. He had the feeling he was making matters worse. Francis was paying the wages and salaries for the workforce; surely he'd know every rule pertaining to holidays?

The thought of taking a fortnight's holiday himself sent shivery thrills up and down Leo's spine. It would be marvellous to get away from here; he certainly needed a rest and the chance to calm his nerves. He would enjoy spending the time searching for the house in which he meant to spend his new life. He'd want it to be near the sea and a small town, perhaps in the Lake District or on the Cumbrian coast, a place where as yet he had no connection. It was to be a permanent bolt-hole, so he'd use his real name to buy it. He'd become an honest middle-class citizen and forget all the nerve-racking things he'd had to do to achieve it.

He reckoned the plan he'd worked out was first class, but at this stage it would be stupid to risk losing what he'd achieved by turning his back on it for a fortnight. He'd put off his holiday to the late autumn. By that time he'd be ready to close down his money-making scheme and never return.

'I'm on holiday for the next two weeks,' Mrs Parks reminded the secretaries one Wednesday afternoon as they were locking up in preparation for going home. 'Only two more days at work.'

'Oh no!' Lydia Tomlin exclaimed. 'Why didn't you warn me sooner? It usually falls to my lot to keep your work up to date.'

'I've been warning you for the last six weeks,' she laughed. 'You take no notice.'

Lydia groaned. 'I can never remember what I'll have to do. Show me again tomorrow.'

'I could do it,' Chloe offered. 'I always worked in accounts until I came here. I quite enjoy figures.'

'That's marvellous,' Lydia said. 'I can't add up for toffee.'

'You can use my comptometer.'

'Thanks a bundle,' Lydia said. 'You'll have to

show me again how that works.'

Chloe laughed. 'Don't worry, I used one all the time at Owen Owens. Show me tomorrow what it is I have to do, and if I can't get through everything, Lydia can give me a hand with my work.'

The following week, Lydia came back from the accountant's office and put some files on Chloe's desk. 'I've told Mr Clitheroe that you've offered to do Mrs Parks's work, but he didn't seem all that pleased.'

'Oh dear, does that mean he doesn't like me?' Chloe laughed. 'I did once douse him with water from my umbrella, but it was an accident.'

She quite enjoyed adding up the large columns of figures as Mr Clitheroe had specified. When she was confident the totals were correct, she took the files back to his office.

'You've been very quick,' he said.

'I'm used to working with figures,' she said.

'Oh!' His eyes behind his heavy glasses looked uneasy. 'Can you spare the time from Mr Bristow's work?'

'He likes us to be flexible and help each other. He says that if one of us is off sick or something, then the work goes on seamlessly.'

'I see.' He opened the top file. 'Where did you learn about accounting?'

'Not accounting exactly. We were all taught bookkeeping at commercial college and I liked that better than the shorthand and typing. When I started work, it was for the Inland Revenue.'

'Oh! Then you'll be good at it.' Chloe thought that that made him look even more uneasy. 'Thank you, it's kind of you to do it for me.'

Leo could feel his stomach churning long after Chloe had left his office. Her beautiful lavender-blue eyes had looked askance at him. Had she noticed his anxiety? The last thing he needed was someone who was used to working with figures. And in particular one of Bristow's relatives. She was stunningly beautiful; he couldn't take his eyes off her face. There was nothing wrong with her body either. He'd just love to undress her and take her in his arms. The trouble was, she was quicker on the uptake than Mrs Parks, and he couldn't afford to let her get close to his figures. She was a danger he'd not foreseen.

The damn job was wearing him down, he knew he needed to pull himself together. He'd always been very careful about the figures he handed out for Mrs Parks to work on. They were pukka; there was nothing fraudulent in them.

Leo returned to his bedsit late on Friday afternoon to find that his bank statement had arrived. The credit balance gave him great pleasure; never had he had money like this before. His salary was being paid in and he was taking out only enough to show some movement through the account. He had several times that amount in Alistair Jackson's account, though he was drawing regular sums out of that. Some, he used to live on, but in addition he was building up cash in embarrassingly large amounts.

He'd bought fish and chips and a couple of cans of beer to take home for his tea. He sat down to eat and gloat over his wealth. This was what made the nervous stress he was suffering worth while.

He'd also brought an *Evening Echo* home with him, and when he opened it and saw advertised a specialist sale of silver in a Liverpool auction room, he felt quite excited. He was missing the collection of antique silver that he'd had to sell. He used to enjoy going to auctions and researching all he could about his pieces.

It would be a good thing to start another collection, because it would lock his cash out of sight in silver. He could and should indulge himself by buying more. It would be safer than having an over-large bank balance that could draw attention to itself.

The advertisement told him that the silver would go on public display in the saleroom for three days before the sale. He went in his lunch hour and was beguiled by the glittering array. He bought a catalogue and mooned over it for hours, longing to own it all. He went again to the preview on the following day to decide which pieces he liked most and what he was prepared to pay for them.

There was the difficulty that the sale would take place during the working day, when he was expected to be at his desk. He immediately let it be known about the office that he had a nagging toothache, and then asked Mr Bristow if he might take an hour or so off on the afternoon of the sale to keep an appointment with his dentist. Old Bristow was quite sympathetic.

Walter was tired when he got home from work. Joan was in the kitchen, scraping carrots for supper. Immediately she stopped to make him the gin and tonic he needed to unwind. She poured a glass of sherry for herself and followed him into the sitting room. It was part of their comfortable evening routine.

'I've kept the local paper for you,' she said. 'Did you see there's to be a big auction of silver tomorrow?'

'No, I haven't had time to open it this week.'

Joan had folded it to the right page for him. 'My goodness,' he said. 'They've got just about everything here. Some very good candlesticks.'

'We did agree we'd get another pair if we could.'

'We did.'

'I'll come with you if you want to go to the auction.'

'I've never been to one before, but I could take an hour or so off.' Walter knew that all collectors craved more, and he was no exception. And he had promised Joan some candlesticks. 'We'll go.'

They arrived just before the sale started. Walter wanted to get a closer look at what was on offer. There was so much silver and it all glittered enticingly. There was an aura of expectation in the hall.

'This is exciting,' Joan whispered.

'There are several pairs of candlesticks, and candelabras too.'

Joan was nudging him. 'There's Adam Livingstone, Chloe's boyfriend. We bought some lovely pieces from him.'

'But he let her down. He's never been near her or his children since she left him.'

'For heaven's sake, he's seen us.' Joan was tugging at Walter's arm. 'He's coming over.'

'Good afternoon, it's Mr and Mrs Bristow, isn't it? Are you pleased with the silver you bought from me?'

Adam was smiling at them, not one whit abashed at what he'd done to Joan's cousin. Walter was not in the habit of showing his displeasure. 'Very pleased,' he said, politely.

'You've come to buy more?'

'Yes, Joan would like a pair of candlesticks.'

'I remember,' he said. 'I wasn't able to find you any. There are several pairs here.'

The sale of silver was due to begin at two o'clock, after the lunch break; other goods had been auctioned off in the morning. Full of eager anticipation, Leo arrived before it started. He'd bought his previous collection of silver at auction and knew the drill. He registered as a buyer and was given his bidding paddle, with the number 234.

Little thrills were bubbling through him as he hurried into the hall to view the silver again. He half expected to find it wasn't as good as he remembered, but he was not disappointed. He couldn't help his audible sigh of admiration.

Within seconds, he had his catalogue out to consider again the prices he'd marked against the pieces he fancied. Leo was fascinated by and felt passionate about good-quality silver, whenever it had been made. What he saw before him would give him a better, more valuable collection than he'd had before.

He'd timed his arrival well. The auctioneer was mounting the rostrum. He slid through the crowd and found a place at the back of the hall, where he could see who was bidding against him. His heart began to pound as the porter held aloft a pair of five-light Victorian candelabra.

The buzz of conversation died down as the auctioneer started. 'A fine pair of silver candelabra in the Adam style. Who will start me at a hundred pounds?'

Leo had worked out how to get what he wanted at the best possible price. No point in taking risks to get the money only to throw it away by paying more than was necessary. He always waited for the bidding to begin, or until the auctioneer dropped his starting price.

Concentrate, he told himself. He knew there'd be dealers here and he didn't want to join a bidding fight and force the price up unnecessarily. One of the bidders dropped out, and then another. Leo held up his paddle. There was only one person against him now. He pressed on and felt a little jerk of triumph as the candlesticks were knocked down to him.

He was bidding again for a pair of George IV wine coasters when he happened to glance at the person bidding against him. The shock made him freeze, although for a moment he wasn't entirely sure. Then the man turned his head slightly so that he glimpsed the side of his face, and he felt his stomach turn over. Walter Bristow was here!

The auctioneer was looking in Leo's direction expecting him to raise his bid, but he daren't. He shrank back and started to edge his way out of the hall. He must not be seen here by the boss; not when he'd asked for time off to go to the dentist. He was halfway down the front steps before he remembered his successful bid for the candlesticks. He paused. He ought to pay for them before he went; he didn't want to be black-balled by this auction house. It was the best in Liverpool for silver.

He shot up the stairs to the office, taking them two at a time. It was probably safer to pay now than it would be later, when a queue could build up. There was nobody here but the cashier. He'd brought cash; they preferred that and it was much the best for him. He knew he wouldn't be able to take the candlesticks from the hall until after the auction had finished. He said, 'I'll collect them after five o'clock.'

'We close at seven, sir. We'll be open again to-morrow between nine and one.'

That done, he crept cautiously down again. He could hear the auctioneer's voice in the distance but there was no further sign of Walter Bristow. His heart didn't stop pounding until he'd been back at his desk for an hour. All afternoon he worried in case the boss had realised he was bidding for those candlesticks. He was very disappointed and cross because he'd had to leave without getting more of that beautiful silver.

The sale was about to start; the porter was holding up a pair of candelabra. 'I do like those,' Joan breathed. 'They'd look lovely on our sideboard.'

Walter felt a shiver of anticipation. 'I like them too.'

'A very fine pair,' Adam said beside him. 'Dating from 1896, if I remember correctly.'

'They look beautiful from here,' Walter said,

'but I didn't come to the preview, so I've nothing to go on but what it says in the catalogue.'

The bidding started and Walter joined in. He wished he'd been able to have a good look at them and wondered how much they were worth. Joan really wanted them and he liked them very much. Bidding was brisk and the price was going up.

He felt Adam put a hand on his arm. 'Don't chase it any further. That's a very good price and they aren't worth more. That fellow's determined to have them.'

As the hammer went down, the auctioneer said, 'Sold for three hundred and twenty pounds to 234 at the back.'

Disappointed, Walter turned round to see who had succeeded in getting them.

'Good lord!' he said. 'Isn't that Francis Clitheroe?' He couldn't believe his eyes.

Joan shook her head. 'I've never met him.'

Adam said, 'No, I think you're wrong. I've done business with that fellow. In fact, he sold me that silver that you bought from me. His name is ... let me think. Yes, Leo Hardman. A strange fellow, he collects silver.'

'I'd have sworn he was my accountant.'

'No, but he's leaving. He must have come just for that one lot. Thank goodness, we don't need him here to drive the prices up.'

Bidding had started for the next lot, a cut-glass powder bowl with a silver lid. 'I love that,' Joan whispered. 'It would look great on my dressing table.'

Walter lifted his bidding paddle and was pleased

when the bowl was knocked down to him. Joan was thrilled, but he mopped his forehead and said to Adam, 'I've never been to an auction before. Not my scene really. It's easier to buy from a shop.'

Adam smiled at him. 'There's a lot of dealers here. They drive prices up and make it more difficult. If you like, I'll buy what I can at the best price possible and bring it round to your house this evening. Then you can choose what you want at leisure and we won't be bidding against each other.'

'Like you did last time?' Joan asked.

'Yes.' Walter was relieved. 'That might suit me better.'

Adam pushed a notebook and biro in front of him. 'Remind me,' he said. 'Write down your address and phone number and I'll ring you later.'

Joan printed it out neatly. They stayed in the auction room and saw several pieces being knocked down to Adam.

'Chloe isn't going to like this,' Joan whispered to her husband. 'He's the father of her children.'

'I can see how he turned her head, a handsome fellow, wouldn't you say?'

'She says he's a cad, a real scoundrel, and he's paid her nothing towards their keep.'

'And he's found himself another girlfriend.'

'Should we be doing business with him?'

'No, but she introduced us to him, didn't she? And he treated us quite well.'

'We needn't tell her.'

In the early evening, Walter let Adam into his sitting room and he unwrapped the newspaper from the pieces of silver he'd bought.

'If you don't like them, don't feel you have any obligation to buy,' he said. 'I'll have no difficulty selling them on to somebody else. It's top-of-the-market stuff. Well, you know that, it was in a specialist sale.'

He gave Walter a copy of the sale catalogue. 'I've marked the price I want against each lot,' he told them, and described each piece as he brought it out.

'There were no other candelabra, but I did get a pair of candlesticks by James Gould. These are hallmarked for the year 1732. George II. A rare find.'

'I do like those,' Walter said.

Chloe was relieved to find that her mother was having one of her better spells. She came home from work on Friday afternoon and met Joan as she was about to leave.

'Your mother's had a good day,' she told her. 'We had a little walk down to the pond and sat in the sun. I asked her if she'd like to come to us for Sunday lunch this week and she seemed quite pleased. Why don't you all come? You're providing countless meals for me here.'

'You know it cheers Mum up to have you here.'

'Yes, but do come, it'll be a change for you all. Bring Rex as well, I know he usually has Sunday lunch with you.'

Chloe smiled. 'Yes, Mum needs him, he's good at helping her in and out of the car. He'll have to drive us too. Mum doesn't feel up to it any more.'

'You ought to learn,' Joan told her. 'Helen's car

is hardly used now. I'll give you driving lessons for your next birthday.'

'Thank you, I'd like that.'

Chloe was looking forward to the Sunday visit. As Auntie Joan had said, it would be a change. There were very few outings now that Mum could manage.

'Come at twelve o'clock, that'll give us time to have a drink first.'

'Mum doesn't drink any more.'

'She'll toy with a glass of sherry, Chloe, if one is put in her hand. She says she enjoys listening to us talk even if she doesn't join in as much as she used to.'

On Sunday, Chloe helped her mother dress in a smart blue dress she'd hardly worn. She looked better than she had for weeks, more her old self. When Auntie Joan led them into the dining room, Helen was full of praise for the silver displayed on the sideboard.

'I've seen it before, of course, it's very impressive. No, I haven't seen it all. Those eggcups and spoons on a stand, that's new, isn't it?'

Chloe got up to take a closer look. 'And the candlesticks.'

'Yes,' Walter said. 'You knew I was going to that big antique silver auction held in Liverpool last week?'

'Yes,' Chloe said. 'Auntie Joan told me you'd both been and bought more pieces.'

'Yes, I was bidding for a pair of Victorian candelabra and I'm almost sure they were knocked down to our Mr Clitheroe.'

'What? Does he share your love of silver?'

'I don't know. He'd asked me for time off that day to see his dentist. I thought I'd caught him out going to the sale instead.'

'He was really there?' Chloe asked.

'I thought it was him, but...'

'Adam Livingstone was there, Chloe,' Joan said. 'He said he knew him, and it wasn't our new accountant. He turned out to be someone quite different, a collector of fine silver.'

Chloe blanched at hearing her speak of Adam. Of course he'd attend an important sale like that. She tried to ignore his name.

'When I first caught sight of him, I was so sure it was Clitheroe,' Walter said. 'But when I was paying for what I'd bought, I could see the name of the person who'd paid for the lot before, and it wasn't Clitheroe. Adam was right.'

Chloe could feel herself stiffening. 'Did Adam say anything? Ask after the children?'

Walter was hesitant. 'I believe he did. Didn't he, Joan?'

'Yes.' She was collecting the used soup bowls and hurried off to the kitchen with them.

'Did he help you?' Chloe demanded. 'Did he come here again and sell you that egg stand and that claret jug?'

'Well, yes, he did.' Joan had placed a leg of lamb in front of Walter and he was noisily sharpening his carving knife on the steel.

Chloe was angry. 'You probably paid more than those pieces are worth. I told you he was dishonest. That's one reason why I left him.'

'He was kind, Chloe.'

'If he was taking money from you, he'd be at his

most charming.'

'I'm sorry.' Joan put an arm round Chloe's shoulders. 'We didn't want to tell you we'd seen Adam. We were afraid you'd be upset.'

'I am upset. I'm afraid he's swindled you.'

'We love what we bought from him,' Walter assured her, 'and I didn't feel we paid over the odds.'

'If you'd taken me with you, I'd have helped you buy it at the auction price, and you wouldn't have had to pay an extra percentage to Adam.'

'Sorry, Chloe,' Walter said. 'It was all a bit rushed, and it was easier for me that way.'

She took another angry breath. 'If–'

Rex put his hand on her arm. 'Let it go, Chloe. Put Adam Livingstone out of your mind. He's not worth worrying about.'

Chloe felt annoyed with herself. Silently she began to eat her roast lamb, but she was no longer hungry. Her outburst had cast a cloud on the lunch party. The happy atmosphere had cooled and couldn't be revived.

CHAPTER TWENTY-TWO

Time was passing and Leo was feeling richer. Up until now, the boss had made no comment when he'd put the monthly figures on his desk. But the result of what he was doing was becoming more obvious. The capital in the company accounts was shrinking.

Leo was growing more nervous about handing over the figures. He told himself he was being silly, that the whole point of him being here was to take the money. He had to do this. He picked up the copy of last month's trading figures taken from his ledgers, slipped it discreetly into a file cover and went to give it to Mr Bristow.

He found him in the secretaries' office, where they were all laughing over some joke. Leo tried to hand him the file and leave.

'Ah, Mr Clitheroe,' he said. 'Come into my office for a moment. I have something I'd like you to do.'

Leo was fighting to look calmer than he felt, but old Bristow hadn't looked at the figures yet, so it couldn't be that. He began to breathe normally again when he found that the boss wanted him to continue paying an employee in the factory his full wage although he was working only half the day. It seemed his wife was very ill and he had to look after her.

He returned to his own office and scribbled a reminder of that. He couldn't settle to do anything else; he'd seen Bristow open the file he'd given him. If he had anything to say about his figures, it would be soon. With his mouth drying, he watched the internal phone on his desk, expecting it to buzz at any moment. When it did, he jumped. Bristow's voice asked him to come back to his office.

'Bring your books with you. I'd like to look through the credit day book, the general journal and the trial balance if you've done it for this month.'

'Yes, sir,' Leo said, hurriedly getting them together. His heart was racing, but he went to knock on the boss's office door, forcing himself to smile.

'I'm a bit concerned about this.' Bristow pushed the monthly bank statement in front of Leo, who hadn't yet seen it. 'We don't seem to be making as much profit as we used to.'

'I had noticed that last month,' Leo agreed, opening the books he'd brought in front of the boss. He knew that he mustn't look as though he had anything to hide. 'I'll do a bank reconciliation.'

'You haven't made a mistake somewhere?'

'I don't think so, sir. I hope not.' He pretended to be willing and obliging.

Together they spent the morning checking through the figures. Leo knew that unless Bristow unearthed one or more of the six fictitious companies now sending in regular big invoices, it was unlikely he'd find out where the money was going.

The following week, Mr Bristow called a mid-morning meeting of senior staff in his office. Leo knew what it was about, though he didn't think it would unearth anything new. He made his way to the boss's office three minutes before the meeting was due to start, with a copy of all relevant figures for each person attending. He'd already voiced his concern at the drop in profits and he thought Francis Clitheroe was still in a fairly safe position. His step was jaunty; he was in confident mood.

Take care, he told himself. He ought to look

329

worried with such bad figures to explain. It was not the moment to let any of them see the satisfaction on his face.

'Good morning,' Walter Bristow was already at the table, sipping a cup of coffee. His secretary was there too.

'Would you like a cup of coffee, Mr Clitheroe?' Chloe asked.

'Please.' He examined her anew. A pretty girl, with her tawny hair done up in a rather insecure bun on the top of her head. It suited her, made her look innocent, though he was sure she couldn't be that. He'd heard she had two children and had never been married. She was exactly the sort of girl that would suit him if circumstances were different.

'Can I take a chocolate biscuit?' he asked.

She smiled; it lit up her face. 'Help yourself.'

He took two and went to sit down. Other men were waiting to get their coffee: John Walsh, Don Tyler and the sales team.

When they were about ready to start, he watched Chloe pour a cup of coffee for herself and pick up her shorthand pad and pencil. As she sat down, her bun wobbled attractively.

The message from Walter Bristow was strong. It was what Leo had expected. Profits were falling, they must practise strict economy from now on: cut back on expenses, cut waste.

'We have plenty of orders coming in, sales are up and we are all busy,' he told them. 'I really thought we were doing well, but our profits are falling.

'Mr Clitheroe and I have been through the accounts with a tooth comb and it seems that running costs have expanded almost out of control.'

Chloe's pencil was flying across her pad. She was taking notes of what the boss was saying. Bristow was trying to motivate them all to do their duty.

The production manager had new ideas on how to cut down waste. The buyer was going to negotiate cheaper contracts when they came up for renewal. He was dealing with two new suppliers who were offering lower prices. The sales manager thought they could widen their market by adding a new line of food for guinea pigs.

'It needn't add much to production costs, since we do a line for rabbits and hamsters already.' He then went on to detail his plan at boring length. The poor sods didn't realise that none of that would touch the problem.

Leo doodled on the paper in front of him. He knew exactly how much he'd managed to seep out of the company coffers. If he hadn't succeeded in doing that, he reflected, they'd have made a very decent profit. He was doing all right here; nobody had the slightest suspicion that he was responsible.

As soon as the meeting ended, Chloe slipped out to her desk and began to type up her notes. Later that day she took them in to Uncle Walter.

'This is worrying me,' he said. 'I've never seen the trading situation change as quickly before. There's no reason for it and there was no warning.'

'The factory is busy.'

'I know, it's positively humming,' he said. 'We should be making a good profit. I don't understand why it's dropping back to nothing.'

'You're running the business differently?'

Walter shrugged. 'No, hardly anything has changed. We're spending more on raw materials, but that must give us more stock to sell. Turnover is much the same as last year, but our cash reserves are draining away.'

'Have you taken it up with the bank?' Chloe asked. 'It's not caused by an error there?'

'No, you made me an appointment to see the manager last month. They've checked back through their figures and sent me duplicate statements for the last six months. Mr Clitheroe and I went through their figures and we can see nothing wrong there.'

'Mr Clitheroe is new,' Chloe said. 'Is he drawing up the figures in the same way? Or has he made changes that are giving you a different picture?'

'That was the first thing I thought of, but no, not that I can see. I even requested a mid-year audit to make sure. Clitheroe says he's following exactly the method Tom Cleary demonstrated to him.'

'He's a strange fellow, Uncle. Not popular with the staff.'

'Why not?'

'He's prickly, on edge.'

'I don't find that.'

'He won't let me near his files and Mrs Parks says the same. She says he won't allow her to file anything away, though she did it all for Mr Cleary.'

'Clitheroe came with good references. I quite like him.'

'I don't, and he doesn't like me.'

'Nonsense, Chloe, you're imagining that. He's very hard-working. Conscientious even.'

'Mrs Parks is very happy to let him get on with the filing. It's a routine chore and a pain if you can't retrieve things when they're wanted again. Why would he want to take that on?'

'You're saying he might be doing something he wants to hide?'

'I'm just saying it's unusual behaviour for a busy accountant.'

'It is.'

Chloe watched Uncle Walter unlock a large drawer in his desk and take out a lot of files. She knew he kept senior staff files in there and that he personally controlled everything to do with them.

He lifted from the pile a file with the name Francis Lovell Clitheroe neatly printed on top, opened it up and pushed it over towards Chloe.

'Because he's drawing up the accounts and he's fairly new here, it's the obvious place to search for an answer. But I can't see it and I've already looked several times. He's very well qualified: a chartered accountant with a degree in economics. He should know what he's doing.'

'I see there's a letter here from the Institute of Chartered Accountants confirming he is a member.'

'He'd lost his certificates, but I took no chances when I took him on. I even did a police check to make sure he had no record.'

'Really?'

'He's handling my money, Chloe.'

'Age thirty-six.' She frowned. 'He looks younger than that. You're not suspicious in any way about him?'

Her uncle gave her a wry smile. 'I was when I first noticed there was less in the bank account than I'd expected. But everything about him seems rock solid. He's polite and very deferential to me. His mother's a novelist. Joan enjoys her books; she's read several of them.'

'Yes, she bought Mum one once for her birthday, and she praised it so much we all read it.'

'How is Helen?'

Chloe shook her head. 'She's not at all well, has a lot of pain. She's not able to read much any more and asked me if I'd read to her. That was the book she wanted. *Serenade at Midnight* by Rosamund Rogerson. We're about halfway through and enjoying it over again.'

'You won't find any clues in that.'

'No, the only way is to have a long, hard look through Clitheroe's files when he isn't around.'

'You think he could be hiding something?'

'I don't know. The only other way is to ask the auditors to run another check on what he's done.'

'But I can't keep doing that. It would tell him I don't trust him, wouldn't it? I've thought about this. I think I'll come in this weekend and have a nose through his books. I wish I knew what to look for.'

'Shall I come in too, Uncle? I know a bit about accounts, and two heads are better than one.'

'Would you mind? You can take time off later.'

On Saturday morning, Aunt Goldie was cross because Chloe was getting ready to go to work. 'Peggy won't be in today, you're leaving me to do everything here,' she complained. 'It's not easy, you know, to look after two children as well as your mother. I expect you find sitting in front of a typewriter more restful.'

Chloe couldn't deny it, and that made her feel selfish. The office gave her something of a social life too; she enjoyed the company of the other secretaries. Uncle Walter arrived to drive her into work and she was pleased to find he'd brought Auntie Joan to stay with her mother.

'I'll have a lovely morning,' she told Chloe, 'playing with the babies and chatting with your mum.'

'That makes me feel better about leaving them.' Chloe smiled. 'I feel I'm being pulled in half a dozen different ways.'

'Walter feels bad about this. That he's sneaking behind the backs of his staff. He needs someone with him and he says you think faster than he can. Anyway, it's keeping it in the family, isn't it?'

When they reached the office, Chloe found the atmosphere very different. It seemed unnaturally dark and quiet, each typewriter hidden under its cover. She shivered. 'It feels full of ghosts.'

'Souls, not ghosts. If the staff knew, they'd hate us doing this.'

'If they have nothing to hide, they won't care,' Chloe pointed out.

'I wish I had a better understanding of accounting. If Tom Cleary hadn't gone to New Zealand, I'd ask him to come in and help.'

'Uncle Walter, I'll do my best for you.'

'I know you will,' he sighed. 'I've always kept a key to every file cabinet and desk I've ever bought.' He produced four enormous bunches of these. 'So nothing can be hidden from us.'

They went to the accountant's office. 'Clitheroe talked me through his figures and said, "I want to prove to you that my figures are correct." At the time, he convinced me they were, but...'

'You think they might not be?'

'If they are, and my business is losing its profitability, I need to rethink how I'm managing it. And be quick too, while I still have a credit balance in the bank.'

'We need to look at everything from a different angle.' Chloe pulled up a chair to Clitheroe's desk and opened the cash books and journals on it.

Walter sat beside her. 'I wish I knew more about how figures can be manipulated.'

'Well, I heard one story of how company fraud took place. Names of non-existent employees were added to the staff and wages were drawn for them. We could start by checking how much is being paid out in wages and salaries.'

'I don't think it's that simple,' Walter sighed. 'I know from looking at the total that it can't be that. That amount hardly varies.'

'Then which totals do vary? Did you say you were spending more on supplies?'

'Yes, we are, but it's harvest time. Some things are seasonal, and we buy more when prices are low at the height of the season; things like barley meal, flaked maize and products made from beans and peas and sugar beet. Things we use to make up the various feeds.'

'We could check what Don Tyler has ordered over the last few months, and whether it's more or less than last year.'

'He's honest, I'm sure. I'd stake my life on that.'

'OK, but we need to check orders against delivery notes. Then the amount delivered against the amount of feed manufactured. And that against sales and the stock being held. And all of that against the figures for the same months last year.'

'That should do it, shouldn't it? Hang on, it'll be impossible to get figures for the current time. Manufacturing is ongoing; there'll be feed everywhere, in the machines, the drying room, in unlabelled sacks and packets.'

'Right, let's go back a bit and check the month of July. You noticed the problem then?'

'Yes, but it's getting worse, more noticeable.'

'Let's find Don Tyler's orders and get started.'

They worked till lunchtime. 'I should take you out for something to eat,' Walter said.

'It'll take up too much time.' Chloe made them tea and dug out the chocolate biscuits, and they carried on until four o'clock.

Her head felt woolly after checking backwards and forwards. Everything they looked at seemed to add up right. They could find no fault with the figures.

'Is disappointment with my business making me a suspicious old man?' Walter asked sadly.

'We have yet to find out,' Chloe told him. 'Shall we come again tomorrow?'

'Perhaps we better had. I'll get Joan to make us some sandwiches.'

On Sunday, they worked harder, and Chloe felt she'd got into the swing of it. But they still failed to find any false figures. 'Clitheroe will be back in the morning,' Walter sighed.

'We've been careful to put things back as we found them; he may not know. Anyway, it's your business.'

'I don't want him to think I'm suspicious of him if he's honest. It would make it harder to work with him. And we're no nearer.'

'We are. We know which figures are correct.'

'They all seem correct.'

'We must give it more thought. I now have a better idea of how your accounts are put together.'

'I don't know about you, Chloe, but right now, I'm too tired to think at all. We've drawn a blank after all that.'

He drove Chloe home, where they found that Joan and Aunt Goldie had postponed cooking Sunday lunch until the evening. The kitchen was filled with heavenly scents of roast beef and Yorkshire pudding. Rex brought Helen in from the summerhouse, where he'd kept her company for much of the afternoon. She was brighter than she'd been for a long time, and with Joan and Walter keeping the conversation going, Chloe felt they had a jolly and sociable evening.

On Monday morning, when Leo sat down at his

desk, he noticed immediately that his beaker of pens and pencils contained an extra biro of the basic sort provided by the firm for its staff. It gave him an uneasy feeling that somebody had been in his office over the weekend. He opened his desk drawers and looked carefully at everything, but nothing seemed to have been disturbed.

He told himself he was being silly. Other staff were in and out of his office from time to time. Any one of them might have left a biro on his desk. The cleaner had been in, of course; he could smell furniture polish. If the pen had been dropped on the floor, she might have tidied it into his beaker. Staff could be notorious careless with anything freely provided.

He opened his file cabinets, but again, nothing was noticeably changed. He couldn't put his finger on anything else that could mean somebody had been searching through his things.

Walter Bristow was showing no sign that he was on to him. This morning they'd arrived at the front door at almost the same moment, and Bristow had held it open for him and wished him good morning. He'd remarked that it was a lovely morning and they'd come upstairs together. Leo had noticed no change in the boss's manner.

Leo was suspicious, yes, but it might just be his nerves; coming here to face Bristow every day was enough to rattle anybody. To be on the safe side, he'd keep his wits about him and his suitcases half packed at his lodgings, so that if his suspicions proved correct, he could disappear at a moment's notice. He must be very careful to leave nothing behind that might provide a clue to his real identity or whereabouts. In the meantime, he'd hang on here and take every penny he could while the going was good.

CHAPTER TWENTY-THREE

As the days passed, Chloe felt that her relationship with Uncle Walter was changing. Until now, he'd been the powerful adult giving her employment and advising her on how to cope with her problems. Suddenly the power balance had swung the other way, and he seemed to be seeking help from her. She knew he was worried about the money his business was losing and he thought her understanding of figures better than his own.

'I left all that to Tom Cleary,' he admitted. 'He set up the accounting system for me and everything worked well while he was here. But now...'

Chloe gave her uncle's accounts a great deal of thought.

He'd got into the habit of coming to his office door and asking her to take dictation. She'd pick up her shorthand pad and pencil and go in, and though he might have the odd letter to dictate, what he really wanted was to talk over the accounts problem in privacy.

'We've checked through almost everything,' he sighed. 'And it looks correct. The books are being carefully kept.'

'I've been thinking,' Chloe said. 'Are you being billed for supplies that aren't coming in? Mr

Clitheroe isn't putting fictitious workers on the payroll, but he could just as easily be sending in false bills.'

'Could somebody outside the company be doing that?'

'I suppose they could, but Mr Clitheroe is making out the cheques to pay them, so he'd have to be in the know, wouldn't he?'

After some thought Walter said, 'Yes, it's his responsibility to make sure the bills he pays are genuine. I know Tom used to check them.'

'If false bills are hiding what's being taken out of the company's bank account, it must almost certainly be Clitheroe who is responsible.'

Walter sighed and stretched back in his chair. 'We buy from many different companies. Some deliver weekly, some monthly, some only occasionally. It isn't going to be easy, but there must be some way we can check them.'

'We could go through the accounts and add up the number of companies that we order from, and we need to check the delivery notes against the cheques paid out.'

He jerked upright again. 'That's it, Chloe, you've got it. That would be proof, wouldn't it?'

'It would. If there's no discrepancy, then Mr Clitheroe is honest.'

Walter was frowning. 'I don't think our profits could go down so quickly unless it was fraud. What happens to those delivery notes?'

'They're checked against the materials delivered to the production department and then they go to Mr Clitheroe to validate the bills he receives. He puts them in the files.'

'What files?'

'He keeps a file for every company. When he sends out a cheque, he writes a covering letter and the copy of that is put in the file too.'

Walter was staring at her in concentration.

'I've typed the letters for him,' she said, 'that's how I know. He gives us the files when we take his dictation.'

'You mean we'd have to look in every file?'

'Yes, and even then... If he's writing a fraudulent cheque for a fictitious company, would he make a file for it?'

'I've got to do something.' Walter looked desperate. 'I think I'll work on tonight after Clitheroe leaves and see if I can pick up something from his files. No, I'll go home and have something to eat and then come back.'

'Collect me, Uncle, and I'll come with you.'

'Are you sure?'

'Of course. As you say, we've got to get to the bottom of this, and if there's two of us working on it, it'll only take half the time.'

Chloe got her children ready for bed, and when Uncle Walter tooted his horn outside, she left Aunt Goldie to read them a story. The Liverpool night was warm and full of bright lights. The streets were still thronged as the car purred through to the industrial area of Bootle.

Once inside the building, the night seemed dark and silent. Walter opened up and they put on all the lights in Francis Clitheroe's office. Chloe was able to find her way round his filing system now, and went straight to the right cabinet.

'All the files of the companies from whom we buy our supplies are here. That's bad news, as we can't both stand here to check them.'

'Good grief, do we have to go through all those? Why does he file like that?'

'It's probably the best way,' Chloe said. 'Questions about deliveries and payment are easily answered; he just needs to take out the file of the company involved. Our problem is, we don't know what name to look for.'

'Or names. There's probably more than one.'

'Right, let's get started. I'll take out all the files in this top drawer and you can sit at the desk to look through them.' She started doing that. 'Then I can check the second drawer by standing here.'

'You want me to open every file and look for a delivery note?'

'Yes, and if there isn't one, that company is suspect, especially if it's putting in regular bills.'

'It's not going to take all that long after all,' Walter said more cheerfully. 'Here's the delivery note in this one and it's bright orange. They'll be easy to see.'

'Some will and some won't,' Chloe pointed out. 'Delivery notes can be any colour and any size too. The company making the delivery decides on that.'

'Oh dear.' Walter's fingers were clumsy, while Chloe's riffled through file after file. Walter breathed heavily as he worked, but suddenly he said excitedly, 'Here's a file without a delivery note.'

'Which company is it?'

'Cheshire Crushing Mills. The copy letter is

343

here, dated eighth August, enclosed a cheque.'

Chloe was searching through the desk drawers for the chequebook stubs. 'Yes, a cheque for four hundred and ten pounds was made out to Cheshire Crushing Mills on the eighth.'

'That matches up with the bill.'

'Let me look in the cash book. Yes, that's recorded here just as it should be. Are we barking up the wrong tree?'

'Hang on, Chloe. Here's another copy letter sending a cheque in settlement of their bill for flaked maize. And here's another.'

'And no delivery notes?'

'No. Four bills here, four copy letters saying cheques enclosed. But no delivery notes.'

'This could be how it's done.' Chloe felt a shiver of excitement as she craned over the desk to look.

'Could they have been mislaid?' Walter sounded defeated. 'Lots of things are. It might not mean anything.'

'One could get mislaid, but not four. Have you heard of this company?'

'Yes...' He paused. 'Well, now I think about it, I'm not sure. We've dealt with one called the South Yorkshire Crushing Mills for years.'

Chloe was staring in frustration at the paperwork for Cheshire Crushing Mills. She straightened up. 'Let me find the file for the South Yorkshire Mills.'

She opened it on the desk and placed the bills and the letterheaded notepaper side by side.

'They're almost identical. The documents for the Cheshire Crushing Mills could be a copy. What d'you think?'

'Yes...'

'And look,' Chloe pointed out victoriously, 'our business dealings with Cheshire Crushing Mills only started at the end of April, after Clitheroe started work here.'

For a moment, they stared at each other. 'This could be the one,' Walter said slowly.

'Let's check it through...'

Ten minutes later he said, 'You're right! We've never had any deliveries from them.'

He leapt to his feet and scooped her up into a triumphant bear hug. 'Well done, Chloe, you've cracked it.'

'No, no. Not entirely.' She laughed and he laughed with her from sheer joy. 'You're missing a lot more money than this.'

'Yes, but this must be how it's being done and therefore ... we know where to look for the rest of it. What a crafty devil Clitheroe is. And I thought him a pleasant fellow.'

'Come on, Uncle Walter. Let's look for another company name that's false.'

They found the Northampton Brown Ale Company, but kept searching. It was midnight before they'd found four more ghost companies and were satisfied that that was all.

Uncle Walter looked incredulous but happy. 'You've solved it for me; you're wonderful with figures.' He laughed again. 'But of course, you worked for the Inland Revenue.'

'I'm so pleased.' Chloe had a wide smile. 'We think we know how it was done and who is responsible, but you want your money back, Uncle Walter. We haven't achieved that yet.'

'No, but I'll do my best to get it.' Walter was rubbing his hands together. 'I'll go to the bank as soon as it opens in the morning. I need to find out who owns the account that is being credited with this money. It must be Francis Clitheroe, mustn't it?'

'There's no other answer,' Chloe agreed. 'And if these cheques are being paid into his account, it's absolute proof of his guilt. You must call in the police. This is fraud.'

'I will, don't you worry. I don't want Clitheroe frightened off too soon, so don't say anything about this to anyone in the office. Better still, you take tomorrow morning off and stay out of the way. After working so late tonight, that's only fair. I can handle this now.'

He dropped Chloe off at her front door. When she went in, she found Aunt Goldie in her pyjamas and dressing gown. She was not in a good temper.

'Where have you been until now? Your mother hasn't felt well this evening and she can't get to sleep while you're still out. She worries about you.'

Chloe crept into her mother's room. It was in darkness. The thin form on the bed turned over. 'Is that you, Chloe?'

'Yes, Mum.' She went to sit beside her and took her hand in hers.

'Did you and Walter find what you were looking for?'

'Yes, he's so pleased. Cheques are being written in payment for false bills.'

'It's fraud, then? Is it that new accountant doing it?'

'It must be.'

'Poor Walter. As if running a business isn't difficult enough in this day and age. He'll have to go to the police.'

'He will in the morning.'

Chloe told her all about what they'd been doing and what they'd found out. It was very late indeed when she kissed her mother good night and put out her light.

Leo had grown increasingly uneasy over the last few days. He'd had a gut feeling that all was not well. This morning he'd taken some figures in to Walter Bristow, routine stuff that he asked to see regularly. Over the last weeks, the boss had usually wanted to discuss the drop in company profits or the economies that could be put in force. Today, Bristow had dismissed him briskly and his manner had seemed cold.

Leo went back to his own office, asking himself if his own nerves were getting frayed and making him edgy. He got out his ledgers and journals. Again he had that creepy feeling they'd been handled and perused. Then he saw a crumb caught between the pages of his cash book. Had he dropped it? He didn't think so. His heart was pounding. He picked it up between his finger and thumb and smelled it. Was it biscuit? He couldn't remember eating biscuits here, but yesterday he'd brought a sandwich for lunch and eaten it at his desk. Had the cash book been open in front of him then? Could this have come from the crust? He tried it on his tongue; it didn't taste of anything but it was still crisp. He didn't know.

One of his fellow lodgers had given him a

paperback thriller, which he'd now read most of. The hero had the same suspicions about a spy searching through his belongings; he'd laid a hair from his head across the lock of his deed box and known immediately when it had been tampered with.

Leo felt he needed that sort of reassurance. It would provide him with an early-warning system, more reliable than gut feelings, or crumbs caught between pages. In the late afternoon before going home, he laid a single hair from his head across each of the first few files in the top three drawers of his cabinet; the drawers that held the files that could implicate him in fraud. He then closed them very carefully. If the hairs were still there in the morning, he'd know he was safe.

That same morning, Uncle Walter rang Chloe while she was eating a late breakfast.

'I've got the proof I need from the bank,' he said, and she thought he sounded triumphant. 'The money shown on the chequebook stubs as going to Cheshire Crushing Mills ... well, the actual cheque was made out to a Mr Alistair Jackson.'

'But who is he?'

'The bank manager thinks it could be a false account set up specially to receive this money. He's given me the cheque and the numbers match up, so there's no doubt about it. The bank collects together all the cheques drawn on my company account and eventually returns them to Mr Clitheroe. All he'd have to do then is destroy it and the evidence is gone.'

'But this account for Alistair Jackson...?'

'It's with a different bank, the Midland. So we can only surmise that Clitheroe is drawing out the money. They won't tell me anything about an account that on the face of it has nothing to do with me.'

'You must go–'

'I did, I went straight from there to the police station.'

'Good, they can delve into all that.'

'It's not so straightforward. It seems that this is a matter for the fraud squad, not the local constabulary, and I haven't been able to talk to them yet.'

'Oh dear, that means a delay. Nothing is going to happen to Mr Clitheroe?'

'Not yet. They've made an appointment for both of us to meet officers of the fraud squad in the local nick at half past three this afternoon. I told them it was you who fathomed this out. We're to tell them of our suspicions and explain our case to them. You'll be here in time to come with me?'

She laughed. 'I'll make sure I am.'

'Say nothing about this to anybody. I'd hoped to have it all cut and dried by now, but this will hold things up for at least a day.'

'Mr Clitheroe has no inkling of this, so will it matter?'

'Probably not. He's been taking money from my company account for the last few months; I don't suppose a few days more will make much difference.'

'Unless he's taking more today and you don't manage to recover it.'

'Chloe! Don't be a Job's comforter.'

She smiled. 'I'm being realistic.'

'I really can't believe he's doing this.'

Chloe had never been in a police station before; it seemed an intimidating place. She thought the surroundings would be enough to make any guilty person feel the force of the law closing round him. As it was, she was glad to have Uncle Walter with her.

They were interviewed by two officers from the fraud squad, an Inspector Halyard, confident, heavily built and middle-aged, and a Constable Benton, beanpole-thin and diffident. They were both friendly and very polite.

Walter set out his case against Francis Clitheroe and Chloe was asked to explain exactly how he'd been able to remove money from Uncle Walter's company account. Questions and further explanations dragged on and on. Constable Benton was writing it all down. Cups of tea were provided to help relax them.

They wanted all the personal information Walter could give them about Francis Clitheroe. He produced the cheque made out to Alistair Jackson as evidence and confirmed that he thought the handwriting was that of Mr Clitheroe. But the officers were not satisfied with that alone, and wanted more evidence.

One of the police officers telephoned the bank where Walter had his company account and made an appointment to see the manager first thing in the morning. It seemed Mr Clitheroe had an account there too, but not Mr Jackson.

Then, as it was after five o'clock and Walter's staff would have gone home, the officers asked to see Clitheroe's office and files for themselves. Chloe produced the six false files from the cabinets. They wanted to take them away.

'Please don't do that,' Walter said. 'If Mr Clitheroe finds them gone, it will immediately alert him. He'll know you're on to him.'

'Yes, better if it comes as a surprise and he doesn't have time to think up false explanations and excuses. We'll leave it until we've made inquiries at the bank.'

That evening when Chloe got home, she found that Joan was on the point of leaving. 'How's Mum been this afternoon?' she asked.

'Quite excited about the progress you and Walter are making about this fraud. I am too. I do hope you're going to catch this fellow and we get our money back.'

'So do I, but it doesn't look straightforward.'

'By the way, I brought some periodicals, magazines and such, round for Helen. Don't throw them out when you've finished with them, I haven't had time to read them all properly. A friend gave me some of them and said there's a piece in one of them about that writer Rosamund Rogerson. D'you remember? She wrote *Serenade at Midnight*, I gave it to your mother ages ago.'

'Yes, we all enjoyed it. Even Aunt Goldie did.'

'I've bought another of hers, it's called *Stroll in the Moonlight*. It's good. I'll bring that round for you when I've finished.'

'Thanks, Mum would be lost without all the

reading matter you bring.'

'So she tells me. I didn't get round to showing the piece to Helen. We were too busy talking about the fraud, and I've forgotten which of the magazines it was in.'

'I'll find it,' Chloe said. 'It will interest her.'

Recently, her mother had begun to have trouble getting off to sleep. Chloe had made it a routine to warm some milk for her at bedtime and sit and read to her while she drank it. Helen said it helped her to relax. To start with, it had been a chapter a night from a book, but recently she'd said she was finding it difficult to keep a long story in her head and that she preferred short pieces.

Tonight Chloe said, 'Auntie Joan has brought a lovely lot of periodicals for me to read to you.'

But she saw her mother's eyes closing as soon as she'd settled her down. She switched off her light and tiptoed away to her own bed.

The next morning at work, Walter called Chloe into his office to take dictation. Before he started he said, 'Joan tells me Helen isn't at all well. I was very sorry to hear that.'

'Poor Mum, I'm afraid she's becoming disheartened.'

'Take some time off, Chloe, and try and cheer her up. I owe it to you anyway, you've worked nights and weekends for me.'

'I'd like to, but at the moment...'

'I know, there's now the problem that I have no accountant.'

'Better no one,' Chloe said, 'than one with his

hand in the till.'

'Yes, but even so, I think you should take some time off to be with your mother. She needs you, and I can manage with the other girls for a few days.'

'Thank you, I will then. A few days...'

'A week, Chloe. I just wish Tom Cleary was back from his trip to New Zealand.'

'When will he be?'

'Another month.'

'We can keep things going until then.'

'I know. I'm sure Tom would give me a hand in the present crisis, but he wants to retire. We'll have to advertise for another accountant as soon as Clitheroe is out of the way. Quite honestly, I'll be glad to see the back of him.'

CHAPTER TWENTY-FOUR

Because Leo was worried, he hadn't slept well. It was a wet and windy morning, and he arrived at the office feeling damp and out of sorts. He was shaking the moisture off his mac in the cloakroom when John Walsh, the production manager, came in, also looking battered by the weather.

'Francis – just the person I need. Would you mind giving me a hand? I've got myself in a bit of a mess. My figures for last month don't balance.'

'What figures?' Leo asked.

'The materials coming in against the amount of food we've manufactured. Unless they do, I don't know what I need to reorder. Tom Cleary used to help me sort things out occasionally.'

Leo was reluctant but felt he had to do everything Tom Cleary had. 'Yes, yes, of course,' he said, and followed the production manager to his office, a small cabin on the factory floor. This was a minor matter as far as Leo was concerned and had no connection with his fraud, but he couldn't relax.

The books were opened on the tiny desk in front of him and he could see that John Walsh was not overly efficient in his paperwork. It didn't surprise Leo. He could hardly hear what the man was saying to him above the grind and rattle of the machines. It made concentration difficult, and though he thought his grasp of accounting had improved beyond belief with the constant practice, it took him some time to sort out the problem.

Walsh was very grateful and walked back with him to the office stationery cupboard, as he needed to replace one of his account books. They stood talking for a time and Walsh suggested meeting at lunchtime. Leo was wary of forming any relationships here, but of all the staff, he found Walsh the easiest to get along with.

It had gone half past ten when he reached his own office. The morning's mail had been opened by his secretary and the letters left on his desk. He glanced through them. Nothing of much importance; a few bills to pay, but it was routine to leave them until the end of the month. He needed to work out the weekly wages today, but before starting on that, he'd check on the early-warning system he'd set up. To know definitely that nobody had touched his files would make him feel safer.

Keeping his eyes open for the hair, Leo slid open the top drawer. He couldn't see it and felt himself go cold. He moved the file pockets apart one by one and peered into them. It wasn't easy to see a single mouse-brown hair; that was the whole point. No investigator would know it was there, or its importance, and it would just blow away and get lost.

Leo could feel himself panicking. This wasn't what he'd been expecting. He told himself the hair might just have fallen inside one of the pockets in the cabinet, but when he checked the other drawers, the hairs had vanished from them too. He was frightened, knowing that without a doubt, his files had been disturbed; that there had been an overnight search in his office. He'd been suspicious that this had happened before, felt it in his gut, but now he was sure it really had taken place.

He could feel himself shaking as he sat down at his desk.

Walter Bristow must be suspicious, but had he worked out what Leo was doing? Had he found the proof? Leo wished he knew. He believed now that Bristow had done this before and found nothing wrong. He couldn't have done, or he wouldn't have returned last night. But for Leo, this signalled that the game was up.

What ought he to do now? He used the intercom to the kitchen to ask for a cup of coffee. When it came, he sipped it slowly, hoping it would settle his nerves. He might still be all right, but one thing

355

was certain: he would not be able to work on here until the holiday he'd booked at the end of September.

Keep calm, he told himself. He had his escape route already set up. He felt sure he could disappear and that they'd not be able to find him to charge him with this fraud. He was disappointed, of course he was, that he wouldn't be able to drag it out for longer. He hadn't accumulated all the money he'd hoped for, but he had quite a sum and he'd have to be satisfied with that. His best plan would be to make this his last day at work. He'd write four more cheques, as large as he dared, and pay them directly into his accounts at lunchtime.

Damn! He'd told John Walsh he'd go to the café with him for soup and a sandwich. He used the intercom to contact him, but nobody lifted up the phone. Walsh would probably be out on the factory floor, and with the noise, he'd never hear it ring. Damn again. He mustn't let frustration wind him up. He was feeling agitated. His nerves always let him down in times of tension like this. He wasn't able to think straight any more; he needed to calm down.

If he wasn't waiting for John Walsh at the appointed time, he was afraid he'd come here to his office. He tried again to contact him and this time he answered. Leo cancelled the lunch date. Apologised and told Walsh he had a prior appointment he'd forgotten.

That calmed him somewhat. Perhaps he was panicking for nothing, but he wouldn't feel safe until he'd left this office and buried Francis Clitheroe for good. Once he was back in his bedsit, he'd be able to relax.

The cheques. No point in leaving without having one more stab at taking as much money with him as he could. He got out the files and the chequebook, then called in Lydia Tomlin to create the paperwork that would hide what he was doing. No point in leaving a trail for the police to follow. Bristow might not have got any further than having suspicions about him. As soon as he'd finished this, he'd take everything he owned from his desk, go to the bank to pay his cheques in and then go straight back to his lodgings and pack up there. He couldn't take pressure like this; better to clear out now.

Miss Tomlin appeared with her shorthand pad. She was bouncing and talkative, and wanted to collect a contribution from him towards a wedding gift for some girl in the kitchen whose name he didn't even recognise. He gave it to her to shut her up and started to dictate the short notes that would accompany the cheques. Except that he'd destroy the originals and just file the copies. It helped that he was doing a logical task for his own benefit. He heard footsteps and voices outside his office, but ignored them and went on dictating.

Two sharp raps on his door made him stop. The next moment his office was invaded by Mr Bristow, looking more a figure of authority than he ever had before. He asked Lydia Tomlin to leave, and then two men crowded in and were flashing warrant cards. It took Leo another moment to realise they were police officers in plain clothes. He felt himself break out in a cold sweat. Things had developed further than he'd supposed. He could hardly take in what they were saying to him; his mind was in chaos.

He pulled himself to his feet. He must not give in to this. He had to stay calm. He had his escape route; all was not lost yet, he could still get away with it.

Bristow, with a face like thunder, was taking files from the cabinet and pushing Leo away to take the cheque stubs from his desk drawer together with the cash books and journals he made his entries in. It horrified Leo to find they believed they had cut-and-dried evidence against him, and that they wanted to take him to the police station.

'What are you accusing me of?' he asked, trying to sound as though he had no idea.

'At this stage it's just to help us with our inquiries,' he was told. But he couldn't help but notice that Bristow was picking up from his desk the six files he'd made for the ghost companies.

Leo knew then that his situation was dire, that they had all the evidence they'd need. It had a sobering effect on him. His mind grew coldly clear, and he knew that everything now depended on him keeping his wits about him.

He protested his innocence, appeared willing to answer their questions, raised no objection to being taken to the police station. His attitude must be one of helpfulness, of let's get this misunderstanding cleared up.

His confidence had taken a knock by the time they were entering the police station. He hated these places, hated these men who were pushing him about. The first questions were about his bank account. He thought he had little to fear here. He'd made Francis Clitheroe's account look as normal as he could, withdrawing enough money for it to look as though he was living on the salary that was paid in.

'Who is Alistair Jackson?' the inspector asked. Leo felt gutted and badly shaken when they began asking him about that bank account, but he stayed icy calm, told them he knew nobody by that name, though he understood now something of the evidence they had to convict him.

He could see them checking the entries he'd written in the cash book against the chequebook stubs, and realised that the whole edifice he'd built up to hide his activities was patently clear to them. He'd stayed too long in the employ of Walter Bristow and was afraid he was going to lose most if not all of the sum he'd built up. He was fighting now for the last and much greater benefit, his own freedom.

The hours dragged on, but he continued to deny any wrongdoing. Eventually he was charged with fraudulently removing money from his employer's bank account. He was told he must appear in court tomorrow morning but that he'd be tried at a later date. He was fingerprinted and photographed and they checked where he was living before they let him go home.

Leo felt reduced to a nervous wreck. He should never have allowed himself to be taken to the police station like that. Despite all his worries, he'd been overconfident. He should have left Bristow's before this happened. Now that he'd been fingerprinted and photographed, they had evidence that could tie him to his true identity. It had been a big mistake to hang on so long.

But he'd admitted nothing to the police and he'd confirmed none of the facts they'd put before him. He was certain they believed him to be Francis Clitheroe, accountant. They'd given no indication that they even thought he might be somebody else. He could still escape their clutches by ditching that identity.

He was very late returning home, and his fellow lodgers had already eaten their tea and gone. 'Where've you been till now?' his landlady demanded.

He was depressed and exhausted, but he knew he mustn't give up yet.

'I had a phone call at the office,' he lied. 'My mother's been taken seriously ill, a heart attack.' He'd previously told her he'd come over from the Isle of Man to work in Liverpool. 'I have to go home. I've booked myself on to tomorrow morning's boat.'

She was sympathetic and had kept his meal hot for him. It was dried up, but he was glad to sit and eat it; he was ravenous. The police had given him a cup of tea but nothing to eat in all that time.

When the evening cocoa and biscuits was put out, Leo had his share and told the same story to his fellow lodgers. Then he went up to his room, pulled his two suitcases from under the bed and systematically packed everything that belonged to him. He was not planning to appear in court in the morning and knew he must leave nothing behind here lest it give some clue to the police. They'd certainly come here looking for him.

That done, he collapsed on his bed and tried to think of what he must do to stay one step ahead. But his brain felt full of wool. He was too tired; he would have to sleep here tonight. Anyway, the buses stopped running quite early out in the suburbs and he couldn't walk far with his suit-cases.

When his alarm went in the morning, he lay back listening to the rush of footsteps and the water flushing in the bathroom upstairs. He felt better; he'd had a good sleep and his head was working again. He was worried about the money he'd worked so hard to get. Since the police had questioned him about the bank account he'd opened in the name of Alistair Jackson, he could only assume that they'd frozen it and he'd never be able to get at the six thousand pounds or so he'd saved up.

He pulled Francis Clitheroe's dressing gown from his suitcase, put on his heavy-rimmed glasses and went down to eat breakfast with the other men. He said goodbye to everybody and found that the landlady wanted him to settle his bill before leaving. Though he knew he could never return here, he wrote her a cheque on Francis Clitheroe's account. Clitheroe wouldn't be the sort to leave without settling his bill, and he still had to play that part. It reminded him that this account might also be closed by the police, once they knew he had not attended court.

When the other men had gone off to work, he picked up his suitcases and went out to the bus stop. The buses were crowded in the rush hour and he felt his cases made him conspicuous. He got off at Lime Street station and found his way to the left luggage department, where he deposited them.

Once he was free of the cases, he caught a bus to Bootle. To reach Lloyds Bank, where Clitheroe had his account, he had to pass the Bristow's building. The sight of it made him shiver, and he was glad he didn't have to go inside and pretend to work; that had really turned sour on him. He almost emptied Clitheroe's account, leaving only shillings in it. Not enough to meet the cheque he'd given his ex-landlady. But he had cash in plenty now, over seven thousand pounds. In addition he'd bled money into the Arthur Worboys account in the Halifax building society. He wanted to kick himself. If he'd left a day earlier, he could have drained the Alistair Jackson account too.

Back at Lime Street, he picked up his suitcases, broke Clitheroe's spectacles and dropped them in a waste bin, then had a cup of coffee in a café nearby. He didn't want to meet the students living in his bedsit building as they rushed out to their classes. By the time he got there, the building was silent and deserted.

He felt safer as soon as he closed the door of his familiar room. He unpacked his cases, made his sofa into a bed and got into it. He reckoned the police would be unable to find him now.

Leo felt much better after two relaxing days in his bedsit. He was enjoying his unaccustomed leisure. Though his get-rich scheme had turned into a fiasco, he had managed to retrieve some of the money. It had been his own fault and it had scared him, but he had nobody to blame but himself. Next time he'd be more careful.

He spent a lot of time adding up the money he still controlled and making sure it was safe. By drawing large sums out in cash and paying them into an account in a different name at another bank, he'd made it impossible for it to be traced through the banking system.

He'd been thinking a lot about his future over recent months. He'd made plans in his head and now was the time to start putting them into action. In order to be Francis Clitheroe, he'd practised an upper-class accent and acquired all the clothes to look the part. He'd found he quite enjoyed being higher up the social scale; people treated him with more respect.

At his lodgings, the landlady had regularly taken the *Liverpool Post* and left it lying around for others when she'd finished with it. Leo had been perusing the properties for sale columns for weeks. He wanted to get away from Liverpool and had decided he wanted beautiful scenery and to be near the sea. He'd narrowed his search to north Wales, Anglesey perhaps. Then he'd seen advertised just the house he'd love to own. It was in the Colwyn Bay area, but he'd got no further than asking the agent to send him particulars. Now that he'd lost the Alistair Jackson account, that house would be more than he could afford, so he was glad he hadn't got round to looking it over and starting to buy.

But he still had enough for a pleasant cottage, and he was looking forward to finding just that. It would be a good thing, as it would be another bolt-hole a long way away from here should he need it. He'd try and book a holiday in Anglesey towards the end of the month and have a good scout round.

In the meantime he was happy to be back in his bedsit. Today he'd eaten a good lunch in the Irish pub round the corner, had a game of darts with his landlord and won. Conor had been very affable, patting his shoulder and saying, 'My friend, you play a very good game. When will I ever beat you?'

As it was Leo's usual drinking hole, he'd met several old acquaintances there and had several more jars of Guinness. It had developed into a jolly social occasion and he'd thoroughly enjoyed it.

Outside, old Billy was selling newspapers as usual on the pavement. 'Early *Echo*,' he cried. Leo tossed his coppers into the cap and took one home. He threw himself down on his unmade bed to read it, but jerked up in horror when he saw his own face staring out at him and the story of how he'd swindled his boss printed alongside.

He could hardly get his breath as he read the piece through carefully. The photograph was the one taken in the police station and made him look like a criminal. The name given was that of Francis Clitheroe, accountant, and he was wearing his heavy-rimmed spectacles, but he would be easily recognisable to his acquaintances in the pub and the students who lived in this house. Perhaps even to the newspaper vendor and the people who'd known him at the Exchange Hotel.

He panicked again; he couldn't think straight. He wouldn't feel safe here now that his face was in the papers. He had to get out of Liverpool straight away, to somewhere he wasn't known and couldn't be recognised. He started to throw some clothes into a suitcase and almost ran with it to the station. Where would he go? Llandudno, he decided on the spur of the moment; he'd never been there before.

Leo always had carefully made plans so that he knew what to expect. He found it scary to be in a train flying along the Welsh coast to a place he could only imagine. He had no idea where he'd sleep that night, and that was adding to his insecurity. When the train pulled into Llandudno station, he found it a busy place. He walked out on to the street. It was all lit up and there were throngs of holidaymakers everywhere.

He walked on, his suitcase bumping his leg; he must look for somewhere to spend the night. He found himself on the promenade, with waves lapping gently on the beach. There were courting couples with their arms round each other, and lights were strung out in a line round the bay. It looked beautiful. Hotel after hotel faced the sea, but they were all too grand for him.

He went down a side street and into a pub. He ordered a beer and asked the barman where he'd be likely to find a room for the night, one that was not too expensive.

He was directed to the outskirts of town. It was

a small and unobtrusive private hotel with no licence for alcohol. More a guest house than a hotel, but just what Leo wanted in his present circumstances. He booked into a room and felt a little better. Nobody would think of looking for Francis Clitheroe here.

CHAPTER TWENTY-FIVE

Rex knew Helen was losing her strength. The days when he could take her out for a meal and then have her spend the night with him had gone. She was clinging to him in a way she never used to. He felt she was looking to him for support and he didn't know how to provide it.

This afternoon, before starting work in her garden, he'd sat with her in the summerhouse for a time. She'd said she felt tired and he'd left her to have a little sleep while he did some weeding. It was half past three when he went to see how she was. She was just opening her eyes. 'Would you like a cup of tea?' he asked.

'That would be nice.'

'I'll go and make it.'

In the kitchen, Peggy was making fish pie for the evening meal. Marigold had pushed the pram down to the local shops for a walk, as Lucy had flushed her toothbrush down the toilet and needed another. Rex made a pot of tea and poured a cup for Peggy. She said, 'There's Victoria sand-wich cake if you'd like some.'

'No thanks,' he said. 'And I don't think Helen will.'

He took the tray over to the summerhouse, and for a moment he thought Helen had drifted off to sleep again. She was lying back on a substantial wooden lounger. Joan had found a mattress to cover the slats and fit under the cushions to make it more comfortable for her.

'I'd better sit up,' she said. Rex helped her, raising the back rest and shaking up her pillows. He put a cup of tea in her hands, pulled up a chair and sat down to drink his own.

He was talking about what he would do next in the garden, but Helen sat there staring straight ahead and gripping her tea cup with both hands.

Suddenly she turned towards him. 'Rex, I want you to do something for me.' Her dull eyes stared into his.

'Of course,' he said. 'What is it you want?'

Slowly she put her cup down on the table. 'I want you to help me to die.'

Rex's hand jerked with shock, spilling some of his tea on his trousers. 'What? I can't do that!' He was aghast. 'I don't want you to die.'

'It's hopeless. I'm not going to get better. I don't want to go on.'

'It's not hopeless. I thought you were improving last month. You were much brighter. When we took you to see that specialist last week, he did some tests and seemed to think so too.'

'No, Rex.'

'Dr Harris thinks you're getting better.'

'No he doesn't. He's been to see me this morning. The tests they did... Well, they think the

367

cancer's spreading. They want me to have another course of chemotherapy.' There was utter despair on her face.

Rex sat on the side of her lounger and put his arms round her. He felt terrible. 'I'm so sorry, love.'

She was clinging, her fingers gripping his shirt. 'I don't want to go through that again, the sickness and the pain.'

He tried his best to sound hopeful. 'This second course could cure you.'

'I think it'll just prolong my... I feel so helpless and useless. I'm making so much work for Chloe and Marigold. Please help me!'

'It's against the law for me to do that.'

'I know, I know. I'm asking an awful lot of you. I'm sorry, but there's no one else I can ask, is there?'

'No, but I don't want you to die. What would Chloe say? She doesn't want that either.'

'I'm going to get worse, and heaven knows how long this will drag on. I'll never be without this awful pain...'

'Dr Harris gives you something for that, doesn't he?'

'But it always comes back.' It was a cry from the heart. 'I'd like to go to sleep one night and never wake up.'

'Helen love...' Rex knew she was crying, and he couldn't hold his own tears back.

'I know it's too much to ask of anyone, but please, please... Help me, Rex.'

Before he left, Chloe poured Rex a beer and they

sat in the sitting room with Marigold and talked about Helen's recommended second course of chemotherapy. He could see they were both in despair.

'Just when her hair is beginning to grow back,' Chloe mourned. 'She won't let me see it yet, but Aunt Goldie...'

'She has to wash, and she can't manage that without help.' Marigold was stoical. 'The other day she wanted me to measure it. It's about half an inch long now. She said that when it reaches an inch and a half, she'll throw away her wig.'

Rex could see that Marigold was fighting tears too. 'She's been so brave. Always trying to look on the bright side. But now...'

Zac let out a scream of rage and started to cry. He and Lucy had been playing together on the carpet.

'What's the matter, love?' Marigold was on her feet in an instant.

'My teddy.' He was angry. 'Take my teddy.'

Lucy was scrambling away with his toy. 'He won't play with me. Won't let me near his things.'

'Give it back to him.' Marigold was stern. 'This minute. You have a teddy of your own.'

Rex pulled himself to his feet and wished them good night. At home alone, he felt in turmoil. He wanted to do his best for Helen, but what was the best? He knew how much she'd suffered during her first course of chemotherapy, and to ask her to go through it again was heartbreaking for them all.

He understood how Helen must be feeling, but to help her take her life? The very thought of that terrified him. If he did, he might be charged with murder, but that wasn't the most frightening thing about it. To take another's life was the biggest decision anyone could make.

She was only forty-eight. That was very young to die. But in her place and her position? Rex asked himself what he'd want to do. There was only one logical answer: he'd want to die too.

The next time he was alone with Helen in the summerhouse, she felt for his hand. 'Have you thought any more about what I asked of you?'

Rex could do no more than nod; he'd thought of little else.

'I'll make it worth your while.' She still insisted on paying his company for the gardening services he gave. 'I'll leave you money in my will.'

'Heavens, no! Not that! If I gain from your death, it'll definitely look like murder. Please, leave nothing to me.' He sat in silence, holding her hand.

'I'm asking too much, I know. I'm sorry.'

'Have you made a will, Helen?'

'I made one when I first came back to live here. I willed everything to Chloe.'

'Much the best thing. Leave it at that.'

'Yes, she's going to need a home for her babies, but now Marigold has no other home.'

Rex smiled. 'Chloe isn't the sort to put her out, she's fond of Aunt Goldie. Anyway, she needs her here to look after her kids.'

Helen sighed. 'Everything changes, doesn't it? I expected Marigold to be another burden, but she's been marvellous since she came to live with us. I don't know how we'd manage without her now. And there's Joan, she's been a very good friend. I'd like to leave my bits of silver to her; she and Walter would appreciate them.'

'That could be done by adding a codicil to your will, and you could leave a legacy to Marigold in the same way. Enough to give her a bit of independence, should circumstances change.'

'Enough to let her know I love her and appreciate what she's doing for us. It's all likely to come back to Chloe or the children in the fullness of time.' Helen sighed again. 'Marigold and I, for a mother and daughter we've had a very strange relationship.'

'That's hardly your fault.'

'No. Can you help me arrange these things?'

Rex thought about it. 'I'll talk to Chloe and get her to contact your solicitor. Better if it comes from her.'

Helen looked up into his eyes. 'Especially if you're going to help me with the other thing. Have you decided yet?'

'Helen, I don't know. I want to do what's best for you, but helping you to die? That's a huge decision to make.'

'I've made it for myself. It's what I want. I'll not change my mind.' She looked defeated.

He felt full of pity for her. 'It's brave of you to face it like this.' He perched on the side of her lounger, put an arm round her shoulders and drew her to him. Having discussed all these intimate details, he felt they were closer than they'd ever been. Now there was a secret between them never to be told.

Rex had spent half the afternoon with Helen. When he was about to go home, Chloe stopped him and asked, 'Will you stay and eat with us? Not just tonight, I mean every night. You come almost every night anyway. Peggy makes generous helpings and Mum's eating less and less, so I know there'll be plenty.'

He wanted to see her kindness as a sign that she cared about him.

'You're very good to all of us,' Chloe said. 'Mum says she looks forward to your coming, and what's the point in you going home and having to start cooking for yourself?'

'Thank you, I'd like that. It makes me feel like one of the family,' he said. 'It's not much fun eating every meal on my own. But hold on, sometimes Helen has other visitors. I'll not stay then, I'd be in your way.'

She was shaking her head. 'Rex, you're very understanding.'

He'd never seen so much of Chloe as he was doing now, and he'd never known so much of the minutiae of her daily life. He felt full of love for both mother and daughter.

She smiled up at him. 'You're as near one of the family as makes no difference.'

Wednesday was one of the days Rex worked in Helen's garden, but today the rain was tipping down, so it didn't surprise him to find the summerhouse empty. He put his head round the kitchen door and found Peggy making pastry and the room full of delicious baking scents.

She looked up, her face red from the heat of the

stove; she had flour on her nose. 'Helen's up in her room.' She smiled. 'She was down here all morning and had quite a good lunch, but after that she said she wanted to lie down and have a little sleep.'

'Best thing for her on a day like this,' Rex said.

'Yes. Marigold and Zac have gone to meet Lucy from nursery school; they're going to get soaked. I told Helen I'd make her a cup of tea about now. I've got the tray ready, will you take it up?'

Peggy was pouring boiling water into the tea-pot. She added another cup and saucer and some home-made biscuits to the tray.

When he pushed the bedroom door open, he could see that Helen was awake. She smiled at him. 'I was hoping you'd come,' she said. 'I want to tell you more about my plans.'

'What plans? Will you have one of Peggy's biscuits?'

'No thanks, just tea. I've told you already really.'

He helped himself to a biscuit. 'I was hoping you'd given up the idea.'

'No, and I'm not going to.'

'I do realise it's a huge step you're facing. But oh, Helen!'

'I've had plenty of time to think about it. I'll not change my mind.'

Rex's mouth had gone dry. 'How d'you intend to do it?'

'I'm going to take an overdose.' She said it so baldly, it made him shudder.

'Of your pills?'

'Yes, at bedtime. I'm on some new tablets for my pain. They're said to contain morphine and they

373

give me a lovely floaty feeling as I go off to sleep. If I save them up and take them all at once...'

'No, Helen! You can't stop taking what's prescribed for you! You need them now to deaden your pain.'

'This way, it'll deaden my pain permanently.' She gave him a wry smile. 'We all have to save up for what we want.'

That she could still joke brought a lump to his throat.

'I take other painkillers during the day; Marigold doles them out for me every four hours. She and Chloe won't let me keep the bottles up here any more. When I was getting over the operation, I had terrible pain and Chloe said I was taking too many. She said the doctor wrote them up to be taken at four-hourly intervals and I mustn't take them until they were due. So now they're kept in the pantry on the top shelf where the children can't reach them. The trouble is, I can't either.'

She squeezed his hand. 'The pain takes no notice of the clock. If I'm in pain, I need them, but if I feel all right, I don't. I sometimes tell them that I'll keep my pill under my pillow and take it later.'

'So you're saving them up?'

'I've saved a few. Do you know how big a dose of morphine I'd need to make sure I won't wake up again?'

'No,' he said. 'No, I haven't the slightest idea.'

'Could you find out for me?'

Rex was beginning to feel desperate. 'I can't ask around about that, can I? Is that the help you're asking me to give you?'

'Yes, amongst other things.'

'What other things?'

'You will help me?'

Rex nodded. He couldn't refuse her and he wanted to protect Chloe from being asked in his stead. 'Yes,' he told her.

'I want you to buy me over-the-counter pain-killers, aspirin or something I can use instead of the pills prescribed.'

'I hate to think of you doing this.'

'I think all my pills are strong; I don't think I'd need very many to kill me. People can die if they take a lot of aspirins.'

Rex hastily drained his tea cup. His mouth was dry again. 'I don't think...'

'There is another way. Every so often Marigold collects new prescriptions from the chemist for me.'

'But she'd know if I took the bottles from the pantry and gave them to you.'

'Marigold can be forgetful too; she's left them by my bed more than once. I'd just want you to take three or four out of each bottle. She wouldn't notice that.'

'To add to your hoard?'

'There's no other way. I've saved two of my sleeping pills and four of the daytime pills.' She took a small green suede Dorothy bag from her pocket to show him. 'I have to collect them in this so I can carry it around with me. They treat me like a child.'

Rex shuddered at the sight of the pills tipped out in Helen's hand. 'It's their way of caring for you,' he told her. They believe it's for your own good.'

'Yes, but I wish they'd listen to me. I keep telling them I don't want any more chemo, that I'd rather things were left to take their natural course.'

'Helen!'

'Everybody else believes that the next course will cure my cancer, and I get encouragement from all sides to go ahead and try it.'

Rex shivered. 'They could be right.' He was still clinging to that hope.

'The doctors talk of surgically rebuilding my breast as though that will restore my body to what it used to be. It won't. Nothing can put the clock back now. I shall take my overdose before they cart me off to hospital again.'

Rex wanted to cover his face with both hands. 'I'm so sorry it's come to this. I wish there was something I could do that would really help.'

'You do help, just listening to me. I couldn't keep all this to myself, could I? I want to make it easier for all of you. I want it to be organised. I hope you don't mind – it's your birthday in two weeks' time...'

'Yes,' Rex agreed. 'Nobody ever did anything to celebrate my birthdays until you started making me cakes and having little tea parties.'

'Chloe has offered to bake your cake this year, and she's going to arrange a little party round my lounger in the summerhouse.'

'That will be nice.'

'I want to make it my send off, my chance to say goodbye to all my family, but only you will know that.'

Rex's fingers tightened on her hand. 'Helen! No!'

'I'll try and stay up for dinner that night. Then I'll say I'm tired, that I've enjoyed it and I'll ask you to carry me up to my room. When Marigold has settled me down for the night, I'll take as many pills as I've collected and hope I'll not wake up again.'

'Oh God, Helen! I don't want you to do that.' He put his arms round her and pulled her close.

'I'm sorry. It'll be your birthday, but...'

'You know it's not that.'

'You did say you'd help me,' she whispered and pulled away from him. He could see the doubt and disappointment in her face. 'Have you changed your mind?'

'If that's what you really want, I'll help you in every way I can,' he promised.

CHAPTER TWENTY-SIX

For Chloe it was proving to be a terrible summer. Her mother had always been small and slight, but now she was painfully thin and frail. Although she still had the occasional good day, she seemed to have many more that were bad.

She didn't complain, but they all knew she was often gripped by pain. Auntie Joan was coming round regularly once or twice a week to keep her spirits up. She used to take her back to her own house occasionally for a meal and a change of scene, but recently her mother hadn't wanted to go. Aunt Goldie was the first to put into words what they were beginning to think.

'Poor Helen, I don't think she's going to get better. She has no energy, and all she wants to do is sit in the garden or in the summerhouse. And even getting out there is becoming more than she can manage.'

Chloe hadn't given up hope that her mother would recover. She talked of their future plans for the garden. Rex didn't need any encouragement to come round. She'd heard him mention the holiday he'd take Mum on when she felt better. Chloe encouraged her to eat a few extra mouthfuls at each meal and tried to buoy up her spirits.

Dr Harris was coming to see her frequently, and prescribing ever more tablets for her pain. Chloe and Goldie made sure she took them and followed all his advice. They'd all tried to believe that Helen would get better, that it was only a matter of time until she did. But when Chloe took the week off work to spend more time with her, it gave her a clearer picture of how things really were.

She was sitting in the garden with her mother when Dr Harris made one of his calls. Chloe looked up to see him striding across the grass towards them. Helen perked up to talk to him, but though he discussed the drugs he was prescribing, Chloe thought his call had no more effect than a social visit. When he stood up to leave, she went with him to show him out through the house.

'Mum seems to be getting worse,' she said. 'All the bounce has gone out of her. Is there nothing more we can do?'

They were crossing the patio to the back door. 'Sit here for a moment, Chloe,' he said.

She perched on the edge of a chair. 'I'm worried about Mum.'

'And I'm worried about you both. Your mother's made her decision. Has she told you that she's refused to have another course of chemo?'

'No!' Chloe was aghast. 'No! Only yesterday Aunt Goldie asked her when she'd be starting it and she said she didn't know.'

'She knows it'll upset you and that you'll try to persuade her otherwise. She feels she can't hold out against you any more. She hasn't the strength.'

Chloe felt tears burning her eyes. 'She has said it makes her feel worse than the disease itself.'

'I know, and we have talked it through. I tried hard to persuade her to carry on with the treatment, but this is her decision and she didn't make it lightly.'

'I know she doesn't think it will cure her and she doesn't want to lose her hair again and be made to feel sick.' She was biting her lip. 'It's as though she's lost all hope of getting better.' She felt a tear run down her face. 'Is there no more hope?'

'There's always hope. Your mother wants it this way; she's decided to leave it to nature. We must respect her wishes and help her to face with dignity whatever comes.'

'It's so unfair,' Chloe railed. 'Why her?'

Dr Harris's dark eyes were kindly. 'Your mother seems at peace, but this is something you have to face too.'

She sighed. 'I wish I were stronger.'

'You're strong enough,' he said. He patted her arm and stood up. 'I'll ask the Marie Curie nurses to come. They'll help you make her as comfortable as possible. Helen likes visitors, doesn't she?'

'Always has.'

Chloe showed him to the front door. She closed it quickly behind him and had to run to the cloakroom. She wiped her face on the towel and then decided to splash cold water round her eyes. She didn't want Mum to see she'd been crying.

She went back to sit with her and hold her hand, but her mother was dozing off. She was doing more of that these days.

Two days later, a Marie Curie nurse came round and introduced herself as Felicity. She made Helen comfortable and sat and talked to both of them. She said that on her days off it would be her colleague Gail who would come. They talked about Helen's medication and what the family could do to help.

When she'd gone, her mother said, 'She's a sweet girl. She's going to give me a bath tomorrow and wash my hair. She says there's a lot she can do to style it. It'll save Marigold the job. I'm afraid she's having to work very hard these days.'

Chloe was pleased that her mother had taken to the nurse, but suddenly she was fading away before their eyes.

Since Chloe had said he must have his dinner with them, Rex had made it a habit to look in on Helen late every afternoon, even when he was working elsewhere. When he thanked Chloe again

380

for this, she said, 'I've got a confession to make. There's an ulterior motive. We need your help.'

'You know I'll be glad to do anything I can.' He smiled. He couldn't do enough for Chloe.

'Mum likes to get up and spend the day downstairs or out in the garden, and while Aunt Goldie and Peggy can get her down the stairs, by evening Mum's tired and the stairs are proving difficult. They're too narrow for us to get one each side of her.' Stair lift needed

'That's easy,' he told her. 'And no bother at all.'

Sometimes when he came, he'd find that Chloe was already home from work and that she'd have walked Helen as far as the kitchen, where the children would be eating a light supper. Peggy had extended her working day to five thirty so she could prepare this for them before leaving.

He knew that Chloe's evenings were busy. She played with the children, bathed them before getting them ready for bed and read them a story before tucking them in. Marigold usually collapsed with a cup of tea in front of the television, exhausted after being on the go all day.

It had been Helen's routine to sit with Marigold and stay downstairs to have dinner with the family, but she said she was so tired these days, she'd rather go straight up to her bed and have dinner there.

Over the last few days, Rex had walked her to the bottom of the stairs and then swung her up in his arms and carried her up to the bedroom he'd once regularly shared with her. He'd sit and talk to her until dinner was ready and then fetch up their meals on two trays.

381

Tonight, when he lowered Helen on to her bed, he said, 'I've been to the library today. I browsed round for ages trying to find out how much morphine you'd need to guarantee a fatal dose. I'm no wiser about that, but I did discover that it's a derivative of opium and that it often causes vomiting. Also, death by poisoning is never pleasant. You're wrong about that, Helen. It's not a matter of floating off to sleep and never waking up.'

'You won't scare me off,' she told him.

Rex told her of what he'd read. 'It'll be painful. You might have spasms or fits and be fighting for breath.' He painted a dire picture for her, in the hope of persuading her not to do it.

'At least it will be over quickly, in hours, rather than waiting months or years for nature to drag out its course.'

'Helen, I wish you wouldn't. We all of us love you and want you with us for as long as possible.'

She was cringing. 'I can't face it. Please get me more pills. It would be too awful if I suffered all that and then woke up again.'

It went against all Rex's instincts, but one afternoon when he was making a cup of tea for them both and there was no one else in the kitchen, he looked on the top shelf in the larder for the two pill bottles. He took four out of each and gave them to Helen to add to her hoard. With what she had, it gave her twenty times her normal dose.

'I think that should do it,' he said as he watched her slide them into her little green suede Dorothy bag.

'I've got to be sure it will.' He could see anguish on her face. 'Will you buy me a large bottle of aspirins too?'

Rex was dreading his birthday and was well aware that it was approaching fast.

He went home to toss and turn in bed. What Helen was doing was giving him nightmares. He should not be helping her in this way, but now he'd done what she'd asked, there was no way he could stop it. He had to admire her guts, but he feared for her too. He was horribly afraid she was going to have a very painful death. Four more days to wait before she staged it.

Rex woke up in a tangle of bedclothes, hot, sweaty and dry-mouthed. He didn't at first realise that it was the ringing telephone down in the hall that had woken him. He lay back, willing it to stop. When it didn't, he switched on his bedside light. It was half past three.

He leapt out of bed, and pulling his eiderdown round him, ran down to the hall still feeling fuzzy.

'Yes, hello,' he said into the phone. Chloe's voice jerked him back to wakefulness. She was crying and hardly coherent.

'Rex, it's Mum. I think she's going.'

'Going?'

'She's slipping away. Dying. She's asking for you.'

He stood half paralysed with shock. This was not what Helen had planned. He almost said, she can't be, not yet, but pulled himself together sufficiently to say, 'I'll be there as soon as I can,' before running back upstairs to throw on his clothes.

His mind raced. Helen knew he wasn't convinced it was the right thing for her to do. He'd never stopped trying to dissuade her. Had she been afraid that at the last moment he'd tell her family about her plan? Was that why she'd jumped the gun?

It was a dark night, and there was no traffic on the road. Rex hardly knew what he was doing; he was in an emotional tumult. Every light shone out of the windows of 8 Carberry Road. Marigold in a scarlet dressing gown had the front door open before he reached it.

'She's at the gates of heaven,' she said. 'I've rung for the doctor.'

He shot upstairs to Helen's room and Marigold followed. Chloe had been sitting by the bed; she rose to her feet. 'Rex, thank goodness you're here, Mum's asking for you.'

Helen was a tiny figure under the bedclothes. She looked half comatose, and her face was deathly pale with a blueish tinge round her mouth. Marigold went to the other side of the bed. 'We're all gathered round you, Helen,' she said in a sonorous voice.

Rex slid down on to the chair Chloe had vacated. 'Helen, love,' he said. 'I'm here now. We're all with you.'

Her eyes flickered open for a moment. 'Rex...' Her breath came out in a long-drawn-out gasp. 'Can't wait for ... your birthday.'

'No need,' he said. His mind was aflame. Had she taken her hoard of pills sooner? Had she been in so much pain she couldn't wait four more days? His stomach churned. But no, this wasn't the painful, agonising death the library books had promised those who took poison. Helen was relaxing into her pillow; she was calm and barely breathing. He took her hand in his; it was icy cold.

'Glad,' she said softly after a few moments. He had to crane closer to hear her. 'I asked ... too much of you.'

'No, Helen, you've never done that,' he assured her, though her last plans certainly had.

Her voice had almost gone. 'Look after Chloe ... and her babies ... for me.'

'Of course I will. You don't have to ask that.'

Chloe was still standing beside him. He heard her sob of distress and got up to draw her closer to the bed with him.

Helen's voice was a faint murmur, a soft whisper. 'I know ... you've always loved her...'

Chloe turned to him and wept on his shoulder. Rex put his arms round her and pulled her closer. The tears were pouring down his face too.

'Oh God,' Marigold said. 'I think she's gone.'

Rex looked down and waited, but Helen didn't take another breath. Marigold was right. Helen was dead. He wept with grief, but at the same time he felt deeply thankful she'd had the peaceful, natural death he'd so much wanted for her.

The sound of the doorbell ripped through the house.

'That'll be the doctor,' Marigold said and went down to let him in. Rex felt numb.

Dr Harris came up to see his patient for the last time. He murmured words of sympathy to them all and drew the sheet over Helen's face.

'I'm afraid there are certain formalities we need

to attend to. I'll make out the death certificate; you can collect it from the surgery in the morning.'

Rex watched both Chloe and Marigold go downstairs to see him out, but he didn't immediately follow. His mind was now on one last service he must do for Helen. He needed to find that green suede Dorothy bag. She must have kept it within her reach. He crept quietly round the bed, opening the drawers in her bedside table, pushing away the neatly ironed handkerchiefs as he looked for it. It was in the last one. He picked it up and found himself sweating with relief to find it still full of tablets. He pushed it in to his pocket.

Before leaving, he folded the sheet back from Helen's face. The lines of age and suffering were gone. She looked young again, as young as when he'd first known her. She looked as though she'd just fallen asleep.

'Goodbye, Helen,' he whispered. 'I'm going to miss you. Sorry I couldn't be what you wanted.'

He turned to go, and found a tear-stained Chloe watching him from the doorway.

She stood staring at him for a moment, then turned and ran from him, along the passage to her own bedroom. The door closed firmly behind her.

Rex hesitated. He wanted to follow her. He knew he could both comfort her and take comfort from her. But it was her bedroom, her private place, and he was afraid he'd say too much too soon. His mind was raging with other things and hers must be too. And she'd closed the door against him.

Marigold had made tea for them in the kitchen and had poured out three cups. Rex hesitated again. He wanted to take Chloe's up to her, but although Marigold's eyes were wet, they were as fierce as ever, and he didn't dare suggest it. Marigold took it up herself.

Chloe got into bed and pulled the bedclothes over her head. It had caught in her throat and made her feel swamped with emotion to find Rex talking to her dead mother. She'd known that Mum loved him; she'd felt their devotion, been envious that they'd found everlasting love while what she'd had had withered and died.

She despised Adam but felt admiration for Rex. She owed him a lot. It was he who'd supported her in her hour of need when Adam had told her not to return to the home she'd shared with him.

'Don't let yourself become a victim,' Rex had said, and she'd drawn from him the strength to do that. Whenever she'd felt weak, lost and unable to help herself, Rex had been there.

'What you need is a bit of gardening,' he'd say, and she'd find herself soothed. Since she'd been a child, he'd been a rock of support.

She heard the tap on her bedroom door, and pushed up through the bedclothes to see Aunt Goldie.

'I've brought you a cup of tea.' She put it down on her bedside table. 'Poor Helen,' she mourned. 'So young, and so sad for you to lose your mother.' The door closed behind her.

Chloe wept, and knew she was weeping for

many things.

Rex went home to grieve alone. Full daylight came quickly. He had work to do that filled his morning, though he felt slower and less effective than usual. Chloe and her grief was filling his mind. He couldn't stay away from her and the house in Carberry Road. He wanted to help with Helen's funeral in the way he had when Gran had died.

When Chloe greeted him, her eyes were red and she seemed numb. He wanted to take her in his arms and comfort her, but she was ring-fenced from him by her family. Uncle Walter and Auntie Joan were there. It was they who helped Chloe decide that her children were too young to go to the funeral. Peggy was going to look after them and lay out a small buffet of finger food for the mourners who would return with them. They all felt held in limbo until the day of the funeral came.

In church, Rex stood between Chloe and Marigold. It was a solemn and sad occasion, but he felt relief, too, that Helen's death had come before she could put her plan in action. If he had helped her die, he'd have felt guilt for the rest of his life, and been left wondering if her cancer might just have gone into remission and allowed her to survive.

Now he could be glad that her pain and suffering were over and that she'd had the calm and peaceful death she'd hoped for. Except that he wanted to weep again that she'd lost her life to illness at the age of forty-eight. That was too young to die.

Rex's heart was heavy. He knew he'd miss Helen as much as any of her family would. She'd been a close friend and his lover for a large part of his life. Yes, he mourned for her, but it left him free now to tell Chloe what he'd always felt for her.

It took him only moments to realise that of course it did not. He couldn't tell her how much he loved her in the days after her mother's death, while she was still gripped by grief. It would seem heartless if he cast Helen aside too quickly. He'd have to wait until Chloe could focus on other things.

The funeral reception was a sad little gathering. Marigold gave in to bouts of weeping and for the first time referred to Helen openly as her daughter. Chloe had red eyes and her children picked up on the atmosphere and cried for their nana. Zac kept asking where she'd gone, and that distressed them all. As the mourners drifted away and Marigold saw them out, Rex felt he should go too.

'No, Rex, don't you go.' Chloe put her hand on his arm. 'You must stay and eat with us.'

That cheered him, as it seemed she wanted him close, but he had to ask, 'Are you sure?'

'Of course. You mustn't go home to an empty house tonight. Mum would never forgive me if I let you do that.'

He found that quite upsetting. Was Chloe seeing him only as her mother's partner? She went on, 'When everybody goes, I want you to walk me and the children round the garden and tell us

389

about the flowers and plants.'

When the last guest left, Marigold went upstairs to lie down and Peggy started to cook the evening meal. It was a cool, damp afternoon and it had been raining. As Chloe dressed her children in macs and Rex pushed their tiny feet into wellingtons, she told them, 'This was Nana's garden. She and Rex made it together.'

The children raced off across the wet grass and Chloe looked up at Rex with a sad smile. 'Mum lived for her garden. It'll always remind me of her.'

She took his arm and they set off after the children. 'Mum's death changes everything for me,' she confided. 'She's left me her house, so I'll always have a home for my children. But you know that, don't you? She said you'd helped her put her affairs in order.'

'Yes.' He could sense the effort Chloe was making to hold her tears in check.

'I'm going back to work,' she said. 'Uncle Walter wants me to; he's worried stiff that so much of his company's money has disappeared with his accountant.'

Rex wanted to take her in his arms and kiss her, tell her not to worry, that he'd help with all her problems. Instead, he dead-headed a few flowers as they passed by, and told her what plants would flower next and how, years ago, he'd dug this pond out from a patch of bog.

'I want you to keep it like this always,' Chloe murmured. 'It will be a memorial for Mum.'

CHAPTER TWENTY-SEVEN

To Chloe it felt strange to be back at work. Not too much seemed to have changed in the office, while her mother's death had caused an enormous difference at home. The girls welcomed her back; they'd kept her work as well as the accounting ledgers up to date, and were being especially kind to her. They were bursting with news of Francis Clitheroe when Walter Bristow came through their office.

'Chloe, you shouldn't have rushed back,' he said. 'Don't you need more time for yourself?'

'No, I'll have less time to think about Mum if I'm working. I prefer to be here.'

'Well, you'd better come in to my office and I'll bring you up to date. Angela, please could you arrange for a couple of cups of coffee to come in?'

'I gather a lot has been going on.' Chloe sat down on the other side of his desk. 'The girls are agog about what Francis Clitheroe was doing.'

'Yes, it's not good news. I didn't want to bother you with all the details at the time. I told you he didn't turn up for his court hearing?'

'Yes, and he's disappeared now?'

'So it seems. Constable Benton went to look for him at his lodging house only to find he'd done a flit.'

'I didn't know he was in lodgings,' Chloe said.

'Neither did I. He told me he was in a rented flat and looking for a more permanent home.'

'That was a lie? It looks as though things are worse than we supposed, Uncle.'

'Yes. The landlady had cleaned his room out by the time the police got there, and said he left nothing at all behind. He told everyone he was going home to the Isle of Man because his mother had had a heart attack and was very ill.'

'I never heard him mention the Isle of Man,' said Chloe, frowning.

Walter was indignant. 'He gave me a London address when he came here. His last place of work was London. They sent me references. Good references.'

'Too good, by the looks of it.'

'Yes, Benton checked and Clitheroe didn't take the ferry to the Isle of Man and neither does he appear to have relatives there. We think that was intended to be a red herring.'

'Heavens,' Chloe said. 'I hope they find him or you'll not get your money back.'

'They've frozen his bank account as well as the one he opened in the name of Alistair Jackson. So I'll get some of it.'

The following day, the police officers came in and asked Walter if they could take another look at Clitheroe's office. 'And then,' Inspector Halyard said, 'we'd like to talk to other members of your staff. Those who worked for him.'

'Yes of course,' Walter told them. 'Chloe will take you.' But he was anxious that little progress was being made, and he went with them.

'You gave him a very private office,' Halyard said, looking round. 'Nobody could watch what he did here.' He opened every drawer in the desk; there was nothing left but articles belonging to the company.

'It looks as though he cleaned up before he left,' Benton said. 'Possibly he's done this before.'

'I don't like this,' Chloe said. 'Clitheroe was telling lies and he seems to have no long term address. I don't like the idea of him getting off scot-free with your money.'

'Neither do I, and Joan's furious about it.'

'So where could he have gone?' Chloe demanded. 'He told us he'd come from London.'

'We checked the address in London that both you and he gave us; it was a false one.'

'What?' Walter was cross. 'That means he deliberately set out to steal from me.'

'It's beginning to look like that. The road on which we thought he lived does exist, but the houses only go up to number thirty-five, and he gave number forty-one as his previous address.'

'He told me that was his parents' home and he'd been living with them up till then,' Walter said.

'You're saying he's vanished?' Chloe asked.

'That's about it,' the constable agreed, taking out his notepad. 'We've drawn no leads at all on Francis Clitheroe. A total blank, in fact. To trace him now we need to know more about him. Is there anything else you can tell us, Mr Bristow?'

Walter spread out his hands, palms up. 'I've told you all I know, really I have. He seemed a pleasant enough fellow, I quite liked him. I had no sus-

393

picions there was anything wrong. I thought he'd do a good job.'

'What about you, Miss Redwood?'

'To be honest, I didn't like him, and I got the impression he didn't much care for me. He wasn't popular with any of the girls; they said he was po-faced.'

'Can you remember anything unusual about him?' Chloe was shaking her head. 'Anything at all, however minor?'

'Well, to start with he used a silver propelling pencil all the time. He fiddled with it while he was dictating. A fancy one, expensive-looking.'

'That might be helpful,' Halyard said. 'He must be intelligent to have worked this system out, would you agree?'

'Yes,' Walter sighed. 'Very intelligent. I reckon he was the sort who could think on his feet. He was articulate, always had words ready in answer to any question. He sounded logical and sincere. Sorry, that doesn't give you much more to go on, does it?'

'No, but if you think of anything else, give me a ring.'

The officers interviewed several members of staff and took away the file Walter had had made for Clitheroe, saying they might find a lead in the information it contained.

The next day was Saturday. Chloe got up late, felt weary and in the morning did little but play with her children. Aunt Goldie made lunch and afterwards went to rest on her bed. In the afternoon, Chloe took the children to the local shops.

Lucy had paddled in the pool wearing the only pair of shoes she had that still fitted her. She bought each of them a new pair. She was pushing the pram along Carberry Road on her return when she saw Walter's car come from the opposite end and pull into her drive.

Auntie Joan had seen her and came back to the gate to meet them. Lucy rushed into her arms and greeted her. 'New shoes, Auntie.'

'Hello, love.' Joan swung her up to kiss her. 'Very smart shoes.'

Lucy's hands stroked the package Joan was carrying. 'For me? Present?'

'No, my pet,' Joan laughed. 'It's a book for Mummy. It's that one I told you about, Chloe. Rosamund Rogerson's *Stroll in the Moonlight*. It's good, you'll like it.'

'Thank you,' Chloe said. 'I need something to read in bed, something to relax me and get me off to sleep. Mum would have liked this. I keep thinking of her, and memories keep crowding back and going round in my head. I'm missing her.'

'I am too.'

'Hello,' Walter said. 'I'm sure you see enough of me at the office, Chloe, and here I am again.'

'Come on in.' Chloe pushed the pram into the porch. 'You're just in time for tea.'

'That would be lovely.' Joan followed her into the kitchen. 'Walter can't settle to anything. He's like a bear with a bad head over this missing accountant. We had to get out of the house for a bit.'

Walter lifted Zac out of his pram; he cooed with

delight to be swung so high. Chloe and Joan made a tray of tea and set out some of the cakes Peggy had made.

'Go upstairs,' Chloe said to Lucy, 'wash your hands and see if Aunt Goldie is awake. Tell her we're having tea in the summerhouse.'

Aunt Goldie came bustling across the grass with Lucy in tow almost as soon as Chloe had poured tea for her guests.

'Joan, I've collected up those periodicals you brought round for Helen. You said you hadn't finished with them, didn't you?'

'Yes, there was an article in one of them about the author of this book I've just brought you. Did you find it?'

'No,' Chloe said, passing round the cakes.

'I'm not sure which one.' Joan began sorting through them.

Chloe picked one up and began leafing through it. She came across an article entitled *'No Happy Ending for Rosamund Rogerson'*, and said, 'This is it.'

She began reading the article aloud. *'Tragedy has struck twice in the life of Rosamund Rogerson, veteran writer of best-selling family sagas, all of which have happy endings. Last week, her husband, John James Clitheroe...'*

Chloe felt a shaft of impatience and broke off. 'There's no getting away from that name,' she said crossly.

'It's only a name, and probably lots of people have it.' Walter was his usual benign self. 'Mustn't let a name put us off. Joan's keen on her books.'

Chloe went on. *'John James Clitheroe, aged fifty-*

nine, a lecturer in political sciences at the London School of Economics, was reported missing whilst taking part in the Sydney to Hobart yacht race. He was a keen and experienced yachtsman, but when some of the rigging on his boat collapsed during a storm, he was swept overboard in mountainous seas. The crew was unable to save him and he is presumed drowned.

'*Last year, the couple's only son, Francis Lovell Clitheroe, aged thirty-six, a chartered accountant...*' Chloe lurched to a halt. Her stomach was churning. 'Oh my goodness! This sounds so like...'

'Like what?' Goldie asked.

'Like Walter's accountant.' Joan's mouth had dropped open.

'The man who's fraudulently taken his money,' Chloe choked. 'Have you read this before? Joan, you must have noticed this.'

'No, I didn't. I just thought how sad for the writer. I don't think I knew the new accountant's name, not until Walter started going on and on about this fraud.'

'Go on, Chloe.' There was a note of urgency in Walter's voice.

Chloe swallowed hard and found her place. '*Francis Lovell Clitheroe, aged thirty-six, a chartered accountant, was killed whilst on holiday in Majorca. He was on an organised jeep safari into the hills in the north of the island when his vehicle went off the road and rolled down the mountain, killing both him and his wife Elspeth.*'

'It's him, isn't it?' Walter asked.

Slowly Chloe read the article through again. 'It's not just his name; other things check out too:

397

he was a chartered accountant and he was thirty-six. But if Francis Clitheroe was killed last year, who was the man we knew by that name?'

'I can't believe this.' Walter was sizzling with excitement. 'It'll open up new avenues for Inspector Halyard. Set him off in a new direction.'

Chloe could feel her heart pounding. 'This man we knew as Francis Clitheroe ... he must have been an imposter. That's why he seems to have disappeared off the face of the earth.'

'I must ring Inspector Halyard straight away.' Walter was already on his feet.

'It's Saturday,' Aunt Goldie said. 'Does he work over the weekend?'

'The sooner he knows about this the better. You don't mind if I use your phone?' Walter suddenly looked lost and was patting his pockets. 'Oh, I need his number, and the card he gave me is in the pocket of my suit.'

'He gave me a card too.' Chloe scrambled to her feet and ran into the house ahead of Walter to get it.

She stood beside him listening while he made the call. It dampened some of their excitement. Walter was able to speak to a police officer but was told that Inspector Halyard was unavailable. He promised to get a message through to him and ask him to make contact.

'It's urgent,' Walter said, giving Chloe's phone number. 'Tell him we have an important new lead.'

Auntie Joan brought the tea trays into the sitting room so that they'd hear the phone ring.

Chloe was trying to think. 'What we need to

know is the identity of the man who worked for you. He wasn't the respectable man we thought he was.'

'A very different person,' Walter agreed.

'A thief and a fraudster.' Joan was angry.

'Halyard should speak to Clitheroe's mother,' Uncle Walter went on. 'Get confirmation of what it says in that article.'

'There must be some connection between Francis Clitheroe and our man.' Chloe munched on a piece of sponge cake. 'We need to find out what exactly it is.'

'Heavens!' Joan was aghast. 'This magazine is three months out of date.'

'You've had it all this time?' Walter was equally horrified. 'We could have found this out soon after he came to us.'

'The point now,' Chloe said firmly, 'is what use we can make of this important fact. We need to know who the impostor is.'

'Could I get that writer's phone number and ring her myself?' Walter was frowning.

'You'd be on delicate ground,' Joan said. 'Better let the fraud squad do that.'

Inspector Halyard rang back within half an hour. Chloe was beside Walter again and thought Halyard was pleased to receive the news.

'Yes,' Walter said. 'I agree, this could be the breakthrough.'

Chloe thought she heard Halyard say that he'd speak to Rosamund Rogerson as soon as he could, and knew they were discussing how she might be contacted.

'Through the editor of the magazine,' she told

Walter. 'Or the publisher of her books.' She held up the book Joan had brought so he could read out their address.

'Yes, yes,' Walter said into the handset. 'I do realise it's Sunday tomorrow and everything will be closed.'

He sighed as he put the phone down. 'I can't see much happening before Monday, whatever any of us does.'

'It gives that fellow more time to cover his tracks,' Joan grumbled. 'I do hope Halyard catches him.'

Nevertheless, they were all much more hopeful. They thought they'd made a breakthrough; their excitement didn't go away. They spent hours discussing what they could do next, going over and over the same ground. The children were bathed and put to bed and Walter read them a story. He and Joan stayed on to eat the scratch supper Chloe and Goldie put together. They felt they were pulling together and that they'd made progress.

Chloe went to bed but she couldn't get to sleep; her head was swimming at this new turn of events. Yes, it was success of a sort, but they would have to find the impostor before Uncle Walter would have any chance of getting his money back.

After about an hour of tossing and turning, she slid out of bed. She was too restless to think of sleep. She paused for a moment at the children's door, but they were both fast asleep. She crept downstairs and made herself a cup of tea, then she wandered from room to room thinking of the

400

accountant's face the day she'd picked up the silver propelling pencil. She'd seen his horror, felt his tension. He'd known he'd betrayed himself. She tried to remember what exactly he'd said. She'd seen initials on that pencil, but what were they?

Chloe groaned. Oh lord, that was the clue to the impostor's identity. She absolutely had to remember those initials.

She shivered, it was cold down here. She put her mug in the sink and went back upstairs. She could hear Aunt Goldie snoring like a motorbike. Chloe settled into her bed, and it seemed only moments before Lucy was climbing in beside her, wide awake in the morning light and wanting to play.

Sunday was a quieter day, but Chloe could think of nothing but the fraud. Rex came round to drive them all over to Auntie Joan's for lunch, and she brought him up to date with the news.

Walter was tired. He and Joan had talked late into the night and hadn't slept well after that. He hadn't been able to stop his mind going over all he knew about the man he'd hired to work on his accounts.

When Chloe and her family turned up to have lunch, the children were noisy and full of fun. Chloe seemed bursting with energy, though she too said she couldn't get the accountant out of her mind.

They were at the dining table and Walter was carving the roast lamb when she said to him, 'I'm intrigued that you thought you saw him at that big silver sale.'

Walter wasn't feeling his best. Lack of sleep had had more effect on him than it had on Chloe. 'I believed I did, but Adam said I was mistaken and it was someone he knew.'

'But he kept playing with that silver propelling pencil. I'm sure he was fond of it.'

'That means nothing, Chloe. Pens and pencils are personal things. It doesn't follow that he's fond of household silver; that's a different kettle of fish altogether.'

'But it might.'

Uncle Walter sighed. 'Are you clutching at straws?'

She gave him a wry smile. 'I think Inspector Halyard is too. That man you saw at the silver sale, did Adam say what his name was?'

'He might have done, but I don't remember.'

'When you bought that first lot of silver from Adam, did he tell you anything about the man he'd bought it from?'

'Chloe, I really don't remember much of anything. I was more interested in the silver itself than the man who was selling it.'

'Did you ever talk to your accountant about antique silver?'

'No, absolutely not. He never gave me any reason to think he might be interested.'

'But he did ask for time off to visit his dentist on the day of the sale?'

Walter was shaking his head in impatience. 'That could have been a coincidence.'

'It could.' Chloe was frowning. 'But I've got this gut feeling there's more to it than that. There were initials engraved on that pencil and they were not Clitheroe's. He told me it had belonged to a friend, but he was suddenly all tense and screwed up.'

'Really? What were these initials?'

Chloe sighed. 'To be honest, I can't remember. I wish I could. There might have been an L, but I'm not sure.'

Walter laughed. 'If you can't remember things, how on earth d'you expect me to?'

'Don't laugh, I'm serious. That day at the silver auction. You mentioned that this man shot away when he saw you. Was it because he recognised you? I'd be interested to know if there is a connection to your accountant. Adam said he knew the man; I'd like you to ring him and ask for his name and address.'

'I'm tired, Chloe, and this business has been going round in my head for days. Why don't we leave it to Halyard?'

Chloe urged gently, 'If you ring Adam after we've eaten, you might catch him before he goes out for the afternoon.'

'I can't see that it will get us any further, but I suppose...'

She was teasing. 'You suppose you have to humour me?'

'Something like that.'

As soon as they'd finished their apple pie and ice cream, Chloe said, 'I'll get Adam on the phone for you. Come on.

'It's ringing,' she said, pushing the receiver into his hand.

Adam's voice answered immediately. As soon as

Walter made himself known, he sounded interested. 'Are you in the market for more silver?'

'Not at the moment,' Walter said, and told him why he was calling. 'I'd like to know the name of the man who sold the silver to you that you subsequently sold on to me.'

There was a pause, then Adam said, 'I remember doing it, of course, but after all this time I can't remember his name and address. Is it important?'

'It is to me, though it has nothing to do with the silver, or, of course, with you. Could you not check through your records and find that name for me?'

'I'm afraid I don't keep records of that sort of thing. No, sorry, it won't be possible.'

Walter had been half expecting that response. 'Drawn a blank,' he told Chloe.

But Chloe's lavender-blue eyes had been watching him closely. She'd gathered what had transpired and said, 'He's pushed you off, Uncle Walter. He writes down names, addresses and phone numbers, and every other scrap of information he has about the people he does business with. They are his contacts and his customers and he knows he can use the same people again and again. He's very organised about it, keeps an alphabetical directory. I know because I helped him in the business.'

She felt like kicking herself. She hadn't wanted to speak to Adam, but knew now that she should have. She was angry with Adam, too. He was protecting his contacts, and of course she should have expected that from him, but Uncle Walter

404

didn't deserve this.

'Leave him to me,' she told him. 'I'll make him tell me.'

CHAPTER TWENTY-EIGHT

Chloe went home to think about the problem again. She wished she hadn't told her uncle that she'd get that man's name for him. She wanted nothing more to do with Adam, but she'd told Walter with such force that she would, that to back out now would make her look a timid mouse. She'd have to do it.

After she'd put the children to bed that night, she made herself go down to the hall and dial Adam's number. To hear his voice, deep and resonant, made her tense every muscle.

'Your Uncle Walter has already asked me that,' he said. 'I'm afraid I've forgotten.'

Chloe felt a rush of anger. She wasn't going to let him get away with that. Either Walter's accountant was a crony Adam wanted to protect, or he was being spiteful.

'Let me remind you then, Adam,' she said. 'If you open your address book, the name I want will have been entered in alphabetical order. Should it have slipped your mind, you'll find it cross-referenced under silver. Finding it shouldn't give you too much difficulty. I'm afraid I have to have it.'

He gave a mirthless laugh. 'And supposing I

don't want to give it to you?'

Chloe forced a note of authority into her voice. She'd stepped back and let him have his way too often; she wasn't going to let him bat her down again.

'Then let me try and persuade you. I'm working for Uncle Walter now, and I think this man has been defrauding him.'

'What? You're working?'

'In the absence of financial support from you, I felt I had to.'

'Oh dear! Sorry! What sort of a job have you got?'

'I don't know whether I'm his secretary or his accountant or something between the two. Anyway, we've got the fraud squad working on it too.'

'Oh!'

'Either you give me that man's name, address and telephone number, or I'll put Inspector Halyard in touch with you and you can tell him what he wants to know. It may occur to you that you'll get more of his attention than you want if he calls on you personally.'

Chloe stopped speaking and there was silence. 'Are you still there?'

'Yes,' he said shortly. 'I'll see if I can find what you want.'

'Thank you.'

'How are the children?'

'They're fine, growing up now.'

'I've missed them.'

'I'd never have known,' she said coldly. 'You'll ring me back with that name? We are in a hurry for it.'

'Chloe! You've just caught me, I'm on my way out for the evening.'

'All right. I'll be in the office tomorrow.'

It was almost twelve the next day when Constable Benton came into the office and told Chloe that he'd like another word with her and her uncle. She knew that Walter was as anxious for news as she was. He had his office door open before they reached it and hurried to settle Benton on a chair.

'We've got an address for Rosamund Rogerson from her publisher,' the constable told them. 'She lives in Wimbledon. We asked the local police to call round and interview her. Her real name is Mrs Rosamund Mary Clitheroe. She is Francis Clitheroe's mother and confirmed that he and his wife were killed in Majorca while they were on holiday, and that the details of the accident given in the magazine are correct.

'We've checked the official records; it seems the accident occurred on the third of September last year. His body and that of his wife were flown home and they were buried in St Michael and All Angels churchyard in Wimbledon on the seventeenth.'

Chloe straightened up in her chair. 'They were on holiday, you say?'

'Yes.'

'And he was working up till then? Where was that?'

Benton consulted his notebook. 'He was in Liverpool, employed as chief accountant at the

Exchange Hotel.'

'Oh my goodness!' Walter said. 'That could be how this man knew so much about Francis Clitheroe.'

'Yes, Inspector Halyard has gone there to make further inquiries.'

They both started firing questions at him, but Benton's manner was officious. 'We'll keep you fully informed about what transpires. I wish we knew more about this man. It would help us trace him.'

Chloe met Benton's gaze. 'He dictated letters to you, Miss Redwood. Did he seem used to doing that?'

She tried to think back. 'He didn't seem comfortable doing it. I think you should ask Lydia Tomlin about that, she was his secretary. Actually, she's told me that he didn't let her near his files. That's unusual; the previous accountant here left all that to her.'

'Thank you, I think we have spoken to her. Mr Bristow, did you believe that he was a qualified accountant?'

'Yes,' Walter said. 'But I was convinced by the certificates and references he showed me.'

'He knew a great deal about accounting,' Chloe added. 'But there were times when he did things I've never been taught. Things that struck me as odd.'

'Give us an example,' the constable said. Chloe had to rack her brains. The questioning seemed to go on for ages.

All that day at work, Chloe kept eyeing the telephone, expecting Adam to ring her. At lunchtime, during a break in Constable Benton's questions; she dialled Adam's number, but he didn't lift the phone. Five o'clock came and she'd not heard from him; she tried again to ring him but he wasn't there.

She caught the bus home. When she came to get off, it had started to drizzle and she still had a five-minute walk. She quickened her step. As she turned into Carberry Road, the drizzle was growing heavier. A parked car hooted as she hurried past it. She turned to see why, and did a double-take. Adam was getting out; he waved and called her back.

Her knees turned to water. She couldn't trust herself with him; she'd always given in and let him have exactly what he wanted. Slowly she went back. 'You've got that name I wanted?'

'Ugh, it's raining,' Adam said. 'Come and sit in the car for a moment.'

Chloe cringed. She didn't want to, but he was retreating. She followed him and climbed into the passenger seat beside him.

'No point in getting soaked,' he said.

'You're doing well, I see.' He had a new Jaguar, which was why she hadn't recognised it.

'Not too badly. Well, I suppose business is looking up. How are you?'

'I'm tired, Adam, I've been at work all day. I just want that name.'

'It wouldn't harm to pass the time of day with me.'

'Sorry, I'm not at my most sociable. What is it?'

'Do you want to come back?'

'What d'you mean?'

'To live with me?'

Chloe was taken aback at the suggestion. 'No thank you.' Her tone was icy.

'It would make sense. We could run the business together and you'd have more time to spend with the children.'

'Thank you, no. We tried it and it didn't work out. Nothing would drag me back. Have you brought me that name and address?'

'Yes.' He patted his pocket. 'Since I'm this close, I'd like to see the children and say hello.'

She was shocked and angry. He'd treated both her and them badly. 'No,' she said.

'For heaven's sake, Chloe, why not?'

'Lucy cried for you, she kept asking when her daddy was coming back. She was upset, she missed you. I don't want to put her through that again. What happened to the new girlfriend?'

'It didn't work out. She didn't stay.'

Chloe smiled. 'Then she had more sense than I had, good for her.'

'Come on, Chloe, we had some good times. Let's give it another go, why not?'

'Absolutely no, no, no. I can't believe you've got the nerve to ask. Nothing would persuade me.'

'No hard feelings. Just let me see the kids. They are my flesh and blood.'

'No. How do I tell a toddler that her father doesn't want her any more? That you found someone you thought you liked better than her mother? That you pitched us out on our necks? No, you cannot see the children. Just give me that name and address so I can go.'

'OK, have it your way.' He produced a scrap of paper. Chloe straightened it out. The name Leo Hardman was written on it, together with a Liverpool address.

'Leo Hardman,' she said. 'That's it.' The initials on that silver pencil had been LH. 'Thank you.' She got out of the car and with a straight back marched on down the road, oblivious of the rain. Her cheeks were burning.

Perhaps she should have given Inspector Halyard Adam's address and told him he could provide a new lead. She could have indulged herself by taking revenge on him by letting the police investigate what he was doing.

But she hadn't, she hadn't needed to. She'd stood up to Adam. After all those times he'd persuaded her to live as he wanted, do as he wanted, she had at last found the guts to refuse. It made her feel victorious. Never again need she fear Adam Livingstone.

She telephoned Inspector Halyard as soon as she walked into the hall and gave him the name and address of Leo Hardman.

'I can't guarantee it,' she said, 'but I have a gut feeling that this is the man we knew as Francis Clitheroe.'

Walter felt altogether more sprightly when he arrived at his office the next morning. Chloe had rung him last evening with her news, and to celebrate, he and Joan had shared a special bottle of wine with their supper. Joan was convinced Chloe was right about Leo Hardman, and now Inspector Halyard had his name and address,

411

she'd persuaded Walter they'd soon see him charged and have their money back.

When he walked into the office, Chloe and Mrs Parks had their heads together in the accountant's room, working out the weekly wages. Clarice Parks had rather taken the wind out of his sails by saying, 'Mr Bristow, I've been very happy working here, but I want to tell you I'll be leaving soon.'

'Oh no! Not you too?'

'I'm not giving in my notice at the moment. My brother's in America, and he wants me and the boys to join him there. He's looking for a house for us, so it'll be a while yet, but I wanted to tell you in plenty of time.'

'That's thoughtful of you, Clarice, thank you.'

'Well, I know you're having awful trouble finding a new accountant. I wouldn't want to think of Chloe being on her own.'

When his phone rang, he recognised Inspector Halyard's voice immediately. 'Have you picked up Leo Hardman?' Walter asked.

'We've ascertained that he worked as night desk attendant at the Exchange Hotel for a time, and that he left without working out his notice very soon after the hotel were notified of Clitheroe's death. That would seem to be the place where Hardman picked up the knowledge he needed about Clitheroe. We think this must be a case of identity theft, but it's very unusual, we haven't come across it before.'

'But you've found him now?'

'No, not yet. We've been to Hardman's address, a bedsitter in central Liverpool, and searched it thoroughly. There were signs that he'd left in a hurry, but he's not been seen there since you reported the fraud.'

Walter felt that his hopes of a quick and satisfactory ending were being dashed. 'So you still don't know where he is?'

'No, but he hasn't cleared out all his belongings and he's keeping up payments for the rent. It seems his intention is to return. A watch has been placed on the premises.'

Feeling somewhat deflated, Walter put the phone down. He wished they'd get a move on.

Leo Hardman had left the private hotel in the back streets of Llandudno after two nights. There were too many families with children there; he didn't fit in and he'd felt they were watching him. He needed to have a place of his own.

He'd spent some time going round the local estate agents, looking at properties for sale. In one of the windows he'd noticed a holiday let, a two-bedroom flat designed to accommodate four people. It was well away from the promenade in a quiet street and provided more comfort than his Liverpool bedsit. He'd decided to take it for a month and pay weekly from the large amount of cash he carried with him.

He'd bought the *Daily Post* every day since he'd been in Llandudno, and been glad to see no further mention of Francis Clitheroe. But the police would certainly be looking for him, because he'd failed to attend his court hearing. It added to his unease that he didn't know if they had found out any more about Clitheroe since he'd left.

If they had, it might not be safe for him to

return to his bedsit. It depended whether they had rumbled that he'd stolen Clitheroe's identity and worked out how that had been possible. If they'd discovered that both of them had worked at the Exchange Hotel, they might well know his real name. Leo didn't think that very likely but he wasn't going to take any risks. That had always been his way.

In the meantime, he had another problem. Being away from Liverpool, he'd been unable to pay the rent on his bedsit. While he'd been in lodgings but coming back each weekend, he'd put the money in an envelope with his rent book and put it through Conor's letter box. His rent book would be duly made up and pushed under the ill-fitting door of his bedsit.

Leo had spent too long thinking about this, and his rent was becoming overdue. He knew Conor was ruthless with tenants who didn't pay up. He had master keys and would be likely to get Maisie to pack his stuff up and clean his room out so he could rent it to someone else. He thought about just letting that happen, but he'd left a lot of good stuff there and it might give the police all sorts of clues about him.

He couldn't send Conor a cheque on his Arthur Worboys account without putting that at risk. A postal order would be stamped with the name of the post office where he'd bought it, and would give a strong clue if the police were look-ing for him. In the end, he scribbled a note telling Conor he was having a short holiday and would be back soon, then folded some bank notes into it, enough to cover the rent for a few more weeks, and posted it to him.

Leo had looked at several houses for sale in and near Llandudno, but none really appealed to him. Now that the leaves were falling and the hills looked bleak in the rain, he began to think that his plans for a new life in north Wales might be a mistake. It was the end of the holiday season and the weather was worsening. It became blustery, and huge waves thundered down on the beach. The promenade was suddenly cold and rain-swept and the cafés and bars were almost empty.

The thought of spending the winter in a country cottage was not so attractive; Leo liked bars and pubs, and games of darts. He was missing his friends and the Irish pub and began to think he might be happier back in Liverpool. He was a city lad at heart and he knew where to hide himself away there.

Had he worried too much about that photograph in the newspaper? He'd been wearing those heavy-rimmed glasses and his hair had been cut short. It was growing now and he looked more like himself. He'd panicked and run when he discovered how much the police knew about what he'd been up to. He'd been shocked at the time, but now he was thinking logically again.

He'd be perfectly safe renting a more comfortable place in a different area of Liverpool in the name of Arthur Worboys. He was sure they couldn't have found that bank account, and he had more money there. He thought about it long and hard, but could see no risk in doing that. If he stayed away from Bootle and Bristow's Pet Foods, he'd be unlikely to have any trouble.

There had been an acute shortage of property to rent in Liverpool, but though it was expensive, it was coming back on the market now. New two-bedroom flats were going up and Leo thought one of those might suit him.

As a temporary measure, he found workman's lodgings in Upper Parliament Street in his newspaper. He packed his suitcase and took the train back to Liverpool. He immediately felt more at home; he knew his way round the city pubs, cinemas and theatres. Here, he could enjoy life again.

The next day he went round the estate agents looking for a flat to rent. He chose a superior newly built one in Woolton and was asked if he wanted a furnished or unfurnished tenancy.

'Unfurnished, please.' This time he meant to make himself comfortable and settle down. He had money in Arthur Worboy's account; he'd use his own name and turn himself into a solid and law-abiding citizen.

'Before a tenancy can be granted, you'll need to fill up this form giving details of your income and present address,' he was told. 'And also supply two references.'

That came as something of a surprise. The landlord of his bedsit had needed no such formalities. Leo took the form and agreed to do as he was asked. He'd think up a background for Arthur Worboys and tell a fib or two on the form. He knew he could arrange references by providing letters much as he'd done when he went to work for Mr Bristow. He went back to his lodgings and set about doing it. A personal reference could be hand-written, but the other was supposed to be from his employer or bank manager, and he would need to type that.

He had a typewriter at his bedsit as well as a lot of other things. To be on the safe side, he should go back and clear it out properly.

Soon he would have a better home than the old bedsit; he need no longer keep that on. Much the safest thing would be to break off all connection with the place, but before he did that he'd empty it of everything that connected him and Francis Clitheroe to it.

Better if he went back when there was nobody much about. He was glad that Conor Kennedy didn't live on the premises, but he had that woman Maisie on the ground floor keeping an eye on the place, and during daylight hours the students would often be coming and going.

He decided the safest time would be after ten o'clock, when Maisie would have locked the front door and would presumably feel she was off duty and could go to bed. If he went at that time on Saturday night, the students would either be out working or enjoying themselves in the bars and restaurants.

He had more stuff there than he could carry; he'd need a taxi to get it all away. The nearest taxi stand he could think of was outside Lime Street station. He'd pick up his typewriter and bring that and one suitcase away. He could get a taxi and collect the rest later. Anyway, he had no space for all his things in these lodgings. He'd need to put most of it in the left luggage place at the station until he moved into his new flat.

At ten o'clock, he stuffed some bags into his empty suitcase and caught a bus into town. He got off near his bedsit, and as he passed the Irish pub, he could hear sounds of jollity; music and singing. He would have liked to have a last session in there; he'd missed the fun. The pubs in Llandudno hadn't been anything like so good. But no, the last thing he needed was to be seen by his old mates, so he gave it a wide berth.

His plan was to pack up his belongings, clear his bedsit and disappear for good. As he approached the building, he could see that Maisie's curtains were drawn and her lights on; he hoped she was in bed. There didn't seem to be anyone else at home in the front of the house. He let himself in quietly and crept upstairs in the dark, but it was impossible to do without the steps creaking beneath his weight. He flinched but told himself it was a solidly built house and sound didn't travel much. Once in his own bedsitter, he drew the curtains and put the light on.

It was an untidy mess, the bed unmade, the air fetid. He set about packing everything that was his and found it hard work. He had two zip bags and three big suitcases packed tight, and was wondering whether the detritus that was left would tell an investigator anything when he heard the front door open.

He froze, listening, holding his breath. Heavy footsteps were coming upstairs. It might just be one of the students, but it sounded like his landlord, Conor Kennedy. If it was, he could hardly have missed seeing that Leo's lights were on. He waited motionless, in a lather of dread and sweat.

The steps stopped outside his door.

'Leo?' The door shook as a heavy fist drummed on it. 'My friend, are you in?'

Leo swallowed hard. He knew he'd have to open the door; the landlord had a master key to all the rooms. 'Hello, is that you, Conor?'

He hurried to push his baggage out of sight behind the bed and opened the door as quickly as he could. What had brought Conor Kennedy here at this time of night? Leo was quaking as he tried to edge his visitor back on to the landing.

A firm hand clapped him on the shoulder. 'My friend.' Conor Kennedy's bald head looked polished under the electric light. 'Home at last, eh? Have you had a nice holiday?'

'Excellent,' Leo said brightly, but inside he was cursing. This was the last thing he needed.

'Llandudno was good, then?'

That made Leo jump with surprise. 'How d'you know where I've been?'

'My friend, you sent your rent money and let me know you were coming back. The stamp had been franked.'

Oh God, was that what had done it? 'Of course!' What a fool he'd been to forget that. But what was he doing here now? 'How did you know I was back?'

'Saw your light on. Come and have a nightcap down in the pub. There's still time for last orders.'

Was it a trap? Surely not, Conor was his friend. 'Tomorrow, perhaps? I'm very tired, the train took hours.'

'Come on, man, a wee snifter will sort you out. Do you good.'

Leo's nerves were shredding; he was panicking, couldn't think properly. This was all wrong. Conor had never done this before. Why was he doing it now?

'Tommy will be glad to see you back.'

'Thanks, then. It's Sunday tomorrow, I can have a lie-in.'

''Tis right you can.'

Leo turned back to pick up his coat, then reluctantly followed Conor downstairs. Two minutes later they were outside the pub and he could feel himself being shunted towards the door. It flew open in his face, releasing a cloud of beer fumes into the night. Once in the warmth inside, Leo looked round furtively. Were the police waiting here for him? Many of the customers had gone home; it looked as though time had been called quite a while ago.

'Welcome back.' The publican, Tommy O'Sullivan, slid a tankard of Guinness on to the bar in front of him. Conor was making much of him, wanting to know more about his holiday.

The door opened and two uniformed police officers came in. Leo had to hold on to the bar; his knees suddenly felt like rubber. He recognised them.

'Leo Hardman?' one of them asked.

He knew he'd lost. He took a great gulp from his tankard of Guinness, and gave Conor a filthy look. 'I thought you were my friend,' he said bitterly.

CHAPTER TWENTY-NINE

Chloe felt the bedclothes being dragged off her. 'Wake up, Mummy.' Lucy's voice was wide awake and full of childish joy. 'Time to wake up.'

Chloe anchored her sheet, craving more sleep. 'Sunday morning,' she gasped. 'Mummy's treat, stay here.'

'No. Wake up.'

'Mummy.' Zac was climbing on top of her, putting baby arms round her.

The curtains were being swished back; the morning sun flooded into her room and a mug of tea thumped down on her bedside table. Only Aunt Goldie would do that; Chloe opened her eyes.

'Morning, Chloe. Such good news: they've caught him at last. Walter wants you to ring him back when you're awake.'

Chloe sat up and hugged Zac. 'Caught him? That's wonderful.' She laughed aloud. Relief, satisfaction and triumph were flooding through her. 'How?'

'He went back to his bedsit. Inspector Halyard thought he would and had told his landlord to let him know when he did. And guess what? Hardman was planning to disappear again. He set about packing up all his possessions, but the tenant on the floor below heard him dragging his suitcases across her ceiling.'

'Marvellous!'

Chloe was pulling on her dressing gown and slippers. She rushed downstairs to the phone and her children followed her. Lucy was jumping up and down with excitement.

Joan picked up the receiver. 'Isn't it splendid news? We're both thrilled. Walter's here, he can't wait to talk to you.'

Walter's voice came on; he sounded overjoyed. 'You were right, Chloe. His name is Leo Hardman. Adam bought silver from him and sold it on to us. He went to that auction and left in a hurry when he recognised me. He passed himself off as Francis Clitheroe, chartered accountant, though he was nothing of the sort.'

'Inspector Halyard got it right too,' Chloe said. 'By talking to Rosamund Rogerson and finding that they both worked at the Exchange Hotel.'

'Yes, he found out Hardman had left about the time Francis Clitheroe was killed, and when he showed me Hardman's security badge, I was able to confirm that he was the man who was defrauding me. He had over seven thousand pounds on him in cash when they arrested him. Can you believe that?'

'A lot of money,' Chloe agreed. 'And it's yours.'

'There's more, of course. Halyard says they'll wear him down, find out where he's hidden it.'

Chloe could hear Joan talking in the background, and moments later she'd taken the phone from Walter. 'Chloe, you were all coming for lunch today anyway. We'll make it a special celebration. Come early.'

'Lovely. What d'you mean by early?'

'As soon as you can. I've got the vegetables done and the joint of pork all ready to go into the oven.'

'Great, we'll come over as soon as I've had a bath and got myself and the children dressed.' She rang off then and immediately dialled Rex's number. She wanted to tell him the news and ask him to come round as soon as he could.

'I'm delighted for you, Chloe,' Rex said. 'Absolutely thrilled. Well done.'

Chloe could hear pure pleasure in his voice.

Rex put the phone down and went back to his tea and toast, but he didn't touch them. He felt full of love for Chloe. She'd tried to comfort him after Helen had died. He hoped she'd found comfort in him too. But now she'd sounded ready to sing and dance, happier than she'd been for a long time.

What a change there was in her. He knew the time was right to tell her of his feelings. He was eager but also fearful to know how she felt about him. He was after all, a widower, fourteen years her senior, and she'd once seen him as a father figure. It was hardly a recommendation for romance. He must look for an opportunity to tell her how much he loved and admired her. Get her on her own.

Up to now, Rex had found it painful to think of the past, but now those troubles were over. Chloe's affair with Adam Livingstone had held him back for years and had been disastrous for her. She'd been very low after Adam had rejected her and the two children he'd fathered.

Rex had held his breath after that, half fearful

423

that she'd live her life as Aunt Goldie had. Especially when her mother's illness and death had followed and she'd been very distressed. But Rex had always known she was a very special person and she'd pulled herself round.

Chloe had wanted to prove she was capable of holding down a job to support herself and her babies. Uncle Walter had given her that job, and his troubles had come at the right time for her. She'd had to work very hard to sort out his accounts, but by fixing her mind on them, she had helped herself over the hard times she'd had.

And now she'd helped to put Leo Hardman behind bars. That must be counted as a great success by everybody. Rex understood what it would mean to her. It would make her feel she could cope with anything life threw at her. It would make her into the confident and well-balanced woman he'd always known she could be.

He knew now they'd both be able to forget the past, put it where it belonged, behind them. Chloe would be able to manage on her own after this.

As he usually did, he drove to Carberry Road in his van, and then backed Helen's car out of the garage. Chloe came running out to greet him, her coat swinging open and her lovely tawny hair bouncing on her shoulders. She was laughing as she threw her arms round him.

'I can't believe they've caught this villain who's been taking Walter's money.'

He would have proposed there and then except that Lucy and Marigold carrying Zac were hot on her heels.

When Rex drew up outside the house in Freshfield, Walter opened his front door before Chloe could reach it.

'Congratulations!' His cherubic face was wreathed with smiles and he came bounding out to sweep Chloe up in one of his great bear hugs. 'She's got her wits about her this one,' he said to Rex over her shoulder.

Joan kissed Chloe and swept them all into her sitting room. 'We're going to start with morning coffee,' she said. 'Walter's overjoyed and so am I, and he's got some important propositions to put to you.'

'Oh goodness.' Chloe laughed.

'No, Chloe,' he said, 'be serious. Quieten down for a moment all of you.'

'Has Mummy done a good thing?' Lucy's childish treble made them laugh again.

'Yes, Lucy, a very good thing,' Walter said. 'This is something I want you to think seriously about, Chloe. You've got a real bent for figures and I'd like you to train as a chartered accountant.'

She clapped her hands. 'That's exactly what I want.'

'You need to get properly qualified; your mother would have liked that too. It upset us all when you wanted to leave school and start work. You were in too much of a hurry to grow up.

'I'm delighted to have you working for me, but it's proved to be a job you could do with one hand tied behind your back. In the long term you'll get bored with it, and you've got responsibilities. You need a job that brings a good salary to enable you to fulfil them.'

Chloe was bursting with high spirits. 'Uncle Walter, that isn't something you have to talk me into. I've been thinking about it for some time.'

'Have you? Excellent.'

'Rex said much the same to me when Zac was a tiny baby.' She smiled at him.

'Did I? I was trying to...'

'Yes, I know. Keep me from sinking into the mire completely. You said all was not lost and I must think about what I wanted to do with my life.'

'Did you?' Walter asked. 'Think about it?'

'All the time. Rex sorted me out.'

'In that case, let me suggest something else.' Walter beamed round at them all. 'I've had a chance now to talk to Tom Cleary. He's home from his trip to New Zealand and has agreed to come back and be our accountant for another year or two, until you can take over. I've told him he'll find that you know more than the average accounts clerk but that he must treat you as an apprentice to start with and then gradually hand over responsibility to you.'

'You're giving me a marvellous opportunity,' Chloe breathed. 'Thank you.'

'You deserve it, Chloe,' Joan said. 'Then once you're qualified, Walter will come to some arrangement for you to help him run the business.'

'Why, that's marvellous. I don't know what to say.' She couldn't stop smiling round at everybody.

'I can't go on running the firm alone much longer,' Walter told her. 'I've really needed you these last few months. This is the best thing for

426

all of us. I know you're capable of doing a good job, and I can trust you.'

Auntie Joan brought in a bottle of champagne. 'We're going to celebrate now and seal that bargain.'

'What a day this is,' Chloe marvelled. 'We really do have lots to celebrate. Especially me, I'm overwhelmed.'

Rex sipped his champagne and made up his mind. He was going to take Chloe into the garden when they returned. He was phrasing the words to tell her he loved her and ask her to marry him.

But it didn't turn out like that. After lunch, Joan suggested they all go for a walk along the beach, which was on their doorstep in Freshfield. It was a lovely autumn day and they were all in the right mood to enjoy the sunshine and the sea lapping against the silvery sand. Rex paddled with Chloe and the children. He couldn't remember when he'd last enjoyed a day out more.

They were hungry when they returned to Auntie Joan's house, and she had a light supper ready prepared for them. They stayed on chatting over glasses of wine until Chloe noticed that both her children had fallen asleep.

'It's past their bedtime,' she said. 'I'm quite shocked, I've never done this before.' They carried them into the car without waking them and Rex drove them all home.

He tried to carry Lucy upstairs when they arrived, but she woke up and was tetchy. Zac too was protesting loudly at being woken.

Aunt Goldie was undressing Lucy to put her to

427

bed. 'No bath, no bath!' she was screaming.

'Not tonight,' Marigold said grimly. 'We've all had enough now.'

Chloe was trying to put Zac into his pyjamas. Rex felt like a spare part because there was nothing he could do to help. He certainly couldn't take Chloe for a walk round the garden and leave Goldie to cope with both children. Not while they were making a fuss like this.

Reluctantly he said good night and went home.

Rex worked in the garden for most of the following afternoon, and worried about how Chloe would view the relationship he'd had with her mother. He knew he had to find out before he left that night how she felt about him.

When Chloe came home from work, the children were playing some ball game with Aunt Goldie and wanted her to join in. Rex tagged on and played too. Afterwards Goldie went to her room to rest.

Chloe took Rex to the kitchen, where Peggy was dishing up the scrambled eggs on toast she'd prepared for the children's evening meal. Chloe poured cups of tea for the adults and they sat down to chat. Later, when Peggy had gone home and the children had been put to bed, Rex carried the beef casserole to the dining table, where Aunt Goldie was waiting to dish it up.

Rex wasn't entirely at ease about continuing to have dinner with them every evening. He thought Aunt Goldie was growing a little frosty towards him, and he found that off-putting.

Tonight he caught her glowering at him across

the table, and was afraid she was thinking that now Helen was gone, there was no reason for him to be with them so often.

On several occasions he'd heard Chloe thank her for looking after the children so well, and tell her how much she was loved and needed. He'd thought Goldie had been happier since she'd come to live with them, but tonight she was prickly and looked sour.

'I do think you're being over-extravagant,' she told Chloe. 'You need to manage your money better. You're spending far too much on running this house.'

Chloe's fork paused halfway to her mouth. 'No more than Mum used to.'

'Yes, but when Helen was ill she had to be cared for. You could cut Peggy's hours down now. She isn't needed five full days a week.'

Rex could see Chloe thinking about it.

'I don't want to do that,' she said slowly. 'Peggy needs a full-time job, and she makes life more comfortable for you and me. I don't want you to have to clean and cook as well as look after the kids.'

'I could...'

'I'm sure you could, Aunt Goldie, but it isn't necessary. And should you not feel well enough to meet Lucy from her nursery class, Peggy's here as a back-up.'

Rex helped himself to another potato; he was afraid Goldie was going to have a go at him. He was right.

'Then there's this garden,' she went on. 'It's big enough and fancy enough for Buckingham

Palace. It's always been a huge extravagance.'

'Mum knew that.' Chloe smiled gently. 'I enjoy it and think of it as a memorial to her.'

'It's no good for children. All they need is a bit of grass to play ball on.'

Rex was uncomfortable. He wanted to cover his face with his hands. He was afraid Goldie meant to cut him out of Chloe's life.

'All these flowers and fancy shrubs take a lot of maintenance.' She flung a dour look at him. 'Rex works more hours now than he did when Helen was alive. It must be costing you a fortune.'

Chloe's lavender eyes met his for a moment. 'It isn't, Goldie,' she said. 'Rex has never charged the commercial rate for the work he does here.'

He felt relief wash over him. Chloe could handle Goldie. He said, 'For me, it's always been a labour of love for friends.'

Chloe smiled at him, but Goldie wasn't ready to give up. 'All the same, now that Helen's no longer with us and you have to work, you have less need of Rex or the garden.'

'Aunt Goldie,' Chloe gave a little giggle, 'you're embarrassing me. Right now, I have more need of Rex, not less. There's something else I want him to do and I haven't yet got round to asking him if he will.'

That made Rex look up and meet her gaze. 'What else can I do for you, Chloe?'

'I've arranged to take driving lessons.' She smiled again. 'I'm having the first one tomorrow evening. I was hoping you'd take me out to practise in Mum's car.'

Rex relaxed, a wide smile spreading across his

face. 'Of course I will. I'll be glad to.'

He knew that would give him lots of time alone with her. Plenty of opportunity for them to say all they needed to in private. Was that why she'd arranged to have lessons now?

He saw her smile at Aunt Goldie. 'Once Mum became too ill, Rex had to drive us all round. I don't feel we should batten on him for ever.'

Chloe had felt Rex's tension at dinner and understood the reason. Since the night her mother had died, she'd begun to see him in a very different light. It had taken her a while to get over Helen's death and she felt she'd been on a roller-coaster ever since. Her mind had been swirling round a dozen things, and she'd had to pay special attention to Uncle Walter's accounts.

But now that was settled, Goldie was prodding at Rex. Only this morning at breakfast she'd said to Chloe, 'It's not as though he married your mother, is it? He's not a relative. There's no need for us to feed him every night.'

Chloe's feelings for Rex were changing; she'd always been fond of him, felt close to him, but now she was growing more sure by the day that she'd fallen in love with him.

When they'd finished their coffee and Rex stood up to say good night, Chloe stood up too. In the hall, he unhooked his coat from the peg, and as usual thanked her for the meal. 'I must tell Peggy how good her rhubarb tart was,' he said. He opened the front door and paused. 'Chloe...?'

'Yes.'

'I'm afraid Goldie thinks I've overstayed my welcome. She's trying to stop me coming so much. I'm glad you didn't let her.'

'Don't worry about Goldie. I'd never let her do that.' Chloe walked out with him to his van. 'You've always understood how things are with me and tried to straighten me out. We should gang up against Goldie, let her see she can't part us. Not after all this time.'

His dark eyes stared down at her. 'D'you feel like a little walk in the garden? We could get started on that right away. And there are other things I need to say to you.'

The house was a black shadow except for the golden light beaming from the windows. Everywhere else was bathed in silvery moonlight. He saw Chloe nod. He unbuttoned his coat and draped it round her shoulders, then, reaching into his van, pulled out a pullover and put it on.

'I don't often come into the garden at night.' Chloe led him through the side gate and away from the house; they strolled down the path towards the pond. It looked very peaceful and very beautiful. Some months ago, they'd sited a garden bench here because Mum was tiring easily and needed somewhere to rest when she took her little walks.

Chloe sat down and tugged Rex down beside her. 'What d'you need to say to me?'

'I was going to lead up to it gracefully, but...'

She smiled. 'Never mind the graces.'

'I love you, Chloe. Have done for a long time. I want to marry you. How d'you feel about having me as a husband?'

'I love the idea, but ... there are things I should

point out to you first. I'm flattered to be asked, but I haven't exactly been what Aunt Goldie calls "a good girl". I've had two children out of wedlock, and she's told me several times that no decent man would look at me after that.'

'I know all that.' Chloe could see Rex hesitating, 'Marigold might not think of me as decent either,' he said. 'I've done things that are morally wrong.'

'Me too, but I did them for selfish reasons. I wanted fun and thrills. If you did them, it was out of love and compassion for others. Not the same thing.'

'Then let's say we've both done things we regret, but the best thing to do is to put them behind us and forget them. Nobody could love you more.'

She felt his arm go round her shoulders and pull her closer. She offered up her lips to be kissed and felt his crush down on them.

A little time later, Rex said, 'I want everything to be open between us, no secrets. I'm not going to list out all my sins, but if there is anything you need to know about me, I want you to ask.'

'Rex, I've know you so long, I think I know everything about you.'

He kissed her again, and it was some time later that she asked softly, 'D'you remember? The night Mum died?'

'I'll never forget it. It was traumatic. I want to explain about me and your mother. I want you to understand how things were between us.'

Chloe hesitated. 'There is one thing I've wondered about. Did she ask you to help her die?'

She knew he was shocked. 'How did you know?'

'I didn't, I guessed. I couldn't help but see that Dorothy bag when I made her bed. She kept it close to her always. One night I asked her what she kept in it, and she said "necessities of life". She showed me a handkerchief, but I think it was just to cover pills. I asked her outright if they were to help her die and she said that I must put that idea right out of my mind.'

'She was trying to protect you, she didn't want you to be worried.'

'I know that. *Did* you help her die?'

She felt him straighten up as though with remembered pain.

'No, but I promised I would. I had to promise, Chloe, because I was afraid she'd ask you if I refused. I didn't want you to take on that responsibility. And also, she was in such pain.' His voice was low and full of compassion as he told her about her mother's plan.

'She knew you'd make me a cake to celebrate my birthday and have a little party round her bed. She told me it would give her a chance to say goodbye to you all and be a happy occasion for you to remember. Later that night she meant to swallow the contents of the Dorothy bag to end her life.'

'That would be a dreadful thing for you to remember. It would give you nightmares.' Chloe took a deep breath, 'She was very brave. So were you.'

'But I'll be eternally grateful,' Rex said, 'that nature took over before she did it.'

'Yes.' Chloe shuddered.

'I was afraid that if she put her plan in action, you and everybody else would think I'd killed her.'

'Rex, no. We all know you'd never do anything to hurt anybody. That's not your way. And certainly you'd never hurt Mum. We could all see you were devoted to her.'

He kissed her again. 'Thank you for trusting me.'

'We all trusted you. But there is something else about the night Mum died. I was in quite a state.'

'So was I, emotional overdrive.'

'I heard Mum say "Look after Chloe and her babies for me."'

He kissed her again. 'She didn't need to ask that.'

'I heard you tell her so, and her last words were "I know you've always loved her." That did surprise me.'

Rex pulled her closer still. 'It surprised me too. I thought I'd kept what I felt for you hidden from her. But she was right, Chloe, I do love you and somehow she'd picked up on it.'

'I knew when I heard Mum say it that she meant real love, not the sort of affection you'd feel for her daughter. But she was in no way upset; in fact I thought she was glad that I'd have you to turn to. That surprised me too.'

'I grew to love you when you were hardly more than a girl, a troubled girl.'

'I was troubled, wasn't I?'

'Very. Your father had been killed in a climbing accident and you were blaming yourself'

'D'you know, you were the first person to tell me it wasn't my fault, that I mustn't think like that. Mum did afterwards...'

'She was troubled too.'

'You've been good for both of us. A real rock, and we both hung on to you.'

'Chloe, you stole my heart. I knew by the time you were fifteen that I wanted you to be my wife and nobody else would do. I didn't dare tell you, or your mother either; she'd have had a fit. I felt I had to wait until you'd grown up.'

Chloe tried to think back. 'I always knew you cared about me. You let it show through everything.'

'Did I? But then Adam Livingstone came into your life and I felt an old fool for letting him snatch you away. I wish I'd had the guts to tell you then that I loved you.'

'I doubt it would have done any good.' Chloe sighed. 'I can see Adam now for what he truly is, but then... No, I wanted to be swept off my feet. Adam was taking me to exciting places, he had plenty of glamour, plenty of style. And I was confusing what you were showing me with fatherly affection.'

'You mean you'd have refused me if I had proposed?'

'Yes, at that time, I think I would.'

The moonlight was just bright enough for her to see his wry smile. 'That makes me feel a whole lot better.'

'I needed to grow up. When I found out I was pregnant with Lucy, d'you know, I pleaded with Adam to marry me.'

'Chloe, will you marry me now?'

'There's nothing I want more.'

'I'd have leapt at the chance to marry you at any time. For years I've dreamed of it. Longed for it.'

Chloe put her lips up to be kissed again. 'It's getting cold out here,' she whispered. 'Let's move into the summerhouse. With the front closed, it'll be warmer.' She clung to his arm as they walked back. All the lights in the house had gone out as they let themselves inside and curled up together on Helen's day bed.

CHAPTER THIRTY

Rex was still with Chloe the next morning. She wanted him by her side when she told Aunt Goldie that they were going to be married. While he cooked a special celebratory breakfast of egg and bacon for the three of them, Chloe rang Uncle Walter to ask if he'd mind her being a little late this morning. It was Auntie Joan who picked up the phone, so Chloe told her news.

'Married? You and Rex?' She was surprised and flustered but offered congratulations and wished them well.

Goldie came downstairs as Chloe was sitting Lucy up to eat her cereal.

'Married?' she screamed, aghast. 'Next month? For heaven's sake, what's all the hurry?'

'There's been no hurry at all,' Rex told her. 'I've taken my time over it. It's over five years since I

437

first thought of asking Chloe to marry me.'

'Don't be ridiculous. Anyway, it would be impossible to get everything ready in a month.'

'Getting ready won't take me long,' Chloe said. 'Not a white wedding, that would hardly be right when I've got two children. No fuss, and not a big event.'

'Not a registry office wedding?' Aunt Goldie was even more shocked. 'Your mother would never forgive me if I let you do that.'

'A quiet church wedding then,' Rex agreed. 'We must book that straight away.'

'It'll depend on when the vicar can fit you in,' Goldie reminded him severely.

'Any weekday morning would suit us,' Chloe said. 'I don't think the vicar should find that too difficult. We'll have the reception here.'

'Here? I'm not sure about that either. Think of the work it'll give Peggy. It'll be too much for her.'

'Perhaps,' Rex suggested, 'we should get a firm of caterers in?'

When Peggy arrived, she was delighted at their news. 'How many people are you going to invite?' she wanted to know.

'The family, of course,' Chloe said. 'And Rex's stepfather and his half-brothers from the garden centre and their families. And some of the Bristow's staff. The girls anyway; they won't forgive me if I don't ask them to my wedding. Say twelve or fifteen in all.'

'For heaven's sake,' Peggy said. 'What makes you think that would be too much for me? I could easily do a sit-down dinner for that number, or a cold buffet, whichever you prefer.'

'Peggy, you're a gem.'

'It's a bit late to make a traditional wedding cake, though; rich fruit cake needs time to mature.'

'We'll manage without a cake,' Rex said.

'Oh, I could make you one, put on all the silver horseshoes and fancy trimmings, but it would probably crumble when you cut into it. I could do a chocolate cake or a sponge if you prefer. Or what about three tiers of different mixtures?'

'That would be lovely,' Chloe said. 'You're good at cakes and the children like sponge.'

'It's better for my digestion too,' Goldie agreed. 'Where are you going to live? Have you decided yet?'

'Here,' Rex told her. 'We talked about this last night. Chloe doesn't want to leave Helen's garden. I'm going to put my cottage on the market.'

Chloe saw Goldie's face fall and knew why. 'We'll need to extend this house,' she said quickly. 'Aunt Goldie, I want you to think about whether you'd like a granny flat, a bit of space to yourself, or whether you'd prefer to stay with us and all be in one house.'

'A granny flat?' A smile was spreading across Goldie's face.

'You think about it,' Chloe said. 'This house was great when there was just Mum and me, but the family keeps growing. We'll be bursting out of it if we go on like this.'

Goldie shook her head. 'You and Rex getting married, that's a right turn-up for the books. What would your poor mother make of it?'

'I think she'd approve,' Chloe said quietly.

By the time Chloe reached the office, Uncle Walter had told the girls her news and they were in a frenzy wanting to hear more about Rex.

'I love him,' she said. 'He's very handsome, very kind and wise and he tells me he's been waiting to marry me since I was fifteen.'

'So that's why you aren't waiting any longer?'

'We don't need to get to know each other.' Chloe smiled. 'Rex has been in touch with the vicar this morning and it's going to be four weeks on Friday.'

'Four weeks,' they squealed in unison.

'To allow for the banns to be called,' Chloe said. 'If I can be ready by then.'

'We'll help you.'

'What sort of a dress do you want? We'll all come with you at lunchtime and try and find you a marvellous one.'

'There won't be time,' Chloe protested. 'We'd have to go in to town to the big shops.'

But Walter heard them. 'You can all take a long lunch break today,' he told them, 'and get Chloe's outfit sorted out if you can.'

Between typing letters, the girls discussed it on and off all morning. They decided that Chloe should look at dressy afternoon gowns.

'Or cocktail dresses,' Rosemary suggested.

At lunchtime they quickly ate the sandwiches they'd brought and Walter sent them into town in a company car.

'George Henry Lees is the department store to try first,' Lydia decided, and the girls were soon picking out floaty chiffon dresses for Chloe to try

440

on. She fancied one in a soft peach shade.

'You look lovely in that,' Rosemary told her. It was full-skirted and of ballerina length. 'I'd choose that.'

'No, too summery,' Chloe decided. 'It looks wrong for early December and I'll freeze in it.'

Her eye was caught by a cocktail suit in heavy velvet, also full-skirted and ballerina length.

'Long sleeves.' Angela smiled. 'It'll be warm, and it's a lovely shade of blue.'

'Cornflower,' Lydia said.

When Chloe tried it on, it felt very comfortable and fitted as though it had been made for her.

'It's gorgeous,' Angela breathed.

'Very smart.'

They marched Chloe from one department to the next and helped her pick out a tiny fashionable hat in the same shade and a pair of dark blue high-heeled court shoes.

Before leaving, they found her a handbag to match her outfit. 'You'll need it for going away,' they assured her. Chloe was delighted with it all.

At home that evening, she unpacked parcels to show Aunt Goldie her wedding outfit.

'It's lovely,' she said, 'and very suitable, but take it up to your room. Rex will be here at any minute and he mustn't see it.'

Chloe was glad to find that Aunt Goldie had recovered from her ill humour and was now trying to help. 'What about your honeymoon?' she asked. 'Where will you go for that?'

'I haven't had time to think,' Chloe said. 'Though Uncle Walter's given me a week off.'

When Rex arrived, he said he hadn't got round

441

to thinking about the honeymoon either. 'Do we need to go away?' he asked. 'There's the children to think about.'

'Yes, you must,' Marigold insisted.

'We could take the children with us,' Chloe said.

'No.' Goldie was adamant. 'You need a rest. At least take a few days alone. You've been working very hard, and now there's all this rush over the wedding.'

'It's hardly the weather for holidays,' Rex pointed out. 'But what about a few days in Snowdonia? We could find a country hotel with blazing log fires and go for walks during the day.'

'That sounds nice.' Chloe smiled. 'A complete change. Goldie, you could come too to look after the kids.'

'On your honeymoon?' Goldie laughed. 'No, forget the children for once. They'd be easier to manage here at home, happier too, and they're used to me and Peggy. You and Rex should have a proper honeymoon.'

For Chloe, her wedding morning was like no other. Usually she was awakened by her children climbing into bed with her. Instead, Aunt Goldie brought her a cup of early-morning tea. 'Don't get up yet. You're to have breakfast in bed. Peggy is setting the tray now.' She drew back the curtains, 'It's a cold frosty morning, but it's bright.'

Chloe lay there listening to the sounds of the household; the distant piping voices of her children and the occasional clatter from the kitchen. It felt strange to be waiting up here on her own.

'Good morning.' Peggy bustled in with her breakfast. Boiled eggs and toast. Tea in the silver teapot and a single late rose in a stem vase. 'Rex cut that for you last night,' she told her. 'He'll make a good husband, that one.'

'I know,' Chloe said, and she sat up to eat and think about her future with Rex. He'd already taken the first steps to legally adopt her children, and had said he loved them so much, he'd like to father another.

When she'd eaten, Chloe got up to have a bath and get ready.

Their wedding was to take place at eleven thirty, and she could hear Auntie Joan and Goldie setting out the buffet on the dining table. Joan had a hairdresser who regularly came to her house. She'd arranged for her to come this morning to fit on Chloe's little hat and make her tawny hair look its best.

Chloe was ready when Lucy came running into her room to show her mother her own blue velvet outfit. It was one shade darker than Chloe's; she and Goldie had chosen it for her one Saturday.

'My flowers.' Lucy held up a tiny posy. 'Rex made for me. Big flowers for you downstairs.'

Chloe led her daughter down. Rex had wanted to arrange the wedding flowers. Every vase in the house was filled with blooms, and he'd made sprays and buttonholes for the whole wedding party. Most had come from the garden despite the season. For Chloe, he'd made a bouquet of white stephanotis and fragrant jasmine. For Lucy, there was a tiny replica.

'You look absolutely stunning in that suit,'

Auntie Joan told her. 'You're more beautiful than ever. And here's Walter coming now, it's almost time to set out.'

Her uncle was going to drive her to the church and give her away. He came in to kiss her, looking very smart in his formal suit with his gold watch chain across his waistcoat.

'Wait five minutes,' Joan told him, 'so we can get there before you.'

Goldie was ready to leave with the children. She draped Helen's evening cloak over Chloe's shoulders to keep her warm on the journey. It made her think of her mother and wish she could be with them today. Rex had suggested she leave her bouquet on Helen's grave as she left the church, and Chloe thought that a lovely idea.

The road shone white with frost. It seemed only moments before she was waiting in the church porch, holding on to Walter's arm. A thrill made her shiver.

'Nervous?' Uncle Walter asked.

'No. I know Rex too well to have nerves about him.'

The music changed, and Walter pushed open the door and led her down the aisle. Chloe knew there wouldn't be many people there, but she saw only Rex standing at the front. He turned as she drew close and smiled at her. A smile that showed his devotion. She had total trust in him.

The publishers hope that this book has given you enjoyable reading. Large Print Books are especially designed to be as easy to see and hold as possible. If you wish a complete list of our books please ask at your local library or write directly to:

Magna Large Print Books
Magna House, Long Preston,
Skipton, North Yorkshire.
BD23 4ND

This Large Print Book for the partially sighted, who cannot read normal print, is published under the auspices of

THE ULVERSCROFT FOUNDATION

THE ULVERSCROFT FOUNDATION

... we hope that you have enjoyed this Large Print Book. Please think for a moment about those people who have worse eyesight problems than you ... and are unable to even read or enjoy Large Print, without great difficulty.

You can help them by sending a donation, large or small to:

**The Ulverscroft Foundation,
1, The Green, Bradgate Road,
Anstey, Leicestershire, LE7 7FU,
England.**
or request a copy of our brochure for more details.

The Foundation will use all your help to assist those people who are handicapped by various sight problems and need special attention.

Thank you very much for your help.